PRAISE FOR FIONA McCALLUM

'Fiona McCallum is one Australia's favourite authors, and *Her Time to Shine* is another inspiring tale about finding strength and overcoming obstacles.'

—*Canberra Weekly*

'A fantastic follow-up that you won't want to miss.'

—*Better Reading* on *Her Time to Shine*

'A master storyteller.'

—*Good Reading Magazine*

'A heart-warming book that deals sensitively with issues of loss, financial uncertainty and emotional repair.'

—*Canberra Weekly* on *Trick of the Light*

'A deeply moving story about loss and the unexpected benefits of having to find your feet when the whole world seems to be conspiring to knock you off them.'

—*Australian Country* on *Trick of the Light*

'*The Long Road Home* is a lovely read that transported me away for the day … this story was as comforting as it is entertaining.'

—*Better Reading*

'It's an inspiring tale about finding hope.'

—*Daily Telegraph* on *The Long Road Home*

T0363037

'*Standing Strong* considers duty, how to do what you know is right even when it's emotionally challenging. With its relatable characters, dialogue and issues, this is a novel that will ring true for many readers.'

—*Better Reading*

'This is a very fine story, well-handled, and does not avoid the hard issues.'

—*Weekly Times* on *Wattle Creek*

'If ever there was a farm-lit book designed for competitive horse riders, this has to be it.'

—*Newcastle Herald* on *Leap of Faith*

'Fiona McCallum wears her literary heart on her dustcovers and with her stories swirling through towns we know and live in, she turns next-door-neighbours into larger-than-life characters – plus a little horse with a big heart.'

—*Riverine Herald* on *Leap of Faith*

'A beautiful novel filled with romance, inner strength and above all, friendship.'

—*That Book You Like* on *Time Will Tell*

'*Saving Grace* is a must-read.'

—*Woman's Day*

'McCallum captures the nuances of a country town and the personalities of the characters that live there.'

—*The Big Book Club* on *Saving Grace*

Fiona McCallum was raised on a cereal and wool farm near Cleve on South Australia's Eyre Peninsula and remained in the area until her mid-twenties, during which time she married and separated. She then moved to Melbourne and on to Sydney a few years later.

Fiona's first novel, *Paycheque*, was published in 2011 and became a bestseller. In the eleven years since, she has written another twelve bestselling novels. *Her Time to Shine* is Fiona's fourteenth book.

Currently residing in Adelaide, Fiona is a full-time novelist who writes heart-warming stories that draw on her rich and contrasting life experiences, love of animals and fascination with human nature.

For more information about Fiona and her books, visit her website at fionamccallum.com. She can also be found on Facebook at facebook.com/fionamccallum.author

Also by Fiona McCallum

Paycheque
Nowhere Else
Leap of Faith

The Wattle Creek series
Wattle Creek
Standing Strong

The Button Jar series
Saving Grace
Time Will Tell
Meant To Be

The Finding Hannah series
Finding Hannah
Making Peace

The Ballarat series
A Life of Her Own
The Long Road Home

The Trick of the Light series
Trick of the Light
Her Time to Shine

Sunrise Over Mercy Court

FIONA McCALLUM
Her Time to Shine

FICTION
HQ

First Published 2022
Second Australian Paperback Edition 2023
ISBN 9781867256007

HER TIME TO SHINE
© 2022 by Fiona McCallum
Australian Copyright 2022
New Zealand Copyright 2022

This is a work of fiction. Names, characters, places, and incidents are either the product of the author's imagination or are used fictitiously, and any resemblance to actual persons, living or dead, business establishments, events, or locales is entirely coincidental.

Published by
HQ Fiction
An imprint of Harlequin Enterprises (Australia) Pty Limited (ABN 47 001 180 918), a subsidiary of HarperCollins Publishers Australia Pty Limited (ABN 36 009 913 517)
Level 13, 201 Elizabeth St
SYDNEY NSW 2000
AUSTRALIA

® and TM (apart from those relating to FSC®) are trademarks of Harlequin Enterprises (Australia) Pty Limited or its corporate affiliates. Trademarks indicated with ® are registered in Australia, New Zealand and in other countries.

A catalogue record for this book is available from the National Library of Australia
www.librariesaustralia.nla.gov.au

Printed and bound in Australia by McPherson's Printing Group

MIX
Paper | Supporting
responsible forestry
FSC® C001695

To all waiting for their dreams to come true: Hang in there — incredible things happen every day.

Part One

Part One

Chapter One

Erica woke with a jolt. Her heart was racing. She sat up and opened her eyes. Nothing. Complete darkness was all around her. She held her breath and stayed completely still, listening. Something was different. Panic began to rise. Her breathing became ragged, gasping.

Where am I?

Oh, yes. Of course. Melrose. It was her first morning waking up in the small town nestled against beautiful and magnificent Mt Remarkable.

She pictured the perfectly put together compact space of the flat with its heavy curtains with a small floral design. She loved how different the décor was from the way her sleek, minimalist home back in Adelaide was designed. Best of all, she loved that she was on a second floor. Even the flat being above Crossley Funerals didn't faze her. She might have moved there out of desperation, but she was excited about starting her new job in a completely different industry.

Just days ago she might have laughed at her ridiculous over-reaction, but now it was reasonable after a few weeks' ordeal culminating in the upheaval on the weekend. She and her young adult daughters, Mackenzie and Issy, had dubbed it *The Kayla incident*. Reasonable, yes, but bloody annoying. Erica hated that the woman was still having an effect, despite being nearly three hundred kilometres away. She really didn't want to think about Kayla at all, but, damn it, there she was now lodged in her brain. Erica still struggled with the fact the girl had been living in her roof space. Well, not *living*, exactly, but there: coming and going, roaming the house at night while Erica was sleeping and during the day while she'd been out.

You're okay; she's locked up and far away.

The tension seeped away and normal breathing returned. But the level of grittiness in her eyes told her it was even earlier than her usual waking time of between four-thirty and five-thirty. The early starts were not by choice, but because she liked to go to bed around nine-thirty, and apparently she only needed seven hours' sleep and no more these days, even though much of those seven hours were spent tossing and turning, fighting the discomfort of hot flushes and night sweats, and attempts to find relief by pushing her feet in and out into the air beyond her quilt. *Bloody menopause*, she cursed as she took several slow deep breaths. Technically she was post-menopausal, but that didn't seem to have made a difference to her symptoms. She wasn't keen on this aging business, or of now being 'a woman of a certain age' – her age being almost fifty. Though, as her parents had said before dementia began eating their brains, it was better than the alternative. Erica knew that all too well, having lost her husband Stuart to cancer six months earlier. Cancer was a cruel beast.

As much as Erica was bothered by some of the various symptoms from menopause's box of assorted horrors, this being dragged abruptly from sleep was a whole new bag of awful – she'd even volunteer instead for more hot flushes if she could.

She was now wide awake and no cajoling would get her more slumber. Many years ago, she'd been able to slip back to sleep due to the sheer exhaustion of new parenthood after getting up and tending to feeding schedules. Now once she was awake, she was awake, regardless of how much her body told her she needed more sleep. In fact, she couldn't remember when she'd last had a full eight hours' interrupted sleep; nor had she woken feeling fully rested in all that time. Despite being somewhat resigned to it, she still regularly craved the long, deep and satisfying sleep of her adolescence.

As she picked up her phone to check the time – she knew it was a bad habit that didn't help matters, but still often did so – she heard a loud clunk and then the scrape of something heavy outside in the otherwise very quiet main street.

She stiffened.

After spending a few moments reminding herself she was safe and successfully easing another burst of ragged breathing back to normal again, she pushed the covers back, got up and went to her bedroom window to look out. With the heavy drapes parted, she could see a truck parked at the kerb near the bakery across the road. *Ah, a delivery. Of course.* Her view was a little obscured and her bedroom was starting to become too cold. Her new boss, and owner of the flat and business below, Walter, had warned her that nights could get cold there in winter and well into spring, and suggested she might want to keep the heating running on auto overnight. She dragged on her bathrobe, tucked her feet into her slippers and moved out into the main open-plan living space to the window above which the air conditioner sat blasting warm air.

Erica pulled the heavy drapes back, and then the net behind, and peered out. She now had a partial view – blocked by the truck – of the side window of the bakery, which was behind a fence. She liked being up high and looking down. It felt safe. And she knew above her was a corrugated steel roof that would be hard to breach – she'd checked on her evening walk the day before.

Erica saw the delivery driver take a trolley piled high with boxes through the open gate to the back door of the bakery. She continued to stand there enjoying the warm air blasting on her back from the air conditioner above.

Before too long the delivery man was putting his trolley away in the back of the truck for the last time, pulling down the roller door, and then getting back into the driver's seat. The truck roared to life and then drove away, leaving Erica with a full view of the bakery's large side window – although all she could see was that the space was brightly lit and there was someone working, coming in and out of sight. She thought there was something on the bench, but couldn't make out what; she was too far away for any great clarity.

Regardless of her limited vision, Erica really liked the idea that she wasn't alone – especially in this dark period before dawn. It reminded her so much of that precious breastfeeding time with each of her girls all those years ago. She'd quickly realised that early morning with its peace and solitude was a great balm for soothing away the fears and exhaustion of fresh motherhood.

Trial and error with feeding had taught her that the less relaxed you were, the more difficult and more stressful everything became. She'd been forced to give up multi-tasking, and in her opinion some efficiency, but in its place had found tranquillity and much joy in bonding peacefully with her child. Warmth and comfort flooded her now at the memory, and she took that with her as she went and made a cup of tea. While it brewed, she took one of the padded dining chairs over to the window.

With warm mug in hand, Erica settled herself in with the company of whoever it was across the way to await enough light to go for a walk. And then was the start of the first day of her new career. She was excited but also a little apprehensive – she really wished she'd slept well last night of all nights.

Squawk, squawk, squawk.

Erica heard the flock of galahs before she saw them moving like a pink and grey coloured kite past her window. Deafening: louder than the truck that had just driven by. Then there was a quiet whoosh of car tyres on tarmac, the rattle of a trailer, and the roar of a motorbike. The town was waking up. She'd watched as the dark grey beyond the window had become pale and then the clouds parted to reveal pockets of blue sky.

She decided tomorrow she'd go for a walk and get back into her routine. Maybe she'd meet and talk to one of the dog walkers she'd seen from across the street on her evening stroll.

Having had breakfast, showered and got dressed, Erica carefully applied her makeup, which she referred to as her seal – somehow it not only covered her complexion but also managed to keep her emotions from spilling over; she hadn't once cried in public when fully made-up since losing her husband Stuart, nor in any of the fraught months of his cancer battle before that.

Sitting on the couch, having checked her watch – still half an hour early – Erica fidgeted. She'd washed her few dishes and put them away and her bed was made and her room tidy, and she'd checked twice through her handbag to make sure all was in order. She tried scrolling idly through her Facebook feed and flicking through TV channels before turning it off after not finding anything to catch her interest there either.

Her phone pinged several times with messages and she grabbed it off the arm of the sofa and pulled it towards her.

Both her daughters and her three dearest friends had sent various words of encouragement and support. She was grateful they weren't phoning – they always knew exactly what she needed. She replied to each with: *Thank you! Feeling great! Will let you know how I go*, along with several heart emojis before tucking her phone into her handbag.

Let's go; better off figuring things out down in the office than sitting up here twiddling my thumbs.

Chapter Two

Erica locked the door to the flat and descended the steps to the business place of Crossley Funerals. She walked along the hallway and paused midway, where the frosted glass door marked *Mortuary* was on her left and the roller door out to the garage area was on her right. She held her breath while listening for sounds from within the mortuary, despite seeing it was dark inside. Nothing. She didn't like how quiet it was back here. She shuddered. It was cold. Or was that her being a silly scaredy cat? Death wasn't something to be afraid of – well, not if you weren't the one facing it. There was no such thing as zombies. It was mind over matter. Erica still wasn't quite sure of her opinion on whether ghosts existed or not. Thankfully the strange occurrences she'd experienced back at home in Adelaide had mostly been adequately explained away.

Righto, there's nothing weird about working with death. It's a privilege to look after the departed and take care of their loved ones, she told herself, bringing her attention back to the present. She hoicked her shoulders up and strode down the hall, turning on lights as she went.

'Hello? Walter, are you here?' she called, going through to the main office reception area. She moved on and around the desk – noting as she did that the door to the front reception room was wide open and the area with its pair of comfortable chesterfield couches and display of caskets and coffins and urns was in darkness. She went into the filing room that led into the kitchen and thus established Walter wasn't in the building, unless he enjoyed sitting in the dark, though he hadn't mentioned he did. But while the place was clearly deserted, it was, thankfully, not freezing cold.

Behind the reception desk she looked around to ascertain which chair might be Walter's preferred spot. She knew he spent a lot of time on the road or out the back, but the area was clearly set up for two people to work side by side. As her slow brain cleared, she realised it was evident which area had belonged to his recently departed wife, Mary. It seemed untouched by anyone but its previous occupant – as if she'd just walked away at the end of the day and not come back: a pump pack of sorbolene cream, mug with *World's Best Mum* printed on it in white, small desk fan, pen with fuzzy pompom on top. Erica also deduced Mary had liked purple; there were touches of it everywhere – sticky notes, the cute pen, the mug, the fan …

Erica pulled the chair out and sat down. Walter had told her she was replacing Mary in the business and he'd been very open about his darling wife and his loss. So it should be fine for her to sit there, she decided, though she was a little uneasy about either packing up Mary's things or using them.

'Right, Mary, where do I start?' She liked having a name to use and, if not a real presence, a sort of familiarity – there in that quiet space. Of course, it could be that she was going mad – or losing it, as Issy and Mackenzie liked to say. Menopause did that to you – she'd had brain fog on and off a lot in recent years, even before all the other stuff had happened. The last few weeks she'd been downright ditzy at times.

Erica bent down and turned on the small fan heater under the desk and then looked at the labels on the stack of four purple in-trays. Going from top to bottom were: *New Bookings, Upcoming Events, Completed Events/Filing* and *Instructions*. She pulled out the black display folder from the bottom tray – that seemed the most logical place to start – and smiled at its label. Written in flowing purple marker across several large white sticky labels was *Mary's Mayhem Manager!*

Oh how I'd like to have met Walter's Mary, she thought with a sigh and after a reverent pause she opened the cover to the first of the clear plastic pockets and began reading comprehensive instructions that went right through each step of the funeral process, with hints and tips in different colours off in the margin of the typed pages.

Erica sighed again, this time with relief, and sent ceiling-wards silent thanks to Mary – not that she believed in heaven, or hell, or organised religion for that matter. She then reached up and took a blank form already on a clipboard from the top document tray and looked it over, making comparisons with what she read in the instructions. She put it aside and went through everything else she could find that corresponded with *Mary's Mayhem Manager!* and did her best to commit it all to memory.

She sat back, satisfied that everything made sense, or if something suddenly didn't, she knew where to find the answer – bless you, Mary! Really, running a funeral seemed a lot like organising any other important event. Not that she was a professional event planner, but she was quite organised and had helped with plenty of functions over the years.

Fiona McCallum

Mary's order suited her perfectly and not once did she stop and think *No, I wouldn't have that with that or do that like that.* They seemed to share the same type of logic. Maybe it was true what Renee – her dear earthy, creative, philosophical younger friend – said about things having a way of turning out for the best. Renee was always also saying that people came in and out of your life for a reason and always at the right time. Maybe this was an example.

Erica was just bending down and adjusting the direction of the fan heater on her feet when she heard a noise behind her. She nearly leapt out of her skin and did bang her head on the edge of the desk as she tried to beat a hasty retreat from her vulnerable position.

'Good morning, early bird,' Walter said, coming through the open door from the kitchen. He must have come in from the door off the hallway rather than around the front like she had. 'Oh god, sorry, I didn't mean to startle you,' he said, clearly noticing the fear Erica was desperately trying to expel from her expression. *Damn it!* Her hand at her chest, which she'd neglected to remove, was most likely a giveaway, too. She cursed her suddenly flaming cheeks and neck.

'No. Sorry. Yes, just a little. My fault …' She was babbling. *Shut up, Erica, the poor man will think you were doing something dodgy. Get a grip.* 'Good morning, Walter. I was just adjusting the heater. Is it okay if I sit here – on this side?'

'No problem at all. Wherever suits. Finding everything okay?' Walter said, dragging the other chair out and sitting down to face Erica.

'Yes, thanks.'

'Oh. Feel free to pack all the bits and pieces away or use them, whatever suits,' Walter said, indicating with a wave of his hand. 'I should have already. I didn't think to. I'm really sorry about that. I have to confess I quite like the little reminders. Though sometimes not so much, too. I still don't want her mug at home. I'm not quite sure why – it really is just a vessel for holding liquid; isn't it? Sorry, I'm jabbering.' He took two deep breaths before speaking again. 'Ah, grief, it's a complicated companion, isn't it?' he added, along with a long sigh. With his lips pressed together, he offered Erica a sad and gentle smile.

'It sure is. I love the colour purple too,' she added. Her heart went out to him: his discombobulation was endearing and comforting.

'Discard or use anything at all. I'll leave it up to you. I'm completely fine with whatever you decide. Really.'

'Okay. I'll see.' Erica wasn't entirely convinced. But it didn't matter; she wasn't bothered by the presence of Mary's things and was happy to leave them where they were. She didn't see any point in getting rid of the useful items. Admittedly she wasn't keen on drinking from her predecessor's mug, but also couldn't say why if pressed. She'd put the fuzzy-topped pen into it and together they could remain as a little shrine to Mary Crossley.

Their gazes both seemed to land on the open book of instructions at the same time.

'Ah, yes, *Mary's Mayhem Manager*,' he said wistfully. Erica was pleased and relieved when he smiled a moment later, even revealing a slightly mischievous glint. 'Feel free to change anything that doesn't work for you, though Mary did seem to have everything down pat. You might want to relabel that.'

'Oh no. I love it. Mary's presence everywhere. Sorry, I ...' What? Erica let it go. She had nothing. She just didn't want to make Walter sad, or sadder than he already was. But as she knew all too well, people often shied away from talking about the recently deceased and doing that – erasing their memory, their being – wasn't healthy either. She remained silent to give Walter space to think and speak if he wished.

'She was great,' he finally said, settling back into his chair. Erica couldn't tell if the big sigh she heard was from inside him or from the padding of the chair beneath. 'But you'll be great too.'

'I hope so. I clearly have big shoes to fill.' Erica cursed the cliché that came out, but it was too late. Anyway, Walter did love an old saying. She might not know much about him yet, but she did know that. And that she liked him and felt comfortable in his close presence.

'So, you settled in and everything with the flat's okay?' he asked.

'Yes. Great, thanks. Very comfy,' Erica said quickly, relieved at not being asked how she'd slept and having to lie to Walter.

They fell into silence and as something to do, Erica inspected the small fan in front of her.

'That's Betty,' Walter said, nodding towards her hand.

'Sorry?' Erica said, turning to look at him, frowning slightly, thinking she'd misheard.

'"Be Gone Betty", to be formal,' Walter said, smiling. 'Mary suffered terribly with her hot flushes. And cold feet – hence the heater under the desk. And Mary ruled over the main air conditioner thermostat. The damned menopause gave her all sorts of issues that never went away. I don't want to presume, but I'm happy for you to take over that mantle too, if you like – for you to take charge of the thermostat, that is. Bloody hormones – as if you women don't have enough to deal with, what with childbirth et cetera.'

'Yes, bloody hormones. All sorts of issues. That about sums it up.' Erica had to admit to being fortunate enough with the condition that she didn't experience hot flushes during the day – though perhaps she had that phenomenon to not look forward to as well. Not only did symptoms vary wildly between women, they morphed and shifted, started and stopped at will, too, by all accounts. She had no idea what other hormone hideousness was in her future.

'Sorry, am I being inappropriate? I don't want to make you feel uncomfortable.'

'No, not at all. I'm not. But most men pull the shutter down when talk of women's issues starts.'

'Well, my view is how can you be supportive without trying to understand it or at least be open about it.'

Erica had the overwhelming desire to tell this dear man beside her how lovely she thought he was, or go over and wrap her arms around him – but that *would* be inappropriate. He seemed much older than his outer appearance would suggest. She had him pegged at early to mid sixties.

'Stuart grumbled about me tossing and turning in bed trying to adjust my temperature; that was the extent of his interest in the situation – though it's quite early days for me. We were both needing time to get used to it, I suppose ...'

'Some things you never quite get used to no matter how long you have,' Walter said in a sage tone. 'Shall I get us a coffee?' he said, abruptly changing the subject and mood.

'Oh, yes, please.'

'Usually it's only instant – out in the kitchen – but I think we need to celebrate your first day with a decent cuppa from over at the bakery. What do you say?'

'Sounds lovely. I'll have a latte, thank you. Here, I'll just get my wallet,' she said, opening the bottom drawer of the under-desk filing cabinet where she'd stashed it earlier.

'Oh no, that's okay. My treat. You can get it next time. Though, as I said, I tend to just stick with instant.'

'I'm perfectly fine with instant.'

'Well, let's get through today and reassess,' he said, smiling and getting up.

'Perfect.'

'Erica, it's great to have you here,' he said, pausing a little way back from the front door and turning to face her. He was smiling.

'It's great to be here, Walter,' Erica said. And she meant it. Right now that was exactly how she felt. Well, while she managed not to let any other thoughts in … *Stay in the moment*, she told herself, and got up to get a glass of water from the kitchen area.

Back at her desk again, she checked the large wall planner above her for upcoming events. There were two in the next couple of days and then nothing after that, but Walter had said things had a habit of changing very quickly in the funeral business.

Chapter Three

Even though Erica was expecting to hear Walter come back through the door, she still lurched in her chair when it banged closed a few moments later. She'd barely sat down – surely it was too soon for him to have been served, the coffee brewed, and for him to be back. Though it wasn't like there would be much traffic to wait for.

'Oh,' she said, looking up and noticing not Walter but a woman standing just beyond the desk. 'Hello. Can I help you?'

The woman was in her mid to late sixties, Erica estimated from her weathered features and dark tan – a farmer, outside a lot of the time? She was also attired in jeans and a navy work shirt with sleeves rolled up to her elbows and a brown quilted oilskin vest.

'Walter's just popped across to the bakery,' Erica said, glancing around her and frowning slightly.

'That's okay. You must be Erica.'

Erica tensed before forcing herself to relax, reminding herself that word spread through country towns like lightning and she'd been seen having lunch with Walter the day before.

'Yes. I am.'

'Welcome to Melrose.'

'Thanks. From what little I've seen so far, it's lovely. How can I help you?' She stood up and wondered if she should be going over and shaking hands, but stayed where she was.

'I'm not sure you can.'

'Oh. Sorry, I didn't catch your name.'

'Peggy,' the woman said.

'It's lovely to meet you, Peggy.'

Erica could see Peggy held a tweed woollen cap – so tightly the knuckles on her tanned, leathery hands looked strained and pale. She could also see from the way the light fell on her cheeks that she'd been crying recently.

'Would you like a glass of water? I've just poured this,' Erica said, leaning down and placing the full glass on the top of the counter.

'Oh, thank you. Yes.'

As Peggy drank, Erica moved around from behind the reception desk and towards the comfortable separate reception room, which was nice and private – not that she thought there was a great chance of much foot traffic in either space.

'Come through here,' she said, standing back to encourage Peggy to enter.

Erica sat down on one end of the chesterfield sofa against the wall, clutching the clipboard she'd grabbed from the desk, and was surprised when Peggy sat beside her rather than across from her on the second couch.

'You're very kind. Thank you. I have to admit to feeling very much out of my depth. Lost,' she said quietly, looking down at the glass she clutched in two hands on top of the flat disc of tweed in her lap.

From the tightness in her jaw and the set of her shoulders, Erica suspected this admission had been made with great difficulty. She weighed up how to approach her – what to say and the tone to take. She could only be herself, speak from the heart. Or stay silent. She knew too often people spoke, filling in the gaps that were necessary for people to order their thoughts and ultimately gain the support they needed.

Peggy sighed deeply but remained silent. Erica was grateful for the silence in this room – no ticking clock. Or should she turn the sound system on? No, something told her this woman would prefer the silence.

'I'm about to lose my wife – to leukaemia – and I don't quite know what to do,' Peggy finally said, putting the glass on the coffee table and looking down at the hat, which she began turning around slowly in her hands as if examining it. Erica found the movement a little hypnotic, her tired eyes closing slightly before she forced them back open and mentally shook her head to clear it and regain focus.

'I'm really sorry to hear that,' Erica said, disappointed with the lack of originality of her words, but reminding herself that whatever this was it wasn't about her.

'Shirley.'

'Shirley,' Erica repeated. 'Tell me about Shirley, Peggy.'

'I don't know what she'd want me to do. About ... you know, this,' she said, sweeping an arm towards the nearby display of coffins, caskets and urns.

'That's okay. We can work it out together. You don't have to have all the answers right away.'

'I don't want her to go at all. Oh god,' Peggy said, and brought her hands, still full of hat, up to her face and burst into tears. She sobbed, her shoulders shuddering. It took all of Erica's strength to

Fiona McCallum

not lean over and pull her in. She picked up the tissue box from the small table at the end of the couch beside her. After a handful were taken, she placed it back down and resumed waiting in still silence.

Gradually Peggy's shoulders stilled and the sobbing was replaced with a few sniffles and then quiet nose-blowing.

'I'm sorry,' Peggy said, finally looking up at Erica through sodden lashes.

'There's nothing to be sorry for,' Erica said.

'I seem to have become a completely different person – I've never cried in public like that in my life.'

'Grief affects us in all sorts of ways. Shirley means a lot to you, so of course losing her is going to hurt. A lot. And unfortunately, probably for a very long time.'

'I'm so scared, Erica,' Peggy said in a hissed whisper, suddenly clasping Erica's hands with both hands.

'Losing your life partner, a big part of your life, is frightening. A lot will change – perhaps everything,' Erica said.

'But?' Peggy said, looking up, frowning.

'But nothing. Grief is hard and it's horrible, no bones about it. Okay, here's a but, or two. *But*, perhaps what might help is choosing the best way for you to say goodbye and honour Shirley and your life together.'

'I don't know how to, though.'

'Yes, you do. I'm sure of it. It's inside you – in the memories built over time; the things you enjoyed together, even the things one of you liked but the other didn't.'

'But what about …?'

'What about what?'

She waved an arm and Erica couldn't tell if the gesture was one of helplessness and defeat or to indicate something.

'This place – the town, district. What people think?'

'It's not their relationship – it's yours and Shirley's. And it won't be their grief to process – it's a very personal journey.'

'But we were not supposed to be … together.'

'Because you're both women?'

'Yes. You're from the city, aren't you?' She shook her head and fell silent.

'Ultimately, I think to find peace inside you you'll have to do what's right for you. Even if it's hard. Otherwise, it will eat you up. And for what – to avoid people's judgement? Are they more important than you? Are you willing to give them that power over you? Will their opinions be a comfort in the lonely days ahead? Sorry, I'm overstepping,' Erica said, cringing.

'Honestly, it's refreshing, Erica. I'm not normally this pathetic. I feel like all my stuffing – my guts – has been pulled out.'

'There's nothing pathetic about expressing emotion, Peggy. Tell me, if you had no concerns, what would you do?'

'We got married earlier this year,' Peggy said, as if not having heard Erica's question. 'We thought it would bring our families together – to us. We did it for us, but we hoped it would change things beyond us. But it just made it worse. Before that everyone could pretend we were just two old ducks sharing a house – maybe two slightly eccentric old ducks sharing a house. I moved in with Shirl, so for years I think they assumed I was her housekeeper, or it was simply to save on the bills or something. Now they know it'll become my house, the anger has really gone up a notch. Honestly, I'd like to tell them to fuck off. Sorry about the language –'

'It's fine,' Erica said.

'It's so disappointing. They're family – Shirl's side and mine. Family is supposed to be everything, support you when you need it. I can handle it, but they won't even visit Shirl. We've been cut out. And that's all fine – well, it's not, but coming back to … you know,' she said, indicating the space around them with her hands. 'Despite all that – our *debauchery*,' Peggy said the word with a roll of her eyes, 'they're insisting on doing her service their way – in a church. I abhor organised religion, as does Shirley. I don't want to pull rank or organise something behind their backs because we've already caused them so much pain – though, that's down to them and their antiquated attitudes. But this is a small community – I don't want it being further divided or create additional embarrassment. I've had it my whole life, so … I also don't want anyone to have any regrets. But I can't go into a church and be a part of all that bloody hypocrisy.'

Erica nodded.

'They think they're going to save her soul; can you believe it? Utterly ridiculous. Oh, and make sure she gets into their idea of heaven. As if – what complete rot.'

'Does Shirley have an opinion?'

'Like me, she's feeling between a rock and a hard place too. Also, too tired to fight any more – they're a lost cause. If our wedding didn't bring them together, well … It's a pretty miserable bunch of people who don't like seeing others in love or celebrating a wedding. It was lovely, but a very quiet affair, as I'm sure you can imagine. Sorry, I'm going off track. Shirl, bless her cotton socks, very unhelpfully says it won't matter to her because she'll be dead. She's worried about me, though. Because, really, funerals are about the living, aren't they? It's our closure, making peace, et cetera.'

'You could have two services – your own; the way you'd like it. Once you decide how that might look,' Erica said. 'And other family members could do theirs their way.'

'I could, couldn't I?' Peggy's sad eyes became a little larger.

'You can do anything – unless it's illegal. You could have Shirley cremated and keep her ashes and decide where to scatter or inter them later. For example, I lost my husband Stuart. His ashes have been in an urn on the mantelpiece in my house in Adelaide for the last six months. My daughters and I quite like knowing he's close by. I can imagine him still being there in a decade,' she said, smiling warmly at Peggy. 'I'm just saying, there's no rush.'

'But there's only one Shirley – there'll only be one body. So, I'd still have to speak to them ...'

'Yes.'

Peggy shook her head slowly. 'I don't want to cause them any embarrassment or be seen as being difficult.'

Erica wanted to point out that by allowing herself to be silenced, she was as good as erasing the fact she was legally married to Shirley. She found it hard to reconcile the words and the demeanour coming from this woman now with what she'd seen just minutes ago in reception. She'd seemed if not brassy and bold, then at least a little determined. But also Erica knew small towns worked in their own ways and she had no first-hand knowledge of any of that on which to draw.

'I think we women have been quiet for long enough on far too many matters,' Erica found herself saying quietly.

'Yes, Shirley would be so disappointed in me.'

'Oh, I didn't mean to –'

'I've been tough – to a certain point – my entire life; I've had to be. But this whole business has quite unravelled me. And my darling Shirley isn't even gone yet – the doctors say it's a matter of days, maybe a few weeks. I've told her it's okay to go, but she keeps hanging on. I don't want her to go, but I can't bear to see the anguish – the pain – in her face.'

'Perhaps her knowing you'll be okay – with this …' Erica tapped the clipboard and waved her own arm to indicate the space they were in '… will help.' They were just words. Meaningless words so she had something to say. Erica felt for the woman and thought, *This is just the beginning – you've got a long way to go. Not knowing which way is up is just the start. The shock. Then comes the confusion – the feeling of knowing what is what but feeling out of kilter. And then the complete scooping out of all your insides, leaving a husk which is not quite knowing how to go on at all – let alone trying to make basic decisions – but doing so anyway. Somehow. Carrying on for everyone else and because you don't know how not to.* A wave of exhaustion swept through Erica.

'Do you know, I think you're absolutely right,' Peggy said, breaking into Erica's thoughts.

About what? Erica wondered. She was a little concerned at seeing the fierceness and determination back in the eyes of the woman beside her. Suddenly Peggy was up off the couch. Trying to hide her surprise, Erica stood and shook the hand that was being offered.

'Erica, thank you for your time,' she said. 'I know what I need to do.'

'That's great. I'm glad to have been of help,' Erica said, suddenly a bit lost herself.

'You're a breath of fresh air in this town,' Peggy said, pulling Erica into a firm and slightly awkward hug, given Erica's hands were trapped by her sides and the clipboard was still in one hand.

They both left the room.

'Oh, there you are,' Walter said from behind the counter. 'Hello, Peggy. Shirley hasn't passed, has she?'

'Hi, Walter. No. Still hanging on. I'd best be off.'

'Okay. Take good care of yourself,' Walter said.

Peggy nodded. 'Be good to her. This one is a keeper. Thank you again, Erica. I'll see you both later.' She turned and strode towards the front door.

'Bye, Peggy. Take care,' Erica called.

'Sorry, your coffee is probably cold now. We could give it a zap in the microwave,' Walter said with a shrug.

'That's okay. I don't mind it as it is.'

'Poor Peggy. She and Shirley have been through the wringer,' Walter said.

'Yes, it sure sounds like it. But she didn't make any decisions,' Erica said, sitting down, pushing the clipboard back into the top tray and picking up her coffee. 'I think it's a complicated situation.'

'Ah, yes, bigotry will do that. *Family* will do that. Well done.'

'For what? I don't think I did anything too useful.'

'Didn't you hear what Peggy said to me?'

'Yes, but ...'

'But what? She's not the easiest to deal with at the best of times – though I like her immensely: definitely more bark than bite. Are you concerned you didn't get her to commit to anything?'

Erica nodded.

'That doesn't matter. Remember, I said we don't do hard sell. And I'm not exactly wedded to the notion that time is money. I'd much rather someone came in and received some empathy and understanding and left a little lighter for it – even if they did decide to take their business elsewhere. We're in the people business – and it's as much about the living as the departed.'

'You're a good egg, Walter.' Again, it was all she could do not to go over and hug the man.

'Thanks, Erica. I can tell you are too. It might not be good financially, especially in the short term, but I can sleep at night. And that's what really matters.'

Oh, god, to get a good night's sleep! Erica thought, sipping at her coffee.

Chapter Four

It was almost the end of Erica's first day – and she was exhausted – when Walter turned his chair towards her and said, 'I've been thinking.'

Erica instinctively said, 'Careful ...' before she stopped herself. It had long been a joke between her and her dad, and Walter, while nowhere near as old as Arthur Tolmer, did have a similar cheeky glint in his eye and playful air about him. 'Sorry,' she muttered.

'Oh, no, don't be! You're absolutely right. Thinking is a dangerous sport, as my darling Mary used to say. But, on a serious note, I've been thinking that since you've clearly got the dealing with people part of the job down pat and are being wholeheartedly embraced, what would you say about me leaving out here largely to you and me sticking to the mortuary and going and collecting bodies?'

'Oh. Okay. It's your business, Walter; I'm happy with however you want to do things.' *I'm just grateful to have a job.*

'I think it's all caught up with me – the tiredness. The burn-out. I've been trying so hard to keep everything together that I hadn't realised just how tired I really am. Not the sort of fatigue that a few decent nights' sleep will fix, but a soul-level, bone-aching weariness. That probably doesn't even make sense.'

Oh, yes, it does. Please don't say you're going to sell up and put me out of a job. Erica nodded.

'I had quite forgotten how exhausting the people side of things really is. Mary used to take care of it and I'd hide away as much as I could – in the mortuary or out in the van driving. We always did the funeral services together – it's important to me to keep on having us both do that.

'You're clearly a natural with the customer service side of things – in fact you remind me so much of Mary, it's quite uncanny. So, would you mind terribly not preparing bodies and just doing the makeup when required after I've finished? You did seem the slightest bit apprehensive about that side of things yesterday – so perhaps it's a win for both of us?'

'Yes, you're right. I'm happy to learn everything and do whatever you want, but I do have to admit to feeling a little relieved at your decision.'

Except I will miss your company beside me. Erica experienced a pang of disappointment. They'd had a great day together, getting to know each other and chatting about all sorts of things between the drop-ins. She'd noticed that after the first few people – perhaps when she'd proven she was fine alone – he'd taken to getting up and disappearing. Often she could hear him fossicking in the kitchen or opening and closing filing cabinet drawers out in the storage room beyond. She'd taken it as him giving her space so she didn't feel unsettled by his hovering. But clearly it was he who'd been feeling unsettled. She hadn't had close relationships with workmates at David Jones, managing her time alone, and today had been a new and fun experience. But she was also happy to go it alone, as she had done at her cosmetics counter, except for the clients that came in and sat in her chair or the browsers who paused to look and ask questions about the products. At least this way they wouldn't run the risk of getting on each other's nerves, not that Erica thought they ever would. But she barely knew Walter. There was always a risk.

'Great. That's a weight off my mind. I do think we should go to see families together,' he added thoughtfully.

'Okay.'

'We'll play it all by ear,' he added, this time almost as if he were speaking to himself. 'Right,' he said, getting up. 'I think we can safely head off early.'

'I'm going to get some groceries,' Erica said, explaining why she was making her way towards the front door instead of the back where the steps to the flat were and also the business's undercover garage and the car park outside. She wondered about getting her own car and taking a drive, but decided against it. 'I need to start making and bringing my lunch from home. Today was great, but ...' She hoped he might get the hint without her saying anything else and avoid any awkwardness tomorrow.

She'd loved her hot pie, but it had to be a one-off. She'd done her sums back in Adelaide and had – through necessity – cut out buying lunch and coffees. She had made such great headway she couldn't relax now. She wanted to drive back and forth to visit her dad. She might even have to retire her dear old Volvo at some point, but couldn't think about that any time soon.

Erica's step was lighter than she'd thought possible considering the lack of sleep dragging at her and a brain that seemed to be full up. In the supermarket she was glad of her habit of always writing her list in the notes app in her phone. With all the interruptions from looking up and nodding hello to people – some faces familiar, most not – she'd never have remembered to get everything. She'd also forgotten how ridiculously long it took to navigate a new supermarket – even if this one was only about half, or even a third, the size of those back in the city. After returning to one aisle three times, she gave up trying to memorise the layout. It was okay just to wander. She had the whole evening alone in the flat ahead of her anyway. It would be nice to cook and waste some time rather than heating something up.

Erica realised she'd have to start looking for a book club or another hobby organisation to join for company in the evenings, otherwise she might go quite mad. She'd survived back at home without joining anything, but perhaps out here it might be a good idea; she didn't have her three dear friends to catch up with. And she was having a whole new start anyway …

Erica had just arrived back at the flat when she heard her phone signal the arrival of a text message. She dug it out of her handbag. The screen told her it was from Geoff, the police officer back in Adelaide. With shaking fingers and quivering insides, she unlocked her phone and read. And then she let out a huge sigh of relief.

Hi Erica. I hope this finds you well. Just to update you, as promised. Court today for K. Good news – she was remanded in custody. Next court appearance 6 December. Rest easy. Will be in touch if anything arises. Here if you need anything from me. All the best, Geoff (SAPOL).

Erica took several deep breaths before replying. She thanked him for letting her know and said it was a huge relief. She then sent a quick text to Issy and Mackenzie before taking several deep breaths and returning her attention to unpacking the groceries.

With the kitchen bench tidy again, Erica fought the urge to throw herself onto the couch and turn on the TV. Instead, she got changed into trackies and was just heading out when her phone rang. It was Mackenzie.

'Hang on a sec,' she said by way of answer. 'I'm just heading out for a walk and need to lock the door. Right, here I am.'

'It's both of us, Mum,' Issy chimed in.

'Even better! Did you get my text just now about Kayla?'

'Yes. And we just heard from Geoff too. Huuuge relief! Even though it's what he said would happen,' Issy said.

'So, we're good,' Mackenzie said. 'How are you, is the more important question.'

'Better now. And, please, let's not think or talk about you-know-who.'

'Suits me,' Mackenzie said.

'Yeah, and me. So, how was your first day?' Issy said.

Erica smiled at picturing them sitting side by side with the phone between them.

'Good. Exhausted with trying to take in so much information. But I really enjoyed it. And I really like Walter. So, all is well here.' She checked each way before crossing the street, taking extra care due to wearing headphones and being distracted by her call. 'It's so friendly here, too,' she continued. 'Though I've been here two seconds and I do feel like I've barely caught my breath yet.'

'That's fair enough. It did all happen very quickly,' Issy said.

'Speaking of which. Are you both sleeping okay? Not, you know …?' Erica asked.

'Not freaking out because of *The Kayla incident*, you mean?' Mackenzie said. Again, Erica smiled – this time at the fingers no doubt above her elder daughter's head signalling quote marks.

'Well, yes. Because you know you can go and stay at Steph's.'

'Yep. We know. We're fine, aren't we, Issy?'

'Totally, Mum.'

'Anyway, we have the advantage of safety in numbers. You were all alone,' Mackenzie said, her more gentle side coming through.

'Okay. Fair enough,' Erica said. 'Hello,' she called to a woman walking her dog on the other side of the street. Her greeting was returned with a call back and a raised hand.

'Who's that?' Issy asked.

'Yeah, do you *actually* know people *already*?' Mackenzie said. Erica couldn't pick if her tone was disbelief, concern or wonder.

'Sort of. No, not really. It was a woman walking a border collie. I think I might have seen her – or at least the same dog – last night.'

'Haha, listen to her. Mum's becoming a dog person,' Mackenzie said.

I could well be. Erica couldn't believe how much she missed Michelle's Daphne after only having her stay for such a short amount of time, though she wasn't sure if it was that she missed her company or her guard-dog capabilities. She shook her head in wonder again at remembering how the dog had behaved the night the whole Kayla fiasco had unravelled – something she was trying hard to not think about. She might sleep better with a dog to warn her if something really was up …

'Can we get a dog, Mum?'

Erica stopped walking. 'What's brought that on? Are you sure you're okay there alone?'

'We're fine, Mum. It might have been the shortest gap year in the history of gap years, but we've just been overseas alone, remember? So, we can handle living in the burbs of little old

Adelaide on our own,' Mackenzie said. 'It was just a thought. We saw how you were with Daphne,' she added.

'But Mum won't get to enjoy the dog if *we* get one,' Issy said, as if the thought had just come to her.

'Hmm, no shit, Sherlock,' Mackenzie said.

Erica was about to scold them, but couldn't find the energy. They were old enough to sort themselves out.

'Can we please just not rush into anything else major right now? I'm not saying no, but ...' she said.

'No worries,' Mackenzie said. 'Hey, shit. Mum, we've got to go. Work.'

'Oh. Okay. Well, thanks for the call. Have fun. And be safe.'

As she hung up, Erica wondered if they'd deliberately called then because they hated speaking on the phone for too long – the young ones all seemed to prefer messaging online as their form of communication – or had been waiting for her to finish work. Either way, she appreciated it. She was very lucky to have such good relationships with each of her girls. Plenty of other mothers didn't. Her friend Michelle, for one ... Speaking of which ... There was her friend's name now on her phone.

'Michelle, hi. How's Daph? My girls and I were just talking about your gorgeous dog. They've announced they want to get one. Can you believe it?!'

'Daphne is great. I'll give her a hug from you. We're all here. And you're on speaker,' Michelle said.

'Hi, Steph; hi, Renee. I'm out for a walk, if you hear any strange sounds.' Erica's heart ached at thinking how far apart they were – a shade under three hundred kilometres suddenly feeling much further away. 'Guess what? The cop just texted to let me know Kayla has been to court and officially remanded in custody.

It's what he'd said they hoped would happen, so was, I guess, a mere formality, but still …'

'Oh, that's great news,' Michelle said.

'Yes. I'm so relieved for you,' Renee said.

'I hope they keep her locked up forever,' Steph said.

'Fingers crossed. So, what's going on with you guys?' Erica asked.

'Just seeing how your first day went – we figured you might be exhausted so thought a group call was the way to go,' Steph said, typically taking charge.

'So, was it, is it, okay?' Renee asked.

'It was good. Walter's fantastic and his wife, Mary, was apparently the most organised woman on the planet. She left behind a brilliant set of instructions. It'll be mainly customer service and event management, so unlikely to be dull. But, yes, I am a bit weary. It's quite a lot to take in and remember.' *What with the damned brain fog …* 'But so far so good. How are you guys?'

'Well, other than missing you terribly …' Steph said.

'I'm missing you guys too,' Erica said, swallowing down the rush of emotion that gripped her.

'I went and visited your dad earlier,' Steph said.

'Oh, thanks so much. How was he?'

'Doing well. I'm quite sure he didn't know who I was, which is completely fine and perfectly understandable, but he didn't seem to mind.'

'That's the main thing,' Erica said.

'He was pretty distracted by a kitten – did you know the nursing home has kittens? They're the cutest little things,' Steph said. Erica was sure she'd mentioned it to them. Oh well.

'I did. He was very attached to one last time I was there.'

'Hard to believe you never had pets as a child. He's quite the doting fur-dad!'

'Yes. I really appreciate you going to see him. It's such a weight off my mind.'

'No worries. I'm happy to. It was fun. I got to play with kittens, too – though I got a right sniffing over and cold shoulder from lord fluffy pants Boris when I got home.'

'Oh dear.'

'Hey, if your girls are suddenly showing an interest in getting a dog, is that because they're scared in the house on their own, do you think? After, you know ...' Renee said.

'I did ask and they said no. But it wouldn't surprise me.' Erica shuddered at a quick flash of images in her mind of *that* night.

'I'll check in with them,' Steph said.

'Thanks. They've just headed off to work.'

'And you're ... okay ... on that front?' Renee asked, lowering her tone.

'I'm fine.'

'Really?' Michelle pushed, matching Renee's serious tone.

'I'm a bit jumpy and still catching up on sleep after the other night. I guess it'll take some time to adjust to somewhere new, too. It's so *quiet* here. Well, except for the occasional rumble of a truck or motorbike going through town – my flat is right on the main road.'

'Yeah, that would take some adjusting to even if you hadn't had that other horrible experience,' Steph said.

'Hopefully you'll be better now with the confirmation Kayla is locked up,' Renee said.

'I hope so. And I'm hoping my brain becomes clearer all round, too. I'm a bit all over the place.'

'Understandable – you've had a lot to deal with recently,' Renee said.

'Yeah,' Steph and Michelle said.

'We'll go and leave you to your walk,' Steph said. 'Call if you need anything.'

'Okay. Thanks so much – for everything.'

'See you. Talk soon,' Michelle said.

'Bye,' Renee said.

After hanging up, Erica felt bad for hogging all the attention – she'd been doing that a lot lately. Though, granted, none of her friends had lost a husband, been threatened by a stalker, lost their job and had to uproot themselves in order to save their home from the bank thanks to said dead husband leaving their finances in the shit. Oh, to have a cruisey life again, though it would never go back to how it had been – too much was missing and she was now too different.

Chapter Five

Again, Erica woke in fright. Thankfully, this time her racing heart was quicker to settle. There was no point staying in bed, though. She'd sit with her new friend, the baker across the road.

Just like the day before, she settled in her window clutching a warm mug of tea. There were worse ways to pass the time while wide awake at stupid o'clock. She was determined to head out for a walk, but couldn't yet – well, definitely *wouldn't* in the dark, though might consider it if she had a dog for company … Her thoughts again went to Daphne, who Erica credited with saving her life a few nights back.

No delivery this morning, she mused. Or maybe she'd missed it. There was light again in the windows and a person moving around, coming in and out of view. She'd thought she might already be bored of this – nothing interesting was really happening – but she still found it a comfort, particularly knowing she had company, even if whoever it was didn't know she was there. She leant back against the chair and closed her eyes.

This morning Erica dragged herself away from the window when it was light enough and, once she was dressed, headed out for a walk.

Brrr. It was icy cold, accompanied by a brisk breeze. She was glad she'd put on her beanie, scarf and gloves. She wrapped her arms around her thick coat as she stood for a moment taking in the morning before heading off.

Her breath puffed trails of white. There was the heavy scent of wood smoke in the air from people's fires. A lot of the houses seemed to have a chimney or more modern steel flue. Thankfully it was a smell she liked. Birds chirped and squawked and fossicked and flapped and rustled in the trees and fought with each other, a cow bellowed somewhere in the distance, and then Erica heard the bleat of sheep. *Lovely,* she thought, and so perfectly rural. Tension she didn't realise she'd been holding drained away and she found herself smiling.

She stuck to the streets and returned to the flat three quarters of an hour later, feeling energised and ready for her second work day.

Half an hour later, showered, dressed, fed and her makeup impeccable, Erica left the flat for the office below.

'Good morning. Ready for your first service?' Walter asked, looking up as she knocked gently on the glass mortuary door, which she knew he was behind thanks to the emanating glow.

'I sure am,' she said, smiling.

'Mrs Cole here will be ready for your deft touch when you've had your coffee, won't you?' he said, laying a hand gently on the forehead of the elderly woman lying on the steel gurney, draped in blue up to her chest.

'Okay. Would you like a coffee?' Erica asked Walter.

'I'm all good, thanks.'

'I'll be with you in a bit,' Erica said. She went through and put her handbag into the drawer under the desk, ready for when they had to leave a bit later. She did a quick check through their running sheet on the desk, even though she knew everything was in order. One of the things Erica found she loved about this whole job so far was how methodical it was; for each funeral everything happened in the same order – give or take – and seemed largely predictable and able to be controlled.

A bit like making up a face: there was the odd blemish once the canvas was cleared, but nothing that couldn't be fixed with a dab or brush of something. Though, granted, she hadn't experienced anything yet. And, of course, with humans there was always the risk of error, but luckily Walter ran a tight ship and was calm, which Erica thought were the keys – both to not showing those present there was a problem at all and to dealing with it in a swift manner. Erica liked to think she was unflappable, and she was sure she had been once. But these days she was so quick to get rattled and when that happened it was really easy to be dragged into a spiral of panic that ultimately saw your brain racing around busy and useless and your body doing likewise – the veritable headless chook.

There was a lot riding on her today.

'Hello, Mrs Cole, I'm Erica. I'm going to make you look even more beautiful for your big day than you already are,' she said, looking over her shoulder from the sink where she was washing her hands.

She was glad Walter had made himself scarce – having someone watch over her while she worked didn't bother her, but she didn't want to feel self-conscious talking to a corpse. Talking to her clients had always been an important part of her work. Knowing Walter chatted to those he tended to didn't help her unease. She was also a little nervous about working on her first dead client – not from a practical point of view, but emotionally. Staring down at the grey lifeless pallor suddenly caused Erica to have a vision of looking down at Stuart just after he'd gone. She gulped back the lump in her throat. Her fingers shook as she laid out her tools on the tray – everything in order, taking the time to steady herself, hoping she could.

Please be able to do this. She'd been employed based largely on her makeup skills and experience – so Walter could keep up Mary's side of things that she was so proud to do and was renowned for locally. *Okay. Just a sleeping client. You've got this*, she told herself, foam block loaded with foundation paused.

'I'm really sorry you had cancer,' Erica said to Mrs Cole. 'It's such a horrible disease. It took my husband too. At least passing means pain-free and at peace, huh? Walter told me your husband is doing okay and your son and daughter were holding up well when he saw them. We've all put together the perfect service for you.'

You would have loved it, she thought sadly. *God, this is harder than I thought it would be*, she reflected as she checked the first stage of her work from several angles before moving on.

'Your family told me you were bubbly and chatty – the life of the party. Well, it's your party and you'll have glitter if you want it! I have your favourite shade of green that matches your gorgeous party frock and shoes. And Walter has done a magnificent job of your nails.'

Erica had been surprised when he'd told her he would be doing Mrs Cole's – and any others – nails himself, saying he'd always done Mary's for her and enjoyed it. She'd stopped herself from pointing out that with such a steady hand and if he enjoyed it he may as well learn how to do all the makeup. She didn't want to do herself out of a job! But if he had the attention to detail and patience, then there was no reason he couldn't.

'That's much better with some colour on your skin.'

As she worked, Erica warmed to her task and stopped babbling incessantly and settled into just the odd comment here and there. It was an ingrained habit she didn't want to break. She could have the radio on or streamed a playlist if she wanted, but she'd always kept her attention on her client and didn't think it should matter whether they were alive and knew she was there or not. It felt right to treat them as if they were listening – to a point. Just as she'd hoped her dear mother and her brother before her had been treated. Thankfully Walter had said she had plenty of time and there was no need to rush.

But in less than half an hour she was finished and Mrs Cole looked as if she were heading out for a night of dancing. Erica nodded with satisfaction after looking this way and that to scrutinise her work from different angles. She was happy with what she'd done, pleased to have this first milestone behind her and ready to face the next part of her big day.

'Are we good to go?' Walter asked from the hall a few moments later, clearly having heard her running the water and cleaning up. Thankfully he hadn't poked his head in and seen how much he'd startled her.

Damn it. When will I stop being so bloody jumpy? Slight menopause jitteriness I can live with, but this is a bloody nightmare.

'Yep. Aren't we, Mrs Cole?' Erica found the woman's hand under the cover against her dress and gave it a quick, gentle squeeze.

Walter came into the room and stood on the other side of the gurney. 'You've done a beautiful job, Erica,' he said, smiling across at her. She beamed back.

Together they lifted Mrs Cole into the casket, closed and secured the lid and then slid it into the hearse. They then did a final check of their list. Despite Walter confirming the floral arrangements were safely in the car, Erica checked for herself. The mass of lovely hot pink gerberas belied the solemnity of the occasion.

They locked the office and Erica grabbed her handbag, had a quick final nervous wee, said, 'You've got this,' to her reflection in the mirror, and met Walter at the hearse that he'd already backed out of the garage and had idling just beyond in the car park.

'Right on time,' Walter said.

'Yep.' Erica wondered if she'd imagined a hint of relief to his tone. Maybe he'd been secretly worrying that she'd be one of those people who faffed about getting ready and kept you waiting.

Thanks to Mary's notes and having watched a couple of videos of previous services, nothing felt too foreign to Erica as they set up for the graveside service. They worked like a well-established team as they put together the portable marquee and positioned it, set out the rows of fold-out chairs and the table with the memorial book and pen. The calm reassurance of the officiating celebrant, Jennifer, who had arrived in plenty of time, helped Erica's composure. Finally, they carefully placed the polished dark timber casket over the grave on the supporting straps connected to the device that lowered Mrs Cole into the ground. Minutes later, and right on time, they began greeting Mrs Cole's family and friends and handing out the printed order of service sheets.

'Well done,' Walter said as they sat in the car waiting for the woman from the district council to finish filling the grave in with her backhoe.

'Thanks, Walter.'

'And you're okay? It didn't bring up too many memories and emotions for you?'

'No, I'm good. Thanks for checking, though.'

Stuart's funeral had been nothing like this. His had been a city cremation – the service in the funeral home's building, the casket rolling between curtains and out of sight. Though they'd had everyone back to the house for a wake, just like Mrs Cole's family was doing today.

'Still fine to go to the wake? Just an hour or so of being sociable.'

'Yes, all good.' Erica had liked the members of Mrs Cole's family she'd met earlier. And she thought the wake shouldn't bring her undone, but as she'd found, emotion had an odd way of being prompted and brought to the surface by the smallest and often the seemingly most benign of things. Hopefully keeping her wits about her would stop it from sneaking up on her, though her too-early start and the brain power needed to memorise all the faces and names and keep the perfect reverent smile on her face was beginning to drag at her. Dealing with masses of people at once was exhausting when you were used to working one on one, Erica was realising. She was also beginning to suspect she was more introverted than she'd thought. Or perhaps she was changing. She longed to go back to the flat, kick off her shoes, take a long hot shower and put her feet up.

Chapter Six

On Friday, Erica was at the desk finishing up paperwork from their most recent funeral service when Walter appeared beside her.

'Hello,' she said, trying to sound as bright as possible.

'A tough one yesterday,' he said. 'Just wanted to see how you're travelling.' He pulled out a chair and sat down back from the desk.

'I'm okay, thanks. How are you?'

The truth was Erica didn't really want to think about the day before. Not the actual service, which had been for an eleven-year-old girl who had died from an asthma attack. Not the quiet presence of children, either – their singing at the first part of the service in the hall had been confronting enough, but the guard of honour at the cemetery by the entire primary school in class order had been positively heart-wrenching to lead the green glittering casket through. All the solemn faces with glistening stripes down reddened cheeks, lips in grim lines, dozens of chins quivering.

As she'd stood with Walter afterwards waiting for everyone to leave, she'd wondered if she'd have let her girls go to a funeral at such a young age as some of the kids had been. Probably. The closure would help. Upfront was always best, wasn't it? But that was her girls; she knew them well, being their mother.

Seeing the small groups of children huddled together sobbing, others standing back with lost, bewildered expressions, had almost felled her. She'd gone to bed and not been able to get to sleep. She must have eventually dropped off – only to wake up even earlier than the usual ridiculous hour she'd become accustomed to. She'd sat in the window with her mug of tea looking down on the bakery, enjoying again knowing she wasn't totally alone and wondering if whoever it was knew she was there. A part of her wanted to meet them properly, but a bigger part didn't want to break the spell.

Her last thought before sleeping and her first that morning had been: *Was I at Mark's funeral?* Her brother. She'd been eleven, too. And she couldn't for the life of her recall being at his service. The hardest part about it was that she knew she couldn't ask her dead mother or her dementia-ravaged father. If she could phone him and believe he knew who he was talking to, would he know who Mark had been and remember the details? She was always very careful to only ask benign questions. She'd heard of so many dementia patients becoming tearful and aggressive. It wasn't a chance she'd ever be willing to take.

She tried to shove all thoughts of Mark back down and put a lid on – in the form of scrolling through Facebook and catching up on the news. The night before she'd remembered she'd left her memento of Mark back in Adelaide when she'd packed so quickly and lightly – the misshapen wool jumper that had once been his favourite; she'd wanted to hug it. She'd got used to vague thoughts of Mark and her mother coming to her and wafting past after the briefest of pauses – like a puff of wind onto dandelion seed heads that sent them flying. Memories of Stuart were still too fresh to be banished so quickly.

She and Walter sat in companionable silence until Erica found herself breaching it with quiet careful words. 'I lost my older brother when I was eleven, so it did bring up some stuff for me.' She looked down and fiddled with the hem of her top.

'Oh dear. I'm sorry.'

'I can't remember being at his funeral. And it's bugging me.'

'You probably wouldn't have been back then, at that age. And there definitely wouldn't have been a guard of honour like today. Times have changed a lot. I'm sure giving kids the closure is the right way to go but …'

'I know what you're saying. Yesterday was very hard to watch.'

'It's difficult feeling so helpless. Not being able to take their pain away. And the old cynical me couldn't help thinking, *Buckle up, kids, life isn't getting any easier from here on in*,' Walter said.

'Yes.' Erica smiled. She liked that she could talk to him like this, and it had helped her push aside her thoughts of Mark and get on with work. What would be the point of dwelling on it? She couldn't let it distract her. Renee would say if she was meant to know, she would. If she asked Walter directly, she thought he might say the same.

The front door opened, and Erica left her thoughts behind to return her focus to work.

'Hi, Peggy.' Understandably, the poor woman looked terrible: ashen, drawn and tearstained. Her wife, Shirley, was in the mortuary; Walter had gone and collected her from the hospital during the night.

'Hi, Erica. I'm afraid it's time to make those arrangements. Shirley passed early this morning. Sorry, you'll know all this since

Walter's already picked her up from the hospital. I'm not thinking straight.'

'I'm so sorry for your loss, Peggy.' Erica stood, grabbing the clipboard she'd already prepared with Shirley's information as supplied by Walter. Both she and Walter moved around towards Peggy.

'We're taking good care of Shirl. How are you doing?' Walter asked.

'No hugs, yet, please. I'm determined to not fall apart,' Peggy said, with her hands raised. 'Shirl's no longer suffering; that's the main thing.'

'Okay. Fair enough. Shall I leave you in Erica's capable hands?' Walter said gently.

'Yes, come through,' Erica said, indicating the reception room as she moved towards the door.

'No. Sorry, I don't mean to be blunt. But if it's okay, I'd rather just tell you. I would have phoned, but I needed groceries anyway. And I figured you'd need me to sign something. I have to keep moving, so I don't … You know,' she added, and shrugged. She took a deep breath and then spoke in a rush: 'Anyway. We – Shirley and I – decided on cremation and for me to have her ashes. No service at this stage; I'll decide later what to do. Is that okay?' she finished, and took a few deep breaths.

'Of course,' Walter said. 'Sounds like a good plan to me.'

'Yes. It's entirely up to you,' Erica said. 'Here we are – just down the bottom,' she said, handing over the clipboard and pen.

'I'm sorry to rush,' Peggy said, handing the form and pen back a moment later. 'I'm a bit all at sea.'

'Would you like a cup of tea?' Erica asked.

'No, thanks all the same. I think I'd better just get home.'

'We completely understand, Peggy, don't we, Erica?'

'Yes, absolutely. You need to do what's right for you.'

'Just take good care and call if there's anything either of us can do,' Walter said.

'Thanks. I really appreciate it – and you. Both of you. I'll see you soon.' Peggy left with her woollen cap raised and without another word.

Walter and Erica exchanged downcast glances before Walter said, 'I'll get us a cuppa.'

Erica nodded and returned to her chair behind the desk.

Chapter Seven

Erica returned from her walk and had a shower, as had become her routine after her cup of tea in the window, with whoever was in the bakery for company, while waiting for the grey light of dawn to appear. She was enjoying the routine. This morning, however, being a Saturday and a non-work day, she was suddenly faced with the question of: What now?

How did one pass the weekend in such a tiny place? The flat was already starting to feel small to her at times – sometimes a little claustrophobic; cosy and comforting at others, depending on her mood in that moment.

With a mug of coffee in hand, she went to the window and looked out. From the activity over at the bike shop next to the bakery it seemed that cycling was the main attraction here. That wasn't her bag; she couldn't remember when she'd last been on a bike. Outside the sky was darkening and she didn't fancy getting wet anyway.

If she were back in Adelaide, she'd be having breakfast with the girls or out with her friends. Spending time with *someone* …

Oh, but who was she kidding: during her last weeks back there, she'd become a veritable recluse. She hadn't wanted to leave the house at all. And, anyway, she couldn't afford to be eating out, and browsing shops was too depressing in her current financial state.

God I miss you guys, she thought. She looked at her phone. It wasn't too early to call any one of her support crew, but she didn't want them to worry about her, or inadvertently make them feel guilty about getting on with their lives or not being able to fix her or her circumstances. And which friend was the right one, anyway? One of the things she loved about her small group was how different each member was. She stared at the list of recent calls on her phone. Renee? No. Erica wasn't ready for her kind of pep talk. Suddenly the device in her hand lit up and began to vibrate. Erica cursed the overreaction it caused in her: a massive jolt followed by a racing heart.

'Hi, Michelle, how's things?'

'All good. Just wanted to check how you're going.'

'Good. All good. I've just been for a walk and now I'm contemplating how to spend my day.' Erica cursed the sudden rush of emotion that caused her throat to cut off part of her last word.

'Are you sure you're okay?'

'I'm fine. Just feeling sorry for myself.'

'You're allowed. What's going on?'

'Oh, I don't know.' Suddenly Erica wasn't sure she had the energy to try to explain, even if she could find the words. She knew that sharing her woes with someone helped and she'd learnt her lesson with keeping everything secret about the finances. But Michelle couldn't solve this; it was a time thing.

'Come on, Erica. What's up?'

Erica took a deeper breath and opened her mouth. 'I'm miserable, Mich.'

'Of course you are; you're grieving and you're a long way from home and on your own.'

'I think I've made a big mistake coming here,' Erica found herself whispering.

'Are you tired from the week? It's been a big upheaval and most likely a lot to take in with learning a new job. You're probably exhausted. When you're on top of things, Erica, you're vivacious and a great conversationalist. You love meeting people and chatting, don't you? Don't let what happened with Kayla change that about you. Though, has something happened? With Walter? With the job?'

'No. I really like my job. And Walter. As I said, I'm just being a sad sack. I'm not sure I'm cut out for being alone in such a tiny, isolated place. I don't know what to do with myself now it's the weekend. I don't want to just sit here. This flat, while very lovely, is *tiny*. It's weird, but I shift between not wanting to leave it and not wanting to be here, but when I head out, I can't wait to come back. I get scared, Mich,' Erica said, her voice still a whisper, not wanting to give more power to these fears by voicing them at normal volume.

'Erica, not only are you grieving, but you had a pretty frightening ordeal the other night – and for a few weeks before that. Of course you're going to be jumpy and afraid. It's part of the experience. You've probably got PTSD. It'll take time to recover from. And be careful of trying to outrun your grief. You need to mourn. Maybe some counselling would be a good idea. Keeping busy isn't necessarily the answer.'

'But I'll go mad if I just sit here.'

'Do you want to just vent or would you like me to try and help?'

'Both, I guess. No: suggestions please. Help me, Mich – save me from myself.'

'Okay. How about reading a book – losing yourself somewhere else and in someone else's life for a few hours?'

'I can't seem to settle. There's a shelf full of novels here.'

'How about getting in the car and going for a drive? In my last relationship, my car was my salvation. There's no lonelier place than being in a bad relationship – even if your partner is sitting right beside you. Human company isn't necessarily the answer. You have to find a way to enjoy being with just yourself. It takes time and practice.'

'But how?'

'Well, if it were me, I'd get in my car and drive to the car park of the local park and sit there and cry.'

'Oh, Michelle, I'm so sorry.'

'Ah, it was ages ago. Anyway, this conversation isn't about me and my woeful track record with men and relationships. I know you won't want to spend the money on petrol or coffee or a meal out, but sometimes that's what you need. If you aren't coping with being alone, just mixing with people anonymously can help.'

'But there isn't anyone here.' Erica tried to laugh but what came out was more like a wail. A self-pitying wail, she cursed. 'See, I'm just being a crotchety pain in the arse. Sorry, Mich, I'm poo-pooing your advice.'

'I understand. If you need to sit and be sad, mourn, do it. But just be aware that doing that at the flat there might make it become a sad place rather than a safe and comfortable and happy refuge. Personally, I think you're better off making yourself leave for a while. Just for a few hours. That way you have something to look forward to and you said you like the décor, didn't you?'

'I do. So I'm not sure why I feel so restless and unhappy.'

'I just told you why: you're sad, lonely and depressed. All very normal, which is in no way meant to diminish your feelings. Each process is different. And please don't think because you've already grieved lost loved ones before you'll sail through this time. Grief doesn't work like that; practice does not make perfect in this case. Though, this is all just my opinion. Is there anything I can do to help, Erica?'

'I don't think so. You're right. I need to be patient. I guess.'

'You also can't stop living your life. Sadly, life goes on. Country people are friendly and especially South Australians, but I think people these days keep to themselves and don't tend to intrude. So you might need to be proactive – knock on some doors.'

'And say, "Do you want to be my friend?"' Erica scoffed.

'Well, yeah. I guess. You've lived in the country before.'

'Yes, but as a kid.' Erica's parents having both been school-teachers, she'd got used to changing country schools. She hadn't liked it but hadn't had any trouble making friends. Renee, who believed everything happened for a reason, would probably say that experience had prepared her for this one … The thought of it just exhausted Erica.

'I just want my mum – you know what I mean?'

'Um. Kind of. You wouldn't want *my* mum. You want *your* sort of mum – the mum who would actually give you a hug and tell you everything will be okay, make you a hot chocolate, wrap you up in a blankie, right?'

'Yep.' Erica sighed. *God, I miss you, Mum.* Though, really, it was the sensation of being nurtured, rather than that actual scenario, which, to the best of her knowledge, had never played out in her childhood – even after losing her brother.

'I've wished for that forever. Mine would just manage to make it all about her – always has – and/or she'd point out how pitiful and embarrassing I was. Either way, I'd feel a whole lot worse.'

'Sorry, I didn't mean to …' Erica's parents had been teacher-like through and through; no-nonsense, get-on-with-things and rarely outwardly warm or emotionally demonstrative. But, still, she'd never doubted their love or support.

'It's not your fault I'm so prickly still. Triggered much? Anyway, best we leave that topic well alone, I think. But being an adult can be hard at the best of times, so I hear you. Sometimes what we all need is a nanny.'

'Yes. Exactly. Someone to tell me *precisely* what to do, and when – to organise me. I know that sounds pathetic and a little ironic given the whole financial situation I'm in and how not being involved got me into it. But I just want to not have to think for myself. God, how bloody pathetic am I? There are people who don't even know where their next meal is coming from and here I am …'

'I'm sure you will be okay, Erica. Don't diminish what you're going through. There's no competition with anyone else – well, there shouldn't be. But make sure if you're going to lock yourself away it's with walls made of cardboard not concrete. You don't want to get stuck in that psychological emotional state forever. Find a way to push yourself in little ways in some areas and every-thing will come together.'

'Hmm.' Erica could see her point, but she was stumped.

'Okay, if you want someone to tell you *specifically* what to do …' Michelle continued, as if reading Erica's mind.

'Yes, please. As I said, save me from myself.'

'Right,' Michelle said thoughtfully after a moment. 'Make your car your best friend – your temporary sanctuary when you're out of the flat. Give it a name. I reckon Vera. As in Vera from the British TV series – no nonsense, smart, dependable. She's a Volvo after all ... Get into Vera – or whatever you want to call her; my dad always insisted cars were female – and talk to her. I know, utter madness, but you've no idea how much my car, Ruby, saved my sanity more than once. Get in ... whoever –'

'Vera works for me.'

'– and just drive down the highway. Or treat it as a mission and have a focus. You could go and gather the tourist brochures from all the little towns dotted about, for interest. People are the key to these places. Go out and chat to the volunteers manning the tourist information offices. Or just head to the next town for a coffee or lunch.'

As if sensing the protestation on the tip of Erica's tongue, Michelle continued, and Erica could as good as see her holding up her hand to silence her.

'There's a chance you're using the penny-pinching as an excuse, even subconsciously, maybe – necessary I know, but – and, Renee will tell you this, but you don't want to develop a permanent scarcity mentality. Remember, the Law of Attraction and manifesting abundance Renee and I are always talking about?'

Erica nodded and frowned. Renee and Michelle had both talked about this philosophy – was it a philosophy? – a lot; though not since Erica had dropped her bombshell about her dire financial situation, and she was grateful for that.

'Of course, I don't know exactly where your finances are at at this point, but maybe just maybe you're ... becoming a tad obsessed? Sorry, I don't mean to sound insensitive. It's just there's a fine line,' Michelle said.

'I think you've got a point. I am probably a bit obsessed. But I feel like I have to be. I won't be paid anything for a couple of weeks ... I hear what you're saying about the scarcity mentality but ...' *Could it be that it's complete bollocks?* '... I've got to be careful.'

'Don't be offended by this, but let me put a hundred dollars into your account. Then go for a long drive and have lunch out on me.'

'I can't do that.'

'Of course you can. Erica, you would do the same for me. I know you would.'

You're right. I would. But ...

'Please text me your bank account details. And we'll have no arguments on the matter.'

Erica's eyes filled with tears. Doubly touching was the fact that Michelle, who worked in childcare, was by no means well off financially herself.

'You're the best, Mich,' Erica croaked. 'Thanks.'

'And just to be clear: this is a gift, not a loan. Promise me you're going to send the details right after I hang up?'

'Okay. I promise.'

'And then you're going to get in the car and you and Vera are going to have a lovely day together – driving around having a look. Cry if you want to. The number of times I drove up the South-Eastern Freeway with no destination in mind, listening to a sad song, floods of tears streaming down my face, I can't tell you.'

'I'm really sorry you went through all that.'

'I know, thanks. But, honestly, a part of me isn't. It's made me who I am and I'm at peace with me now. And I reckon Renee would say that maybe I had to go through it to help you.'

'I love who you are, Mich.'

'And I love you. You'll get through this, Erica. You'll see. Just be kind to yourself and don't be afraid to reach out and lean on others, and be vulnerable.

'Okay, I'm going to go now and you're going to text me those details. Have, if not a good day, at least a better day than ten minutes ago. I'll check on you later.'

'Thanks, Michelle. You're the best. Give Daphne a big hug and an extra treat from me. God, I miss her.'

'Oh god, I've had you on speaker,' Michelle said, 'and now I have said pooch sitting glaring at me insisting on being given a t–r–e–a–t.'

'Oops, sorry about that.' Erica smiled. The serious red kelpie would stare up at her mistress and refuse to move until she was rewarded with a treat. Because Michelle could rarely resist *that* look.

'Oh well, it might distract her from noticing me getting ready to give her a b–a–t–h. Okay. I'm going. See you.'

'Bye.'

As Erica was in her online banking looking for the BSB and account numbers, which she didn't know off by heart, a text came through from Michelle reminding her to send them. Erica was uneasy as she did, but also had to acknowledge she felt lighter after their conversation. And it was true. She absolutely would have done the same for Michelle – or any one of her friends in the same position. She finished her text with a row of kisses and hearts. It felt so inadequate.

As Erica got dressed to go out, she pondered her friend's words and realised that, while she was very grateful for the money, what she'd gained more from their chat was a plan for the day. Without allowing herself to reconsider, she grabbed her handbag and keys and headed out.

Downstairs with the flat and external door to the main building closed behind her, she looked at her dear old Volvo with a new mindset — it was not just a vehicle of physical transportation but a means of freedom and companionship. Vera now represented mental and emotion freedom — well, she hoped. She experienced a surge of affection for the relatively nondescript white car.

Right, Vera, let's see what's of interest around here, she thought, closing the car door behind her with a solid thunk.

Michelle was right in that there was comfort in the familiarity. It was just the two of them. And that suddenly felt not only okay but good, as reliable-as-ever Vera roared to life.

Chapter Eight

Erica deliberated for a few seconds whether to head left – further north from Melrose – or to turn right – back towards Adelaide. No, left it is – she'd go to Orroroo. She'd had a year of primary school there. Couldn't remember which one, nor any actual details about the place. Each of the towns they'd lived in had been visually very similar, as far as she could remember, due to being laid out by the same surveyor.

South Australia was full of towns with big wide main streets, divided in two by large loops of concrete-edged median strip, out from which a grid of straight streets radiated. The perimeter of the original town had streets that tended to be unoriginally named North, South, East and West. Some were given the differentiator of street, road or terrace, just to shake things up. Things got positively wild as subdivisions were added later and curved roads and cul-de-sacs were included and road names took on the surnames of important people in the area or other place names. It was almost as if someone or several somebodies had been positively spiteful towards the order of things at some point since the early days.

What Erica did remember – and again, not specifically of a particular town – was the discomfort of starting as a new kid each year, further highlighted by being the child of two teacher parents. She'd got quite good at meeting people and forming friendships, but not so good at keeping in touch when they moved to the next school and town the following year. She didn't have one friend from her school years – well, except Steph. But she didn't count because they were cousins and hadn't ever been at the same school anyway.

Erica remembered now how much she'd loved starting school in grade one. And how she'd begged her parents not to move at the end of that first year – and the next few. Then she'd stopped because what was the point? It just caused arguments and didn't change anything. At the end of every school year, she'd hug her friends goodbye. They always vowed to keep in touch – to write, via snail mail in those days. And call; the one landline in the house. But they never seemed to – or not beyond the first few times. Sometimes Erica had a few weeks of the summer holidays before they left. Sometimes not even that. But it always seemed to happen fast – not without warning, because inside she always remained on tenterhooks, but without warning in the sense that her parents didn't ever ask her or Mark's opinions about leaving or if they had a preference of where to go. Not that Erica would have – but it would have been nice to have been consulted.

A wave of sympathy towards her parents swept through her. It wouldn't have been easy on them either. Erica had cried and sulked a lot. So had Mark.

But then, she remembered, he'd also started getting into minor trouble – caught underage drinking, out late with friends.

Hanging with the wrong crowd. She'd heard that phrase through the walls in arguments. Also, 'Brighten your ideas up else you'll be in serious trouble.' Perhaps that was one of the reasons they had moved so often – embarrassment at their elder child's antics plus removing him from temptation. It wouldn't have been a good look for two schoolteachers, being unable to control their own child. Erica could see how that might backfire, too: damned if you do, damned if you don't. But they were the eighties; it was a completely different time with very different influences.

As well as the towns looking much the same, all the schools had too. Back then it had been classrooms with horizontal timber slats painted in glossy cream. Later the weatherboard was the wider boards of simulated timber – cement sheet probably, with quite possibly plenty of asbestos in there too – also painted, but showing the manufactured texture of simulated timber lines and squiggles of knots. Inside, all rooms had blue or beige carpet with low pile. No air-conditioning: instead large fans whirled overhead, rattling and shuddering unevenly when on high speed. The constant wondering if and when they would fly off their mounts was always a major distraction in high summer. As were the boys who tossed up sodden chewed paper – spit bombs – leaving the girls to roll their eyes. 'Only small minds do that,' the swots in class would say, including Erica. 'Smaller minds notice,' was the retort.

Erica did admit to having had some fun times. But the cloud of moving was the dominant memory: leaving friends, trying to make new ones, wondering what everyone she knew was doing while she was packing and unpacking and starting over. It didn't help that her brother was six years older, and nor that she wasn't given the same leniency due to the dark cloud of recent and not-so-recent abductions of girls in South Australia. With no one else to play with, and her brother off exploring on his bike, free of the constraints of his younger sister, Erica remembered wanting to hang out with her parents, but they had always been too busy getting ready for their own new start.

Her bedroom had become her sanctuary. Perhaps that's why she loved the little flat back at Melrose so much; it reminded her a little of those days.

Maybe she was unsettled due to being back in the country and having feelings and memories from her past brought up. Or perhaps it was all mixed up in her grief or yearning for a time that was meant to be fun and carefree. It had had its moments – the good and not so good.

It didn't help that out here was short blue-grey saltbush as far as the eye could see – well, that's what she assumed it was. Beneath it was brown dirt – almost an ochre colour. It was winter, but she suspected this was how the countryside this far north looked all the time – maybe just a little darker and fresher after rain. This really was the edge of the outback, wasn't it? She knew people loved this type of landscape. Erica couldn't understand why. To her it was depressing; it wasn't helping her mood at all.

For a moment she considered turning around. But when she checked her mirrors, there was a truck looming up behind her. She'd chosen this way for a reason – if not consciously – Renee would probably say. Maybe reminiscing and being melancholy was what she needed, despite the discomfort.

The truck zoomed by with a loud whoosh, roar and rattle. *It's okay, Vera, just a bloody big truck.* And then she laughed at herself. A slight sour stench of livestock stayed with her in the car with its old, leaky seals.

Seeing a sign pointing to Orroroo Giant Gum Tree, she pulled in, keen to see something other than the expanse of dreary land-scape all around and the straight bitumen road ahead with its white dashed centre line. It was all a little mesmerising; how did long-range truck drivers do it?

As she drove at a crawl on the dirt road, surprised to discover some puddles that were wet and squelchy beneath her tyres, splashing as she traversed them, she marvelled at the enormous tree looming up ahead – the only stately living thing for miles. No wonder it was considered so special as to be celebrated with a plaque and signage.

Very impressive, she thought, coming to a stop. She turned off the car, got out and walked over to the information board facing the giant specimen, which was apparently over five hundred years old. Initially in awe, Erica became sad in the silence surrounding her and the majestic lone tree. This tree had once been accompanied by many more, and should still be. Industrialisation and progress were depressing right then, though if not for all that had come before, she'd not be there at all. And nor would Mackenzie and Issy – and they were true gifts to be treasured.

Feeling a little buoyed, and determined not to become completely depressed, she returned to her car, drove back out to the road and then turned left to carry on to Orroroo. It must be close, mustn't it? She hadn't taken note of the number of kilometres from Melrose to Orroroo on the map or the numbers on her speedo when she'd started; she'd just looked at the two dots on the map relative to the length of her thumb.

Driving into Orroroo, Erica felt unsettled. Nervous even. *What's that about?* she wondered. *Bloody hormones. Go away.* She concentrated on pulling off into the forecourt of a small rustic petrol station and up to the bowser.

As she filled up, she looked around. *God, what's up with you?* she thought as the unease started up again. She'd spent a year here but it was only vaguely familiar. And not in a happy, nostalgic way. She didn't even know which direction the house they'd lived in was, nor the primary school. And she felt no desire to drive around and look for either landmark. *Is that weird? Probably.* Erica thought it would make sense if she'd been bullied at school — or outside of it — but she hadn't. Well, not that she recalled. And she wasn't sure just how well she could trust her memories these days.

Just not enough sleep. And you're a bit jumpy all round. Your mind is playing tricks on you. Let it go.

Back then these towns were all livelier, weren't they? she thought, forcing herself onto another tack.

She'd almost filled her tank — from a quarter — before the next vehicle rolled past, a shiny dark-grey four-wheel drive towing a modern caravan with tinted windows.

The town hadn't even been touched by the corporate hand of one of the big fuel conglomerates. The building attached was clearly a workshop — through the back she could see shelves filled with small boxes that she imagined held nuts and bolts or maybe fan belts and whatever other consumables cars needed. *No*, she thought, looking around, *not completely a mechanics* — perhaps it was part hardware and part rural supplies store too — the sort for machinery needs not animal care. In there were no aisles of grocery essentials, bright lighting, lurid branding.

No food or snacks at all that she could see.

There were a few lawnmowers and drums of something in varying sizes with different-coloured labels — more a haphazard, left unattended feel than careful placement.

There was a man sitting behind a wooden counter with dark stains, but no lollies — not even a box of charity sweets with a slot for donations — no fridge for drinks, and no pie warmer. Erica's stomach gave a grumble of annoyance, and she experienced another quiver of disquiet.

'Just the fuel, thanks,' she said brightly to the man, who barely looked at her when he took her card and silently processed her purchase before handing it back without so much as a grunt. She thanked him and also silently sent more gratitude to Michelle.

As she got back into the car, she sighed loudly in an effort to regain her composure. She really wished budding artist and very imaginative Renee was there; she'd love to give a commentary on what this place and the man's inside stories were – what bodies were being hidden, what money laundering was taking place. It felt very much like a scene in a movie in which a slow rusty sign swung slowly and let out an eerie squeal as it moved back and forth. *That's what it is.* Erica laughed at her ridiculous imagination. *Just too many tales about Snowtown and Truro*, she thought, though was unable to shake the unease rippling away under her ribs as she drove out.

She pulled in a little further down the street in front of the information centre. She took advantage of the aged but clean toilet facilities next door, before heading into a recently renovated building housing clear plastic displays of brochures, most of which she'd already collected in Melrose. She felt a bit bad about leaving so abruptly, but there was nothing but tourist booklets and a little reception desk behind which was someone hard at work on a computer. She said thanks and left.

A gaze up and down the street told her the town was not thriving – not just empty of people today. She could see no interesting shops to explore, further highlighted by the absence of advertising material in the information office. Lots of the buildings seemed empty – no signage, windows so dirty they were almost mirrors. Nonetheless, ignoring the jangle of unease inside her, she forced herself to take a stroll. *It's the people who make it*, she told herself, recalling Michelle's pep talk. She saw someone in the front yard of the police station and headed that way.

'Hello,' she said to the small black short-haired border collie that put its paws up on the top of the woven-wire fence. A young woman in navy-blue T-shirt with *POLICE* written in white on the chest came around from the side. Erica stepped back and lowered her hand.

'She's fine – won't bite. Loves a pat.'

'She's gorgeous. Aren't you?' Erica said, lifting her hand to pat the dog's head. But she received so many licks she couldn't get anywhere near fur. The young woman opened the gate and the dog rushed out and jumped up on Erica's legs.

'Ooh, you're lovely.' Erica patted the dog.

'Hop down, Milly. Sorry, she's young,' the woman said when Milly took no notice.

'She's okay. She's gorgeous.' At that moment the dog got down and took up a position on her back with her legs in the air in front of Erica, who couldn't resist rubbing her stomach. 'Are you going to be a crime fighter, Milly?' she asked, rubbing the smooth skin.

'I keep telling my boyfriend to take her out with him.' Ah, so not the officer in charge. And what was her accent? Erica thought she'd detected one, though she was terrible at picking them – always muddled Canada and the USA and Scottish and Irish. Fancy being out here if you were from a lush cool climate – summer must be hell. *The things you do for love*, she thought.

'Come on, Milly, we have to go in now,' the woman said, opening the lid of the post box and checking inside before closing it again. Erica noticed the first spots of rain.

'Thanks for the cuddle, Milly. You've made my day. Thanks,' she said, smiling, to the human. 'Enjoy your day.'

'You too.'

Erica crossed the wide street and made her way up the other side. Just the basics – chemist, deli, pub. Probably best, she thought. She didn't have money to spend and didn't need anything. Her intermittent hunger pangs had even gone. She wasn't sure what she wanted to eat, anyway, or whether she fancied sitting down in an establishment or getting something to consume in the car.

As she drove around and through the town, it still didn't seem familiar. What year had she been here? She couldn't remember.

She headed towards Peterborough but instead took the turn-off to Jamestown. Just because. She was suddenly really hungry again. She drove past a couple of places that looked like old-fashioned cafés, but still nothing piqued her interest. She became annoyed with herself for turning this into a ridiculous and quite possibly unsatisfactory quest.

Instead of travelling on to Laura she decided to head back home to Melrose. She'd make a sandwich at the flat and save her money. She'd keep a visit to Laura and the other towns further south for another time. Content with her decision, she settled back into the drive. The landscape now had some lovely trees and a generally lusher look. This suited her much better and brightened her mood again. Except for her stomach. It was now protesting and she was exasperated with herself for not eating earlier.

She came to the main road to Melrose, which was about twenty minutes away, she reckoned, and after checking for traffic turned. And there right in front of her was a big red sign announcing *Bakery*.

Yes! Her mouth watered encouragingly.

She pulled over and went in, letting out a sigh of relief at seeing it was bustling with people and there were tables to sit at and a big blackboard menu up on the wall behind the counter, which included a display case of hot baked goods on one side and cakes and pastries on the other.

A freezer with the Golden North insignia stood near a fridge full of drinks.

No more procrastinating!

She lined up and tried to look at the blackboard, though it was now blocked from her view by the people ahead of her. Her mouth watered as a plate with a pie and a squirt of tomato sauce was carried past by a waitress also holding a mug of coffee. Decision made! She heard her dad's voice in her head: you'll start to look like a pie if you're not careful. *You're probably right, but too bad.*

Erica tucked into her steak and mushroom pie as if it was her last meal – it tasted almost *that* good too. After a few forkfuls, she forced herself to pause and take her time.

But while the meal was lovely, she didn't like sitting and eating alone, so soon headed off.

Chapter Nine

'Good morning,' Walter said, coming in looking slightly dishevelled, followed by a waft of icy breeze. From upstairs Erica had seen the trees down the street moving, though it had been calm when she went for her walk earlier. She'd almost convinced herself to turn right at the western end of the street, just past the historic brewery where farmland began, but had found herself instead turning left and continuing along the streets rather than going next to the creek. Just like every other morning. But at least this time she hadn't had a rush of anxiety at the thought of heading into the cover of the trees. Maybe tomorrow she'd conquer that too.

'Good morning.'

'Bit brisk out there,' Walter said, standing beside the reception desk and unwinding his scarf.

'Did you walk?'

'No,' he said with a laugh. 'Ridiculous level of layering, I know. I have no explanation, except to say we elderly need to protect ourselves from the elements − even when barely out in them.'

Erica wondered if he had made so much noise from way back down the hall for her benefit because she'd been so clearly startled whenever he came in. She was surprised and relieved to realise the clattering of the back door hadn't caused her to jump this time. Maybe she was getting better.

'It was cool when I walked this morning, but it was calm.'

'It's the wind that annoys me,' Walter said. 'Shouldn't let it, given it's out of my control, but there we are; it does. At least the fire season's a good way off yet. That's when you start taking serious notice of the wind and its direction. It's okay – we haven't had a major emergency here for years,' he added, waving a hand dismissively when he saw the alarm on Erica's face.

She hadn't given the fire risk of country living a thought or even really realised just how rural this place was until she'd arrived. Her anxiety gripped, until she reminded herself that there were some lovely old buildings in town and there wouldn't be if a fire had gone through at some point. No, she wasn't going to let that plague her.

Walter pulled out a chair from the desk and sat down. 'Erica?'

'Yes.' Erica cursed the apprehension that caused her voice to squeak. He was always so jovial. If not upbeat, all the time – he was usually smiling and that could be heard in his voice. Now his tone was just like her previous bosses' when she'd been asked to join them in the conference room and then moments later been told she no longer had a job; she had been retrenched due to the company going into voluntary receivership. She cursed her immediate jump to the negative and to it being about her. She was working in a funeral home; this *was all* serious business.

'I owe you an apology.'

'Oh? What for?'

'I should have checked on you over the weekend or at least made sure on Friday that you would be okay left to your own devices. It quite slipped my mind that it was your first one here – you've so quickly become such an important and welcome fixture. So, I just didn't think that you would be at a loose end. More, I just didn't think. I've become so set in my ways – so keen to keep myself to myself when I get the chance … I hope you can forgive me.'

Erica frowned slightly to herself. Had one of her friends said something to him? No, she was being paranoid. 'Oh no. Not at all. I'm a big girl, Walter – I can entertain myself. There's nothing to forgive.'

'You're too kind. Still, it was very remiss of me. So, you were okay?'

'Perfectly fine. Great, thanks.' Erica was glad she wasn't having to sit there and lie – she had been perfectly fine after all. Thanks to Michelle. 'I went for a drive and had lunch at Stone Hut.'

'Ah, yes, the best pies this side of the Black Stump, or something – isn't that the claim? They are rather good. Did you partake?'

'I did. And while I can't yet claim to be a connoisseur in the meat pie department, I did enjoy my steak and mushroom hot baked delight very much.' Erica couldn't remember when she'd last had a meat pie before the one she'd had with Walter the previous week. 'I also treated myself to an ice cream.'

'Our local Golden North brand, I hope.'

'Absolutely.'

'The factory is just down the road in Laura, but alas they don't open for tours these days. I'm sure my son's school class did a visit back in the day.'

'I've left Laura for another time.'

'It's gorgeous. I particularly like the bronzes commemorating CJ Dennis. They have a lovely art gallery, too. There are some very pretty towns around here, but unfortunately none is really thriving in a shopping or browsing sense any longer. Well, not like they used to. Mary and I loved to visit antique shops many years ago on our free days; they used to be dotted around everywhere – at least two or three in most of the towns about.'

When Walter fell silent, Erica said, 'And then yesterday I had a lovely quiet day reading – one of the books on the shelf in the flat.'

'Mary loved her books,' Walter said. 'Reading was her go-to when she got the chance. Nothing too high-brow; popular fiction she could dip in and out of. In theory. Most of the time she got hooked and didn't put the book down until she'd finished. I'm so pleased your weekend was okay.' He was clearly relieved.

'Better than okay, Walter, it was great. How about yourself? What did you get up to?'

'Nothing special. But my weekend was wonderful.' Erica noticed the last word was drawn out like a long, contented sigh. 'Thankfully no one died and I got to potter around the garden. Thanks to your presence here and you being so good at picking everything up quickly and efficiently, I was able to fully relax for the first time in ages. It was very good. Other than Mary being missing, it could have been the old days. But I did feel her presence sitting on the bench nearby reading. Mary wasn't much for gardening, but she always kept me company. I did overdo it a bit pulling weeds because I'd left it so long. So, I had a long soak in the tub and then spent Sunday in front of the box watching some golf.'

'That sounds like a lovely weekend.'

'It was. And I have you to thank.'

'You're far too generous, Walter. I'm glad to be of help,' Erica said, not really sure what to say. 'Thank you for the job' is what she should have said, she realised too late.

'Right. I've got a few things to do out the back, so I'll leave you to it for a bit,' he said, getting up and leaving Erica.

Chapter Ten

Wednesday morning Erica woke feeling glum. She couldn't shift the heaviness, which she decided wasn't tiredness even though she still wasn't sleeping well. But this gloomy feeling was bothersome because not only was she unable to shift it, she couldn't figure out what was causing it. Not really convinced it was part of the general grief following her shadow-like, she went through in her mind the anniversaries of loved ones she'd lost and birthdays she'd memorised. Nothing.

She was surprised and a little disappointed to realise she'd missed acknowledging her mother's date of death – just days earlier – but managed to not dwell on it. Reluctantly she was forced to give up, the words of Renee echoing in her mind as she headed downstairs to work: 'Trying to force it out wouldn't help: it'll come when you've given up and are least expecting it. And if it doesn't, then it doesn't matter and you weren't meant to remember.' Renee also reckoned illness manifested when you stressed over things. That Erica could believe – Stuart had been a stress-head, despite his veritable mantra of, 'It'll be fine, don't worry about it.' He'd tossed and turned at night, had plenty of startled awakenings from frightening dreams. He always laughed everything off – and he'd ended up with cancer. So Erica did her best not to worry, but far too often found herself worrying about worrying.

She'd tried years earlier to learn to meditate from a book she'd bought but had given up. She still wasn't quite sure what meditation really was and how you knew when you were actually doing it right. She could stare out the window of a bus not seeing or taking note of what was passing by, losing chunks of time such that she suddenly wondered how she'd got to where she had and so quickly. That was kind of meditative, wasn't it? Letting go, giving in. Giving up on meditation had at least given her mind fewer things to worry about, she'd said with a laugh to Stuart at the time. Though maybe she'd tried to learn at the wrong time in her life – when the kids were little and Stuart was bustling about and she couldn't find enough peace for herself – not even long enough to eat a full piece of toast without it going cold. That was probably exactly when she'd needed to learn, but maybe now at least she could give it another shot. She shook it all aside and went downstairs, her heavy black cloud trying to drag her down at every step.

'How's things?' Walter said, appearing and slumping heavily into the empty chair behind the desk beside Erica.

'Good, thanks.' Today was looking like a quiet day. Older people – and the majority of their workload – tended to pass overnight or in the early hours, which meant they would be aware by now. Today they were having a stock delivery so she thought she might see about changing the display around to keep her from being bored. Walter hadn't been lying when he'd said right upfront that the job was a bit feast or famine.

'Are you okay, Erica?' Walter said, bringing them both mugs of coffee – their second; she'd done the first run back into the kitchen as had become their habit.

'Hmm.'

'You seem a bit down this morning.'

'I don't know. Something is bugging me but I can't put my finger on it. It's not the sense I've forgotten something – well it kind of is – but I'm sure not something recent, like anything to do with work or the flat, if that makes any sense. Probably not.'

'No, it does.'

'Anyway, you don't seem all that cheerful yourself. Is something up?'

'I missed my wedding anniversary – well, you know what I mean. Thirty-eight years it would have been.'

'Oh, I'm so sorry. Is there anything I can do?'

'No, I don't think so. Thanks. Just these reminders pull the stuffing out of us grieving souls. Hopefully it'll get easier as time passes. Unfortunately, it took an email from my son to remind me,' he said ruefully.

'Ah, so you're feeling a bit guilty too, then?'

'Yes. How could I have forgotten it?'

'Did you remember every year when Mary was here? My husband and I had a terrible record of acknowledging on the actual day. I'm not sure what that says about our marriage,' Erica said sadly.

'You're right, though – Mary always remembered, but I can probably count the number of times I did on two hands, if I'm being generous.'

'Well, there you go. I think you're being extraordinarily hard on yourself. And knowing what I do about Mary, I think she wouldn't want you beating yourself up on her account.'

'Yes, you're probably right,' he said on his way back out to the mortuary. But to Erica's ear his mood wasn't any lighter. And neither was hers. If they hadn't automatically done their coffee already, she'd have suggested they treat themselves, as a circuit breaker – they'd been very restrained and not succumbed to the lure of real coffee and bakery treats in the café across the street since that first time.

'So, none the wiser about what's eating you, then?' Walter said, reappearing an hour later.

'Nope.'

At that moment Walter's mobile rang. Erica turned and watched him while he took the call, trying to read his expression.

'Yes. Right. Okay.' He made a note on the pad of paper in front of him. 'We're on our way.' And then he hung up and sat back into his chair for the briefest moment. Erica's stomach flipped. Was this work? Or had something happened to his son? No, he'd said, 'We're on our way.'

'What's happened?'

'That was the police. There's been a drowning a bit further north. A young lad. We're needed to go and get the body. Are you okay to come with me?' he said, getting up.

Something in Erica shifted, but she couldn't grasp what or how or what it might mean, and the tiny piece she had held disappeared. She looked at Walter as she tried to reach for it again, pull it back, make it bigger, while also trying to comprehend his words.

'There'll be plenty of people there to help me load the body, so I won't need you in that way. But it would be a good idea for you to see and know how this part of the job works. Also, your company would be very welcome,' he added gently.

Erica's brain suddenly cleared so much it seemed completely empty and she couldn't form much in the way of thought at all, other than the reality that she was shaking inside.

'Erica? If you're coming, we have to get going,' Walter prompted.

'Sorry. Yes. Of course.' She took a deep breath and got up, and as if on autopilot gathered her scarf and jacket from the nearby hook and then grabbed her phone and handbag. Her legs were quivering and unstable and her skin clammy as she followed Walter out the back to the garage and into the white delivery van.

Chapter Eleven

She settled in her seat and did up her belt, trying to ignore what was going on inside her, but it was hard. Her heart now seemed to be doing weird things: tumble turns one way, pausing, and then tumble turns the other. And the jittery feeling around it was increasing in intensity and spreading right through her, way beyond where her heart was. *Shit, am I about to have a panic attack?* She'd never had one before but had heard of lots of women her age suddenly starting to have them.

Okay. Just the bloody hormones. Get a grip. She looked out the windscreen and tried to ignore the physical stuff going on inside her and remember what advice she'd read for dealing with it. She must have. What, other than trying to breathe slowly and deeply? That was a struggle as it was at times. Random images of her fearful last few weeks in Adelaide and first mornings here suddenly flashed into her mind. She was becoming better at getting her fear back in check.

Thanks to Kayla.

Christ, where did that come from? I wouldn't be in this state if not for that.

Fuck, I'm arguing in my own head. Damn it.

Focus.

Despite seeing it coming towards them from the other way, a truck roaring past startled Erica. The sound was unusually loud and the van's shudder in the whoosh of air was frightening in her heightened state.

But it also served to nudge her out of her reverie, and it was like coming back online. Her senses rebooted. Ah yes, the senses. Concentrate on them. *Ground yourself in the here and now and by focussing on what you can hear, taste, smell, see, touch.* Wasn't that what she'd read somewhere?

As they drove in silence, Erica stared out the windscreen, concentrating on breathing and taking an inventory of her senses. Gradually the sharp, ragged drag of breath up and down inside her smoothed and she was left with an overall slight vibrating feeling. Still not ideal, but this she could cope with. Calmer and with her brain clearing, she returned her attention to work and the job they were on.

She now remembered Walter telling her the other day that a journey such as this meant, after collecting the body – wherever that was and however long it took – they sometimes came back to the funeral home and left the drive to the coroner in Adelaide until first thing the next day. Or, if the detectives had finished with the scene and the body in situ when they got there and had already identified the deceased, they might immediately begin the drive to Adelaide. Once at the forensic centre, they might wait a few hours for the autopsy to be completed and the body released to them or leave without it if there was a delay for some reason.

They drove in silence punctuated by the occasional moment of small talk – mainly chat from Walter and automatic replies from Erica.

Erica longed to engage properly but the only topic that came to mind was the one at hand and she knew from the brevity of the conversation Walter had had with the police he didn't have much more he could tell her. She was also aware that her desire to now chatter and fill the space was down to nerves, so she forced herself to stay mainly silent. The radio was turned low.

Eventually they pulled onto a rough track – two bare-earth tyre-width lines either side of weeds and foliage that brushed against the underneath of the van. They stopped just before a police car with its lights flashing. An officer was standing beside it.

'Go a little further on, over the rise,' the officer said, indicating with a wave of his hand before Walter even spoke; his window had barely gone down far enough. Erica wondered if Walter knew him.

'Okay,' Walter said, putting the van back into gear and moving forwards slowly again.

Or that's what Erica thought had been said; she was too busy dealing with a new rush of anxiety that had caught her unawares at seeing the flashing lights. It was a sudden and stark reminder of the scene outside her home that dark night not so long ago – though today it was daylight and there was no fire truck.

A few moments later they arrived at a vague clearing. An ambulance was parked nearby just off the track, alongside several other vehicles wedged right up against the closest trees. Several people of differing shapes and sizes, clad in orange overalls with *SES* across the back in black, stood beside three lads with mussed hair shrouded in blankets and with their arms folded across their chests. Erica couldn't see their expressions. One of the people clad in orange was comforting another SES colleague.

A long lump draped in white was a little way away, just up from where the edge of the creek lapped at the dry stones and fine gravel. Looking closely at the ground around the body were two people in black pant suits – a woman and a man by the looks. Detectives?

Erica stared and was only vaguely aware of Walter getting out of the van, opening the back door, closing it again – the sounds seeming hollow and a long way off. Had he spoken to her – told her to stay there or asked her to go with him or maybe do something else?

She blinked in her search for clarity and a flash of something shot across the back of her mind like a flare. She tried to force it forwards, but it was gone.

A strange vague déjà vu strolled into her, causing her pulse to skip and then feel as if it had stopped.

Then clarity lit her up inside, like storm clouds parting for a beam of sunlight.

Mark. Erica let out a weighty sad sigh. She hadn't been there when they'd fished his body out of the water hole, but this was very close to the scene she'd imagined in her mind's eye.

Anxiety rose again and she worked hard to dispel it. Her frozen state suddenly ended with the desperate need to escape the cabin and take in fresh air. Her hands struggled with the handle for an extraordinary amount of time before she finally opened her door and stumbled out – as carefully as she could without drawing any attention. Erica leant against the van breathing in the cold morning air while staring at the water, trying to appreciate its beauty and ignore the body it had claimed.

The air was still. Strangely, she realised, there was zero bird life – not in the trees nor overhead. Though she couldn't be sure for she realised her ears were filled with white noise. And just under that was the thumping of her heart in her chest like a drum.

Her ears emptied of the cotton wool in a moment and she heard instead loud cracks of twigs and crunches of dried leaves. Erica turned around to see people moving around or shifting their weight. A few voices could be heard murmuring. No actual words. Nodding heads. Gesticulating hands and arms – those of the lads, the uniformed police officers now over talking to them, Walter with his hand on the shoulder of an SES person. An ambulance officer clad in green overalls stood with an arm around their similarly dressed colleague. Was it a relative – an uncle, the victim's father? Were the two people being comforted both parents or close relatives of the deceased? They all probably knew each other.

She wondered if that had been the case when Mark had had his accident. How many friends had been with him? She couldn't remember. Where exactly had it happened? She couldn't remember that either. She frowned. Tried hard. Nothing. Had her parents told her? They must have. Did she ever go there? Did they? Again, probably, but she had no idea.

The next thought that lodged in her mind and this time refused to shift was: where had it happened – near what town? She couldn't remember. How could she not? It was one of the biggest events of her life.

Erica frowned as, in her mind, a bright light shone into her eyes. *Clarity? What are you trying to tell me? Car headlights?* She closed her eyes and concentrated. Flashes of light in several directions joined the solid yellow light shining upon her. *Camera flashes?*

A bolt of fear gripped her – a hundred times more intense than the regular but short bouts of menopause-related anxiety and heart palpitations. While she wanted to complete the memory puzzle, she also wanted to physically separate herself from this – from whatever it was. But she was frozen; her whole body was rigid and seemingly anchored to the ground. She took several deep breaths, willing the fear to subside.

Okay. I'm ready. Come on, tell me.

But the harder she fought to tug the memory free, the more it retreated. And then the light was gone and her mind was dark and empty again.

She opened her eyes and focussed on regaining her composure, glad no one had noticed her, or at least commented. Her heart rate returned to normal and the fear seeped away. But frustration and questions remained. *Jesus. Where did that come from? What was with the lights? Was I at a media conference? On TV? About Mark? Or something else?* She rubbed her face, exhaustion taking over and pushing everything else aside.

New movement grabbed her attention. Walter was walking towards her. Behind him were two SES volunteers carrying his trolley on which was the mound of bagged body.

Erica moved to the back of the van, ready to help slide the trolley in – this bit she could do, even in her zombie-like state. But she was too slow and had to stand back out of the way, looking on helplessly and feeling guilty and annoyed with herself, while Walter instructed the SES members.

Erica got back into the front of the van as the back doors closed with a clunk, and was immediately comforted by the familiarity and being away from the silent yet still tight and grim atmosphere outside the car.

'I'm so sorry if I've let you down, Walter. I ...' she said when he got into the driver's side and closed the door. *I ... what?* Erica had no words and also too many words. Ultimately, she supposed, she'd let herself down.

'You haven't. Not at all. It would have been good for you to meet some of the people, but, Erica, it's okay. Really. I understand how confronting it might have been for you. Don't worry about it.'

Chapter Twelve

After the police officers had guided them with waving arms as Walter had performed a careful several-point turn in the tight space they drove slowly back out the way they'd come, so slowly Erica could hear the twigs snapping under them and the creak and hum of the rubber tyres on the smooth track.

Erica stared into the side mirror at the group they'd left behind, still standing, mainly motionless. She continued watching as they became gradually smaller and smaller and then disappeared from sight when Erica and Walter turned into a slight bend.

She barely took in the journey and it was ages before she managed several deep breaths. She hadn't realised she'd been holding her breath, but she was now struggling for air.

'They've finished with the scene – it happened really early this morning – and I have the identification details, so we're going straight down to Adelaide. Sadly, that was both his parents back there.'

Erica nodded in response to Walter, unable to find words. *His*, Erica mused.

'Are you okay?' Walter asked. She blinked and tried to sharpen her attention. They were on the highway at full speed and they might as well have been teleported there for the time she'd lost.

'Honestly, I don't know, Walter.'

'Understandable,' Walter said with a nod. 'Poor Todd.'

'Sorry?'

'That's his name – our precious cargo.'

Oh.

'Fifteen.'

'God. Yes. Horrible.'

'It's times like these you are reminded of how fragile life is.'

Erica nodded. They lapsed into silence.

A few minutes later, Walter said, 'It's winter – why would anyone be out here swimming? Another tragic accident resulting from youthful skylarking, I suppose.'

'Hmm.' She stared out the window at the farmland now whizzing past the window. A farmer was rounding up sheep.

'Depressing, huh? How life just carries on,' he said, nodding in the direction out of the window to the farmer toiling away.

Erica nodded; she didn't have the energy to exclaim he'd read her mind, and the mood wasn't right for the pronouncement either.

'But also wonderful – that it is.'

Erica frowned and turned back to look at him.

'They could be relatives of our friend back there, Todd, and they get to enjoy the last few moments of normal life before the point at which nothing will ever be the same again. Or maybe they already know and are relying on doing something they know how to do – practically automatically – to keep them upright until they allow themselves to acknowledge the truth. Do you want to talk about it? This or the other thing that's bothering you that's related to this?'

'No. But if you need to talk about it, I'm happy to listen,' Erica said. She hadn't found the words, wasn't sure she wanted to, now or later.

'Thanks. I'm okay – I need a bit of time to process. Would you rather I drop you off in Melrose? It's okay with me if you're not up for this, Erica. Like I said, it is quite confronting.'

Erica suddenly realised they were entering Melrose. She'd lost a chunk of time. She desperately wanted to go up to the little flat and hide from the world, but to Walter she said, 'No. Thanks – I really appreciate the offer. But I don't think avoiding it will help.' She also remembered he'd said he wanted the company. That she could do, even if she was doing it badly.

'Okay. If you're sure. The long drive might do us good.'

They drove on. Erica thought the silence was becoming more comfortable.

A bit later, Walter said quietly, 'There are some items in the glovebox to help you pass the time – and under the seat.'

Desperate for a distraction and something to do with her hands, Erica felt under the seat. Her fingers found the edge of a book. She dragged it out and onto her lap – it was a battered old Nora Roberts paperback. Mary must be a big fan of Ms Roberts's work because the shelves in the flat had a whole row devoted to her books.

She smiled weakly at Walter, who smiled sadly back.

As she opened the glovebox, Erica marvelled at having never done this before in the several times she'd travelled in the vehicle.

Oh, but this isn't the hearse. This is the white delivery van. I really am losing it.

She rummaged through the contents: squashed flat box of tissues, bottle of hand sanitiser, spare small bag for collecting and containing any garbage, several spare pens, a roll-on deodorant, a book of puzzles with a pencil tucked inside marking the last page. Opening it, Erica's heart ached slightly at seeing a half-finished crossword in handwriting she knew to be Mary's. *Oh god*.

'Check right at the bottom,' Walter said, without taking his eyes off the road ahead. 'Underneath all of that.'

Erica shot him a quick frown and leant forwards against her seatbelt to get a better look. Sure enough, tucked down in a groove was a packet of boiled individually wrapped yellow sweets. Barley sugar. She pulled it out and held it up to show Walter, waggling it just as her father had done to silently ask if he wanted one.

'Yes, please,' he said, holding his hand out. Erica undid the twisted wrapper ends and held it out, still contained, for him to take and then put the wrapper in the small tray under the dash before unwrapping one for herself.

She savoured the sweet taste on her tongue: it took her right back to road trips with her parents. They used to suck Menz Crown Mints and had competitions over who could keep theirs the longest and resist biting it. No DVDs or iPads in those days for entertainment! Back then it was all games like I Spy and counting numberplates and tallying up groups of coloured cars. Talking had also been limited because it meant shouting to be heard over the roar coming in from the rolled-down windows, necessary in a car without air-conditioning. All their cars *had* been air-conditioned according to Mark – four (meaning the number of windows) by sixty or one hundred (or whatever speed they were doing when he said it).

Ah, Mark, she thought sadly. He'd been cut down too soon, like the boy in the back. What would Mark have done with his life, as a career? What were his interests? Had she been present during such discussions? She frowned. Nothing. A new bout of sadness pulled her down into the seat. *But at least I'm calm*, Erica thought as she nibbled on the inside of her right cheek, the hard barley sugar resting comfortably inside her left. She'd often won the family competitions with the Menz Crown Mints; she was good at ignoring it and savouring the sweetness flowing from it into her mouth with no interference from her.

She fiddled with the pages of the book on her lap, but didn't bother to open it – she knew she'd never concentrate and wasn't sure she wouldn't become car sick like she had as a kid if she did. Though did barley sugar help with that or was it something else? That didn't quite sound right. No, she suddenly remembered, it's ginger that eases nausea. She felt ridiculously triumphant for remembering so quickly. Why didn't they make boiled sweets out of ginger beer, or did they? She'd never heard of them if they did exist.

'How are you travelling?' Walter suddenly asked as they sped up after slowing to go through one of the small towns. Erica couldn't have said which one. She knew she'd seen the welcome sign but it had immediately dropped from her memory.

'I'm okay, thanks. How are you doing? Sing out if you want me to drive.'

Walter nodded. 'Thanks. I like the distraction.'

Erica nodded. *Yes, why do you think I'm offering?* The last time she had done a long trip in the car as a passenger it had been beside Stuart, she realised with a thud. God, she was hating all these reminders.

'Do you want to talk about what went on back there?' Walter said. 'I couldn't help noticing your reaction. Tell me if I'm out of line, but I got the feeling it wasn't just about Todd.'

Erica rolled the lolly around in her mouth for a moment, trying to choose her words. 'I ...' she started, but nothing more came out. She stared out the windscreen for a moment and then took a deep steadying breath. 'My brother Mark died in the same way. He was eighteen. Back in the nineteen-eighties. Obviously,' she added.

'God, you've really been through the wringer, you poor thing. You mentioned you'd lost him, but I wasn't sure how – not that it matters. Particularly rough at that age, regardless. There? It happened back there?' Walter was a little incredulous. He looked at her briefly before returning his full attention to the road.

'No, not back there. Well, I don't think so.' *Maybe it was, and that's why I felt what I did.* 'I'm not actually entirely sure where it happened. I can't seem to remember anything about it. Or him.'

'Ah. That's tough. But go easy on yourself, Erica.'

'I have images in my mind – which is pretty much just like what was back there. But I don't know if my parents took me there some time or I saw it on TV. It's bugging me that I don't know. And of course, I can't ask them – Mum's gone and Dad's ... Well ...' She lifted her hands off the book in a gesture of helplessness and dropped them again.

'Those with dementia often go backwards and can recall with great clarity events from certain periods of time,' Walter said, thoughtfully. 'But then perhaps it wouldn't be wise to bring up something like that in case it causes upset.'

'Yes. Exactly. I don't know where Mark's buried, even – if he's buried or scattered. Or if I've forgotten or never knew in the first place. I don't even remember my parents talking about him. Ever. Not after the first few days. But they must have, mustn't they?'

She frowned deeply, could feel the lines etching sharply into her skin. 'Mustn't they?' she implored, looking at Walter.

'I don't know,' he said. 'What *do* you remember? Maybe that's a better way to tackle it – in order to potentially shake something free.'

'His jumper. A tatty old brown one that has now shrunk and become felted and tiny and misshapen. I still have it – back in Adelaide. It was his favourite. Or at least one he often wore. So, to me it was him – the epitome of him. Mum took me into his room to choose something to keep as a memento. But I can't ever remember going in there again after that.'

When Erica's mother had encouraged her to choose something special from her brother's room, she hadn't realised it was because everything was going to be tossed. She'd thought it a rare moment of sentimentality and gentleness. She might have saved some of his things – railed against their decision instead. Perhaps that was the point in doing it the way they had. Now she felt deceived and disappointed. Once she'd admired their stoicism, but now it felt wrong and cold. She kept these thoughts to herself. She was grateful for her full face of makeup, which meant she wasn't in floods of tears. Though perhaps that release would be helpful in excising the frustration and dislodging a memory or two.

'Why can't I remember him, Walter? I can't even remember what he looked like, the colour of his eyes,' she said, her voice dropping to a whisper. 'I know they were blue, but I can't picture which blue. I can't tell you if they were blue like the deep ocean or more a pale clear blue like an aquamarine.'

'Perhaps your parents chose to protect you with out-of-sight-out-of-mind. I think back then there wasn't the focus on or recognition of the need for closure and facing emotion like we have now. Remember we discussed how differently the young are included in funeral services now than previously? Perhaps it was the same story with talking about your brother,' Walter continued thoughtfully, almost as if talking to himself. 'Sadly, back then there was a tendency to just get on – completely generalising, of course – and not openly grieve or show emotion as is becoming more acceptable now, even encouraged. Where did you live at the time – was it in the city or the country? That will most likely be where Mark was buried. And, again, back then burial was more likely than cremation, especially if it was rural.'

'My parents were both teachers and we moved around a lot, all over the state – often a new place each year.'

'God, that must have been hard on you, too.'

'Yeah, it probably was. But that bit was no harder than both your parents actually being teachers at the same school. *That* didn't endear me to many of my peers or prove an incentive for having anyone for sleepovers, or weekends, or holidays,' she said sardonically.

'No, I can imagine,' Walter said. 'Crikey, so many events in your early life would have profoundly affected you.'

'Yes. Well, I guess – I don't know any different, so …' Erica said.

'I'm sure a lot of your schooling must be a bit of a blur, especially where you were and when.'

'But surely I'd remember – be able to picture where I was and who I was with, when Mark died and afterwards … Oh.'

'What?'

'I vaguely remember us moving again straight afterwards.' *Maybe that's why I can't remember going back into his room.*

'Maybe your parents needed a fresh start away from prying and pitying eyes and whispering tongues, which are such a part of small-town life.'

Erica fought to hold back the frustration building inside her. She was glad when Walter spoke again, distracting her.

'You know,' he said, 'there's a fantastic online site where you can search cemeteries and gravesites worldwide. It's even got photos. Incredible, the effort people have gone to. You can search just a name or narrow it down and select a particular cemetery. Though, obviously, it relies on someone in the area having done the documenting and also that your loved one was interred. Helpfully, it's called simply Find A Grave – easily found via our friend Google.'

Erica nodded. She wasn't sure what was stopping her reaching into her handbag for her phone to try searching right now, but something was.

'Anyway, something to think about when you're ready. If you ever are. No pressure from me,' Walter added.

'That sounds great. Thanks for letting me know.'

They lapsed into silence again and stayed that way for what seemed ages to Erica. Walter finally broke it again by saying, 'Any chance of another one of those barley sugars?'

'Of course,' she said, diving back into the glovebox. 'Would you like me to take the top off the water for you, too?'

'Oh, yes please, good idea. I hadn't realised, but now you mention it, I'm quite parched.'

Erica busied herself with getting the green stainless-steel water bottle, which they'd designated his, from the footwell behind Walter's seat, undoing the lid and handing the open bottle to him.

'Ah, that's better. Thank you.'

'My pleasure.' Erica was so grateful for the change of subject. Having put Walter's water bottle back when he'd finished, she selected the purple matching stainless-steel water bottle beside it, opened it, and took a long slug.

Gradually higher density population signalled they weren't far from their inner-city destination.

Chapter Thirteen

Erica tried to commit to memory all the turns Walter took, but her mind was still distracted by her inability to remember Mark or any details around his death, or of him. When they turned into a narrow laneway and had to carefully negotiate past jutting-out police vehicles parked along their route, she became very thankful Walter hadn't asked her to drive. When he stopped and then began to back up towards a brown nondescript roller door, she silently sighed with relief and her slight anxiety floated away. She could occasionally perform a reasonable reverse parallel park, but hadn't needed to for ages. She wasn't sure how she'd go in a vehicle she didn't know and in this tight area with all the weirdness going on inside her.

Erica watched as Walter pressed an intercom button and then heard him as he gave Todd's full name and date of birth. She heard the groan of a roller door – a sound she knew well – and looked in her side mirror. Behind it was an empty space with another roller door behind. Walter reversed further and again Erica heard the familiar groan of a roller door. The one behind them was still, so she looked back to the front. That door was now coming down. When she heard more groaning start up, she looked in her mirror to see the door behind them coming up. They were sandwiched between two roller doors – the one in front down and the one at the back up to reveal a white space like a hospital corridor. To the side stood a person dressed in black – *very much like a security guard*, Erica thought. Perhaps that was who had answered the intercom.

'If it's a bit whiffy in there, just remember to breathe through your mouth.'

Erica nodded. 'Got it,' she said.

'Okay?' Walter said, turning with his hand on the open car door.

'Yep,' she said, opening her door, though she wasn't entirely sure. She was nervous; she didn't like hospitals at the best of times, particularly not their smell.

Together they dragged their trolley out of the back and into a spotlessly clean corridor with zero welcoming aesthetics – no touches of colour here on the laminated surfaces or highlights of honey-coloured timber exuding a little warmth like there had been in the hospitals of Stuart's stays. Nor were there any of the occasional fresh and pleasant aromas that managed to sneak through – flowers being moved around perhaps, staff's delicate scents of deodorant, moisturiser and shampoo as they swept by in their swift, smooth, efficient movement.

Despite expecting it, the strong smell of ammonia wafting around caused Erica's eyes to water, her head to become light and her stomach to protest.

It's okay, just breathe through your mouth, she told herself.

Their footsteps were loud and there was a slightly rhythmic creak, rattle and groan from the gurney they pushed, echoing slightly in the empty space. She watched as another door opened up ahead. A stronger waft of ammonia swarmed around Erica. *Oh god. Yuck.* She gulped, trying to stop the bile that was rising up painfully inside her.

'Are you okay?' Walter asked, looking across the trolley at her.

Not really. She nodded her response, concerned that if she spoke she might vomit. At that moment Erica's stomach tumbled and she swallowed in anticipation of warding off bile or gas rising. Her head began to spin.

'I hope I'm not overstepping, but you don't actually look okay,' he said. 'You're very pale. Go and wait with the car. There's no shame in finding this difficult. Seriously, Erica. I'm fine here. Go out and sit in the car. Please. I'd feel better – remember I have a duty of care to keep you safe and healthy; can't have you cracking your head open if you faint,' he said, smiling wanly.

She nodded again. 'Thanks. I think I had better wait outside.'

'Here are the keys,' Walter said, handing them over. 'I won't be long. Just a matter of signing Todd in and then I'll be out. Be with you in a jiffy.'

With her hands over her mouth, Erica made her way on shaking, weak legs the few metres to the roller door where the security guard still stood. He nodded to her as she went past him.

Safely inside the car, she took great gasps of the closest to fresh air she had available and then took some sips of water from her steel water bottle before holding its cold surface to her face. The change of sensation was a good circuit-breaker.

To distract herself further, she got her phone out and scrolled idly through her Facebook feed, not really taking any notice of what she was seeing. Away from the smell, she began to feel physically better quite quickly, though the background irritation of the gaps in her memories of Mark didn't seem to be going anywhere. It was right back at the front of her mind now the assault on her senses had seeped away. Should she look on the Find A Grave website for Mark? Why not? What harm could it do?

As she put his details in the boxes for a general search, she paused to acknowledge the wave of sadness that gripped her at realising neither Stuart, nor her mother, nor her favourite auntie, Irene, would come up if she searched for them; her mum's ashes had been scattered at her favourite park and Stuart's remained in the urn on the mantelpiece back at the house. It was good he was with Mackenzie and Issy, but suddenly it seemed terribly sad and wrong that her loved ones weren't somewhere people could visit and sit quietly beside them.

It really said something about how disconnected society as a whole was becoming, didn't it? If she weren't feeling so low, she might have laughed at how profound her thought, how like Renee, too. Should she inter Stuart somewhere she could place a plaque? But perhaps the non-specific, random nature of scattering ashes meant you had them in your heart always, wherever you went. And of course you could go to where they had been scattered, she supposed, though knowledge of their location would probably die with those who had done the scattering; it was unlikely anyone would record the details for future generations. A piece of memorial jewellery made from a portion of the ashes – like diamonds or glass beads – was a nice idea, too; though wouldn't provide a physical context either.

God, it was all so final. Yeah. Like death, really, Erica. Der. And she smiled at her own ridiculousness. Oh how she longed to be with her small tribe of friends and have them rolling their eyes at her and all bursting into laughter until they almost wet themselves. She missed it. When had they last laughed like that? When did life get so serious? Again, rather obvious: when loved ones started getting cancer and other serious ailments and then dying, especially those who did so well before their time. *Damn you, Stuart*, she silently cursed. And then, *Sorry, I didn't mean that*. And then, *I miss you*, as guilt prodded between her ribs like a branding iron into her side burning her with shame. She took a deep breath, pressed search. She wasn't sure what result she was hoping for.

She stared at the results, shocked that so many Mark Tolmers around the world had died. As she scanned the results for Australian cemeteries she wondered if they could have buried him overseas. *No, don't be ridiculous. You were eleven; it was years before you left for the US and even longer before your parents visited that once.*

She was both disappointed and relieved to find no results for locations in Australia. Definitely disappointed, she decided, because she was no closer to any answers and now had even more questions. Well, if not more, the same ones remained. Well, one that mattered, really: where was he? No, make that two. There was also: what were his favourite places? What could be considered clues as to where he had died? Oh, shit, there were so many questions, she thought, hating the rolling stream of them coming in. He'd been eighteen. Did he have a girlfriend? Anyone serious? A fling? What were his hobbies other than hanging out with his friends – at watering holes. Was it somewhere near where they lived?

Okay. Stop. Where was I at school in 1984 – year seven – last year of primary school? She closed her eyes again and tried to force her recall. Why the hell couldn't she remember something as simple as that? All years and all schools seemed to be blended together. It didn't help that most years she'd had one of her parents as her teacher, so she couldn't use the teacher as an anchor to the year or particular classroom. *Why can't I remember?*

She leapt in her seat when she heard the back doors open and then the trolley being slid into the van with a metallic clunk. She was still clutching her chest from her fright, as if trying to actually hold her heart and stop it from jumping out somehow through her ribs, when Walter's door opened and a moment later he sank into his seat and closed the door behind him.

'Shit. Sorry if I startled you.'

'I'm so sorry about back there, Walter.'

'It's okay. You didn't miss much – just swapping the trolleys and signing a form. Are you okay, though – feeling a bit better?'

'Yes, I'm fine. The smell just got to me.'

'I admit it was pretty strong in there today. Sometimes it's not too bad,' Walter said, starting the vehicle. Erica noticed the roller door opening up in front. She checked in her side mirror to see the one behind coming back down.

'What now?' she asked.

'We navigate our way out of this rabbit warren without scraping any police cars and find somewhere to park to catch our breath for a minute. Now, you must have been deep in thought if I startled you, given I was only gone a few minutes,' Walter said as they crawled their way back down the narrow alleyway.

'Yes. I was searching the Find A Grave site.'

'Oh. Did you find anything?' he said.

'No. He must have been cremated and scattered.'

'Or perhaps the cemetery with his particular grave hasn't been surveyed or recorded yet,' Walter said.

'Or that. God, I think that's even worse than him not being anywhere to be found.'

'Maybe you're not meant to learn all this right now. Or maybe ever?'

'You sound like my friend Renee – that's what she would say. She's very, um, wise,' she added after a beat.

'Thank you. I'll take that as a compliment.'

Erica took a deep breath in an effort to force back her frustration. She wished none of this had come up. She wished today had never happened. That thought brought her up short: she was being self-centred. Todd's family and friends would be thinking exactly the same thing. And their hearts will be being ripped out and trampled on, shredded – hers was just having a fingernail run over it, irritating a scar. No harm had been done to her.

She lost track of where they were until they went past St Andrew's Hospital on South Terrace and down to the car park against the Victoria Park Racecourse, where they pulled into a space and Walter turned off the vehicle.

'Again, I'm so sorry about back there,' Erica said, feeling the need to fill the silence.

'Seriously, don't worry about it. There was no harm done.'

'I thought I'd be fine – I am in the mortuary back at work. And I was at the hospital with Stuart all those months.'

'Well, in there is a different level of clinical altogether, so I'm not surprised it threw you for a loop. And you probably have some residual trauma from losing your husband, so being back in a place with similar sounds and smells …'

'And taste; I could practically taste the cleaning chemicals in there. I can still smell it on my clothes,' she said, dipping her head to her sleeve and sniffing. 'It's like it's stuck in my nostrils. But you lost Mary in a hospital as well – so you'd be triggered too.'

'True. And I am a bit.'

But someone had to pull themselves together and do the right thing by Todd, she thought, burning with shame.

'We're all different. For me being able to focus on the task at hand helps, but for others that in itself could well be the trigger. Do you meditate, Erica?'

'No. I've tried. Years ago. I couldn't seem to get the hang of it. Not sure I'm any good at it.' She couldn't be bothered going into it.

'I had lots of tries and failures too. But persisted out of sheer desperation. You know *Mary's Mayhem Manager*?'

'Yes. Of course.' Erica looked at Walter, frowning.

He sighed before continuing. 'She put it together so someone else could take over and we could have a break. Same with renovating the upstairs flat. She wanted us to go and visit our son in London. I kept promising her we'd get around to it. And then suddenly one day it was too late.'

'Oh, Walter. I'm so sorry.' While the words were completely inadequate, Erica wasn't sure what else to say. And silence seemed all kinds of wrong.

'Thanks. So, for me, turning to meditation was a desperate attempt to ease my guilt. And to come to terms with the loss and the loneliness. It's helped me enormously – though it took some trial and error. Trying alone to visualise, following instructions in a book, didn't work for me at all. But then I discovered guided meditation on my phone; there's a great app – well, probably lots of them, really – with heaps of teachers to choose from. Some you pay for, but a lot is free. I found a few I really connect with and I enjoy half an hour most mornings now. I tell you, if I don't get to do it, I feel all out of kilter for the day. I don't know if it works or I'm doing it right but I figure you can't go wrong with simply listening to a soothing voice and focussing on your breathing and relaxing. Stilling a racing mind and taking a break from the energy of the world for a bit. I'll show you what I'm into if you like. But first, did you remember anything about your brother Mark? Has anything been shaken loose?'

'No. It's weird. I can't even tell you where we lived or what school I was at when it happened. I feel like I'm losing my mind – or I did a long time ago when it comes to him.'

'It was a traumatic event at a young, impressionable age and stage of development. The brain and soul can be very good at protecting us.'

'Actually …' Something became clear for Erica. She frowned.

'What is it?'

'I've got a box of old school photos and report cards.'

'Great. They'll tell you what school you were at in each year.'

'Yes. You're right.' Excitement rose in Erica momentarily, but just as quickly ebbed away to be replaced with the discomfort of another question. 'But what's now bugging me is … Mark would have had the same – he'd finished school and was still living at home. So his box – our parents kept them up to date, adding any immunisation records, important papers – would have still been in the house when I went through everything to get Mum and Dad organised to move into the nursing home. But it wasn't there. If it was, I would have had all these questions then, wouldn't I?'

'Hmm.' Walter nodded slowly.

'And, actually …' Erica's heart slowed. 'None of his stuff was in the house. I can understand clearing out his room and getting rid of his clothes et cetera. But I've got an awful feeling they got rid of all traces of him. Ages ago.'

'Maybe they did. That wouldn't surprise me at all. Some people are sentimental and keep movie ticket stubs, for instance. Others are just content with the memories. And then there are those who fall somewhere in between. And as we're always having to acknowledge, it takes all kinds and grief takes all forms. So please don't be too hard on your parents. Whatever they did they did because that's what felt right at the time.'

'I need to let it go,' Erica said, taking another deep breath.

'I think you'll find that easier said than done.'

'Yes. So just roll with it, right?'

'It might also help to remind yourself that whether you remember or not doesn't really change anything.'

'You're right. Nothing I do or don't do will bring Mark back.'

'Sadly, not.'

'Enough about me, Walter; please change the subject. What did they say back there – are we waiting for Todd to take him back?'

'Yes. Two to three hours is the estimate. Now, I'm happy to take you somewhere or to call you a cab or an Uber, or whatever it is you young ones do for transport in the city – on me – if there's somewhere you want to go.'

'It's been a while since I was called young, Walter. Thanks for that.'

'You could go and visit your daughters or one of your friends?' he suggested.

'Oh. I hadn't even thought … What do you normally do in this situation?'

'Well, this doesn't happen very often. But when it does, I usually just sit and enjoy the quiet time. Listen to a podcast or read a book. Mary used to use the time to shop – take advantage of a trip to the city.'

Erica realised this might be the first time he'd made the journey without Mary beside him.

'But it's entirely up to you what you do, Erica.'

'You're really kind, Walter, but it wouldn't feel right to leave Todd. Does that sound strange?'

'Not at all. That's how I feel.'

'I'd love to see one of my friends or the girls, but they'll all be at work. And we are too. It feels right to stay put.'

'Me too. I made a silent promise to Todd's family to take care of him.'

'I feel like we both did – we're in this together. I want to be able to look his family in the eye, if we do their service, knowing he truly wasn't alone – I know he's not aware of it, but I am. And it's important to me.'

A part of Erica yearned to go to her house, just a fifteen-minute drive away, and look through her box of school mementos, or even phone the girls and see if they were home and if so ask them to do it for her, but that would … The thought brought her up short. Did they know about Mark? She couldn't recall having ever mentioned him or discussing him with them. Ever. Shame burnt again as she realised she'd been as instrumental in eradicating memories of him as her parents.

But then a gentle voice inside her told her she had followed their lead. And things were probably different back then, like Walter had said. And what would she do with knowledge of where she'd been at school – or where he'd died – anyway? Again, as Walter had said: What would it change? She might go on a long drawn-out quest that ended with her being none the wiser. Or worse, experiencing further heartbreak.

What if she went and tried to find people who had known him and might have memories of his accident? It would be worse than finding no one if she found people who didn't remember it – or them – at all. Yes, best to let sleeping dogs lie. Not knowing hadn't hurt her all these years.

Chapter Fourteen

'Okay, I'm just going to put my window down a bit for some fresh air,' Walter said, turning on the key.

'Good idea,' Erica said, putting her finger on the window button by her arm and lowering hers a bit. The gentle sun beamed into the space from Walter's side, lighting up the dark faux-leather console. Outside she could hear the quiet energetic hum of the city bustling about its business – the whispering whoosh of cars, hum of engines, the occasional deeper throaty stop-start groaning of another vehicle: a bus maybe.

Walter then pushed his seat back and reclined it. Erica looked around, wondering how to occupy herself. She wasn't good at sitting still for long periods of time, and was starting to regret choosing to stay. The car was becoming a little claustrophobic now too. She didn't feel like reading, nor idly scrolling Facebook. She knew there were stacks of podcasts but she didn't know where to start. And she didn't want to fiddle with her phone and disturb or annoy her companion. So, just as Walter was getting

out his earbuds from their box she asked him what he was going
to listen to.

'Oh. It's a meditative sound track – this one's just sound. Would
you like to try it? No pressure from me.'

'I think I would, actually.' She fossicked in her handbag for the
little box of corded earbuds and opened it.

'I'll send a screenshot of the home page of the app I'm on and
the particular track.'

A moment later Erica's phone pinged twice.

'Got it okay?'

'Yep. Thanks.' She put her earbuds in while the app down-
loaded and then searched for the particular track Walter was
listening to – it seemed as good a place as any to start.

'Now don't mind me if I fall asleep and start to snore; it's
happened plenty of times before. And apologies in advance if my
breathing bothers you,' Walter said, shuffling in his seat a little
and getting comfortable. Within seconds his eyes were closed and
his hands were clasped on his stomach, rising and falling with his
slow and steady breathing. His features evoked serenity.

I want some of that, Erica thought, reclining her own seat a little
and settling in. *Now, no fidgeting. Just sit.*

As she got settled with her eyes closed and the track at a
comfortable volume, Erica realised it was really nice to just be
still – to have nowhere to be, nothing to do for the next few
hours. Gradually the stifling sensation inside her was replaced
with comfort.

For three hours Erica pressed the play button whenever the track
on her phone ended and managed to stay in her blissful state – until
Walter's phone pinged. Not wanting to leave her silent mindful
state she kept her eyes closed for a few more moments. Walter

shifted beside her making a quiet creaking, and then she heard the clunk of his manual seat being adjusted back into his driving position.

'That might be the coroner,' he said, checking the device. 'Yes. They're ready for us,' he said quietly, but stayed where he was. 'How are you doing?' he asked, turning to look at Erica.

'Oh my god, Walter, that was amazing. I can't believe I just sat here for all that time without fidgeting. I feel so rested – like I've been asleep, but I haven't. I'm all energised and ready for whatever is next.'

'Incredible, huh?'

'Sorry. Here I am going on as if I've just invented it!'

'I love your enthusiasm. And I'm so glad it helped.'

Erica again had the strangest sense she'd been through something profound. There had definitely been a shift inside her. A thought occurred: *Stuart, you'll never guess what.* It pulled her up, her breath catching in her chest momentarily as she waited for the inevitable wave of sadness and then the ache of pain to settle back inside her. But neither of these things happened. The thought came, rolled around, then left, taking any residue with it. She took a slightly deeper breath. *I'm okay. It's all okay.* She thought, almost idly: *You're gone. I love you, I miss you. But I'm okay. Actually, better than okay. I'm good.* Even Erica's face felt softer – her muscles relaxed, her lips sitting in a gentle smile.

'Good to go?' Walter said.

'Yep.'

Walter drove back into the heart of the city, down the narrow alleyway again, pulled into the cut-out to reverse, pressed the intercom button, gave his details and then backed through the now open roller door. As the door in front came down and the back one opened, Walter turned to Erica.

'You stay here. I'll be back soon.'

Erica opened her mouth to protest.

'I know you're feeling better, but I'd like you to stay that way.'

Erica nodded as he got out. She was both relieved and disappointed in herself.

A few minutes later when she heard the trolley slide into the back with a clunk, Erica was again glad she'd stayed and waited the three hours with Walter for Todd's body to be ready. She experienced a renewed surge of respect for her boss.

They made a few turns and were soon on the main road out of the city. At the traffic lights Erica looked back in the direction of her suburban home and had no yearning to go there. Everything was well by all accounts with the girls taking care of things.

Melrose was home now and she felt like she was going home; that knowing familiar welcoming. This time as she made this particular journey, she was able to take in the sights from the car, devoid of the slight nervousness she'd felt that first day that was just over a week ago but could have been a lifetime. It didn't matter.

'I love the feeling of going home after being away – no matter how long it's been: hours, days, weeks,' Walter said suddenly with a long drawn-out contented sigh. They'd had the odd brief bout of chatter, but had been silent for ages, and had been on the road for a couple of hours, having left the built-up areas. More trucks than passenger vehicles passed them now. Erica nodded.

'Hmm,' she said.

'Sorry, you're probably feeling a little strange driving away from *your* home. I'm sure you're probably experiencing the odd bit of homesickness too. My apologies – that was a little insensitive of me.'

'Not at all. I feel like I'm going home too, actually. I really do.'

'That's great to hear, Erica.' Walter beamed. 'I'm so pleased.'

'This is one of my favourite sights in the world,' Walter said when Mt Remarkable loomed large up ahead.

'It's beautiful,' Erica said. 'It's like an enormous hand cupping the town – being safely held and protected.'

'Yes, it sure is a magical and spiritual place – in a non-religious way, that is,' he added. They exchanged a smile; one of their shared qualities was a disdain for organised religion. 'I think it has an energy all of its own.'

Erica nodded. *Just like Hanging Rock*, she thought. She and Stuart had done a road trip there years back with the girls – as a homage to one of their favourite books and movies, *Picnic at Hanging Rock*. They had all been stunned into silence, which was no mean feat with two young teenagers, by its beauty and strangely hypnotic and mystical aura. This place had the same eerie, reverent atmosphere, she thought, suddenly remembering their trip clearly.

'Have you ever been to Hanging Rock in Victoria, Walter?' Erica asked.

'Oh yes. That's a magical place, too, in the same vein as here. Mary said it was too spooky. I could see what she meant, but I liked it – the mystery.'

'Me too. Until I came here to Melrose, I thought the feeling I had with Hanging Rock was something to do with the intrigue around the book – whether the story was in fact true or a brilliant work of fiction. But I have the same sense here in Melrose.'

'Hmm. I bet some sinister secrets are hidden up there too. I'm glad it's treating Melrose and its current living inhabitants well,' Walter said.

'Yes,' Erica said.

Once again parked in the garage at the back of the office building, they unloaded their precious cargo gently from the vehicle and into one of the refrigerated compartments in their mortuary.

'I'll get Todd settled in and be there in a sec – you go on,' Walter said.

'Would you like me to have a tea ready for you?'

'Yes, please.'

Erica didn't question him or feel the need to ask; he probably had a private ritual he liked to use in circumstances like these – for himself and for Todd.

Chapter Fifteen

Erica was just tidying up her desk and turning everything off ready for the weekend when she heard the front office door open and then close. She looked up and was so surprised she looked down and blinked before looking back up again, to make sure her eyes or brain were not deceiving her. They were not. Her mouth became fixed in an O formation, her voice unable to squeeze out any words.

'Hi, Mum. Surprise! We've come to visit,' Issy said, waving both hands jazz style.

'Yes. Here we are. God, it's a bloody long way. And this place is *tiny*,' Mackenzie cried. 'Sorry,' she added sheepishly as Walter appeared from down the hall.

'No need,' he said cheerily. 'It *is* a bloody long way if you've come straight from Adelaide and it's your first time. And, yes, it *is* tiny, if you mean the town. But we like it that way. You must be Issy and you must be Mackenzie. Walter Crossley. It's a pleasure to meet you both,' he said, holding out his hand to each girl standing

119

before him. Erica was slowly coming to and was thankful for him stepping in. And he'd named the girls correctly.

'W-wow,' Erica finally managed to mutter with a bit of a stammer when Walter had moved towards the reception room. She stood up and held the desk for support.

'What, no hug, Mumsy?' Mackenzie chided playfully. 'We've driven all this way for one of your famous hugs,' she said, grinning cheekily.

Erica noticed Issy was looking shy and a little lost. She stepped out from behind the reception desk and gathered her daughters to her, melting inside as she did. God, she'd missed this. And when had they got so tall? She'd only been away from them for a matter of days, and they hadn't seemed any different when they'd come back from their 'shortest gap year in the history of gap years'. But then they'd seemed vulnerable and that night had been such a shitstorm she hadn't had a chance to really look them over like this. Now they were the epitome of strong, independent young women. *Stu, you'd be so proud of our girls*, she thought, her heart expanding to the point of slight pain.

'Lucky we packed the iPads,' Mackenzie said.

'What is there to do around here? Oh, but is there wifi and mobile coverage?' Issy said, looking a little stricken. *There are my girls*, Erica thought, smiling to herself.

'Der. How do you think we speak to Mum and text her and everything, Is?' Mackenzie said, rolling her eyes.

'Girls. Really?' she chided.

'Sorry. We're a bit tired,' Issy said.

'Yes. It's a long way.'

'We've established that. So why didn't you tell me you were coming?' Erica said.

'So you could spend hours, days, whatever, worrying about us being on the road?' Issy said.

'And freaking out if we were three minutes later than expected because we stopped off somewhere interesting?' Mackenzie stared her mother down, her eyebrows raised.

'I ... Yes, you're probably right,' Erica conceded. 'But I'm so glad you're here, even if you are ganging up on me,' she said, putting out her lower lip in an exaggerated pout. 'So, is everything okay? Has something happened?'

'Here we go. Told you,' Mackenzie said, nudging her younger sister. 'Nope, all good. We just fancied a drive and both managed to get some time off work at the same time.' She flapped a hand. 'And don't forget we've just been through Europe on our own.'

'But not in a car,' Erica pointed out.

'Oh, you don't know the half of it,' Mackenzie said. 'Just jokes, Mum.'

Walter laughed.

But Erica wasn't completely buying the joking around; Mackenzie was clearly deflecting from something. Her heart contracted as she looked at Issy, who had never quite grasped the art of lying, white lies or otherwise, like her elder sister had.

'Issy? What's up?'

'Nothing.' But her voice was practically a squeak.

'Is something wrong with your grandpa?' Suddenly there was a lump caught in her throat.

'Of course there's something wrong with Grandpa; he's lost his mind, remember? Dementia. Remember that horrible disease? He's fine – the usual.'

Erica relaxed a bit. While Mackenzie was clearly avoiding something, they would have phoned her, or the nursing home would have, if something had happened with her dad. Perhaps both girls were a little uncomfortable with Walter there. Out of the corner of her eye she noticed him trying to hold back more laughter. Mackenzie was pretty funny, exasperatingly so at times.

'Right. So, shall we go and have a drink and an early dinner?' she said. *And you can tell me what's really going on.* She stopped herself from uttering the words by nibbling on the inside of her bottom lip. 'It really is wonderful to see you both – a fantastic surprise. Walter, would you like to join us at the pub?'

'Oh. Thank you – that's very kind – but I think you lovely ladies don't need this old git cramping your style. We can catch up over the weekend if you fancy – feel free to call if you need anything. You know where I'll be. Meanwhile, you have fun.'

'Yes, and you call me if I'm needed, too, Walter.'

'I'll do nothing of the sort – you enjoy your time with your girls. I'll be off. Cheerio,' he said, walking down the hall with his hand raised.

'See you on Monday, if not before. Have a good weekend,' Erica said.

'Bye, Walter, it was lovely to meet you,' Mackenzie said.

'Yes. Hopefully we'll see you again before we leave,' Issy called.

'I like him,' Issy said.

'Me too,' Mackenzie said.

'Yes, he's a good egg, as your grandpa would say,' Erica said. 'Right, wow, you've given me quite a shock.' She leant against the desk.

'Well, I'd like to think it's actually a nice surprise, Mum,' Mackenzie said haughtily, hands on hips, making a show of looking put out.

'Of course it is, Mackenzie.'

'I missed you so much, Mum,' Issy said, wrapping her arms around Erica's waist and laying her head on her shoulder.

'Yeah, all right, I missed you too,' Mackenzie said, coming up and kissing her mother on the cheek. 'Like you wouldn't believe,' she added in a serious tone. 'But not like you need to come home or anything.'

'So, what's going on? I know there's something. I'm your mother, remember – I can practically read you like books.'

'It's okay, it's nothing too drastic,' Mackenzie said thoughtfully. 'But there is something we want to talk to you about. It's okay – we're not pregnant, ready to elope, on drugs or out on bail, or anything else, um …'

'Illegal, immoral or unsavoury – none of that,' Issy added.

'Okay then,' Erica said. 'That's something at least. Let me just get my bag, and then I'm good to go,' she said, going back around the other side of the reception desk. She paused with her handbag on the desk and her finger on the light switch for the back half of the building. 'Oh, or do you want a tour first?'

'Are there any dead bodies here?' Issy asked quietly, looking around her with trepidation etched in her features.

'There is actually – in the mortuary, out the back.'

'Yuck. No thanks, then,' Mackenzie said.

'Same,' Issy said. 'Are there, um, ghosts?' 'Probably,' Erica was about to say. But Issy spoke again. 'Like, in the flat?' she said, raising her eyes towards the ceiling.

'No. None that I've come across, anyway.'

'Brilliant. Phew,' Issy said.

'Well, thank goodness for that,' Mackenzie said. Erica nearly laughed out loud at their obvious relief. But it was a valid concern. Hadn't she had the same thought when she'd arrived?

'Maybe tomorrow for the tour – when it's, um, lighter outside,' Issy said.

'It's called electricity, Issy – lights, you know? You flick a switch and voilà!'

'Piss off, Mackenzie. You were thinking the same thing. She was, Mum – she was going on and on about ghosts when we were in the car.'

And just like that they were her babies again – bickering siblings, seemingly much younger than they'd appeared moments earlier.

'No ghosts, no ghoulishness. Nothing icky. It's an office building with another room out the back – not much different from a commercial kitchen except there are no ovens or cooktops and instead a row of refrigerated compartments. And a gorgeous flat upstairs. Where are you parked? Do you want to get changed?'

'We're right out the front. It's not like it's a struggle to find a parking spot. There's no one here!' Mackenzie said.

'There is in the mornings – the place becomes quite the metropolis with people getting their coffee fix,' Erica said.

'Yeah, right, Mum, whatever you say,' Mackenzie said.

'Anyway, you can park out the back next to Vera – move your car after we've eaten.'

'Cute name, Mum,' Issy said.

'Thanks. It's a bit of a long story.'

'Oh, we already know it, kind of,' Issy said.

'Oh?'

'We saw Michelle arriving when we were leaving Grandpa's the other day,' Issy said, blushing. She quickly shut her mouth.

'Don't worry, Mum, she wasn't saying anything bad,' Mackenzie said. 'Just that she was worried about you that day. I think she was flustered because she'd just hung up from you and then practically bumped into us.'

'Okay. Fair enough. Right, so, this whatever it is you have to talk to me about – is it okay in the pub or would you like to go up to the flat where it's private?'

'The pub's fine,' Mackenzie said.

'Yeah, I reckon,' Issy said.

She had to take them at their word. While Mackenzie could be prone to a little too much bravado at times, they were both sensible and sensitive enough to do the right thing.

'And do you need to change first?' Erica asked.

'No, I'm good to go,' Mackenzie said.

'I'm good too,' Issy said.

'Come on then, this way,' Erica said, ushering them towards the front door. When they were outside, she locked it behind them.

'Is there room for both of us to stay in the flat?' Issy asked while Erica fiddled with the key.

'Yeah, without sharing a bed? Because we brought our tents and sleeping bags and everything,' Mackenzie said.

'It'll be fine. It's cute and cosy – which you'll be glad of later, because it gets damned cold here at night – but the second bedroom has twin beds, so there's plenty of room for you both.'

Facing the street, Erica pointed left and then right. 'Your choice – there are two pubs. And I haven't been to either yet, so have formed no bias.'

'That one,' Issy said, pointing to their right – towards the building with the quainter appearance. They turned and started walking.

'Australia has a drinking problem if a place this size needs two pubs,' Issy added.

'Well-known fact, Issy,' Mackenzie said.

'Well, don't forget this district is much bigger than just the town,' Erica said, feeling the need to defend her new turf.

'Yeah, point taken,' Issy said.

'And there aren't any other options for an evening meal. So, it's not all about alcohol,' she added. She wasn't *sure* this was correct – she hadn't looked for other dining options – but she hadn't seen any ads for local eating establishments in the tourist brochures, not that were open for dinner.

'Listen to you defending the place, Mum,' Mackenzie said. 'I thought we'd get here and you'd be begging us to kidnap you.'

'Haha, very funny, Mackenzie,' Erica said.

'So, you're okay? You're not homesick? Not going mad with nothing to do? You can tell us,' Issy urged.

'I will admit I had a few wobbles in the first few days. Hence, Michelle, you know … But it really is a lovely place. Everyone I've met has been friendly enough. And Walter is the best boss I could have ever asked for. Honestly, I think the quiet life and alone time are good for me – just what I need. So how are you both? You okay?'

'Yep. Working, adulting – you know how it is,' Mackenzie said, linking arms with Erica.

'Same-same,' Issy said, linking up with Erica's other arm.

'Not wishing you were back overseas?' Erica asked.

'No,' Issy said.

'Nope. That can wait. I don't care if Adelaide is considered dull and provincial – I like it. And we're allowed to say that now we've had an opportunity to get a different perspective,' Mackenzie said.

'God it's good to have you guys here,' Erica said, squeezing her arms to her.

'It's so good to see you too, Mum – all jokes aside,' Mackenzie said, giving her a nudge.

Issy leant a little closer to Erica.

They crossed the empty street to the footpath in front of the quaint stone two-storey building. 'Here we are – after you both,' Erica said, untangling her arms and stepping back for them to enter.

'That took less than three minutes,' Issy said. 'And we were dawdling!'

'Yes, it'll be an easy stumble home when we've got absolutely hammered,' Mackenzie said.

'Except for the stairs up to the flat,' Erica pointed out.

'Party pooper,' Issy said over her shoulder as she pushed open a heavy glass door.

'Yep. That's me,' Erica said with a laugh, following Issy and Mackenzie inside.

They went straight up to the bar directly in front of them and ordered drinks and meals after a quick perusal of the laminated menu. Erica couldn't believe she hadn't eaten there yet – and then she remembered her financial status. For a moment there it had been like old times before Stuart had died, when he might have just been away on a business trip. She pushed it aside. This counted as a celebration for that as well as her surprise guests, and also came under the category of self-care. And of course, she still had some of the money Michelle had sent. Her heart swelled such a lot whenever she thought of that generous gift.

'My treat,' Mackenzie said, as Erica reached into her handbag for her wallet.

'Oh, you don't have to do that,' Erica said.

'I know I don't, but I am. Because I can,' she said defiantly.

'Even me?' Issy said quietly.

'Even you, grasshopper, even you,' Mackenzie said, stroking her younger sister's hair. 'It's cheap here compared to Europe, anyway.'

'Where we were for, like, two minutes,' Issy said. 'It's not like we got used to anything over there, but Mackenzie's now comparing everything to European prices,' she said, rolling her eyes. 'What are you like?' she said with another roll of the eyes. Erica had to try very hard not to laugh.

'Well, it was *shocking* – you have to agree with that, Issy.'

'I do. But I don't feel the need to point it out like some wannabe sophisticate.'

'Yeah, righto, point taken,' Mackenzie said, tapping her card on the machine.

'Anyway, thanks very much for dinner, Mackenzie,' Issy said.

'You're welcome, little sister.'

'Yes, that's very generous of you, Mackenzie. Thank you.' She beamed inside.

'Least I can do, Mumsy. You're welcome too.'

Chapter Sixteen

They'd sat where directed and had taken several sips from their drinks and put them down on the lacquered wooden tabletop when Erica said: 'So, do you want to tell me now what Grandpa said that's upset you?'

'We didn't say we were upset,' Mackenzie said.

'No. Not really,' Issy said.

'Darlings, you've just driven more than three hours. Clearly it isn't something you want to tell me over the phone,' she said, placing a hand on each of their legs. 'It's okay, there's not a lot that can shock me or upset me these days.'

'Well ...' Mackenzie started and then stopped and looked at Issy with her eyebrows raised. 'Do you want to tell her?'

'No. You go.'

Mackenzie took an obvious deeper breath. 'Mum? Did you have a miscarriage or a stillborn baby? A boy?'

What? Erica was stunned. Of all the things in her mind they might be about to tell her, this was not one of them. 'No. Why do you ask?'

'I mean, it could just be Grandpa babbling,' Mackenzie said.

'Well, he does do that,' Erica said.

'Yes, but he seemed so sure – adamant. And now he's got that kitten, he seems quite lucid.'

'Though in a slightly different time zone,' Issy added.

'Yes, there's that. Oh I don't know.' Mackenzie frowned.

'You obviously thought there was something in it because here you are. So, what exactly did he say?' Erica prompted.

'Well, he kept saying, "your brother", as in *our* brother. Like he was talking about us having another sibling. Mark.'

Erica felt the blood drain from her face and was glad she was sitting down. Even still, her thighs began to quiver. She swallowed. 'What did he say about him?' she said, her voice little more than a squeaky croak.

'Something about it being his birthday,' Mackenzie said. 'He seemed worried that it had been forgotten.'

Oh! Could that *have been what was bugging me the other morning – when we went and got Todd?* Erica frowned. Once she'd known his birth date. Had she repressed it, along with everything else about him? Was that because her parents hadn't ever really mentioned him since his death? *Until now, I couldn't even have told anyone the month of his birthday.* Shame swirled around inside her. *And maybe still not; I can't rely on anything Dad says.* Sadness seeped in, and then another layer for her dad. She hated to think of him being upset, especially about choices made so long ago that couldn't be undone. Was this distress in his old age what some people meant by karma?

'Do you know who or what he was talking about?' Issy said.

'Oh my god, you do,' Mackenzie said, clearly scrutinising her mother.

Erica nodded. 'Mark was *my* brother. He died when I was eleven and he was eighteen. He drowned.'

'God, Mum, that's awful. You poor thing.'

'Yes, that's so sad. And must have been really hard,' Issy said.

'That kind of makes sense, though. Grandpa kept apologising for not doing the right thing, or something. And he said he was really sorry for not being more sympathetic for not … um … Issy, do you remember?'

'Not remembering him, not acknowledging him. That's what he said. It sort of seemed all encompassing – not just about his birthday.'

'How come we don't know? You've never mentioned him. Have you? He would have been our uncle. That's weird, Mum.'

'Yeah. Remember Katie's brother died – Katie from the year below me – they celebrate his birthday every year,' Issy said.

'Commemorate, not celebrate,' Mackenzie corrected.

'Yes. Commemorate it. But still …'

'I know it seems odd and almost unbelievable, but it was the eighties and things were different then,' Erica said.

'We might not have been there, but we know all about the eighties – big hair, clothes in lurid fluoro with matching eyeshadow …' Mackenzie said.

'Don't forget the great music,' Erica added.

'Yeah, all right, we'll give you that, won't we, Is?'

'Yep.'

'So …?' Mackenzie prompted, serious again.

'Remember the tatty old brown jumper that lives in my bedside drawer? That was his; it's all I have of him.'

'Oh. I thought that must have been one of Dad's,' Mackenzie said.

'Other than that, I don't remember Mark at all or his funeral. Nothing. Not even his birthday or the date he died. Mum and Dad didn't really ever talk about him afterwards. And you know how they were teachers in country schools and we moved around a lot?'

The girls nodded.

'Well, I can't remember which town we were living in when he died, and where he might be buried – if he even is buried.'

'That's the olden days – he would have been buried, I reckon,' Issy said, nodding knowingly. Erica held her breath a little waiting for Mackenzie to admonish her. But she didn't. Nor did she look at Erica like she was worried her mother had lost her mind. Because, really, as Erica was fully aware, all this was quite unbelievable. And coincidental, if it turned out Mark's birthday *was* the same day Todd had died. Spooky. Though Renee was adamant there was no such thing as coincidence; that everything was connected. Erica became overwhelmed with the enormity of that thought and was relieved to let it go when Mackenzie spoke again.

'It must have been really traumatic. That's why you can't remember. Your brain has blocked it,' her eldest said.

'Yeah, we've been reading up on it online – you know, after the whole Kayla palaver,' Issy said. 'There's a thing called trauma by proxy.'

'Are you okay?' Erica asked, suddenly worried.

'We have had a few sleepless nights, haven't we, Is?'

Issy nodded.

'Why didn't you tell me? You said you were fine,' Erica said.

'We are. We're okay, Mum,' Mackenzie said.

'Yeah, totally.'

'I'm so sorry,' Erica said.

'It's not your fault,' Issy said.

'Do you need to see someone – someone professional?'

'No, I don't think so.'

'Maybe guided meditation would help – Walter put me onto an app. I'm really enjoying it; it's calming me and helping with focus.'

'Hmm. There are bits about that night that I can't remember and some things I do but at first they aren't in the right order, until I really make myself stop and think about it,' Mackenzie said.

'Yeah, same.'

'Oh god,' Erica said.

'It's okay, Mum. We're just telling you because it does kind of make sense that you might have forgotten about your brother. And I'm guessing back then death, and kids for that matter, were treated differently – hence what Grandpa was on about, I guess,' Mackenzie said.

Erica nodded.

'What's weird,' Issy said slowly, 'is why you wouldn't remember what school you were at. Because surely he'd be buried in the local cemetery. Eleven is year seven, isn't it? I can clearly remember the classroom I was in and where we all sat.'

'Yes, but, Issy, you left school not long ago. Mum's …'

'Ancient?' Erica suggested.

'Well, yeah. Sorry, but …'

'I don't think it's helpful to worry about the fact you can't remember. Maybe there's a way to figure it out. I did try to get it out of Grandpa, but he was fixated on apologising and that's all. And he got a bit upset, so we left.'

'Walter mentioned a website called Find A Grave – and I searched, but couldn't find anything,' Erica said.

'What about school photos or reports?' Mackenzie said.

'Well, actually, this is all really spooky – the timing, that is. Because the other day we had to collect a body of a boy who drowned –'

'Oh no. How awful,' Issy said.

'Yes. That's so sad,' Mackenzie said quietly.

'Sorry. Go on.'

'And it's just that it reminded me of my brother Mark and how little I actually recall about him – or even really knew, maybe, for that matter. I do have a box of old papers and my school reports – either in the garage or up in the roof – so that might help for figuring out the school, but I didn't want to raise all this at the time. I can't get over how strange the timing is – with me and your grandpa. Sadly, I think Mark's box of school photos and reports – if he ever had one; I can't remember – must have been thrown out years ago. It wasn't there when we went through the house,' Erica continued.

'No. If we'd seen it, we would have wanted to have a nosey for sure,' Issy said.

'Mum, would you mind us going through your box without you being there? Because, if you're cool with it, that could be our mission – to find out whatever we can,' Mackenzie said.

'That's fine. I wouldn't mind at least knowing where I was at school that year.'

A moment later their meals arrived. Erica picked up her cutlery and began to eat. *A problem shared is a problem halved*, she thought idly, and then made a vow to try to stop keeping things to herself. *I'm a chip off the old block, Dad. Look where it's got us*, she thought sadly. Though, there was still no way she would have announced any of this to the girls over the phone ...

'Yum. Oh my god, this is so good,' Issy said.

'Yeah, there was nothing like this in Europe,' Mackenzie said, deadpan. 'Just kidding. There was, but we couldn't afford it.'

They all laughed before diving back into their meals.

Chapter Seventeen

As Erica strolled with her girls back down the street, she thought how full her heart was – as full as her tight stomach. At that moment all felt completely right in her new, changed world. She didn't even mind that Mackenzie and Issy would be leaving again on Sunday morning. Right now was what mattered.

'Well, they certainly lived up to the hype about their schnitzels,' Mackenzie said.

'Yes, the food was fantastic,' Issy said.

'Thanks again for buying dinner,' Erica said.

'My pleasure, Mummy dearest.'

'Yeah, thanks again,' Issy said.

'My pleasure, little sister. I'm going to do an online review when we get inside,' she said. 'Brrr, it's cold,' she added, wrapping her arms around her.

'Do you want to put your car around the back?' Erica said, standing beside the white hatchback parked out the front of the office of Crossley Funerals.

'Probably a good idea,' Mackenzie said.

'Just go up there and turn left,' Erica said, pointing.

'Well, we may as well all hop in, since we're all going to the same place,' Issy said.

'Yes, you're quite right,' Erica said.

'Look at you two, one glass of wine and you're useless, light-weights,' Mackenzie said, shaking her head as she fossicked in her handbag.

'Well, in my defence, I am relatively new at being allowed to drink,' Issy said.

'Ah, yes, but not new at actually drinking, right, Issy?' Mackenzie said, holding up the keys and unlocking the car so the indicators flashed orange twice.

'Actually, I'd better drive. Just in case,' Erica said, holding her hand out for the keys.

'Mum, it's fine – I've been off my Ps for ages,' Mackenzie said. 'And, look, you could stand in the middle of the street and not be run over here, let alone hit anyone else,' she said.

'Um, gutters, poles, parked cars, Mackenzie,' Issy said with her eyebrows raised.

Mackenzie coloured a little. 'Yes, well, I got distracted momentarily,' she said, placing the keys in Erica's outstretched hand.

'Exactly,' Issy said.

'And, actually, you've both technically been drinking for years – since you were around thirteen, remember?' Erica said, getting into the driver's seat and closing the door.

'I'm not sure the odd sip from your and Dad's glasses quite counts,' Mackenzie said.

Erica still wasn't sure about Stuart's wisdom in introducing them early to alcohol in the hope of taking away the mystique and power of the substance. It hadn't worked on him – he was still very capable of getting absolutely hammered, until he'd become sick. It didn't help he reckoned he didn't get hangovers.

'It would if you got caught over the limit,' Erica said while adjusting her seat.

'True. I miss Dad,' Issy said.

'Me too,' Mackenzie said.

'Do you want to talk about it – him?' Erica said, turning in her seat towards them both seated on the passenger side of the vehicle.

'No. It's okay, thanks. It is what it is,' Mackenzie said with a shrug.

'Hmm. What she said,' Issy said.

As she started the car, Erica's mind drifted back to the girls' early alcohol consumption. She supposed it had helped because she hadn't once come across them stumbling in late unsteady on their feet, or giggling, or loudly whispering.

Though, perhaps it was a case of what she didn't know didn't hurt her and they did it while staying with friends. Not that they'd ever done all that much of that, either. And Erica was sure she'd have heard from other mothers – at least a hint or dropped word.

Or Issy would have confessed quick smart, she thought, checking her mirrors and then pulling out onto the road. They'd both been open books the whole way through childhood and adolescence.

Sometimes Erica had cringed at what she learnt, and wanted to say 'Too much information' while covering her ears with her hands. But she always wanted to be the sort of mother they were comfortable coming to – with anything, no matter what – so the odd inappropriate thing heard was a small price to pay. She'd had to work hard at not crossing the line into attempting to be their friend, though it was sometimes difficult. It was necessary.

One thing she and Stuart had both believed was that kids needed boundaries.

As she prepared to turn the corner, she caught sight of Mackenzie beside her and then Issy in the back in the rear-vision mirror. Erica's heart swelled again. And she once more uttered the silent words: *We did good, Stu.* She expected a wave of sadness to creep in but warmth and a sense of completeness remained. Maybe she was becoming stronger, easing her way through her grief. Was this acceptance? Maybe. There was really no point in not accepting it – nothing would bring him back. *Perhaps this was the effect of the meditation I'm doing each day now*, she thought as she indicated and then pulled into the car park behind Crossley Funerals.

'Okay, fingers crossed there really are no ghosts,' Issy said, looking up at the two-storey old stone building looming above them from where she stood at the green-painted wooden door with their bags waiting for Erica to unlock it.

'Issy, people are already dead when they come here,' Mackenzie said.

'Yes, but it's an old building. The previous generations might have died in here,' Issy said.

'True. But not exactly a helpful thing to say, Issy, is it?' Mackenzie said.

'No. Sorry,' Issy muttered.

Inside the first door Erica noticed Issy staring down the hall where you could see the frosted door clearly marked *MORTUARY, STAFF ONLY.*

'Seriously, Issy, it's fine,' Erica said gently. 'But would you rather stay somewhere else? I wouldn't be offended.'

'Come on, Issy: if Mum's not spooked, we're fine. She's the one who had the full Kayla experience. And remember we've been –'

'To Europe!' they both cried – Issy with less exuberance. The tiny phrase was quickly becoming a catch-cry.

'I imagine it's too late for the caravan park office to be open, anyway,' Issy said.

'It's probably too late to disturb *anyone* around here – don't country people go to bed early?' Mackenzie said.

'Do they?' Erica said.

'Oh yes. On account of working with the daylight. Or is it the fresh air?'

'Oh, what are you?' Issy said, laughing.

'What? Here we are coming home at, what –' she checked her phone '– eight p.m. – I rest my case. See, Mum's already got into the swing of it.'

'To be fair, I've never been much of a night owl,' Erica said. 'Well, not by choice. Anyway, we don't have to go to bed yet – it really is very early for that. Unless you're tired from your big drive,' she added, beginning to make her way up the stairs.

'But what is there to do?' Erica heard Mackenzie mutter behind her. Thankfully she could pretend to have not heard.

'Welcome to my humble abode,' she said, after unlocking the second green door at the top of the stairs, throwing it open and standing aside once she was in. She put her keys and Mackenzie's in the bowl on the bench. 'Compact, as you can see,' she said, holding her arms out.

'Oh, it's gorgeous. So cuuuute,' Issy said.

'Hmm,' Mackenzie said, turning around and taking in the space. 'It is, actually. I like it. I don't even mind all the old-world chintz. It's like right out of a Laura Ashley catalogue, though nicer, I reckon.'

'I'm dying for a wee,' Erica said. 'And a quick shower. I'm suddenly feeling all grimy,' she added. 'Can you two amuse yourselves for a bit? I won't be long.' Erica didn't wait for an answer.

Ten minutes later Erica returned to the main area, dressed in her flannelette pyjamas with a thick bathrobe on top, to find the girls with their heads buried in their phones.

'Bathroom's free if you want to have a shower,' she said. 'Ah, that's better.'

'We're just doing our reviews,' Mackenzie said, not looking up.

'I'll go,' Issy said, putting her phone down.

'I'm going to put the kettle on – would you like some tea?' Erica said, going to the kitchen bench by the sink. 'Sorry I don't have any wine. I didn't even think to get a bottle.'

'We don't need wine, Mum, do we, Mackenzie?' Issy said. 'I'd love a peppermint tea after my shower though, if you have it.'

'No, I'm good,' Mackenzie said.

'Peppermint tea I can definitely do.'

'Same for me, then, thanks, Mum,' Mackenzie said. 'And don't be too long, Issy, I don't want a cold shower,' she added.

'Oh. Yes. I'm not sure how much hot water there is,' Erica called.

'Got it,' Issy said, and disappeared into the en suite that joined the two bedrooms.

'There are towels in the robe,' Erica called.

'All good, Mum, we came fully self-sufficient. Didn't know what you had. There, five stars. Great review, if I say so myself,' Mackenzie said triumphantly, and put down her phone.

Erica was stunned at how quickly the girls showered and returned. She was still standing at the kitchen sink waiting for the peppermint tea to steep well, getting lost in her own thoughts and dragging herself back only to be lost on another tangent.

'You know, Dad would hate this place,' Mackenzie said, standing beside Erica, a whiff of fresh apple body wash joining them.

'Yep, he so would,' Issy agreed.

Erica tensed slightly, wondering where this was going, hoping the wonderful vibrant mood of the evening wasn't about to be dropped like a stone.

'Which makes it perfect for a new start, Mumsy,' Mackenzie said, sidling up to Erica and wrapping her arm around her mother's waist.

'Dad would be really proud of you, you know, Mum – for taking this chance, and having the courage,' Issy said.

'Thanks, darlings. I'm doing my best.'

'That's all any of us can do,' Issy said sagely.

'And it's enough. It's always enough,' Mackenzie said, with equal solemnity.

Erica looked up quickly and then away again. Mackenzie wasn't exactly flaky – just not prone to expressing deeply profound statements very often. It took her quite by surprise, as did the tears that suddenly filled her eyes and began cascading down her cheeks. A heartbeat later Mackenzie's arm was around her again and squeezing her shoulder.

'Sorry,' she said, wiping her nose and dabbing at her face with a now-damp tissue.

'What for – being human?' Issy said, her own eyes red and wet.

'Yeah, better out than in, Mumsy,' Mackenzie croaked and then cleared her throat.

'I'm just feeling sorry for myself for a moment.'

'You're allowed,' Issy said. 'We're all allowed,' she added, blowing her own wet nose. 'But, seriously, Mum, we didn't come up here to make you all sad and depressed.'

'I'm fine. Just checking my release valve is working correctly,' she said with a wan smile.

'I don't know how you deal with all the death and upset and grieving people day in day out,' Mackenzie said, her arms folded. They were all now standing apart and leaning against different areas of the bench in the small galley kitchen, mugs in hand.

'I think knowing I'm helping, um, helps,' Erica said. 'I haven't embarrassed myself yet.' *Well, not in dealing with our customers in the usual manner* ... 'I actually really enjoy feeling useful,' she added, taking a sip from her mug.

'Mum?'

'Yes, Issy.'

'You know that just because we don't need you to ferry us about or cook meals, or whatever, that it doesn't mean we don't need you, right?'

'Yeah, Mum,' Mackenzie said.

'Oh, darlings. I didn't mean ...' Erica was lost for words. 'I know ... Thank you for saying, though.'

'And while we're being serious,' Makenzie said, 'you do know you can talk to us – like, confide, cry, yell and scream – if you need to, don't you? Because we're adults now.'

'Yeah. We can handle it,' Issy said.

'I appreciate that.' *But you'll always be my babies and I'll always protect you the best way I know how.* 'What did I do to deserve you two?' she said, gathering them to her again.

'Okay, enough with all the melancholy. I spy Scrabble over on the shelf – who's for a game?' Issy asked a few moments later, when they'd parted.

'Okay. But only if we can promise there'll be no fighting,' Erica said, looking from one daughter to the next. 'And no phones, no

Googling for obscure words. Only the official Scrabble dictionary is allowed.'

'Deal,' Mackenzie said. 'I hope you've improved your vocabulary, Issy.'

'Might I remind you who did most of the translating and deciphering overseas?'

'Yeah, point taken,' Mackenzie said good-naturedly, and laughed.

'But no foreign words – only what's in the dictionary, remember?' Erica warned.

'Yup,' Issy said, going over to the bookshelf and retrieving the game with dictionary on top and bringing it over to the table where the others met her with their mugs.

'Be prepared to lose, losers,' Mackenzie said, setting up the game.

'Famous last words – the higher you are the further to fall, remember. Beware of being too cocky,' Issy said.

Erica sat back beaming at them. 'Thanks for being here. What a great night,' she said.

'You won't be saying that in a few hours when you're lost for words and tiles,' Mackenzie said.

'Yeah, game on.'

That wasn't quite what I meant. 'We'll see,' she said, and made a show of pushing up her sleeves.

Chapter Eighteen

Erica woke with her muscles already taut and her heart racing. She could hear movement in the flat just outside her door. She opened her eyes in the hope of still being caught in a dream of some sort and also losing the intensity of her senses. She'd forgotten to put in the earplugs she'd started wearing. Hadn't she? No. That's right; she'd left them out in case … Ah, the girls.

Gradually her body tension loosened and her heart returned to a normal steady beat. But what would they be doing up? She checked the time, despite already knowing it would be around five a.m. Sure enough, it was what was considered a ridiculous hour by most, but to Erica her normal wakeup time. It didn't seem to matter that she'd gone to bed later last night – almost midnight – after several rounds of Scrabble.

She pushed the covers off and dragged on her robe and then socks, noting the weight in her limbs and overall sluggishness as she did. Out of bed, the grittiness in her eyes burnt and there was a slight ache of tiredness behind them. If she hadn't heard movement and hushed voices out in the main room she'd have lain there and listened to a meditation or something. Oh, who was she kidding? She'd have still got up. And gone and sat in the window …

She found Mackenzie and Issy sitting on a dining chair each underneath the split-system air conditioner, feet tucked up under them, a quilt around their shoulders, looking out the window. Just as Erica did each morning. She always returned the chair to the dining table to be tidy; one thing out of place in the small area made everything look a mess.

'Are you okay? Did you get cold?' she asked.

'Sorry if we woke you. There was a noise – well, several, actually,' Issy said.

'And, yes, it's bloody freezing – not under here, obviously,' Mackenzie said.

'Sorry, I should have suggested you leave your door open.' Erica liked sleeping in a chilly room, thanks to the changes that had resulted from menopause. She'd forgotten the younger generation liked their spaces warm.

'I guess we're not used to how quiet it is here,' Issy said.

'Yeah. Every noise is *so* loud,' Mackenzie said.

'It's most likely the bakery down there,' Erica said, leaning between them and peering out the window. 'They have deliveries – but not every morning. And a baker must start work early. It almost scared me witless my first morning here, until I realised what the noise was. I wear earplugs now most nights.'

'Oh, look, there's someone working in there,' Mackenzie said.

'Yes, I get up and sit and watch him. He's quite good company, actually. Well, I'm assuming it's a he – I can't really tell from here.'

'Creepy much, Mum?' Mackenzie said.

'Well, it's not like I know who he is or anything. And I doubt he can see me up here from down there.'

'Well, he wouldn't need to if you weren't creeping the poor bloke out by looking down on him,' Mackenzie said.

'It is a little weird, Mum,' Issy said.

'Cup of tea, anyone?' Erica said, going to the kitchen.

'Are you serious?' Mackenzie said.

'Yes. Completely. I'm up now. I'll sit and be peaceful – the last few mornings I've been listening to a calming music track or guided meditation, which is quite nice. Better than the silence I used to sit in. Stops me thinking.'

'But you still sit here and watch him?' Mackenzie said.

'Well, yes. I like it.' *He's become my friend, my protector. Silly, I know, but still.* 'And, might I point out, Mackenzie, that's exactly what you and Issy are doing right now. *Actually,*' Erica said, her eyebrows raised.

'Oh, yeah,' Issy said, and got up, taking her chair with her.

Mackenzie silently followed suit, pulling the curtains together behind her when she left.

'I don't turn the light on – he probably doesn't even know I'm here,' Erica said.

'Mum, you've got the light on right now,' Issy said, settling herself cross-legged on a dining chair.

'Yes, but only over here,' Erica said. 'And I'll turn it off in a bit. So, no tea for you two?' she asked, having to raise her voice over the kettle, which was very loud in the tiny space.

'Oh, all right. White English breakfast, thanks,' Mackenzie said, joining Issy at the table.

'Yes, thanks: when in Rome ...'

Erica smiled to herself. Clearly they were too tired and too embarrassed by their mother to seize the opportunity to team up for their catch-cry.

'Mum, the poor man probably thinks he's got a stalker,' Mackenzie said.

'Oh, don't be ridiculous, Mackenzie,' Erica said.

'Er, Mum, remember Kayla,' Issy said gently.

'Yes, but that's, that was –'

'Different?' Mackenzie said.

'Oh god. You're right. Poor man.' Erica delivered the girls' teas and then experienced a sense of loss as she sat down at the table with her own rather than in her usual spot in the window. *They're right, aren't they? I have to stop looking out.*

'Why would you actually get up now and not try to go back to sleep, anyway? You know you've trained yourself into these early starts, don't you?' Mackenzie said, blowing on her tea.

'Darling, you wait until you get to my age and experience all the joys of menopause and thereafter. There *is* no more sleep to be had. Yes, I've probably had less than usual due to us being up late, but five-thirty is seven hours after my usual bedtime.'

'So this isn't about Kayla and PTSD or any of that?' Issy said.

'I don't know. At first I got a terrible fright because of a noise – pretty sure it's a delivery.' *And I'm still a bit jumpy a lot of the time, but you don't need to know that.*

'Yes, I can imagine you thought Kayla had found you or you were back at home and going through all that again, or something,' Issy said.

'Exactly. It's actually quite nice to know there's someone right over there,' Erica said, nodding towards the now hidden window.

'Hate to burst your bubble, Mum, but he'd never hear you if you needed him to save you, or whatever,' Mackenzie said. She looked over her mug at her mother.

'Especially if he's wearing earbuds, which he probably is. I would be,' Issy said.

'Oh no. I couldn't work in the dark alone without some music, but not via earbuds,' Mackenzie said, visibly shuddering.

'Well, he's not in the dark – he's got lights on. Obviously. But, yeah, you're probably right, actually – about wearing earbuds,' Issy said. 'Though, he's fine – he's in the country, with no one else around.'

'So? Plenty of horrible things have happened in country towns in South Australia,' Mackenzie said.

'Hmm. True, I suppose. I can see what you mean, Mum,' Issy said, 'how it could be a comfort. So, you don't know who it is?'

'It'll be the baker, I expect,' Mackenzie said, joining them at the table.

'Well, der, Mackenzie,' Issy said.

'I thought you knew everyone around here, Mum – didn't you say it was that sort of place.'

'I don't remember saying that – I think that might have been your assumption. I've only met a few people.'

'And, anyway, if the baker is near the end of their shift, they'll be off to bed. Chances are your paths would never cross,' Issy said, before taking a sip of her tea.

'Yes, that's true,' Mackenzie said.

'I like the intrigue of not knowing,' Issy said, a little dreamily.

A part of Erica longed to meet the person toiling away over there, but another part didn't want her bubble of solace and dreamy speculation shattered.

'When it's light I usually go for a walk,' Erica said, changing the subject. 'There's a lovely creek below the mountain that runs right beside the town.' She wasn't about to admit to them that she still hadn't been able to make herself go there. She might be able to if she had company … 'And there's always the streets, too. A few people walk their dogs.'

'So, Mum, are you seriously up now, as in, not going back to bed? At all?' Mackenzie said.

'Nope. As in, I'm serious that I'm up and not going back to bed.'

'Oh god. It's going to be a long day,' Issy said.

Welcome to my world and that of countless other women, darlings.

'Yes, how do you survive?' Mackenzie said.

'Girls, nothing and no one is stopping you going back to bed. I don't need the company and I promise I'll be quiet. And you're young – you still need your sleep. Do you want to go for a walk with me in a couple of hours?'

'Uh, maybe. Depends.'

'If I'm not here when you wake up, that's where I am and I won't be long and not far away. And if you're up you can come, or not. Entirely up to you.'

'Good night. I need some more sleep,' Issy said, putting down her mug. She yawned as she unfolded her legs.

'Me too,' Mackenzie said, catching Issy's yawn and also putting her mug down and getting up. 'Fingers crossed I can,' she added, rubbing her eyes.

'Good night, sleep tight,' Erica said, and also got up. She took her mug over to the window and looked out and down to the bakery. The girls were probably right, she again conceded reluctantly: maybe it was a bit creepy. Anyway, she wasn't quite the same person she'd been when she'd arrived. She was so much calmer and could take comfort in listening to a meditation track in her room instead.

Bye, baker person, she thought. A touch of sadness followed her to her room. *I'll miss you.*

Chapter Nineteen

Erica was surprised to wake and find bright light instead of the soft, filtered pale grey of dawn peeping in from behind the heavy curtains in her room. She'd actually gone back to sleep – while listening to a meditation track. She took the silent buds out of her ears and closed down the meditation app and paused, listening, trying to detect whether the girls were up.

She stretched, checking if she felt like a walk or not. Not, she decided. She was sure the girls would be up again soon, anyway, and together they could have breakfast and decide how to spend the day.

They'd never been the sorts to laze about in bed until the afternoon like many of their peers. Still, she didn't want to wake them. She was mindful they had a long drive back to Adelaide the following day and that fatigue was a potential issue if they didn't get enough sleep in the days beforehand.

She put her earbuds back in and selected a healing guided meditation track. She was probably going to be addicted, but there were worse things, she decided.

The track had finished and she was still lying in the silent relaxing bubble when she heard the toilet flush and then the water running in the basin. And then she thought she heard the distinct sound of a mug being placed on the bench out in the kitchen. And there was definitely the roar of the kettle. She got up and went out.

'Good morning, Issy.'

'Morning, Mum.'

'Did you get some more sleep?'

'Yep, thanks. All good. Cup of tea?'

'Yes, please. Good morning, Mackenzie,' she said, catching sight of her elder daughter out of the corner of her eye, emerging from the second bedroom.

Mackenzie's response was an undecipherable grunt. She plonked herself down at the table, squinting and frowning.

Erica resisted laughing at her dishevelled appearance. 'What would you like for breakfast?' she instead asked. 'I'm afraid I don't have anything fancy – toast and cereal. No bacon and only one egg,' she said, looking in the fridge.

'Sounds good to me – either,' Issy said. 'Perhaps toast and save the milk for our teas – unless we remember to get some more along the way.'

'Ah, yes,' Erica said.

'Toast is good with me, if there's enough bread,' Mackenzie said, sounding a little brighter.

'Any idea what you'd like to do today? If not, we can go for a drive and visit the nearby towns,' Erica said.

'I was thinking a walk in the Alligator Gorge – have you been there? It's just up a bit, near Wilmington – north of here,' Mackenzie said. 'It looks beautiful. It's the perfect time to visit, according to the website, and it's going to be a nice day. How about we leave visiting the towns for another weekend when it's too warm for walking or there are likely to be lots of tourists about?'

'And when there are no snakes. We're in the country now, remember?' Issy said.

'Yes, we don't want to be wandering about in the bush when it's hot,' Erica said.

'Here,' Mackenzie said, handing her phone over to Erica.

'Looks lovely,' she said, admiring the images of huge rock formations, and then handing it back. 'A great idea, girls.' It wasn't something she thought she'd go and do on her own, so it sounded like the perfect thing to do together.

'We brought our water bottles and coats,' Mackenzie said.

'Yes, even some muesli bars − enough for all of us − just in case,' Issy said.

'Ooh, you are organised. Brilliant,' Erica said.

'I'll just go online and pay for a permit now in case there's no mobile coverage − I read a warning on the website somewhere about the signal being patchy.'

'Are we definitely okay in a car, or do we need a four-wheel drive?' Erica asked.

'Nope, definitely says two-wheel drive is fine.'

'I think we'll take Vera, though, just in case it's a little rugged.'

'Oh, Mum, you really are so cute naming your car and talking to her,' Issy said.

'Oh wow, it's gorgeous,' Issy said, looking around them.

'Yes, what a great idea of yours, Mackenzie,' Erica said. She tried not to think that they weren't far away from where young Todd had drowned. It was further north, she thought.

'You might not be saying that later when you're knackered, Mumsy,' Mackenzie said.

'Don't write me off just yet, missy,' Erica said, walking over towards the information board. 'I think I can manage a two-hour modest hike.' She pointed to the green line. 'It says *most abilities.*'

'Ah, yes, I read a TripAdvisor review from a retired couple who said they did it with no problems. Sorry, Mum, I'm not saying ...' Issy said.

'No, you're right, best to be cautious. I'm being overly prickly. I think we've got all we need,' Erica said, checking off the list on the sign with what they were carrying. 'So, good to go?'

'Yep,' Issy said.

'Come on,' Mackenzie said, moving off.

They oohed and aahed over the breathtaking surrounds for a few moments before falling silent to concentrate on descending the steps.

Erica appreciated the girls stopping at the seats along the way. It hadn't taken her long to feel a little puffed. She was glad they all owned sturdy hiking boots because the trail wasn't really a trail, in Erica's view, but more rocks in a creek bed. And plenty of times they had to make their way around or over patches of water via rocks else risk getting their feet wet and putting their boots' waterproofing claims to the test.

'Oh no,' Mackenzie, who had been walking ahead after several lead changes, said, stopping. 'I think we're going to have to turn around.'

Erica, with Issy by her side, looked at the water pooled right across the rocky path-slash-creek bed in front of them. There was no way around and it really was too deep to get through without getting seriously wet. And she wasn't keen on that.

'Sorry, girls, but I think we're going to have to finish this another day,' she said.

'Oh well, something to look forward to for another time,' Issy said.

'Yeah. Let's go back and do those quick walks to the lookout,' Mackenzie said.

They reluctantly turned around and returned the way they'd come. They'd just arrived at the parking area when a big black cloud covered the sun and Erica noticed a change in the atmosphere. A cold breeze made her shiver. She was slightly hot and damp under her clothes and had taken off her rain jacket and tied it around her waist, but now she untied the sleeves from around her stomach and put it back on.

'Do you think we'd better leave the other walks for another time too?' she said, looking up.

'Yes. I reckon that's going to dump a shitload of rain onto us in a few minutes,' Issy said, also looking up. 'Come on. Let's at least get into the car.'

They'd just settled themselves in the car and drained their water bottles when the large black cloud overhead released a long, heavy shower of rain. It was so powerful Erica could feel the drumming on the roof of the old Volvo in her chest.

'Phew, just in time,' she said.

'Yes. Wow, brilliant timing,' Issy said.

'Lordy, that's loud,' Mackenzie said as a long, deep rumble of thunder made its way right around them, seeming to permeate the car and even their bones, and then several shards of lightning lit up the sky.

'I'm glad we're not out in that,' Erica said, turning the key and starting the engine.

As they made their way back out to the main road, water was already running across the road in the dips and the distinctive smell of fresh wet asphalt was coming in through the vents.

They'd eaten the muesli bars the girls had brought and some nuts along the way, but now Erica was suddenly ravenous. She checked her watch and realised it was one o'clock – they'd set a slow pace on the trail and stopped lots of times to rest and enjoy and soak in their surroundings.

They seemed to remain right under the storm cloud and the rain had become heavier not long after they'd turned onto the road back to Melrose.

'I think we'll just stop for a bit. Best not to chance it,' Erica said a few moments later, pulling off the road to wait it out.

'Good idea,' Mackenzie said.

'Yes, it's pretty ferocious. And no one else seems to be taking the dangerous conditions into account,' Issy said, as a car, and then another very close behind, roared past.

With the rain pelting down hard on the roof and the wipers at full tilt groaning and squeaking and scraping, Erica didn't hear her phone. But she did feel it vibrate against her thigh where it was in the pocket of her jacket, which she'd left on in the rush to get into the car. *God, I hope no one has died and I need to go to work*, she thought, surprised to see Walter's name on the screen.

'Hi, Walter, how's things?' she said, having to slightly raise her voice.

'Sorry to bother you. I hope you and the girls are having fun. Goodness, what is that sound?'

'We're in the car on our way back from Alligator Gorge. It's bucketing down – so much that we're pulled off the road.'

'Oh. I'd better get the washing in – no doubt it'll be here soon,' Walter said. 'Thanks for the warning! Anyway, the reason I'm calling – and please don't feel at all obligated, any of you – is I've decided to be spontaneous and have a dinner party tonight.

Well, it might have been a barbeque but I'm thinking not now the weather is coming in inclement. The Bureau of Meteorology did say chance of showers, but they're so damned unreliable with their forecasts. Anyway, sorry, there's me babbling. I'm calling to invite you and the girls. Just bring yourselves – no need for anything else as there'll be plenty of food and drinks. I will completely understand if you're not up for it – for any reason. No pressure, but I just thought ...'

'Hang on a sec, Walter, and I'll –'

'Oh no, please don't put the girls on the spot – just call or text me back in a bit,' he said cheerfully. And he was gone. Erica was left wondering if he'd hung up or the phone had cut out.

'What? Mum?' Mackenzie said.

'Yes, what did Walter want?' Issy asked. 'Has someone died?'

'Do you have to go to work?' Mackenzie said.

'No. He was calling to invite us to dinner tonight. But it's entirely up to you. There might not be anyone your age. I don't know.'

'That's cool,' Mackenzie said. 'Do you want to go or do you want to use us as an excuse?'

'When have I ever ...?' Erica closed her mouth. Mackenzie was looking knowingly at her. She couldn't put a finger on specifics, but there had been the odd occasion with Stuart's networking events when she'd stayed at home with the girls under the guise of them being a little peaky or unsettled. 'Yes, you're right. I'm a terrible human,' she said with a laugh.

'Ah, the odd white lie is perfectly fine,' Issy said.

Says the kid who couldn't lie to save herself, Erica thought, smiling. 'I'm keen to go and meet a few people,' she said. *And it might be a good idea career wise*, she pondered. 'But you don't have to.'

'Seriously, Mum, what else are we going to do around here? Other than go to the pub or stay in the flat and play more Scrabble? No and no. Thanks. No offence, Issy.'

'None taken. I wouldn't mind going. I'd be happy to hand out food and drinks for Walter if he wants, or help in the kitchen, or whatever,' Issy said.

'Me too,' Mackenzie said.

'So, shall I call him back and tell him to expect all of us?' Erica asked.

'Yep. Sounds good,' Issy said.

'Same,' Mackenzie said.

Erica did and was pleased to hear how thrilled Walter sounded at having his invitation accepted by them all. 'Wonderful. Any time between five and six would be perfect. Just yourselves,' he reiterated before ending the call.

After hanging up, just as Erica began to wonder if she actually had his home address, she received a text containing said address and a link to Google Maps.

'What do we need to take?' Issy asked.

'He said, nothing,' Erica said.

'Sorry, Walter, but I'm not doing that,' Issy said.

'Yes, that's not going to happen,' Mackenzie said.

Erica was again reminded of how grown up her girls were, and enjoyed another moment of parental pride in their manners.

'Hmm,' she said. 'There's apparently a good tourist information centre with a selection of handmade goodies back in Laura. I don't think there's anything much here.' Erica thought, searching her memory.

'But Laura's over forty-five Ks away – half an hour's drive,' Mackenzie said, looking up, aghast, from her phone.

'Welcome to the country,' Erica said. 'Come on, let's go on a mission to find something nice for Walter.'

'And some lunch? I'm starving,' Issy said.

As she drove, Erica marvelled at how quickly she'd got used to driving vast distances – well, vast to her – for seemingly quite inconsequential reasons. And also out of necessity. She'd drive back to Stone Hut for another pie and ice cream in a heartbeat ...

Oh. 'Girls, how starving are you? Can you wait a little while for lunch?'

'I can,' Mackenzie said.

'Yes, do you have somewhere in mind?' Issy said.

'Do you fancy a meat pie? A good one?' Erica said.

'Oh god, yes!' Issy said.

'Definitely,' Mackenzie said.

'We passed a sign along the way saying something about famous pies,' Issy said.

'Yes, it was right on the highway,' Mackenzie said.

'That's where I'm thinking. I went there the other week. Very tasty. But they have other things too.'

'Yum. Crank up Vera. And let's go, then,' Issy said.

'I really hope they haven't run out now you've planted the seed, Mum. I'll be devastated!' Mackenzie said.

When they went to pull back onto the road the rain had gone and the sun was out, leaving the asphalt darker and the leaves of the trees nearby glistening in the breeze. Behind them was blue sky and up ahead, in the direction they were heading, shades of purple and dark grey.

They raved their way through their meat pies and then ice creams in cones – rejecting the notion that it really was too cold for the frozen delight – and then headed on to Laura.

Chapter Twenty

After browsing for gifts and being unable to decide between the handmade jams, chutneys, sauces and chocolates, they grabbed a selection and headed back to Melrose with barely enough time to get showered and changed for their evening at Walter's.

'I told you people go to bed early in the country,' Mackenzie said, as they were about to leave the flat.

'Just because we're to be there around five doesn't necessarily mean an early night – we might not eat until much later,' Erica said.

'It's probably all going to be oldies, too,' Mackenzie said.

'Well, it probably is. And it's not too late to change your minds.' Erica looked from one to the other.

'I want to go,' Issy said. 'I like Walter.'

'Yes, okay, we'll be grown-ups. Time to sit at the grown-ups' table,' Mackenzie said, pretending to be miffed. 'Okay. Ready?'

'Are you? That's the question,' Erica said with a laugh.

'Yes, I've got the goodies from Laura,' Issy said, holding up the brown paper gift bag by its handles.

'God, don't forget that after the insane amount of time we spent deciding,' Mackenzie said.

They'd also grabbed a bottle of red wine, which Issy had tucked under her arm, but weren't too sure about the quality. Wine had always been Stuart's domain. And since his death Erica had drunk very little once she'd emptied the stock back in Adelaide. It was an expense she didn't need, so she hadn't even set foot into a bottle shop in the last six months.

'He's not far away – just up the other end of the street, really – but I'd rather drive, if that's okay with you. It'll be dark when we come home,' Erica said, as she held the door open for the girls to leave the flat first.

'That's perfectly fine with me,' Issy said.

'I wonder if there'll ever be a time when women will feel and actually *be* as safe as men out and about on their own when it's dark,' Mackenzie said with a sigh as she began descending the steps.

'I really hope so,' Erica said.

'At least we carry mobile phones now – not like in your day, Mum – though I wouldn't mind being legally allowed to carry pepper spray, too,' Issy said.

'Nah, I reckon I'm too much shoot-first-ask-questions-later. I probably end up being arrested or sued,' Mackenzie said with a laugh.

'Yeah, totally,' Issy said lightly.

As they piled into the car, Erica was glad they weren't taking gloomy dispositions to Walter's.

'This is it,' Erica said, pulling up beside a white weatherboard cottage with black highlights and a welcoming porch light aglow by the door. Out the front was a large kidney-shaped patch of lawn in the centre of which was a bed of rose bushes with plenty of foliage but no buds or blooms as yet. Everything was neat and in place.

'We're early,' Mackenzie said.

'No, we're right on time – Mum said he said between five and six,' Issy said.

'No one arrives right on the first time – it's just an indication, Issy,' Mackenzie said.

'Yeah, whatever,' Issy said, opening her door and getting out of the car.

They rang the doorbell and waited. Erica noted the smell of woodsmoke in the cold air and wondered if it was coming from Walter's house. It was quite strong. Being the last days of winter, it was still in the air most of the time. Erica still liked it.

Walter cried, 'Welcome, welcome,' and hugged Erica. 'Hello, Issy, Mackenzie. Good of you all to come,' he said. He momentarily looked a little awkward, as if not quite knowing how to greet the young women, and then looked very relieved when Issy darted forwards and gave him a quick hug, and Mackenzie did the same.

'This is for you,' Issy said, handing him the paper bag of goodies from Laura. 'Thanks very much for having us.'

'Oh, that wasn't necessary, but very lovely of you all the same. Thanks so much.'

'And we brought some wine,' Mackenzie said, holding out the bottle. 'Though we've no idea what it's like.'

'Yes,' Erica said, 'a sommelier I am not.'

'Join the club,' Walter said. 'It's South Australian and it's red, so that's a great start,' he said, looking at the label. 'And it's a Shiraz, so, yum. You're very kind. Thank you. You're the first to arrive. Come on in.'

'Something smells divine,' Erica said, unable to resist, as the scent of roast hit her nostrils when Walter closed the front door behind them.

'Slow-cooked lamb. God, I've just realised I didn't check if any of you are vegetarian,' he said, suddenly looking with concern at Issy and Mackenzie.

'No, I love roast lamb, Walter. It sounds – and smells – perfect,' Issy said.

'Me too. We have no dietary issues, so all good, Walter,' Mackenzie said.

'Phew, that's a relief,' he said, making a show of dragging the back of his hand across his brow. 'Though there are stacks of vegetables. I'm actually not a huge meat eater these days, but I do love a roast, especially when it's cold out. We're just going to put it all on platters when it's cooked and we can all help ourselves.'

Erica noticed he was slightly flustered – not quite the unflappable Walter she was used to seeing at work. She thought perhaps he wasn't used to entertaining alone. She had the strange and slightly unsettling sense that she knew Walter quite well on one hand, but also not at all on the other. Perhaps he was still figuring out who he was as a singleton too, just like she was.

Inside was much bigger than the house's façade had suggested, Erica saw as they followed Walter down a long wide hallway and out into a large open-plan space with an exposed brick feature wall. A fire glowed orange through the glass of a built-in slow-combustion wood heater and the opposite wall was lined with timber floor-to-ceiling bookshelves. Walter placed the paper gift bag and wine they'd brought next to a collection of bottles on the shelf set up like a bar, including ice buckets with bottles poking out. They all moved towards the fire.

'People magnet,' Walter said, nodding at it. 'Everyone gravitates to a wood fire – even when it's not on and the weather isn't cold, I've noticed. They're so good for the soul. Bit messy to deal with, but worth it.'

'You have a lovely home, Walter,' Issy said, looking around.

'Thank you. It's all my late wife Mary's doing, and it's possibly a bit big for me now,' he said, also looking around, as if seeing the space for the first time. 'But it's home.'

As Erica took in the area, taking special note of the expanse of plain linen curtains in an oatmeal colour that she assumed was covering a bank of glass doors leading out to more lovely lush garden, she had a whole new respect for Mary's interior decorating skills. Just like in the flat, the décor here all worked perfectly. Erica thought Mary might have been wasted in the funeral industry. No, that wasn't fair – it was a very worthy and fulfilling occupation. But she hoped she'd been truly happy. Erica checked herself. Not everyone had allowed their husbands to curb their dreams. She was just reacting to the reminder of Stuart's influence over her life path thanks to choosing the wine, she supposed.

And really, it wasn't Stuart's fault if she hadn't stood up for herself or even voiced any career aspirations. Anyway, she'd loved being a mother to Issy and Mackenzie. And she was enjoying her new life now.

Stop thinking, Erica, she told herself, and almost laughed aloud.

'Can we help with anything, Walter?' Erica heard Issy ask.

'Yes, I'm happy to help too – or stay out of your way. Whatever works,' Mackenzie said.

'Oh. Right. Um. I'm quite on top of everything, I think, and a little out of practice with delegating, to be honest.'

'But don't you organise Mum every day at work?' Mackenzie said, causing Erica to prick up her ears from over at the bookshelves, where she was looking at an arrangement of photos in silver frames of various sizes.

'Oh, no, not at all – well, not really. Your mother has grasped things very quickly. We've settled into a great groove, haven't we, Erica?'

'We have. But, Walter, you're being far too generous. It's thanks to your Mary having written such comprehensive instructions and your calm, patient attitude.'

'Ah,' he said, waving a hand dismissively. 'Let's just agree we make a fabulous team.'

'Definitely. Agreed,' Erica said.

'Oh, that's right, I was putting the platter of nibbles together when you arrived,' he said, moving back to the large kitchen area.

'I can finish that,' Mackenzie said, going over to where he now was.

'Thank you. Yes, please,' Walter said.

The doorbell rang.

'Oh,' Walter said. 'Actually, I seem to have got well and truly distracted and completely lost my manners. Issy, would you please organise a drink for yourselves while I get the door? Everything should be right there where the bottles are. There's water and soft drink in the bar fridge, which is hidden in the cupboard below. I'll be back in a sec.'

Issy moved over to the bar in the bookcase near their mother.

'I'll have a glass of the red wine we brought, thanks, Issy,' Erica said.

'Me too, thanks, little sister,' Mackenzie called from behind the kitchen bench.

'Everyone's arrived at once,' Walter announced as he stood aside at the end of the hall and a group of people entered the space, with him introducing them as they did. It reminded Erica of a slightly less formal version of the grand occasions she'd seen on TV where people were announced by some dignitary or other and then stepped forwards. *Though no one's bowing or curtseying, thank goodness*, she thought.

'Erica, Mackenzie and Issy – many of you will know of Erica, my new right hand, even if you haven't already met. Erica, Mackenzie and Issy, let me introduce Gemma and her dad Roy – they run the wonderful bakery across the street from our office. Phillipa and Lloyd – our local real estate agents and my next-door neighbours to the left. Erica, Peggy you know and Jennifer, who you also know.' As they all exchanged handshakes, Erica was left wondering if Peggy and Jennifer had come together or had arrived separately. Perhaps they were related – or old friends. She did know that Jennifer wasn't a true local, but considered a blow-in, like Erica. Walter had told her she'd moved to Port Pirie from Sydney. Or maybe Jennifer had officiated at Peggy and Shirley's wedding. She was so warm and engaging, Erica thought she'd develop firm friendships wherever she went.

'How are you doing, Peggy?' Erica said when the initial hubbub of introductions had ebbed away. Peggy had popped into the office briefly to collect Shirley's ashes. She'd seemed tired and sad, but had assured Erica she was doing okay. Erica and Walter hadn't discussed Peggy beyond the purely professional. Walter's discretion was one of the many things Erica appreciated about him.

'Today is one of the better days, thanks, Erica. It's such a help to have something to look forward to, bless darling Walter.'

Erica thought she looked very well for someone who only a few days ago had lost her wife and partner of many decades. Perhaps Walter had encouraged Jennifer to call Peggy – or vice versa – so she didn't have to arrive alone. That seemed a very Walter thing to do.

Erica was glad she had arrived with Mackenzie and Issy, but felt certain she'd have been very comfortable arriving here on her own – or at least not been uncomfortable for very long.

This going out and meeting new people – dinner parties at people's homes, too, for that matter – was different. She and her friends always ate out, declaring they preferred to avoid all the palaver.

Stuart had hosted plenty of events at their sprawling home back in Adelaide, but he always insisted on having them professionally catered – a tax deductible expense. Whenever Erica had offered to take care of the food herself – as a more than competent home cook – he'd gently rejected the idea. She'd never given it much thought. But now she was questioning everything about their past and relationship together. Had this been another subtle way he'd shut her down and controlled her?

At least she was doing something about it; she had a whole new career – had got a job of her own volition with someone with no connection to Stuart. That was a satisfying thought. She was trying very hard to put the past behind her – as guided by the meditations – and that also included thoughts and frustration around her brother Mark, which annoyingly still kept popping up. It didn't help that they were preparing for Todd's funeral on Monday.

Concentrate, she told herself, after she'd had to ask Roy to repeat himself.

'How are you enjoying Melrose?' Roy asked.

'Oh, very much, thank you.'

'Nibbles, anyone?' Mackenzie said, holding up a platter with a selection of dips, crackers and vegetable sticks.

Issy appeared. 'What can I get you to drink, Roy?'

'Oh, actually, I brought some beer,' Roy said, pulling a six-pack out from under his arm and looking at it as if he'd only just remembered it was there. He handed it over to Issy.

'Would you prefer a glass?' Issy asked.

'Yes, please: I'd better be a bit civilised.'

Erica and Roy chatted about the weather and their visit to Alligator Gorge and close call in getting wet until Walter called out, asking everyone to please be seated in the dining room. They made their way through the large brick archway and selected a seat.

Over dinner – a plate piled with succulent lamb and wonderfully caramelised roast vegetables – Erica chatted with Gemma, complimenting her on the lovely baked goods Erica had enjoyed that first day and her coffee.

She longed to ask about the bakery employee who worked in the early hours, but was stopped by the earlier discussion with Issy and Mackenzie. It was the beginnings of a potentially awkward conversation to reveal you were perving on someone's husband. Erica had just heard Walter tell Gemma it was a shame Jimmy couldn't make it. She assumed Jimmy was Gemma's husband or partner. He must be the guy across the street – her new friend across the street, as she still referred to him in her mind. She'd really better stop that.

'That's a shame,' Walter said. It was the way he said it, the extra gentleness and regret in his tone, that caused Erica to take notice. And Gemma's reply even more so: 'Oh well, maybe next time. It is what it is.' She sounded a little weary, or maybe frustrated or disappointed, given the addition of a shrug.

'Is your husband unwell?' Jennifer asked.

'He's not my husband. Jimmy's a younger guy staying in a van behind the bakery. I don't want to talk behind his back, but he's new in town and struggling a bit.'

'If he's looking for some company, I'd be happy to help,' Erica said. 'You're welcome to give him my number.' The words had been uttered before she could stop them. Oh well, too late now. She was very curious about the guy.

'Okay, thanks. He might really appreciate that. He's mentioned seeing you across the street. But he's pretty shy, though, so don't expect him to ...' Gemma shrugged.

'No worries. Just if it helps.' Erica hoped her face wasn't giving her away as embarrassment coursed through her.

Walter handed Erica a pen and notepad and she concentrated on writing down her number while hoping the heat she felt was just a hot flush. She rarely experienced this phenomenon outside of bed and was lucky that when she did, while very hot, prickly and uncomfortable under her clothes, her skin didn't seem to change colour. She wasn't sure if that was the same for other women in her position, but was very grateful for it.

She tried very hard not to look at Issy or Mackenzie lest they embarrass her or she do that all by herself. Jimmy might not be Gemma's husband, but Erica still felt as if she'd been caught out doing something improper.

Chapter Twenty-one

Partway through the meal, when they were sitting back having had their plates collected by Issy and Mackenzie, letting their food settle before dessert, Jennifer, seated to Erica's left, leant towards her and spoke. 'I wonder, Erica, if I might ask a favour?'

'Oh, sure. Fire away.'

'Well, I'm putting an amateur theatre group and production together as a way of meeting people – being as I'm newish in the general area – well, not even quite this area, but well, anyway … I was wondering if you'd do the makeup for everyone. Voluntarily, I'm afraid, but I'm sure it will fun,' Jennifer said.

'Oh. Okay. I don't see why not.'

'Perhaps you might like a part as well?' Jennifer prompted.

A jolt of fear shot through Erica like a bolt of lightning – and was gone just as quickly. But she was left with a slight quiver of tension inside. *Christ. What's that about? What's up with me? Am I going to start having full-on panic attacks now, too?* She forced her attention back to answering the question and not blurting out what was on her mind: *Hell no!* 'No, thanks for asking, though. What play are you doing?' Erica said.

'It's by a new playwright – a friend of an acquaintance. It'll really help get her career off the ground to have it produced. Plus, I'm looking for a social outlet or two to keep me occupied in the evenings. There's only so much TV, online rambling and books I can consume. And some human company would be nice.'

'Sounds like a good plan,' Erica said. 'Keep me in the loop.'

'Walter, are you going to try your hand?' Jennifer said.

'You know, I think I'd really like to. I probably shouldn't commit, given the nature of our work, but I'm throwing caution to the wind – I'll deal with and/or juggle whatever comes up. Count me as all in!'

'Oh. Of course,' Erica said.

'No, Erica, you'll be fine. I'll make sure of it,' Walter said.

'Okay.'

'Brilliant, Walter. Thanks,' Jennifer said.

'My pleasure,' Walter said.

'I'd love to do it,' Phillipa said.

'And I hope it doesn't sound too egotistical, but I would too, actually,' Lloyd said.

'Fantastic. Thank you so much,' Jennifer said.

'I've not the foggiest about acting – or anything to do with the theatre, for that matter – but I could do with keeping busy and being around people,' Peggy said. 'So, I wouldn't mind being involved – in whatever capacity you see fit – but I also don't want to bring the mood down.'

'I'm not having caveats. Thrilled to have you on board, thanks, Peggy. Good for you. Gemma? What say you?' Jennifer asked.

'Oh yes. I loved drama at school.'

'Brilliant,' Jennifer said.

'Dad?' Gemma said, giving Roy, who was slumped in his chair and looked very close to drifting off, a nudge.

'Why not? If you need an old town drunk or hobo – someone lounging around not saying much. Not sure my old noggin is up to remembering too many lines.'

'Good on you, Roy, that's the spirit!' Jennifer beamed while she added a note to her notebook. 'Issy and Mackenzie, would you like to join us old fogies?' she asked.

'Sorry, we live in Adelaide, so it would be a bit tricky to rehearse,' Issy said.

'Oh, that's a shame,' Jennifer said.

'But we absolutely will be there on opening night cheering you all on,' Mackenzie said.

'Yes, definitely,' Issy said.

'Ooh, and maybe you can sell tickets down in Adelaide and we can have an audience from further afield. Why think small?!' Jennifer said.

'Absolutely,' Issy said.

'Yes, totally. We'll do our best,' Mackenzie said.

'Sorry, folks, I'm getting quite ahead of myself. But, ooh, this is exciting – I've always wanted to do amateur theatre and life's been in the way for forever. You lot are brilliant – thank you for your enthusiasm. Please send anyone my way who you think might be interested in being involved – in any facet. The more the merrier,' she said, closing her notebook and tucking the small pencil back into its spine. 'I'll let you know when I've got enough ducks in a row for our first meeting.'

'Right, who's for some dessert?' Walter said, getting up. 'We have on offer sticky date pudding and a cheese platter with fresh and dried fruits. So, hands up for option one. Okay, then, too easy,' he said.

'Sorry, Walter, it seems I've quite taken over your dinner party,' Jennifer said.

'Oh, no, not at all,' Walter said. 'It's wonderful to have something interesting to talk about other than hatches, matches, dispatches and the weather.'

'Speaking of which,' Gemma started. 'Can anyone put me straight? I've had people tell me the death of young Todd Jackson is being investigated as a possible crime but then someone else told me that's not true. And if there is anything untoward, why would his body have been released so soon? His funeral is on Monday – that I do know for sure. It's bugging me.'

'I heard a whisper, but put it down to gossip – for basically the same reason,' Peggy said. Erica took a sip from her wine glass and hoped to be kept out of the conversation.

'You don't get told anything, do you, Walter?' Lloyd said, looking over at Walter who was at the kitchen bench. 'Erica?'

Erica shook her head.

'No. And I – *we* – wouldn't say if we did. Would we, Erica? Sorry, folks.'

'And that's why you're so well respected around here,' Roy said.

'Well, I was there – as part of the SES search and recovery,' Phillipa said. 'And those lads all looked shifty as hell, if you ask me. But it's lucky my opinion doesn't matter because one of the detectives told me it was definitely a tragic accident. Misadventure. Nothing more.'

'Ah. Thank you, Phillipa! As I say, it's been bothering me,' Gemma said. 'While it doesn't bring him back, in some ways I suppose that's a relief. I guess we all react to trauma and reveal our shock differently.'

'Yes. Though I still can't help thinking it was strange to be out swimming when it's this cold still,' Roy said. 'Oh well, another of life's mysteries.'

'I also heard he was bullied badly at school. For being gay. I really hope it's not true,' Gemma said. She shook her head slowly.

'You didn't hear this bit from me, but, yes, I can confirm that – from the same reliable source,' Phillipa said.

'Sadly, that's what I was told as well,' Peggy said.

'It's all so awful,' Lloyd said.

'Yes,' Jennifer said.

'Why is being gay a bloody issue still – it's twenty-twenty-two for Christ's sake,' Mackenzie said, interrupting the silence as she leant over to deliver dessert to the table. Then she muttered, 'Sorry, I'm not having a go at anyone here, but …' She sat back down and stared at her plate, shaking her head.

'No, you're quite right, Mackenzie,' Walter said. 'It's ridiculous.'

'Exactly. Well said,' Gemma said, picking up her spoon.

'You'd think people would be over persecuting others for things out of their control by now, wouldn't you?' Lloyd said.

'Yes,' Phillipa said.

'Now, sorry to all the men present – you're each wonderful,' Jennifer said, 'but I saw a rather poignant meme on my Facebook feed the other day on this very subject – well, sort of. Anyway, it said something like: *The fact I am still attracted to men proves sexuality isn't a choice.* Haha, how do you like that!?'

There were titters around the table.

'The notion that *any* women are sexually attracted to men has always mystified me!' Peggy said, lifting her wine glass.

'Haha. Touché, Peggy. I'll drink to that,' Roy said, raising his glass.

'Yes, quite,' Walter said. 'You know, sometimes I'm embarrassed to be of this gender. We're far too often given credence and power due merely to our chromosomes.'

'I agree,' Lloyd said.

'And don't get me started on mansplaining,' Peggy said.

'What's mansplaining?' Roy asked.

'I'll explain it later, Dad,' Gemma said, patting his arm.

'Thanks, I'd appreciate that.'

'Sorry, girls, we're leaving the world in a right mess for you to sort out,' Jennifer said.

'I reckon it's going to take a whole lot more than our generation to make any headway,' Mackenzie said.

'Yes, and we're the lazy, entitled ones who aren't capable of thinking of anyone else's needs, remember?' Issy said.

'Well, I think you're both lovely, and a great credit to your mum here,' Peggy said.

'Thanks,' Issy said. 'We haven't decided what to do with our lives yet, have we, Mackenzie?'

'No. I'm pretty sure I want to go to university at some point, though,' Mackenzie said.

'Yes, me too,' Issy said.

'Ah, plenty of time,' Jennifer said with a sweep of her hand. 'Personally, I think seeing some of the world first adds richly to your studies – different perspective and maturity are always wonderful ingredients. No rush,' she added.

'Actually, they've both just been overseas,' Erica said.

'Mum, it's hardly worth mentioning since we got homesick and only lasted a few weeks.'

'Ah, yes, but you went. And you admitted you weren't ready – there's no shame in that. And hadn't you just lost your dad?' Walter said.

The girls both nodded.

'Well, I think that was very brave of you,' he said.

'Yes. Sometimes you need to leave to appreciate what you had, too,' Roy said.

'Thanks, everyone,' Mackenzie said, beaming at those gathered around the table.

'Yes, I really appreciate you not giving us a hard time,' Issy said.

'Well, if anyone does that, it says more about them than you,' Lloyd said.

'Exactly,' Erica said. She watched on proudly as Mackenzie and Issy collected the dessert plates from around the table.

'Oh, leave it – I can do that later,' Walter said.

'We don't mind, really,' Issy said.

'No, not at all,' Mackenzie said.

'Oh, what a lovely evening,' Peggy said. 'Thank you, Walter. And Jennifer for dragging me out and away from my self-pity.'

'You're healing, Peggy – that's not self-pity. And we all here have lost someone and or have been a little lost ourselves,' Walter said.

'Yep. No shame in reaching out,' Lloyd said.

Gradually a chain of yawns made its way around the table and Erica was surprised to find it was nearly ten.

'Would you like us to make tea and coffee, Walter?' Mackenzie asked from the kitchen bench where Issy was stacking a dishwasher.

'Oh, that would be lovely. You should be able to find everything in that cupboard to your left.'

'A tea would really hit the spot,' Jennifer said.

'Yes,' Peggy said.

'You lovely ladies can come again,' Walter said, as Mackenzie and Issy, having taken orders, delivered each beverage to the right person.

'Yes, it's been such a delight to have you two young ones to add a different perspective – no offence, Walter,' Jennifer said.

'No offence taken. They've been a wonderful breath of fresh air.'

When they finally all hugged Walter and each other goodbye and headed outside and got into their cars, it was almost midnight.

'That was fun,' Mackenzie said.

Erica searched her words for hints of sarcasm, but found none. She sighed contentedly to herself.

'Yes, I'm so glad we went,' Issy said.

'Thanks for being such a big help to Walter,' Erica said.

'You don't have to thank us, Mum – Walter did,' Mackenzie said.

'At least we can leave with the knowledge you are being adequately looked after,' Issy said sagely.

Erica beamed to herself, a little lost for words.

'Yes, our work here is done,' Mackenzie said, making a show of wiping her hands on each other. They all laughed. 'And life has officially come full circle – the children are now the parents,' she declared, imitating Sir David Attenborough's deep tones.

'Very funny, Mackenzie,' Erica said. 'Just no looking for nursing homes for me just yet, okay?'

'Roger that, Mummy dearest. But, seriously, what a lovely group of people. I thought country people didn't tend to welcome newcomers.'

'There you go again with your generalisations, Mackenzie,' Issy said.

Erica couldn't see her eyes in the dark car as they drove, but her tone told her they'd be rolling around in her head.

Just a few minutes later they were parked once again behind the office building below the flat.

'By the way, thanks for not mentioning my brother Mark when they were talking about Todd Jackson's drowning,'

Erica said before opening her door. 'I just couldn't be bothered explaining it.'

'Again, no need to thank us, Mum,' Mackenzie said.

'Yes,' Issy said. 'That's your story to tell if you want to – or not, if you don't. It was nice of you to offer your number to Gemma's guy with problems, Jimmy, by the way.'

'I'm not sure,' Mackenzie said. 'Do you think that was wise? We don't know what sort of *problems* Gemma was referring to.'

'I think someone would have said something if there was a major issue or it was inappropriate. I just think it's nice to reach out – I know what it's like not knowing anyone. Thankfully I've had Walter,' Erica said.

'Hmm. Fair enough, I suppose,' Mackenzie said.

'I can't believe we were there so long and didn't get bored,' Mackenzie said, kicking her shoes off once they were in the flat and throwing herself onto the couch.

'It really was a great night,' Issy said, pulling a chair out from the dining table and plonking down.

'I'm pleased you enjoyed yourselves,' Erica said. 'Thanks for coming with me.'

'I'm kind of jealous about the play,' Issy said.

'I'm sure you could find a theatre group back home if you want to,' Erica said.

'Yeah, maybe.'

Chapter Twenty-two

Erica was surprised and pleased to find it was seven a.m. when she woke on Sunday after Walter's dinner party, until she remembered how late they'd gone to bed. She'd mostly slept soundly until easing into her early wakeup time. But then she'd managed to drop off to sleep again, so that was something. There were no deliveries, she didn't think, to the bakery on a Sunday morning – that's why she'd slept so peacefully. But the previous Sunday she'd been jolted awake, hadn't she? She couldn't recall. Perhaps this was a sign of progress – that she was recovering from her mild PTSD, if that's what she had.

Oh, she thought, pausing with her legs out of bed, on the cusp of leaving it, *but I have company. Perhaps that's why I slept so well – and right through.*

A little depressed sigh left her; she wished her girls could stay, but they had work and lives in Adelaide. She didn't want to pop her bubble of contentment and get out of bed. But then she heard movement on the other side of her door. The girls were up.

183

She dragged on each piece of her walking attire, laid out in order on the back of the chair in the corner of her room.

When she arrived in the main room of the flat, she was a little surprised to see both girls had their overnight bags near the door.

Issy, seated at the table, must have noticed her pause and followed her gaze, because she said: 'Sorry it's such a quick visit.'

'Yeah, sorry, but we have to get back for work,' Mackenzie said.

'I know. It's okay,' Erica said.

'But we'll absolutely be back before too long,' Issy said. 'I love this place.'

'Me too.' Mackenzie went over to the window, pulled the curtains apart and looked out. 'No baker this morning,' she said. 'But, brrr, you can feel it's cold out – it's coming off the glass,' she said, closing them again.

'I checked just before,' Issy said. 'I guess he doesn't work on a Sunday,' she said with a shrug.

'And you told me off for looking,' Erica said.

'I know. Couldn't resist,' Issy said.

'The struggle is real, Mum,' Mackenzie said.

'See,' Erica said with a laugh, and rolled her eyes. 'Do you want to go for a walk or do anything before you head off?'

'No. It's too cold for a walk,' Mackenzie said.

'Yeah, just a leisurely breakfast?' Issy said.

'Sounds good to me. Coffee, anyone?' Mackenzie said, making her way to the kitchen.

'Yes, please,' Erica said.

'And me, thanks,' Issy said.

Erica wished she'd thought to get bacon and eggs so breakfast could take a bit longer. 'I'm very glad I didn't have that third glass of wine last night,' she said.

'Hmm. Me too,' Issy said.

'Toast or cereal?' Erica said.

'Toast please,' Issy said.

'Yes, thanks, same,' Mackenzie said.

Erica got the loaf of sliced bread out of the freezer and then the tray for the oven's grill. Best to toast them all at once so they could eat together, she decided. And also standing and watching them so they didn't burn would be a good distraction.

'I'm really glad you've made some new friends and you're happy here, Mum,' Mackenzie said, stepping aside so Issy could squeeze in between her and Erica to get out plates and cutlery from the drawers.

'Yes, that group last night was lovely – all of them,' Issy said. 'Roy seemed quite grumpy at first, but I think he's just a bit of a thoughtful character: careful with his words.'

'We were a little worried about how you were settling in – especially after seeing Michelle the other week,' Mackenzie said.

'Yes, because we know you wouldn't tell us if you were unhappy,' Issy said.

'Well, I ...' Erica wasn't sure how to proceed.

'I know you don't want us to worry,' Issy said, as if reading her mother's mind.

'Exactly,' Mackenzie said.

'But you can be honest – tell us anything,' Issy said.

I'm not so sure about that. I'm the adult here – well, the parent – remember? But she kept the words to herself. 'In my defence,' Erica said, 'I needed time to get my footing – to settle in.' *Because there's too much at stake for me to fail.* 'I love that you're concerned, but I really am fine.'

'Well, we know that now, don't we?' Mackenzie said in a scolding tone.

'Anyway, just promise you'll tell us if at some point you're not – fine, that is,' Issy said.

'Absolutely,' Erica said.

'Promise?' Issy urged.

'I promise. And the same goes for both of you. Okay?'

'Yep,' Mackenzie said.

'Yes,' Issy said. 'But don't forget, we're all grown up now because we've been to …'

'Europe! Alone!' Mackenzie cried.

'Yes, Europe! Let us not forget Europe,' Issy said.

'How could I possibly?' Erica said cheerfully. They all laughed. 'Right, here's the toast – watch out, the pan is hot,' she said, taking it to the table where a large cork mat was ready to protect the timber.

Mackenzie put their mugs on the table and stood surveying the area. 'Are we missing anything, before I sit down?'

'Nope, we're good to go,' Issy said.

They were silent for a few minutes while they prepared their slices of toast, took a couple of bites and sipped from their mugs.

'Now, you haven't really told me how things are with you both and everything back home,' Erica said. 'Have you found someone else to move in?' She wasn't sure she wanted another young person in the house, but the extra money would really help with the mortgage and other bills. She reminded herself the girls were sensible, and had amply demonstrated that these last couple of days.

'Hmm. Destiny showed an interest, but when we checked her references … I don't know, something just didn't feel right. You know the one, Mum – from the year above me. Ben G's sister?' Mackenzie said.

'It's okay, we're keeping an eye on the spreadsheet you put together, and the bank account. But we're being very discerning about who we take, because once they're in it'll be so much harder to get them out if it doesn't work – in the sense of having the conversation. Don't worry, Mumsy, you won't end up with squatters,' Issy said.

'Hmm, right. I'd appreciate that,' Erica said.

'Anyway, we know a friendly cop from *The Kayla incident* now, so we'll just call him if we have any issues,' Mackenzie said.

'Which we won't,' Issy said.

'Exactly. Don't worry – it's all good,' Mackenzie said, waving her hand as if batting a fly away.

Erica thought about pointing out that the more they tried to reassure her, the worse she was feeling about it all, but kept it to herself.

'Are you okay with us having a boy in?' Mackenzie asked.

'If we can find one who's tidy and not too stinky, that is?' Issy added.

'It's your home, girls – you're adults now; it's up to you who you share it with. Just as long as you look after the place.'

'Which we will. Like you said: it's our home,' Mackenzie said.

'Yes, we're being very picky,' Issy said.

Erica longed to remind them that they couldn't take too long due to the expenses, but instead concentrated on taking a deeper breath without it being obvious to the girls and telling herself it would be just fine.

'A new guy at my work is looking for somewhere, but I was just waiting to check him out a bit more before suggesting it,' Mackenzie said. 'Anyway, don't worry, Mum, it's all under control.'

'Okay. Sorry, I didn't mean to nag.'

'Also, Mum, what did you decide about Mark?' Mackenzie said.

'What do you mean?'

'Yes, now you've had a chance to think about it some more, do you want us to go ahead and do some digging? Or not?' Issy said.

Erica wasn't sure. The topic kept passing through her mind. On the one hand, it felt wrong that Mark might be forgotten. On the other, what would knowing more achieve? 'I don't know. Nothing will bring him back,' she said.

'But maybe knowing something might help?' Issy said.

'Or not?' Mackenzie said.

Erica almost laughed. *Real helpful, girls.*

'How about if *you* want to know you look through the boxes of stuff at home, if you can be bothered,' Erica said. 'There's my old school stuff and some boxes of photo albums from your grandparents. I'll leave it up to you. I think I'm fine with whatever you choose to do. I can understand you wanting to know.'

'I know it shouldn't and I don't quite know how it changes things, and it doesn't really, well not in a practical sense, I guess, but, well, learning you were not always an only child is … I don't know,' Issy rambled before giving up. She shrugged and raised her open hands, palms up.

'I suppose I can see how it might change things a little, in your eyes,' Erica said.

'It's weird that it does, because it shouldn't, I know …' Mackenzie said.

'I get it,' Erica said. She didn't at all, but wanted to give the girls the freedom and reassurance to follow this through or not, whichever they chose.

'So, we'll have a look through your box – if we feel like it. And then see,' Issy said.

'Okay. Yep. Sounds good to me,' Erica said.

'I don't feel all that compelled to know, actually,' Mackenzie said thoughtfully.

'Clearly I'm not that fussed, either,' Issy said.

'Does that make us terrible human beings?' Mackenzie said.

'No. Not at all,' Erica said.

'We never go and visit Granny at the wall,' Issy said. 'Perhaps we should – perhaps *I* should. Sorry, I didn't mean to lay on a guilt trip. But she did mean a lot to me.'

'I think about her all the time and she meant a lot to me, too, but I don't think that means we have to be visiting some wall with a brass plaque engraved with her name and some dates on it,' Mackenzie said.

'Hmm,' Erica said.

'Visiting or not doesn't mean we loved them any more or less when they were alive,' Mackenzie said. 'It's really just to provoke a memory, I suppose, isn't it? Have an actual connection?'

'Yes. I guess,' Erica said.

'And if you have strong memories in your heart you might not need to do that – forever, right?' Issy said.

'Exactly,' Mackenzie said.

'Speaking of which, what are we going to do about Dad? I mean, his ashes, obviously,' Issy said.

'What would you like to do?' Erica said.

'I don't know,' Issy said.

'How about nothing? Can't we just leave him where he is? I like him being in the urn on the mantelpiece – it's like he's still watching over us,' Mackenzie said.

'I agree. It doesn't matter how long he's there, does it?' Issy said.

'No, not at all,' Erica said.

'I don't know why I mentioned it,' Issy said.

'Because you wanted to,' Mackenzie said.

'Well, that's settled then,' Erica said. 'We'll just leave his ashes where they are. And when things change – if you change your mind; either of you – then we'll talk about it. Okay?'

'I bet he'd like to be scattered at the New York Stock Exchange, given his obsession with money,' Mackenzie said idly.

'True,' Issy said.

'Maybe that's something we can save up for,' Erica said.

'Don't people like to be scattered somewhere they've actually been?' Issy said.

'I don't think it matters, as long as it's meaningful to them or their remaining loved ones,' Erica said. 'Someone told me the other day they're scattering their dad's ashes in the sheep yard because that's their strongest memory of him. There are no rules. And there's nothing wrong with doing nothing, too, I don't think.'

They finished their toast in thoughtful silence.

'I've had such a lovely time,' Issy said wistfully, pushing her empty plate away from her a little. 'I don't want to go back to Adelaide. It's so peaceful and that bit slower here.'

'Well, you're welcome to stay as long as you like,' Erica said.

'I can't let my boss down since she was good enough to give me my job straight back, *and* give me a promotion,' Mackenzie said.

'Yeah. Oh well, we'll just have to visit again soon,' Issy said. 'I wonder when the play will be.'

'No idea. It might not happen,' Erica said.

'I reckon it will,' Issy said. 'I think Jennifer will get everything under way quick smart. She seems very keen. And very organised.'

'Well, I'm sure she'll hold you two to trying to sell tickets, so you'll be kept in the loop,' Erica said.

'Sounds good to me. Maybe she'll need a chorus,' Issy said, 'and I can join in.'

'You can't sing, Issy,' Mackenzie said.

'I can so. Everyone can sing.'

'I mean, you can't sing in tune.'

'Maybe not, but I could fill a space in the back.'

'Anyway, she'd have said if it's a musical she has in mind – it's clearly not,' Mackenzie said.

'Pity,' Issy said.

'There's nothing stopping you finding a choir back at home, remember,' Mackenzie said.

'No, you're right.'

'I didn't know you harboured ambitions to be onstage, Issy,' Erica said.

'I didn't know either – I wasn't remotely interested in drama at school.'

'Well, we all change,' Erica said.

'You're going to love being in that fold again, Mum,' Mackenzie said.

'I wasn't ever in the theatre, Mackenzie.'

'Film's not *that* different, surely.'

'Yeah, maybe you'll restart your career ambitions,' Issy said.

'I have a new career, remember?' Erica said.

'Yes. Sorry. I didn't mean to imply …' Issy said.

'What? That I'm flaky? I've committed to Walter. Anyway, I wouldn't know where to start with getting back into film makeup and special effects, even if I wanted to. I think it's probably a younger person's game now.' Erica cursed how defensive she was getting.

'Mum, you're hardly old,' Issy scoffed.

'But she has been out of the loop for ages,' Mackenzie said.

'Yeah, so much so we didn't even know about that part of her life, remember?' Issy said.

'Yes, well ...' Erica said, a little lost for words. It was uncomfortable having your own daughters pointing out your limited ambition and lack of career progression – even if they didn't realise they were.

'Women are always putting their careers aside for men,' Issy said a little huffily.

'God, Issy, where did that come from?' Mackenzie said.

'Well, they moved back from the US for Dad – well, for his family.'

'Hmm. You're right. And then she stayed at home for us,' Mackenzie said.

'Exactly. It's her time now. Well, it should have been. And it would have been if Dad hadn't left her in the shit financially,' Issy said.

Excuse me, I'm right here. 'Darlings, I appreciate your ... concerns ... but I am perfectly fine. I am happy with where things are for me right now, even if it's not exactly what I had imagined,' Erica said.

'Sorry, I didn't mean to be ...' Issy stopped.

Patronising? 'It's okay. Do either of you want a second coffee?' Erica said, getting up and collecting their mugs.

'No, thanks. We should hit the road. I need to do some washing when we get back so it dries in time for work in the morning,' Mackenzie said. 'How's that for peak adulting?'

'Very good. But don't be in too much of a hurry to grow up. You need to have fun and enjoy life too,' Erica said.

'Roger that, Mumsy,' Mackenzie said.

'Got it,' Issy said.

'Can we just fill our takeaway mugs?' Mackenzie said, getting up.

'Of course you can.'

'Thank you so much for coming all this way – and for the wonderful surprise,' Erica said, tears in her eyes, hugging both girls to her tightly. She didn't want to let them go – not because they were leaving, though there was that, but because she was so grateful to have two such fabulous humans as daughters. She was very proud of them.

'It's been lots of fun. And I'm so glad you're happy here,' Issy said, looking intently at her mother as she paused with her hand on the open car door before getting in.

Erica waved them off, waiting until the white hatchback had turned out of the car park area behind Crossley Funerals and had disappeared from sight.

She looked around her for inspiration, suddenly a bit lost and bereft. A moment later, some of Renee's wise words came to her: 'One hour at a time, and work in five-minute increments when it's a difficult day.' She'd go back upstairs and have a cry. And put some washing on.

Chapter Twenty-three

On Monday morning Erica was again awake in the pitch dark of early morning, though she didn't mind; she was resigned to this being her new normal. It was a lovely quiet time of day to collect one's thoughts. And at least this time her rousing had been smooth – no jolting, fear or racing heart. And no gritty eyes, so it mustn't be ridiculously early. A wonderful morning indeed!

Resisting opening the curtains to look out over the bakery, she instead sat with a cup of tea at the dining table waiting until it was light enough outside to go for a walk. Though she wasn't enthused about that. She could hear the wind occasionally catching one of the windows and making it rattle. It was probably freezing out. She considered going back to bed, but ended up staying where she was.

Suddenly the phone beside her chirped with the announcement of a text message. She turned it over.

Erica's heart began to beat harder and faster at reading the message staring back at her on the lit phone screen. It read: *Hi Erica, I'm Jimmy.* Included was a waving emoji. She frowned.

Jimmy? Who's Jimmy? Jimmy who? The name rang a bell but her brain was fuzzy and not cooperating.

A moment later another text came through: *Sorry — across the street at the bakery. I saw your light on. Gemma gave me your number.* Another waving emoji.

Oh! Jimmy! That *Jimmy.*

You only know one Jimmy, Erica.

Actually, you don't even know one — you know of one.

She closed her eyes hard in an attempt to get her head to clear, and then began typing out a reply before quickly pressing send: *Hi, yes, I'm Erica. Lovely to 'meet' you, Jimmy.* She also added a waving emoji.

A quick succession of messages back and forth followed:

Jimmy: *Sorry if the deliveries wake you.*

Erica: *That's okay. I'm a bit nocturnal.*

Erica: *Long story.*

Jimmy: *Me too.*

Me too, what? Erica wondered. *Long story? Obviously nocturnal — but by choice or not?*

Jimmy: *How are you enjoying Melrose? You're from the city, right? It's quiet here, huh?*

Erica: *Yes — from Adelaide. It's quiet — except for the early morning deliveries!* She added a laughing face emoji so he knew she was joking.

Jimmy: *Hey, fancy a cup of something? I'm having a hot chocolate. Come over?* A steaming cup was the emoji included this time.

Erica: *Yes please. Be there in a sec.* At the last moment before sending, she added a thumbs up emoji.

She raced back to her bedroom and quickly threw on her casual walking clothes, laced up her runners and, with keys and mobile in hand, left the flat.

Downstairs, to save walking around the block, Erica made her way through the funeral home to the front door, pausing to listen and tensing in the shadows. Damn it: she thought she'd be fine because she knew the building so well now and it was just a matter of racing through the main corridor.

Struggling to keep her nerve in check she turned to retreat and take the long way around instead. But it was too late now; the darkness had closed in around her and going back was just as frightening a prospect as carrying on. She bolted forwards.

At the front door, Erica struggled to get the key in the lock, all the time practically feeling the shadows closing menacingly behind her. After what seemed an age, she was out in the street bathed in pale orange street light with the shadows and menace safely behind her. She concentrated on taking deep breaths and willing her heart rate to settle while she locked the door.

Having checked the street in both directions several times, Erica jogged across, her footsteps pounding with the same intensity as her heart, which was still beating a little erratically in her chest. Apprehension and excitement roared around inside her like the cold gusting wind ripping at her clothes and hair.

With another quick pause and a few more steadying breaths, she went through the gate and closed it behind her. She knocked lightly on the back door of the bakery.

A moment later a very tall, blond, broad-shouldered young man stood in the open doorway, smiling at her – he was slightly nervous like her, she thought, judging by the two big red patches on his cheeks. Or maybe he'd just been standing in front of an open hot oven. Erica estimated him to be around twenty-five.

'Hello there,' he said.

'Hi.'

'I thought you'd changed your mind. Which would have been perfectly fine. Oh, god. Awkward much?' he added, and then laughed self-consciously. 'Sorry, I didn't mean to say that out loud.' His ears now began to turn red.

'Yes, totally awkward,' Erica said and matched his laugh. 'Glad someone said it.'

'Do you want to stand here or come inside?' he said, standing back. 'I promise you'll be perfectly safe. Oh god, said the spider to the fly. Is this a really bad idea?'

'No.' Instead of being alarmed, Erica found his concern and bumbling endearing and disarming. Her unease seeped away. 'Come on, you offered me hot chocolate. Is the offer still there?' she said, stepping inside.

'Of course,' he said, closing the door behind her. 'Take a seat,' he said, waving an arm at the stainless-steel bench with a stool either side. 'Do you want all milk or half and half water? Sorry, but it won't be frothy: just heated in the microwave.'

'Just however you have yours is fine with me. God, it smells good in here,' Erica added, taking a deep whiff of fresh baking, her mouth watering at seeing the racks of baked goods over the far side.

'I'm sure it does, but I've stopped smelling it.'

'I know what you mean,' Erica said, settling herself on the nearest stool. 'I used to work on the ground floor of David Jones – you know, where all the perfumes and cosmetics are?'

'Yes, I heard you're a makeup artist.'

'It was so strong there and I completely stopped noticing it. Though my sense of smell now seems to have gone the other way and it's super-sensitive. So, there you go.' She pushed aside the memory of the city forensic centre visit with Todd Jackson last week prodding at her and trying to force its way in. 'Anyway …

Not many secrets around here, are there?' Erica said, laughing off her unease.

'Oh, there are plenty of those, believe me, but it all depends on who's holding onto them and why. I bet you learn all sorts of things in your job.'

'I'd say the same to you, but I've never seen you working in the café, not that I'm in there much. Do you work in there too?'

'No. Right, try that and see what you think. Shouldn't be too hot,' he said, handing her a mug and sitting down on the stool across the bench from Erica.

'Yum,' Erica said after taking a tentative sip and then a long slug of the silkiest liquid that she thought had ever slid down her throat and which was perfectly bitter and sweet and creamy. She didn't often drink hot chocolate and now wondered why.

'Ahh,' he said, putting down his mug after his own long sip.

'How do you not constantly sample, or do you?' Erica said, nodding towards the racks.

'One sure does need an iron will – certainly to begin with. I just try to keep busy and pretend they're not there. I'm so grateful to Gemma for giving me the job – and so much more – I'd never eat into her profits. The odd hot chocolate is okay, though. So, any idea how come you're an insomniac?'

'In part, my age or, more specifically, menopause. It has a lot to answer for!'

'Ah, yes,' he said, nodding. 'My mum said she suffered terribly with the night sweats and then brain fog during the day. Sounds totally awful. Sorry. It's probably weird of me to say. I'm an only child and Mum was on her own and told me all about it. She said it should be spoken about more generally, and that she owed it to my future wife and any daughters to educate me so I wasn't a typical clueless and insensitive man.'

She smiled at him. 'Yes, menopause absolutely should be openly talked about so everyone knows what we're dealing with,' she said, waving an arm. 'It really mucks up one's sleep, but I also had a scare back in Adelaide just before I moved here. An intruder in the house. So I'm a bit jittery.' Erica noticed Jimmy's previously reddened complexion was suddenly quite pale, verging on ashen.

'Oh god, you poor thing. That's awful,' he said.

'Yeah. I'm used to waking early, but lately it's been even earlier and usually with a massive fright, since the stalker incident. I had a few nightmares when I first arrived, too. I'm getting better, though,' she said, taking another sip. As she did, the thought, *I can't actually believe I'm here – have come out in the dark alone*, wandered through her.

'So, someone was actually in your house?'

'Yes. It's a bit of a long story.'

'I've got plenty of time, but will completely understand if you don't want to talk about it.'

'Well, the shorter version is that at first I thought I was going mad. I was hearing noises, being forgetful – menopause does that too, so knowing that didn't help. Anyway, thankfully the police turned up right at the perfect moment and arrested her. And it just so happened I wasn't actually there right then because I had a friend's dog staying and she'd insisted on me taking her out for a wee. When I got back there were flashing lights all over the place. And then they brought her – the intruder – out in handcuffs. Scared the bejesus out of me, I can tell you.'

'*Her?* It was a woman?'

'Yep. You don't really think of it – young women doing that. Well, I didn't. She's in her twenties. Had a knife and everything.

At the station she admitted she wanted to kill me. Thankfully she's now safely locked up.'

'Fuck. I can't believe you're fine with it – well, so matter of fact.'

'Um. You're here sitting with a complete stranger drinking hot chocolate at silly o'clock, too,' Erica said, raising her eyebrows.

'Not really – not really strangers, that is. You've met Gemma and Gemma knows your boss Walter ...'

'True. You're right. But, seriously, I'm still a bit jumpy all round – nearly leaping out of my skin at the slightest noise, even during the day. And I did also struggle to leave the house for a bit – though that was while I thought I was going mad, before I knew what was what. But here I don't really have a choice. I needed this job. I got retrenched from DJs and thanks to my husband who died a few months ago, I'm as good as broke. Shit, sorry about my verbal diarrhoea.' Erica concentrated on her hot chocolate.

'God, you've had your life seriously turned upside down.'

'That's pretty much what it feels like. But enough about me. How come I've never seen you out and about?'

'I'm kind of in hiding. Not in witness protection or anything,' he added at seeing her huge eyes. 'I had a stalker, too.'

'Really? Wow. What is wrong with people?'

'Yup. I guess I'm just not doing quite as well as you. And, you're probably not going to believe this, but mine was a young woman around that age, too.'

'No way. But ...' Erica stopped the insensitive, judgmental question in its tracks.

'But ... how could I be afraid of a young woman? A bloke my size?' He looked at her with raised eyebrows.

Erica nodded. It was her turn to blush. 'Sorry,' she said, cringing.

'It's a fair question and not too unreasonable an assumption. But can you imagine my need to explain me doing something in self-defence? I'd most likely have done damage, too. Maybe even killed her. I walked away instead. Well, I tried to. Over and over. She was relentless – coming into the house, moving stuff around. Basically, just messing with my mind, which I nearly completely lost.'

A shudder raced through Erica and then cold fingers tapped a path up and down her spine as images of her experiences flashed in her mind like a quick slideshow, leaving her quivering inside. She swallowed and nodded, waited for him to continue.

'I didn't even report it; I thought no one would believe me. I'm not sure I would have if someone had told me it was happening to them. But Kayla completely gaslighted me. Google it – gaslighting,' he said. 'Very scary stuff.'

'Did you say Kayla?'

'Yes. She was my girlfriend. What's wrong?'

Erica was suddenly light-headed and clammy – green around the gills, she reckoned her dad would have said. *No. Don't be ridiculous. That would be too freaky.*

'Kayla was the name of *my* intruder-slash-stalker,' she said. 'Although probably every second baby girl born around the late nineties was named Kayla,' she added with a wave of her hand. 'I'm sure the police must have told me her surname or I've seen it written down, but I can't remember it now.' Erica racked her memory but came up empty. 'That's weird.'

'Kayla Jones? About your height, lean, dark reddish hair – probably dyed, though – sharp pixie-like features? Comes across quite intense? Oh, and her parents are both doctors – does that ring any bells for you?' Jimmy said.

'Yes. That's the one. I can't believe it.'

'I can. Of course it'd be the same one – there's only one degree of separation across the whole of South Australia,' Jimmy said in a sardonic tone accompanied with an eye-roll.

'That is true. And at times completely ridiculous and very frustrating!'

'I know, right?'

'Well, the good news is you don't have to hide any more, Jimmy. She's locked up.'

'Really?'

'Yes. She's in custody and goes back to court in December. The police officer I'm in touch with is a really nice guy. He's promised to let me know the moment anything changes. I could probably get him to call you if it would help.'

'I'll think about it. God,' he said, rubbing his hands over his face, 'I'm not sure what it means for me. I've been scared for so long – well that's what it feels like. She destroyed my life,' he said quietly. 'I lost my job – I was a chippie. Her antics got me fired. I had to give up all social media – not that that's probably a bad thing, though.'

'Except it should be your choice,' Erica pointed out kindly.

'Yeah. She hacked my email. And even messed with my bank account.'

'Oh my god. Why wouldn't you have gone to the police over *that* at least? Sorry, I didn't mean to sound judgmental.'

'With the email I wouldn't have been able to prove she hadn't found my password lying about or have access to my phone. And with my bank account, she didn't actually technically hack it or steal any money – she couldn't have found *that* password; I'm not stupid.'

Erica frowned in confusion.

'Can you believe she'd pay me, like five cents every few days – sometimes more than once in an hour. Kind of clever of her, but pretty fucking annoying.'

'Sorry, I don't follow.' Erica frowned deeper.

'Internet banking?' 'Yes, I'm not that old,' Erica wanted to say, but nodded instead. 'Pay anyone? Well, that's what it's called with my bank – when you pay someone using their BSB and account number?'

'Right, yes, that I get,' Erica said, and nodded.

'Well, she must have seen a statement showing my account number and started paying me tiny amounts and using the description part to leave messages.'

'Oh, yes. I know what you mean now!' Erica had suddenly remembered Michelle's deposit – how she'd written in the description, *Love from Michelle Xx*. 'Fuck. That's bloody intrusive. Wow.'

'Yes. Exactly. There was no escaping her. I blocked her on my phone, on social media – but with friends in common she'd still somehow manage to pop up. Then she started on the internet banking. I had to shut my bank account and open a new one – a major bloody pain in the arse doing the notifications for all the direct deposits.'

'Who even thinks of that?!'

'Kayla.'

'Yeah, sorry, *obviously*. But you could have taken *that* to the police – that would have been evidence, wouldn't it?'

'By then I was too worn down. I closed the account. And then when you do that everything disappears. I know if it came down to it the bank could be subpoenaed or whatever. But I just wanted it over and her out of my life without ending up in jail or court myself. She was incredibly manipulative. And very good at using those cute features to appear very demure. Butter wouldn't melt in that mouth!'

'Yes, I know what you mean. That about sums her up. She broke into my house through the terracotta roof tiles – had been camping up in my attic space. I'm pretty sure she watched me sleep,' Erica said, shuddering as icy fingers walked down her spine again.

'Bloody hell. Though nothing would really surprise me about her. Sorry you had to go through that.'

'Sorry you did too, Jimmy.'

'So, I dated her for a while. How did you meet her – or is she a relative?'

'No, thank god! She came in to have her makeup done in DJs with a friend – Matt.'

'Oh. Matt, as in her flatmate?'

'That's the one. Did you know him?'

'Yes, but not all that well. Just met him a few times. He seemed nice enough, though. I hope he's okay – you know, in relation to Kayla. I probably should have warned him, but I had enough going on. And, to be honest, it took me ages to realise what the fuck was going on. When I did, I just got the hell out of there.' He rubbed his face. He shook his head before resuming talking. 'Sorry, go on. You were saying Kayla came into DJs with Matt to get her makeup done.'

'That's right. Anyway, she got pissed off and fixated on me when I encouraged Matt to pursue his dream of studying film makeup. That's what the police said. I still don't really understand why she targeted me.'

'I guess that's kind of the point with personality disorders ...'

'I'm not a health professional, so I'm not sure what was or is wrong with her,' Erica said, shrugging.

'Other than being a spoilt, privileged, attention-seeking brat? That's a big part of it, I reckon. I really hope Mummy and Daddy can't get her off.'

'Don't worry, the police are taking it very seriously. They've assured me she's not going to be out any time soon,' Erica reiterated. 'She was also in possession of the drug ice when she was arrested at my house. But the biggie is she admitted to wanting to kill me.'

'Oh god, Erica, I'm so sorry. Maybe if I had gone to the police, what you went through wouldn't have happened.' Jimmy looked at Erica with big sad eyes. She noticed his face was pale again.

'Maybe, maybe not, but don't even go there, Jimmy. What happened to me is no one's fault but Kayla's. And, like you said, if you had gone to the police, she might have been let out anyway because she wasn't considered dangerous enough. She's committed a whole list of really serious offences now. So, don't worry. Please concentrate on recovering. That's what I'm doing. How did you come to be here in Melrose, anyway – are you related to Gemma?'

'No. I got in my car one night, about six months ago, and drove until I almost ran out of fuel. I saw a light on in the bakery here and knocked on the door. Poor Gemma. I scared the shit out of her.'

'I can imagine.'

'I begged her for a job doing the grunt work at night-slash-early mornings so I could hide out during the day. Other than Gemma and her dad, you're the only person I've met. They even brought the van into the backyard for me. I have to confess that the first time I saw your light on and you in the window I nearly had kittens, as my mum would have said. I thought you were Kayla – that she'd found me.'

'God, you poor thing. Sorry about that. I have a confession, too – I sat in the dark watching you, enjoying knowing you were over here. You being up and about and so close was a great comfort.'

'I've felt that too.'

'But then my daughters visited on the weekend and told me off for being a stalker, so I stopped.'

'I'm so glad you gave Gemma your number.'

'Me too. It was on a whim. The urge to meet another newcomer, maybe. So, at the risk of sounding creepy, what do you make – anything other than what I see here and in the café?' she said, looking around.

'Cakes. Fancy cakes. I'm still learning. Here are some pics,' he said, dragging his phone off the nearby bench and bringing up an image of a round cake covered in what looked like cream frosting with a pile of white flowers on top.

'Wow, that's fantastic. Are those flowers real?'

'No. They're made of icing – I did them. It's for a small wedding for a friend of Gemma's.'

'Wow. You're very clever.'

'Thanks. I'm a newbie with a lot to learn, but I'm enjoying having something to focus on. I've become pretty obsessed, but figure there are worse things ... I like being able to give something back to Gemma, too.'

'Have you always baked? I know you said you were a carpenter, but did you bake then too – in your spare time?'

'Oh yes. Mum was a great cook and taught me from an early age. I hadn't baked for years, though, until I got here. But I had too much time on my hands, even with helping out Gemma, and didn't want to head outside. She's teaching me a lot – not as in a formal apprenticeship, or anything; maybe we'll do that down the track. Meanwhile, I'm also spending hours on YouTube and Insta figuring out how to do some things. There are heaps of incredible hobby bakers creating amazing cakes for fun – just another medium of art, really. I wouldn't mind making a career out of it somehow, combined with catering. If I could get over this agoraphobia, I might be able to do something ...'

'You will. Just take it one step at a time, I reckon.'

'I hope so.'

'I was actually planning to go for a walk – I do most mornings – just around the town. Would you like to come? It might help.'

'Oh. Um. I ...'

'No pressure, but I'd be happy to come back with you if it all gets too much. I do understand what it's like to ... you know,' Erica said with a shrug.

'Thanks. But maybe another time? Sorry. I think I need to quietly process everything I've learnt this morning.'

'I'm not surprised. My mind is pretty blown by the coincidence that is Kayla, too; that's a whole other level of wow. There's no need to apologise. Let me know if there's anything I can do to help. But I'd better get going. I don't want to be late for work. You take good care.'

'Thanks. You too. Maybe see you tomorrow morning?'

'Yep. Sounds good.'

Erica left the bakery with mixed feelings that swirled around and shifted back and forth during her walk. She was thrilled to have made a new friend – she really liked Jimmy. But her mind kept shifting from astonishment at the strange happenstance – which took South Australia's already strange connectedness to a whole new level – and sadness for Jimmy at what Kayla had reduced him to. She'd been a one-person wrecking ball. Incredible to think that someone so small in stature could wreak so much havoc.

She experienced a wave of intense gratitude for and pride in how far she'd come with her recovery as she lifted her arm to wave to the woman with the border collie and sent more silent thanks to Daphne.

Part Two

Part Two

Chapter Twenty-four

Sitting at her desk, lost in thoughts flicking back and forth and around and around about Kayla, Jimmy and Issy and Mackenzie, Erica almost jumped out of her skin when Walter appeared in front of her, having come from the back hallway. She looked up at him. The way he was wiping his hands and the focussed look on his face told her he'd just come from the mortuary. She hadn't even noticed the light shining behind the frosted glass door when she'd passed by just before, nor any noises coming from within.

'Good morning,' he said.

'Good morning. Have we had a new arrival?' she said, trying desperately to drag some buoyancy up and through the dark lump inside her.

'We have. A Mr Barrow. Milton. Seventy-one. Stroke. I don't recall having met him or his family before. Would you like a coffee while I'm up?'

'Yes, thanks. That would be good.'

Erica stared back down at the desk, her to do list becoming a blur again as her mind drifted once more.

It seemed that just a second had passed and Walter was back and putting a steaming mug in front of her with a clunk and then sitting down on the next chair.

'So, your girls got back to Adelaide okay?' Walter asked.

'Yep. All good.'

'What a wonderful surprise for you having them visit.'

'Yes, it sure was.'

'I'm sure they'll be back before too long.'

'I hope so.'

'Chin up,' Walter said gently.

'Sorry. I'm not sure what's got into me.' Damn. It had been an automatic response she hadn't really meant to utter. And it was a lie. Of course she knew what was bugging her – bloody Kayla! And the positively freaky coincidences arising from her meeting Jimmy that morning. She wanted to be honest with Walter, but couldn't without betraying Jimmy's confidence. While she hadn't wanted to give in to her sudden paranoia at wondering if this was a warning for her – and Jimmy, for that matter – she'd relented and sent a text to her police contact, Geoff, to double-check Kayla's whereabouts. Hearing straight back from him and getting his reassurance that the young woman in question remained in custody had helped, but Erica was still a little out of kilter. It suited her to leave Walter assuming her mood was to do with her missing her girls.

'Oh, there's no need to apologise.'

'Thanks.' Erica tried to offer him a smile, but it was weak.

'I thoroughly enjoyed meeting Mackenzie and Issy – what delightful young ladies.'

'Yes, they're good, most of the time.' Erica couldn't help smiling at picturing their faces: Mackenzie's often slightly sceptical expression, Issy's open features a little wide-eyed with wonder and concern for others. 'Thanks again for the other night, Walter. I had such a lovely evening. And so did the girls.'

'You've very welcome. Thank *you*. And for bringing two such wonderful helpers.'

'That was all them – I didn't even suggest they offer.'

'And that's one of the reasons they're such a credit to you.'

'Thanks.'

'I have to say, I'm a little excited about Jennifer's play idea.'

'Yes, it'll be fun.'

He drained his mug. 'Come on,' he said, standing up. 'Bring your coat and handbag. Let's go for a drive to cheer us up.'

'Oh. Walter, that's lovely, but I'm fine. I'm just …'

'Glum? I know. And it's okay. I'm not telling you off. I'm a bit out of sorts too. Your gorgeous girls got me pining for my Peter, all the way over in London, and, well, you know, I'm a bit sad about how things have turned out – losing Mary …'

'I'm sorry, Walter.' But Erica stopped when he held up his hand.

'It's okay. And not your fault. Just the way of things. Some reminders pass through okay and some pluck at the tiniest raised piece of scab and tear it open again. Normally I'd just get in the car and drive – I find great comfort in the metal beast.'

Does everyone *know about driving being a panacea – how come I didn't?* 'I know what you mean. About the scab, and being in the car.'

'You're welcome to head out on your own if you like. But I have something in mind that I think will help both of us. Anyway, we might need to fortify ourselves before dropping in to see Mr Barrow's widow – our friend in the mortuary – on the way back. Unless you really don't want to,' he said, pausing, looking concerned.

'No. Come on. It sounds like a good plan.' Erica retrieved her handbag from the drawer and then got up and dragged her scarf and coat from the rack and followed Walter down the hall to the car out the back. As she did, she again felt a little guilty about her slight dishonesty with him about why she was glum.

'I'm sure the girls visiting has brought up all sorts of feelings for you,' Walter said, as he got into the car. 'Grief is a complicated business. As is, well, simply being human, really,' he added thoughtfully.

'It sure is,' Erica said, snapping her seatbelt on.

'Have you been to Port Pirie?' he said.

'Not for many years.'

'You probably won't recognise it then; it's not the quaint town it once was. Now the big stores have moved in. But useful nonetheless. I'll give you a bit of a tour.'

Erica enjoyed the drive and gradually began to lose her black cloudy disposition and become brighter again. It helped that the sun was shining brightly through the car as they made their way. And she became interested in the different surroundings – not so different from Melrose and the other towns close by and where she'd been lately, but intriguing to go somewhere fresh. She hadn't come in this direction or this far on her day out the other weekend, or with the girls on Saturday.

'Right, everything you need,' he said after driving around and pointing out various businesses and other landmarks. 'And, see, not all that far away once you're used to it.'

Erica was a little startled when he slowed right down and came to a stop out the front of a business with a sandwich board on the pavement advertising counselling services. *Oh, Walter, bless you.* She ached with remorse over having potentially caused him to worry about her. The poor bloke was probably desperate to stop her leaving.

'Just in case. No harm in reaching out for a different perspective on things,' he said, and put his foot down again. 'Though, remember, I'm always here.'

'Jennifer's in Port Pirie, too, isn't she?' Erica said.

'Yes, she is. We could see if she's up for a visit,' Walter said, significantly buoyed. 'It's always nice to see a cheerful face and soul.'

He pulled into a park and got out his phone. 'Jennifer, it's Walter. Erica and I are in your neck of the woods, if you're available ... I understand you might be officiating at Mr Barrow's service on Thursday – we can go over the details ... Brilliant. Can we bring you a cake and coffee? ... Oh, okay, please don't go to any trouble on our account ... Great. We'll see you soon.' An even more chipper Walter placed his phone back in the front console. 'Jennifer will cheer us up,' he said.

'Do we need to take anything?'

'No, she's just baked scones, apparently, so it's our lucky day,' he said, grinning, as he put the car in reverse and checked his mirrors. 'And she has a whizz-bang coffee machine – her words – so insists we just bring ourselves.'

'Hello, you two,' Jennifer said, beaming from the porch of a small stone cottage.

They made their way through a cream woven-wire gate onto a red-brick path dividing a lawn in which stood a steel post painted in gloss cream. From it a sign swung, also in cream but with a purple border and neat lettering in the same purple colour, advertising her services as a celebrant.

'I'm so glad you called.' She welcomed Erica and Walter with quick hugs. 'Welcome. Come in. Gorgeous day out, but still chilly,' she said, closing the door behind them and then leading the way down a long carpeted hallway. The space was warm and inviting. There was the faint scent of baking in the air, which became very strong when they went through a door with etched frosted glass panels into a large kitchen and casual dining area.

'Yum,' Walter said, sniffing the air contentedly, gravitating towards the tall golden scones on cooling racks. 'These look fantastic,' he said.

'Yes. Wow. Lovely,' Erica said.

'Thank you. I just felt the urge this morning – subconsciously I must have known you were coming.'

'You have a gorgeous garden too,' Erica said, moving past the island bench and over to a wall of glass doors overlooking a large and very pretty garden with an expanse of neat green lawn surrounded by curved beds filled with rose bushes and under-planted foliage Erica assumed would provide a stunning floral display in the warmer months. There was also a small area paved in old red bricks containing a table and two chairs and covered in a frame with a well-established climbing rose. Her mouth practically watered at imagining it in full bloom. In her mind she pictured white flowers – suitable for either a small wedding or a small funeral ceremony if necessary.

'Thank you. Another labour of love. Though I'm a fair-weather gardener so I haven't been out much yet. And it's not nearly as pretty as it can be – you'll have to come back when it's looking its best.'

'I look forward to it,' Walter said.

'Right, coffee. You'll see I have Gabriel, my saviour,' Jennifer said, indicating a large shiny coffee machine on the nearby bench. 'So, we can offer you a short black, long black, latte, flat white, cappuccino … I think that's all of them covered, isn't it?'

'A latte would be wonderful, thank you,' Erica said.

'Yes, please, same for me. Fabulous,' Walter said. 'Can I help with anything?' he added.

'No, thanks. Easiest for me to get everything out. Take a seat. Pity it's too chilly to sit outside, but still ...' Jennifer busied herself with collecting crockery and cutlery, linen napkins.

'Oh, please don't go to a lot of trouble on my account,' Walter said.

'No, please,' Erica said.

'It's no problem at all. It's nice to have a bit of finery occasionally,' she said. 'A good excuse. Not that I really need one.'

Walter and Erica sat and watched as Jennifer bustled about putting jam and cream into beautiful fine bone china dishes and adding silver spoons in between attending to the coffee machine, which at times made conversation impossible, given the loud sounds it made.

'I was going to head your way in the next day or so and see if you were up for coffee, since we've crossed the line into socialising,' Jennifer said. 'What a great evening Saturday night was. And how delightful are your daughters, Erica? Here we are,' she said, finally bringing the last mug over and plonking herself down on a chair. 'Tuck in, everyone,' she said, grabbing a scone and cutting it in half.

'This is wonderful, and so unexpected. Thank you,' Walter said, slathering the first half of his scone in jam.

'Yes. This is perfect. Thank you so much,' Erica said. 'And, thank you, Gabriel, your coffee is fabulous,' she said after taking a sip. She smiled and raised her mug in the machine's direction.

'Yes, cheers, Gabriel,' Walter said, also raising his mug. 'We were a bit in need of cheering up this morning, too, weren't we, Erica?' he said, changing tack.

'Hmm.' *Please don't say any more, Walter.*

'A chinwag with a cheery soul sometimes is just the tonic,' Walter said, before taking a large, decisive bite out of his jam and cream laden scone.

'I'm very honoured to be chosen for the job,' Jennifer said cheerfully.

'Yum, your scones are incredible, Jennifer,' Erica said, having taken a bite too. 'And so is your coffee.'

'Yes, thank you again. Utterly sublime,' Walter said. 'I think we're going to have to look into getting ourselves a Gabriel, Erica.'

'Sounds like a good plan to me, Walter,' Erica said.

'I know a guy – well, a girl, really, and that's not even kosher to say now, is it? Anyway, I can hook you up. Just say the word,' Jennifer said, flapping a hand above the table.

'I'll let you know. Need to crunch some numbers first.'

'I completely understand. I can help you sort through the guff if you like. It's quite the minefield once you start looking.'

'Brilliant. Thanks.'

'Walter is very keen on your play idea, Jennifer,' Erica said after they'd been silently eating and drinking for a few minutes.

'Well, it's early days. So, fingers crossed.'

'Anything I can do to help, just shout,' Walter said.

'That goes for me also,' Erica said.

'See, that was just what we needed,' Walter said after they'd bade farewell to Jennifer and were back in the car and on their way out of Port Pirie. 'Never underestimate the power of reaching out without letting on why.'

'Hmm. Yes, that was a very good idea.'

'And, scones! How lucky are we? Yum. I'm as full as a goog, though,' he said, patting his stomach and grinning with childlike glee.

'Yes, incredible timing,' she said, and smiled at how like her dad Walter was in that moment.

'Now, sadly, we have to come back down to earth with a thud and go and talk to Mrs Barrow.'

'Yes.'

In the silence Erica wondered whether it was her imagination or had there been a romantic spark lit in Walter. Of course, she'd never say anything. She also wondered if Jennifer was gay and/ or this warm and effusive with everyone, or if she too had an ember being fanned inside her. Erica really hoped Walter, who had become so dear to her, wasn't about to be hurt. But he'd say so himself: I'm a big boy. And he wouldn't want her worrying needlessly on his account.

Her thoughts turned to idly wondering if she'd ever be interested in finding a partner again. The fact no images of handsome – or otherwise – men came to mind or any pictures of her with someone else in a romantic type situation told her she was a long way from that eventuality.

No, she decided. No way. In among the burn of grief and getting her mind around her new job and location and every-thing were the rumblings inside her that she was actually really quite enjoying being on her own – not having anyone enquiring about what she'd been up to. Well, maybe not quite *enjoying*, but close …

Often Stuart had had a way of asking about her day, quite possibly out of innocent interest, but Erica found it intrusive – like he was actually checking up on her. It especially jarred while he was sick and it took all her will not to snap at him – say, 'What of it?' and the ilk. They were tense times – mainly due to him being bored and feeling useless – and her strung out and exhausted with trotting back and forth and spending time at the hospital in between everything else she'd always done in her life. It had been like having an extra part-time job. Of course she was only happy to do it – no, not exactly happy: committed. He was her husband and she'd said vows and meant them when they got married. But it didn't mean it wasn't difficult and very taxing – mentally and physically.

Sometimes she longed to have him beside her watching TV – or less so, hovering over her shoulder when she was on Facebook and browsing online, giving a running commentary. But far too often she didn't actually miss him at all – and she felt a right shit for thinking it every time she did. Perhaps this was a sign she was moving to a different – a more comfortable – part of her grief.

While she couldn't – or, rather, wouldn't – speak these words aloud, twenty-odd years in a relationship was unlikely to be good fun one hundred per cent of the time. They'd had rows along the way – usually about Stuart trying to tell her what to do and how to live her life. He'd been a good father and most of the time a good husband. But he'd also been a pain in the arse plenty too. And she knew he'd pissed people off with his work as well – she'd heard his side of enough heated phone conversations. Sometimes even both sides if the other person was being really loud, despite not being on speaker. 'It takes all kinds to make the world work,' had been her mother's answer to any criticism – quickly uttered when she'd idly slipped into a criticism of someone. Often Erica had assumed it was a mantra – note to self – as much as a reminder to or scolding of Erica.

Chapter Twenty-five

'Phew, we're not late. I was thinking we might be pushing it,' Walter said as they turned off the main road onto a corrugated potholed driveway. This part of the journey seemed to go on forever and Erica thought her bones might be shaken loose on the ruts despite Walter navigating it at practically a crawl. Finally, a brick house appeared ahead and they were greeted by a barking blue heeler. It was still barking and showing its teeth, hair on its hackles raised, when Walter had turned off the engine. Erica looked at her boss with big questioning eyes.

'We'll just wait a sec. Edith is here – well, she should be – so she'll call the dog off. Hopefully,' he said.

Suddenly they heard the squeal of rusty hinges and then the slap of a wooden screen door and a woman's voice shout: 'Bruce! Come out of it. And sit down!' Erica felt a little sad for the dog as it shrank and then slunk off to settle in the sun against the edge of the verandah in a hollowed-out patch of dirt, looking dejected. Having been distracted by the dog, it was only at the last moment

Erica remembered her compendium and reached back into the car to grab it after they'd exited.

As they walked towards Bruce, the blue cattle dog flapped its tail and writhed a little, trying to get closer. Erica experienced a mix of longing to offer comfort and fear at how he might react.

'Good dog. You're a good dog,' she said as they passed. A part of her heart stayed with him and she was sad thinking how different a farm dog's life might be from that of a city dog like Daphne – also a working dog breed.

They shook hands and Erica was introduced and then they made their way inside and straight into the kitchen. They sat at one end of an enormous table. The other end seemed reserved for bills, newspapers and assorted paperwork. Erica accepted the offer of a cup of tea after Walter had. She smiled, nodded and quietly said thank you when a mug was placed in front of her, and again when a plate of Arnott's YoYo biscuits was put down. She hoped she wouldn't offend by not eating anything.

'Sorry, can't bring myself to bake. These were Milton's favourites anyway. It's funny how you crave the opposite to what you were raised with. His mother was one of the best cooks in the district – won with biscuits, cakes – clean sweep at the local shows most years. Even the Royal Adelaide Show. But oh no, would rather a bikkie from a packet was my Milton. Bless him. I was the same with handmade clothes by my mother, too, back in the day,' she added with a shrug. She dragged a crumpled floral hand-kerchief from inside her sleeve, dabbed her red eyes and blew her nose softly.

'I'm so sorry for your loss,' Erica said, just in case she hadn't said it earlier when they'd arrived. She was sure she had.

'Thank you, dear. Sorry Aiden isn't here – my son – he's meant to be.'

They sat through two cups of tea – the second of which Walter got for them – and stories from their long marriage spanning droughts, floods, bushfires, mouse plagues, good years and the occasional brilliant season. Finally Edith told of how they were meant to retire at the end of the year, invest in a caravan and grey-nomad their way around Australia. The edge to Edith's voice during that part of the conversation told Erica she felt let down. Ripped off. In how many ways? she wondered.

Was Edith the sort to rant and rave and beg for what she wanted, or one to silently hope and wait for her turn? And what might she have desired? New clothes, an outing to wear them to, a kitchen renovation perhaps. In this space, no major updating had occurred probably since their marriage, forty years before. Perhaps the kids as adults – or Edith – had given the place a lick of paint or two. But not a lot more. Was sitting here a constant and depressing reminder of her place and lack of status and power?

They had three kids – one son and two daughters – and seven grandkids. These details Erica had learnt along the way, as well as the fact Milton had loved history and had been on the museum committee and had appeared in one of the videos Erica had watched the other week during her visit.

She had in front of her a photo of him – brought in by Edith for them to take to put on display at the service, so she didn't forget later – but still she couldn't place him in the clip. Of course he might have looked much younger in the video, because from memory she thought they'd been made a couple of decades before, when that part of the museum's display was set up.

Eventually Erica was going through her notes and confirming the details of the upcoming service. A few minutes later they were out on the verandah saying goodbye. This process seemed to take ages, as if Edith didn't want them to leave. Was she unsteady on her feet? There was a walker nearby. Erica wondered if it had been Milton's or was Edith's and she didn't want to use it due to vanity or some other reason.

'Hello there,' Erica said, bending down to pat the dog who had appeared beside her, having practically crawled across the dirt. As he rolled onto his back, exposing his belly for her to rub, she realised with surprise, at seeing the prominent nipples, that he, Bruce, was in fact a she. *Huh?*

'Get out of it, Bruce!' a booming male voice shouted.

Erica, still stooped over the dog, turned and looked towards the sound. A tall dark angry-looking man of around forty in khaki work wear with an Akubra on his head strode on long legs towards them.

'Bruce is fine. Really. Not causing any trouble,' Erica said, standing up.

'Aiden, these are the people from the funeral home,' Edith Barrow said. 'You were supposed to be here earlier.'

Aiden Barrow glared at his mother.

'Hi, Aiden, Walter Crossley and Erica Cunningham from Crossley Funerals,' Walter said, interrupting the stretching silence. He extended his hand. 'Sorry for your loss.'

'Yes. Sorry. I'm Erica,' she said, feeling suddenly disconcerted under the brooding gaze.

He shook her hand loosely and briefly. 'Bloody dog,' he muttered.

'We were just going over the details for the service, if there's anything particular you wanted to include,' Walter said.

'Nope,' was Aiden's response. Again, his brusque tone caused Erica to cringe.

'Right. Well, we'd better be off, then, if there's nothing else we can do, Edith?' Walter said. 'Call if you think of anything,' he added, and they made their way back to the car.

'You could find a home for the dog,' Aiden shouted.

'Sorry?' Walter said, turning back around. He and Erica looked at Bruce, back in her dirt hole, curled up and looking warily at Aiden. Erica's heart lurched.

'The dog. It needs to go,' Aiden said.

'Aiden,' his mother warned.

'I'm serious, Mum. It's either now or when you go into town.'

'Yes, please, Walter, if you know of anyone who needs a dog. She's not bad with sheep,' Edith pleaded, her eyes doing more of the work than her words or tone.

'Mum, that's crap. She's too nippy for sheep. It's a bloody stupid useless mutt. Dad was too soft. Should have got out the gun years ago.'

Erica just managed to catch her gasp in time. She'd heard – from where, she couldn't remember – that farmers put down injured and unwanted dogs by shooting them. Sometimes for a transgression as minor as not coming quickly enough when called. Perhaps it was Michelle. Daphne had been a rescue. Perhaps she'd come direct from a farm rather than via an organisation. Erica couldn't remember. Or perhaps Michelle had learnt her history. A shard of memory tugged at Erica's frazzled brain.

'I'll take him, er, her,' Walter said suddenly. 'You said Bruce, didn't you?'

'Yeah. Stupid dog. Stupid name. For a bitch.'

Again Erica cringed at the venom. She longed to leap into the car and lock the doors.

'Does she have any things? Bedding?' Walter said, looking around.

'Nope. Dad used a forty-four-gallon drum and some old wheat sacks, but I'll be keeping them.'

Suddenly Bruce was sitting to attention between Walter and Erica, her tail sweeping the dirt below in a smooth rhythmic back and forth motion. The dog looked from one to the other, just like Daphne, Michelle's dog, did when begging for treats or to go for a walk. *How lucky is that dog compared to this one?* Erica thought.

'Um. Okay,' Walter said, looking anything but sure. 'Guess we'll just take the dog then.' He looked at the dog then to the car and back again.

'Up to you, but I've got stuff to do. Mum?' Aiden said.

'Bye, Aiden. We'll see you Thursday,' Walter called, a moment too late. The screen door had already slapped shut.

'Please take Bruce with you,' Edith said, suddenly grasping Walter's hand in both of hers. 'I've got to go. Thanks. For everything. And you, Erica. See you both on Thursday.'

Chapter Twenty-six

Erica and Walter were left looking at the dog.

'Well, then,' Walter muttered and went over to the back door of the car and opened it. 'Come on, Bruce, in you hop.' The dog leapt in and Walter closed the door as Erica got into the front passenger's seat.

'So I take it you've been in a car before, then,' Walter said, turning from his position in the driver's seat to where Erica assumed the dog was curled up on the floor. She couldn't see Bruce, but longed to take her in her arms, to tell her everything would be okay, and never let go. This despite just weeks back being definitely in the no pets camp.

'Thanks, Walter,' she said, as he started the car and put it in gear.

'What for?'

'For taking Bruce.'

'We weren't leaving her there, Erica. I don't think Aiden was joking and most likely wasn't bluffing. What an intense soul – positively scary.'

'Yes. It takes all kinds,' Erica muttered.

'Yup. Grief affects us all differently, that's for sure.'

'Do you think Edith will want Bruce back when things settle down? And did you hear Aiden say she's moving into town?'

'Yes, I did hear. Perhaps she's going into aged care. She seemed a little unstable on her feet. I really hope she's not being bullied into anything, though,' he said sadly. 'And what are we going to do with you, Bruce? Do you fancy being a business mascot? Bit nippy with the sheep is a worry, though, miss,' he added. 'You're a good dog, really, aren't you? Don't worry, we'll figure it out,' he said, while looking into the rear-vision mirror.

I love you, Walter, Erica thought while she listened to the friendly one-way conversation going on around her. Warmth flooded through her.

'You'll be blamed for turning me soft, Erica,' Walter said as they shuddered and bumped their way slowly back down the driveway.

'Oh. Sorry.'

'Just kidding. I will readily and proudly put my hand up to always having been soft in the middle. But, somehow, I've managed to never be lumped with a client's unwanted pet before. This is a whole new bag of tricks. I just hope all and sundry don't suddenly think we're the equivalent of the local lost dogs' home. Not much call for a branch of that around here. Less humane, less expensive methods really are used, I'm afraid, for unwanted animals. Sorry. Takes a bit of getting used to – the brutal reality of life out here. Sometimes it doesn't feel all that different from the wild west in some ways. Bit confronting. You'll get used to it. Just try not to react, is my advice.'

Erica sat in silence and hoped she'd never get used to something like that. As they drove, she thought about how strange this place was compared to Adelaide, which was just three hundred kilometres away – not all that far in the scheme of how vast the state was. Eye-opening. Her thoughts went to Renee, budding artist, who always said all experiences, good and bad, were necessary to add to her knowledge bank. Come out here, Renee.

'Are you going to keep Bruce or try to find another home?' she asked when they turned onto the road.

'I'm not sure yet. I think I'm in a state of shock,' he said with a laugh. 'But I need to stop and get some food and a bed for the poor thing. Better give her a bath and some flea treatment, too. Who names a female dog Bruce, anyway? That's strange.'

'I agree.'

'Thank goodness my place has a decent fence. There really is a lot to take into account. One thing is for sure, Bruce: your days of living out in the cold are over.' Again he spoke while looking into the rear-vision mirror.

Erica smiled.

'I think we need to think this through a bit,' Walter said, slowing down and then pulling onto the shoulder of the road and stopping the car just before the fifty kilometre speed sign on the outskirts of town.

'Have you changed your mind? Are you thinking of taking her back?' Inside, Erica grappled with what to do if he was. She didn't have any power in the situation.

'God no! She's not going back there. Don't worry, Bruce, I'm not doing that to you,' he said, turning in his seat and looking back at the dog Erica assumed must still be in place on the floor behind her seat. She thought she could feel the vibration of the thick tail thwacking against the floor, but it might be her own heartbeat she could feel. She relaxed a little. 'I don't suppose you know anything about dogs, Erica?'

'Nope. I'm afraid not. Well, practically nothing. Never owned one.' A day taking care of Daphne didn't count.

'Okay. So, first we'll need food, water and shelter. We can get food at the supermarket. Hopefully they'll have a dog bed, too. Though maybe Bruce here isn't too fussy what she sleeps on. But I would like to make her feel special from the outset. I'm not sure we should take her into the office until we know she's toilet trained for inside, though.'

'Are there any health regulations with having her in a funeral home?' Erica asked.

'Good question. No, I don't think so.'

They drove the few hundred metres and parked at the small supermarket with café attached and petrol station forecourt.

'Do you mind staying here and making sure our new friend doesn't destroy the car's interior?' Walter said.

'No, not at all.' Erica watched Walter go inside and then undid her seatbelt and shuffled over so she could look back at the dog.

'Aww, aren't you gorgeous?' she said, looking down at Bruce, who had her head resting on the lump between the two sides of the car's floor. Now Erica could definitely hear the thump, thump, thump of a tail.

'You've got really beautiful kind eyes. Or are you sad? I hope you're not sad,' she said, stretching down and stroking the dog's smooth head. She felt her back tightening and her neck beginning to crick so withdrew her hand. As she did, she received a lick.

'Darling girl, you're going to be just fine with Walter. And me. You're very well behaved,' she said, now back in her seat and facing forwards but still feeling the need to keep the dog company by talking. 'But you're actually a bit smelly. Is that your normal aroma or did you just fart? Was that contentment on your face not about me at all?'

Erica smiled at picturing how her girls had grinned – more pride than contentment when they had filled their nappies as littlies. She sniffed her hand. Yuck. She couldn't identify the odour other than labelling it as rank.

I hope they've got dog shampoo and Walter remembers to get some. She thought about sending a text reminder, but then noticed Walter's phone sitting in the front console. By her elbow, poking out of one of the cup holders, was a pump bottle of hand sanitiser. Relieved, she squirted some out. She might have the odour of decaying animal on her hands and all sorts of horrible bacteria.

Walter soon returned carrying a box and what looked like two squishy dog beds tucked under one arm.

'Stay, Bruce,' he commanded, having opened the back door. 'And no peeking in the box – everything is sealed.'

'Did you happen to get shampoo? Our new friend is a bit smelly.'

'I tried. There wasn't any dog shampoo but I got some organic human stuff with no nasties. Probably what I have at home would have been perfectly fine, but Chantelle was keen to help. I think the term "she saw me coming" might apply,' he said with a laugh as he shut the door. 'She even insisted on me getting two dog beds – one for the office and one for home. I was powerless, I tell you.' He got back into the driver's side and then started the car. 'Oh, yes, I think our friend has rolled in something a bit ripe. Dead fox maybe. Sorry, Erica, I didn't think to leave a window down.'

They pulled into his driveway and up to a roller door. 'Actually, I think we'll drive in so she can't escape,' he added. The roller door in front of them began to rise. Walter turned the car back on and then drove into the garage.

They waited until the roller door behind them was fully closed before exiting the car. 'I'm sure she won't run away, but … No,

scrap that; I'm not sure of anything right now. This is a whole
new ball game for me,' Walter said.

'I'll grab everything and you keep your hands free to unlock
the door,' Erica said.

'Good plan. Thanks. It's not heavy: just a bit cumbersome and
awkward. Right. Come on, Bruce, there's a good girl,' Walter
said. 'This is your new home. I hope you'll be happy here.' The
dog hopped out of the car and then trotted around the garage,
sniffing the floor, zigzagging back and forth and taking in the
whole space, before heading out the open door into the garden.
Out on the lawn she squatted and did a wee. 'Well, you're a good
girl to wait. Thank you. I think, Erica, we should be very glad
Bruce is a girl and won't be cocking her leg on everything she
comes across.'

'Yes, that's one less thing to worry about.'

'I wonder if we have to worry about her attracting male dogs –
and if she's desexed or not, that is.'

'Oh dear, yes.'

'One thing at a time. Stop dithering, Walter,' he told himself.
He opened a glass door into the house beside a fold-up clothesline
attached to the nearby fence.

Erica placed the box and dog beds on the top of the washing
machine and then washed her hands at the trough.

'Oh, you're such a good dog,' Walter said, looking down to
where Bruce sat to attention in the space below them. 'I think
it's safe to say she's not going to run away – she's sticking to us
like glue. So, we can relax a little. You wait here, Erica. I'll just
get us a couple of old gardening shirts to protect our clothes from
whatever carnage is to come.'

With both attired in navy shirts with their sleeves rolled up,
they stood for a moment with their hands on their hips. While

Walter had been gone, Erica had got the shampoo out ready and placed it on the windowsill above the large square stainless-steel tub.

Walter opened the cupboard behind them and brought out a stack of beige towels.

'I think we'll need a jug or something to pour water since we don't have a hose type attachment,' Erica said.

'Right. Good thinking.' Walter disappeared and moments later reappeared with a stack containing several plastic jugs of varying sizes. 'Covering all bases,' he said by way of explanation. 'When we get started, we don't want to have to try to press pause. I hope she isn't going to mind this. I can just imagine it turning into a *National Lampoon* style comedy. Yes, I'm stalling.'

'Do you think I should set up my phone to film us? We might get a viral hit,' Erica said, grinning at Walter.

'Don't you dare,' he said, grinning back. 'I'm not so old as to not know what that means, young lady. Okay. Can't put this off any longer. Oh, do you think run the water and put her in or put her in and then run the water?'

'Dog definitely in first in case she struggles, I reckon.'

'Yes. Good point. Right. She suddenly looks very heavy. Okay. Bend the knees. And, here goes,' Walter said.

Erica had to work hard to stifle her rising giggles at seeing the bewildered look on Bruce's face when picked up around the middle by Walter.

'Just make sure her legs go over the edge okay because I can't lift her much higher. Lordy, you're a heavy girl. No offence,' he said, puffing slightly with exertion.

Erica carefully lifted the four feet after which there was a short clatter of claws as the no doubt startled dog got her footing in the shiny tub.

'You're okay. Good girl. Just stand there,' Walter said. 'You hold her and I'll get the water running.'

Erica patted the dog, who now looked very disconcerted. 'It's okay, we're not going to hurt you,' she soothed. *God, I hope you're not going to bite us.*

'Nice and warm but not too warm,' Walter said, fiddling with the taps and then putting the plug in. 'We'll be as quick as we can,' he said, pouring a jug of water carefully over the dog. 'Okay?'

Erica wasn't sure if he was asking her or Bruce. 'All good my end,' she answered, just in case. The dog was fully wet when she began to quiver.

'Aww, poor thing. You're a good, good girl. Sorry, but this has to be done. You're smelly and we need to check for fleas. So far so good in that department,' Walter said.

Both Walter and Erica massaged the soap through her coat, working quickly, and then rinsed twice.

'Let's dry her as much as we can so she won't catch a chill.'

'Good plan. It's just like bathing toddlers, isn't it?' Walter said, as they both quickly towelled the dog off. 'Just as wriggly, aren't you, missy?'

'I hope she doesn't mind not smelling like a dog,' Erica said.

'Yes. You're a little bit floral, Bruce. At the risk of undoing our good work, I'm going to let her out onto the lawn and in the sunshine while we get out of our wet things and clean up. Goodness, we look as wet as the dog.'

They took off their overshirts, hung them on the line, and went out into the sun to watch Bruce, who was on her side rubbing her face along the neatly clipped lawn.

'Oh. I got her a squeaky toy, too,' Walter said. 'As I say, Chantelle saw me coming.' He ducked inside the laundry to the box and then brought out what looked like a green dinosaur.

He squeezed it and it squeaked. 'Ugh. I might have to perform some surgery on that and remove the noise maker. It will drive us batty in the office.'

Erica laughed when Bruce looked up towards the noise with her head tilted, and then resumed her snuffling. 'I doubt she'll know what a toy is,' she said.

'Yes. She'll probably recognise a large bone, but the shop didn't have anything looking like that in the toy department.'

While she watched Bruce, Erica's gaze was drawn to a round purple object in the nearby garden bed. She moved over to it and realised it was a rock – about the size of her two cupped hands together – painted purple, the same shade as many of the objects on her desk at work. A wave of sadness swept through her.

'That's for Mary, as I'm sure you've gathered,' Walter said, now next to her. 'She's buried in the cemetery, but I wanted a reminder closer. I talk to her – it – while I garden and when I sit out here when it's warm enough. Call me mad, but still …'

'I think it's lovely. And absolutely perfect.' Erica thought it might be a nice idea for her and the girls to do the same for her mum and Stuart.

'I'll just get her ladyship, Bruce, some food and water and then I think you and I have earnt ourselves a cuppa and a sit down,' Walter said, moving away.

Erica eased her gaze away from Mary's rock and took in the rest of the lovely garden.

'Goodness, I'm exhausted,' Walter said, reappearing a few moments later with two bowls. One contained some dog biscuits and the other he began filling with water from the outside tap.

'Bruce, here, girl,' he called. The dog looked up at hearing her name and then trotted over. She checked out the water, had a brief slurp and then ate a few biscuits before moving away again. 'I'll leave your toy here, too,' he said, placing the squishy green object by the bowl. 'I guess we can't really change her name now, can we?' He stood, hands on hips, looking after her.

'No, probably not.' Erica grinned. Walter was a hoot and reminded her so much of her dear dad before dementia had taken hold.

'We'll be just inside,' Walter called to Bruce, who again looked up for a moment before returning to her snuffling.

Chapter Twenty-seven

'Ah, that's better,' Walter said when they each had a mug in front of them and were seated at the small table in the space adjacent to the kitchen. 'Goodness, what a morning. I did say your job would be varied, with no two days exactly the same, didn't I?' he said, with a cheeky wry look at Erica.

'Yes, you sure did.'

They sipped their drinks for a few moments in silence, lost in their own thoughts until Walter spoke again. 'You know, I don't fancy leaving her behind when we go back to work – not because I think she'll do any damage here or come to harm. I just ...'

'Yeah, I know what you mean. I feel the same way,' Erica said.

'So you definitely wouldn't mind a canine companion?'

'Nope. Not at all.'

'You said you don't have any experience with dogs, but I thought you seemed to know what you were doing back there.'

'Well, I'm not sure about that. I've never owned a dog, or any pet, for that matter, but I had my friend Michelle's red kelpie,

Daphne, stay with me for a couple of nights recently. Which actually turned out to be less than twenty-four hours, in the end.'

'Oh? Did something happen?'

'You could say that.'

'What happened? Sorry, there's me prying and being nosey. Don't feel the need to tell me if you don't want to.'

Suddenly it felt right to Erica to tell him. 'No, it's okay. It's quite a story, though.' *Just don't mention Jimmy.*

'Okay. I consider myself forewarned.'

'She actually saved my life – Daphne, my friend's kelpie. Not long after my daughters had left on their gap year overseas, I thought I was going mad. I was hearing things, smelling things. I thought it might be a possum in the roof. But that didn't explain the scent – my husband's – so I then thought maybe he was haunting the place. Don't worry, Walter, I don't even believe in ghosts.'

'Hey, no judgment from me,' he said, raising both hands in a surrender pose. 'I've often thought I've got a fleeting whiff of Mary. And there've been plenty of times I've been sure she's standing right behind me, only to spin around and … nothing. That causes disappointment all over again. But, sorry, I digress. Please, go on.'

'And of course menopause,' Erica said, rolling her eyes, 'seems to do all sorts of annoying things with memory, forgetfulness et cetera. Well, it has for me. Though maybe it's not menopause … But, well, anyway.'

'And pure grief does that too, so don't be too hard on yourself. There have been times when I've found my keys in the fridge. Go on,' Walter said.

'I got scared, like *really* scared. And completely lost my mojo. It got to the point where I was afraid to leave the house. And when

I did, I'd be looking over my shoulder the whole time, jumping at shadows. Basically, completely losing my mind and grip on reality. Or that's how it felt.'

'God, you poor thing.'

'It didn't help that I was trying to keep my dire financial situation secret from my dear friends.'

'Yup. Secrets will eat you from the inside out.'

'So, I was stressed. And then I got retrenched. Which, apart from the obvious problem – money, bills to pay et cetera – got me to the point where I seriously struggled to make myself walk outside. Then my dear friend – who's also my cousin, not that you need to know that, sorry – Steph, had me take care of her cat Boris.'

'Hang on, you're losing me slightly. Daphne is the kelpie, right? Dog, not a cat?'

'Yes.'

'Right.'

'Keep up, Walter,' Erica said with a laugh.

'Go on.'

'Well, Boris was supposed to be no trouble, and perfectly calm, being older,' Erica continued. 'And he so wasn't. He was skittish and a few other things happened. I tell you, Walter, by then I was seriously frazzled and exhausted from not being able to sleep. So another friend, Michelle, decided I needed to have her kelpie stay for a few nights to look after me. Daphne. She's beautiful and very clever. And great company.'

'And a good protector, I'm guessing?'

'Exactly. That was the theory. So, I'm fast asleep and suddenly I wake with a big fright to find this dog, Daphne, standing on my chest and scratching at me.'

'God, I'm getting serious anxiety just listening to you,' Walter said, putting a hand to his chest.

'I knew she would demand to go out for a wee or a poo, which she shouldn't have needed until the morning. But I figured I'd better deal with it, rather than her have an accident. So, I took her out.'

'Christ. In the dark? When you were already terrified in the daytime?'

'Yup. But I found there was something very reassuring about having Daphne beside me – she's not a huge dog but she makes her presence known. So, we get to the park a few streets away and then she just sits. Apparently doesn't need to do anything at all. I think, oh my god, you cheeky thing, you've dragged me out just because – taken advantage of me because you know I know diddly squat about dogs, blah, blah, blah.

'But then, as if someone's given her a command, after about twenty minutes of me sitting on the bench in the freezing cold – luckily I'd grabbed my coat on the way out – she suddenly squats, does a wee, and then turns and tugs on the lead to head back towards my house.'

'Excellent,' Walter said, clearly enthralled by the story.

'She stopped at each street crossing perfectly but I was basically just following, being taken for a walk myself,' Erica continued. 'And, actually, having her to focus on and the quietness, I started to enjoy being out. Weird, I know, given everything else.

'Anyway, I came around the corner at the end of my street and there're flashing blue and red lights and every type of emergency vehicle parked not far away from my house.'

'Oh god. Your house was on fire?' Walter said, putting his hands over his mouth.

Erica shook her head. Walter removed his hands and flapped one as if waving her on.

'I'm strolling along thinking something was up with the neighbours. Then I see the police are at my door.'

'Ah, a doorknock?' Walter said.

'Nope. Apparently, the neighbours behind me, who I've never met, had reported suspicious activity on my roof. I arrived home to find a house full of police and firefighters who've gained access and arrested a stalker.'

'A what?'

'A stalker, an intruder. A young woman had gained access through the roof tiles and had been staying and coming and going from my attic space – not a real attic space, just storage, really, but anyway …'

'Christ. But why? Did you know her? Are you famous and attract that sort of obsessive attention?' Walter said.

'Nope. I'd met her a couple of times. She has some issues.'

'I'll say she does. Far out.'

'And she later admitted she'd planned to kill me.'

'Oh my god, Erica. I'm so sorry you went through that.'

'Thanks. It was pretty harrowing, but could have been so much worse. And she's locked up and won't be out any time soon, according to the police.'

'Phew. I'm exhausted just listening to that. So, did you find out why she targeted you?'

Erica nodded. 'Because apparently I encouraged her fictional boyfriend – they were just friends, but she wanted more – to pursue his dream of doing film makeup and special effects, which meant him moving to Sydney to study.'

'Which meant him leaving her, I presume?'

'Exactly.'

'Seriously? That's all it took.'

'Apparently. I know, it doesn't make sense, does it? But that's because we don't have her sort of "issues" – or addiction problems. She was caught with the drug ice.'

'Oh. Apparently that stuff causes all sorts of brain wiring issues and aggression. It's a huge problem everywhere. Thank goodness she's off the street. Hopefully she can get the right sort of help and turn her life around.'

'Yes. Exactly.'

'I'm so glad you're okay.'

'Yeah.'

'I'll never forget hearing of that pensioner whose neighbour gained access through her roof tiles and killed her hoping to get her hands on her house and pension. Thankfully she was caught, too. Horrible. And she looked so normal on the TV – someone you wouldn't look twice at if you passed her in the street,' Walter said.

'No. Same with this girl – Kayla is her name. Anyway, that's the story of how my friend's red kelpie Daphne saved my life. And I truly believe it.'

'I'm surprised you didn't race off to the RSPCA the next day and get a dog for company.'

'I might have if I didn't need to pack and get myself organised to move up here to Melrose.' Her thoughts went again to Jimmy. She longed to share the strangest part of all with Walter – say, 'And you'll never guess what!' – but that bit wasn't hers to tell.

'What, this all happened just a matter of days ago?'

'Yes, the Saturday night and into the Sunday morning before I left.'

'Christ, Erica. Why didn't you cancel me, or at least postpone?'

'I desperately needed the job. And I didn't want to let you down – I felt such a connection with you and you sounded like you really needed me too.'

'I did. I do. You're an absolute godsend, Erica.'

'And you're a lifesaver, Walter.'

'Even though we're always dealing with death and the dead?' he said, raising his eyebrows and offering his trademark cheeky smile.

'Yeah, well, there's that,' Erica said, chuckling. 'But, seriously, I reckon Bruce would say you're a lifesaver, too.'

'Yes. I really do think that Aiden fellow would have done something terrible to her. There was a look in his eye. More than just anger. It was like he was looking for somewhere to unleash his rage or something. Oh, listen to me being all melodramatic.'

'No, I agree. I noticed it too. It was a similar look to that in Kayla's eyes – the young woman who stalked me. Maybe he's on drugs too.'

'Or perhaps just worn down with life and disillusioned.'

'Being a human is hard sometimes.'

'I agree. Can I tell you something, Erica?'

'Yep.'

'Please don't take this the wrong way, but I have been a bit worried about how jumpy you are. It makes sense, of course, now, having learnt what you've been through. And you've seemed a little calmer these past few days. I wish you'd told me right from the outset. But I understand why you didn't.'

'I'm sorry, Walter.'

'No need to be, Erica. Thanks for telling me now – for confiding in me.'

'Can I tell you something else?'

'Of course. Anything.'

'I still struggle to leave the flat – I do, obviously – but some-times I find it quite difficult. And so far, I've only walked around the streets because I'm too scared of the shadows near the creek, or rather what can be lurking in them or behind the trees. Even though I know there's no threat – that's the frustrating bit,' Erica said, her voice practically a whisper.

'I think that's understandable. It will take time to regain your equilibrium. You've been through trauma, heaped upon the trauma of losing your husband. I think you're doing well. But if you need time off to see someone, you let me know.'

'Thanks.'

'And I'm always here to listen – I might be your boss, but I hope you consider me a friend too.'

Erica smiled at Walter, who smiled back.

'Here she is,' Walter said when they heard the *clip*, *clip*, *clip* of dog claws on the large textured cream tiles on the floor of the open-plan space. Bruce trotted over and sat between them, looking up from one to the other.

'What else do you think she wants?' Walter said.

'I have no idea. Maybe she's trying to round us up – or is pleased with herself because she *has* rounded us up,' Erica said with a laugh.

'Well, I think we'd better get back to the office and organise Milton's service. We'll just keep missy here out of the mortuary and hope she can adjust to being an inside dog. She was fine in the car, so fingers crossed,' Walter said as they got to their feet.

'Yes. Walter?'

'Yes, Erica,' he said, pausing and turning back to her.

'Please don't treat me any differently now. I'm not fragile,' she said quietly.

'Erica, we're all fragile in our own way. But I'll try not to patronise you or treat you with kid gloves. And if I overstep, then you are to tell me. But don't mistake me caring and making sure you're okay, because I won't apologise for that, or change that about myself. Okay?'

'Okay. Thanks.'

Back at the office Bruce trotted around checking out the space, Erica put the dog bed – complete with soft green dinosaur toy – behind the reception desk and Walter set up the second pair of pet bowls he'd bought in the kitchen. He then joined her at the desk, where they stood watching the dog.

'I can see she's going to be quite the distraction,' Walter said, with a laugh. 'We'll be lucky to get any work done at this rate.'

'I really hope she's going to be good with people, because I think it would be great to have her calming presence – in here and at funerals. An assistance or therapy dog – I don't see why she couldn't become one of those,' Erica mused.

'Hmm. If she behaves well enough. Actually, didn't I read something about assistance dogs now being used in court to comfort vulnerable witnesses giving evidence?' Walter said.

'I don't know. I don't recall that, specifically. But I have heard assistance dogs are being used for all sorts of situations. And I'm pretty sure all sorts of breeds. Even different animals, I think, not just dogs. How good would it have been to have her the other day at little Elsie's funeral for the kids to cuddle or simply to distract, diffuse the fear a bit? It might have helped. I don't know. Maybe it's a silly idea or totally unworkable.' She finished with a shrug. 'She – or any dog – might just cause complete mayhem, which would be very bad for business.'

'Hmm. I think you might be onto something. And not just for kids. It might have helped dear old Mrs Kanute last week,' Walter said.

Erica nodded. The dear old lady with dementia had buried her husband and had been so confused and kept looking around and asking for her Stephen. When her daughters had led her away, she'd initially refused, insisting she was waiting for him. It had been so hard to watch.

'My dad's nursing home has some kittens and he's really taken to them. It's been beautiful to watch – him being so gentle and loving with them, despite never having had pets, well, as far as I'm aware. Maybe he did as a kid and he's back there. I don't know. All I do know is they seem to keep him focussed and calm.'

'It's definitely food for thought, Erica. We'll see how she settles in.'

At that moment Bruce appeared in front of them. Walter reached over to give her a pat, but she darted away. 'Hmm. She doesn't seem to like me very much,' he said, sadly. 'I hope I haven't traumatised her by giving her a bath. Or maybe it's because I'm a man. I can't help wondering how Milton treated her. And Aiden, of course. Or everyone else.'

'It's early days,' Erica said. 'She'll need time to settle in.' Though she had noticed that Bruce had come close to her. 'Let's sit so she doesn't feel so scrutinised,' she said, dragging her gaze from the dog and sitting down behind the counter where she was out of sight.

'Good idea,' Walter said. 'Let's go over the details we've got for Milton's service on Thursday.'

'Oh, look,' Erica whispered a few minutes later. Out of the corner of her eye she'd caught sight of Bruce. She slowly turned her chair, hoping it wouldn't squeak and give the dog a fright. Walter did the same. They watched as Bruce picked up the green dinosaur and then with it still in her mouth flopped down onto her bed.

'Oh, bless,' Walter said.

'Yes. So far so good,' Erica said.

Chapter Twenty-eight

Erica had just got down to the office and settled at her desk and was a little disappointed because she hadn't heard from Jimmy that morning. She'd texted him saying she was going for a walk and would collect him if he was interested but again reassured him that there was no pressure. She hadn't heard back and hoped he was okay. But she hadn't texted him again – the last thing she wanted was to be overbearing, as much as she wanted to help him. She knew all too well that these things had to be done in your own time. Maybe she'd already scared him off. Or he'd simply retreated again. Hopefully he was calmly processing the positives from their conversation or, better yet, had taken such a leap of recovery he was out and about somewhere.

She picked up her phone when it rang, hoping it was Jimmy. It was Walter.

'Hi, Walter,' she said.

'Hi, Erica. Do you fancy going for another drive?'

'Yes. Sure. Always.'

'I'll meet you out the front – be there in a sec.'

Erica grabbed her things and found outside the front door that something had been left on the step. Oh. It was a two-thirds empty large bag of dry dog food, secured with a piece of string. Hooked under the string was a folded piece of paper. She carefully dragged it out and unfolded it. It appeared to be a dog registration form containing Bruce's details. Down the bottom was a note saying ownership was transferred to Walter Crossley and then a signature. At that moment Walter pulled up in his car.

'What's that?' he called from the open car window.

Erica stood back. 'Dog food,' she said. 'I'll just pop it inside and lock up.' She tucked the form into her handbag, lifted up the bag of dog food – getting a meaty whiff, as she did – and took it inside, and then locked up behind her.

'Good morning,' she said to Walter. 'Hello there, lovely girl,' she said to Bruce, as the dog's head popped up between the seats. 'There was also a registration form, with her details. Look,' she said, dragging it out to show Walter and pointing out the hand-written note.

'Well, that answers that, then,' Walter said.

'Yes. So, how was – is – she?'

'Okay-ish. I'm sure she's afraid of me.'

'Oh. That's not good.'

'No. I hate seeing her cringe and step away. I can tell she's trying, but I'm struggling with those big brown eyes – they look sad to me, and it's breaking my heart. I don't think I'm cut out for owning a dog. Or maybe it's just her.'

'Aww, are you sad, Bruce? You poor thing. Walter, I don't think you can take it personally.'

'I'm trying not to.'

'She probably just needs time to adjust. Maybe it's the experi-ence she's showing fear of, not actually you. I'll bet being inside buildings and cars is all very foreign to her.'

'You might be right. But still, would you mind taking her – having her with you overnight, that is? See if she's better then?'

'Of course.'

'If she isn't, we can rethink it.'

'Okay. So, where are we off to?'

'The vet.'

'Oh. Do you think there's something wrong with her?'

'Not as far as I know – other than the fact she doesn't like me.'

'Oh, Walter, I really don't think that's the case.'

'Sorry, I'm feeling a little maudlin. We had a bit of a restless night, didn't we, Bruce? And it made me miss my Mary all the more – she would have known how to handle it. Ah, don't mind me. I'm being a sad sack.

'So, anyway, I've managed to get an appointment at a vet in Port Pirie to check her over – make sure there's nothing to worry about, get some flea and worm treatment and whatever else we need. She'll probably need desexing, too.'

They drove in silence.

'My apologies in advance of any indignities you're about to undergo, Bruce,' Walter said, as they parked.

'See,' he said as Bruce moved over to Erica's side to wait for her, instead of exiting through Walter's side where he was already holding the door open.

Erica didn't know what to say. She opened the door and grabbed the lead, which had remained attached to Bruce. 'Come on, girl, out you come,' she said, and the dog jumped down.

The vet's door gave a squeak as they went in. They closed it behind them with a clunk.

'Hello,' Walter said at the counter. 'I'm Walter Crossley with Bruce here for a general check-up. I rang earlier this morning.'

They were instructed to wait. As she sat, Erica experienced the same uncomfortable and slightly anxious sensation of taking one of her girls to the dentist or doctor. She almost shared the thought with Walter, but he was still at the counter talking to the receptionist. She reached down to pat Bruce, who was next to her. She wasn't sure if the dog realised she was sitting on Erica's feet – not beside them, but on them. She liked Bruce's closeness – it was calming – and wondered if it was normal behaviour, though resisted getting out her phone to do a check with Google. Until she learnt otherwise, she'd take it as a sign of affection.

Erica looked around. She'd never been in a vet surgery before. Out here was just like the reception area for a human doctor, except for the bags of cat and dog food displayed on one wall and the collection of bright toys, leads and harnesses et cetera hanging from hooks on another. The clean smell was slightly different, too – gentler. No doubt chemicals with reduced toxicity and scent were used. On the floor was shiny lino or poured PVC or something, instead of low-pile carpet squares. She watched Walter take a stroll about, looking at everything. He seemed nervous. She wanted to quip something like her dad might have – What, you got ants in your pants or something? – but then he sat down beside her.

Just a few moments later Bruce's name was called, so they both stood up.

'Actually, perhaps I'll stay here, since … you know …' Walter said.

'Up to you. Though maybe it might help to come in – you can ask the vet for advice,' Erica suggested.

'Hmm. Fair enough. You don't mind, do you, Bruce?'

Erica was a little relieved the vet was female, for Bruce's sake. She was looking at a computer screen.

'Hi, I'm Bronwyn,' she said.

Erica and Walter both said hi.

'Hello there, Bruce,' Bronwyn said, coming over to Bruce, bending down to give her a pat and then gently lifting the dog up onto the counter.

Walter stayed back and sat on one of the two chairs.

'You're a lovely girl.'

Something in Bronwyn's tone piqued Erica's interest, but Walter got in first.

'Do you know her?' he asked.

'Oh yes. We're old friends, aren't we, Bruce?' she said, stroking the dog. 'Well, not exactly friends, and not actually old,' she added with a laugh. 'Yes, we know each other – let's leave it at that, shall we?'

'We've just acquired her. I'm Walter and this is Erica. Her owner died recently. Oh, we're funeral directors – over at Melrose. His widow, well, more accurately his son, insisted yesterday that we take her. He was adamant, if you get my drift? Neither of us have been dog owners before, so we thought we should get her checked out.'

'Right. I see. Okay, then, let's have a good look at you, Bruce,' Bronwyn said.

'Does she have a microchip?' Erica asked.

'Yes. And is she desexed?' Walter asked.

'Yes, and yes. It's noted on her file and she has all the right tattoos in her ears.'

'Oh, well, that's something,' Walter said.

'Hmm. Desexing is mandatory now unless you're a registered breeder. And desexed dogs attract a cheaper registration cost. So, from memory – it's not recorded on the file – but I think it was a daughter or daughter-in-law who brought her in for her annual shots. Sad to think they didn't want her. At least she's landed on her feet with you – haven't you, Bruce? That's the main thing.

A lot of them aren't as lucky. In so many ways. Right. Sorry, Bruce, a bit uncomfortable now, but it'll soon be over. You hold the front end,' she said to Erica as she gently held Bruce's tail up to insert a thermometer.

'I'm staying right out of the way,' Walter said. 'She doesn't seem to like me all that much.'

'I think you'll find she just needs time to settle. You said you got her yesterday, didn't you?' Bronwyn said.

'That's right,' Walter said.

'It's early days. These work dogs primarily spend their time with men and they're often not appreciated for their hard work and skill, if you get my drift? It doesn't help that they can't speak English and stand up for themselves. It can be a tough life, depending on which establishment they find themselves in.'

'I don't think she's ever even lived inside,' Erica said, stroking Bruce.

'Oh no, she won't have. I rarely come across a work dog that lives inside as a pet as well. Doesn't help that they love to roll in anything smelly. Right, Bruce, that horrible bit's all over now, there's a good girl. Her temperature's fine,' Bronwyn said, looking from Erica to Walter.

Erica watched while Bronwyn listened to Bruce's heart with a stethoscope and then looked in her ears, eyes and mouth. She also checked her all over – including stretching her legs out to their full length.

'There. The picture of health,' she said, rubbing the dog's ears. 'Would you like me to give her a worming tablet now to save you doing it? And also treat her for parasites? She's a bit early for her annual vaccination.'

'Yes, please – both,' Walter said, getting in just before Erica.

'You shouldn't have any problems doing it yourself – she really is a very good dog. There, not so bad, huh, girl?' Bronwyn said, holding Bruce's mouth closed after popping a tablet down her throat.

'They said she's a little nippy,' Walter said.

'Oh. Not in my experience. I wouldn't worry. Perhaps someone mistreated her at some point? Just take her easy and introduce her to things slowly and gently. Remember, everything you do with her is probably a new experience, and we all can get anxious in that situation. Just watch her body language – ears down and tail tucked between her legs will tell you she's afraid. That's when they can nip.'

'I can't look her in the eye; she seems morose to me,' Walter said, sadly.

'Yes, if you're not used to it – or dogs at all, for that matter – I suppose it can get you in the feels,' Bronwyn said with a laugh, before putting the spot treatment onto the back of Bruce's neck.

'Right, just separate the hair, so you get to the skin, and then empty the tube, like this,' she said, holding up the tiny tube and then demonstrating. 'It's not cheap, but it's important to give her one of these each month – and it's the most convenient way to do it. Okay. All good, Bruce?' The dog shook herself, causing her paws to slip on the counter. 'That's me all done. Do you have any questions?'

As if understanding the ordeal was over, Bruce lay down. Erica smiled at her.

'Is dry food okay?' Erica asked. 'She came with a bag.'

'Yes – she seems in good nick. No cooked bones. Ever. They can become brittle and splinter and cause serious internal damage. Raw bones are useful for keeping them mentally stimulated and helping clean their teeth, but go for large ones to lessen the risk of ingestion – in part or completely. And I always recommend supervision.'

'Oh. Goodness. I'm glad you told me – I could have got that all wrong,' Walter said.

'We have a range of other chew options, too. Remember, there's a lot of useful information on our website and you can always phone and ask our staff if you have any questions.'

'Great. Thanks. Do you happen to know why she's called Bruce? Being a she and all …?' Walter said.

'No. Sorry. Maybe her owner was a Bruce Lee fan? I wouldn't go changing it at her age. Could be too confusing. But she's your dog, so …'

'How old is she, as a matter of interest?' Walter asked.

'Five and a half.'

'You said she has a microchip. Do we change the details for that here?' Erica asked.

'Oh. Yes. Good point. No, there's an online database – it's a national registry. It's separate from council dog registration. I'll just get the scanner and check it's working okay, and print out the details for you. I'll be back in a moment.'

'You're being such a good girl,' Erica said, cuddling Bruce.

'Right, miss, let's see,' Bronwyn said, re-entering the room carrying a white device with a handle and a piece of paper. 'Just stay there, Bruce, there's a good girl.' She moved the scanner over the dog until it beeped. 'There we are. It definitely works. Here are her details and where her chip is recorded,' she said, picking up the piece of paper from beside the computer.

'Phew, it's a lot to take in and remember. Like having children all over again,' Walter said.

'Yes, but without the education expenses. Or the clothes,' Bronwyn said. 'And she won't need the level of exercise of a younger dog, which can be an issue if you're new to dog owner-ship and especially with a working dog breed. Well, good luck. Just call if you need any other information.'

'Thanks very much, Bronwyn,' Walter said.

'Yes, thank you.'

'It's my pleasure. Are you okay to lift her down or would you like me to?' Bronwyn said.

'No, thanks. I'd better get used to it. She's coming home with me. You're a chunky monkey,' Erica said. 'Meant not as a criticism at all,' she added, as she lifted the dog and set her carefully onto all four paws on the ground.

They headed out the door to the reception area, leaving Bronwyn behind.

'Now, Erica, I'll get this,' Walter said, taking out his wallet. Erica let out a gentle sigh of relief. 'We'd better take some chew thingamajigs and one of those toys you put food into,' he said, going over to the display and reading the label. 'I was Googling last night – apparently they're great for keeping them entertained. Will be good for in the office, I think.'

'Yes, good idea. I've heard of those,' Erica said.

'And if you can suggest anything else for new dog owners,' he said to the receptionist. 'Is this the right size one of these things?' he said, holding up the red Kong toy. 'For a blue heeler?'

'Yes. That's the one. Um. Do you need some treats?' the recep-tionist said.

'Oh, yes, definitely,' Walter said.

'Just remember not too many – they're high in calories,' she warned when Walter put two packets on the counter.

Erica shuddered at hearing the total, but Walter didn't seem to flinch and cheerfully thanked the receptionist.

'That's us all sorted,' Walter said, holding the door open for Erica and Bruce.

'Lordy, that was quite an ordeal, wasn't it, Bruce?' he said as they settled back into the car. This time Erica noticed Bruce's face was equally between them, not favouring Erica. 'Oh. Hang on a sec. We forgot to get her a harness to be safely clipped in while in the car.' Walter was out of the car and closing his door before Erica could say anything.

'I'm going to miss you being right here, Bruce,' she said, stroking the dog's face beside her elbow. 'But we'll also be much safer.'

A few moments later Walter was back. 'Sorry, folks, I need Bruce so they can teach us how to put on the harness. You'd better come too, Erica. False alarm, Bruce – sorry.'

A few moments later they were back in the car with Bruce secured on the back seat. 'Right. Take two. I hope she won't get car sick from that position,' Walter said. 'But I do like that I can't see her sad eyes.'

'Listen to you, the devoted fur-dad,' Erica said. 'Do you want to keep trying with her – having her at your place, I mean?' She hoped not, and found herself holding her breath as she waited for his response.

'No. You know, I think she came to us for you, not me – you're perfect together.'

Erica beamed and her heart swelled. 'I'll do the microchip and registration when we get back,' she said, for something to say.

Chapter Twenty-nine

'Now, you're absolutely sure you don't want to take Bruce home with you?' Erica asked as they were packing up for the day.

'Quite sure. No offence, Bruce,' Walter said.

The dog looked up at Walter, her tail waving back and forth slowly behind her.

'See, she's relieved.'

'Oh, Walter, stop it. Don't be ridiculous. She'll be happy with anyone who feeds her and treats her well.' Erica wasn't sure this was true – well, she hoped not. She remembered the look on Daphne's face – scepticism, maybe disappointment, a touch of resignation perhaps – the knowledge that her real master was not there but she had to accept this imposter, pander to her, even, if she were not to starve.

There you go again, Erica, putting human emotions and thoughts into creatures.

Who's to say they don't think that, anyway? They're domesticated: hardly wild animals for whom each day is a life and death struggle.

True – some have been said to sit on their former owner's graves, grieving.

Bruce looked at Erica, tail swaying. 'Are you okay to come with me?' she asked the dog. The tail became a little more animated – or Erica thought she could have imagined it.

'Right. There's our answer,' Walter said. 'I'll see you both in the morning. Cheerio,' he said with a wave.

Erica waited until Walter had disappeared down the back corridor before bending down and giving the dog a big cuddle. 'You're a beautiful girl, and you're coming home with me. Yay,' she said quietly. Erica's heart swelled. She hadn't felt this depth of nurturing and protective instinct since Issy's birth. Wow. And in that instant, she totally got why pet people were pet people. And how some of them – like Michelle – with no sense of irony referred to their pets as their surrogate children. Also, right in that moment, Erica knew that if she had to, though hoped it would never come to it, she would throw herself in front of a car or another dog to save Bruce.

She picked up the plush green dinosaur and the red Kong toy along with her handbag. 'Right. Come on, miss, home time,' she said, getting up and turning off the lights as she went. Bruce trotted happily beside her.

At lunchtime after their return from the vet, Erica had set up Bruce's second bed in her bedroom in the corner out of the way where she wouldn't trip over her at any point. A part of her really hoped the dog might choose to share her bed, though that was probably a bad precedent to set.

She probably should be more master-like and commanding, but was keen to show Bruce just how good life with humans could be. She figured the poor dog had some catching up to do.

While eating dinner, with Bruce tucking into her own on the floor nearby, Erica looked down at the dog several times and marvelled at how lucky she – Erica – was. Not only to be the proud owner of a dog, but one who very clearly had impeccable manners. A big part of her was glad to not have to go through the teething or any of the other puppy stages where all manner of objects might be chewed up and spat out. She hadn't munched on the dinosaur, simply picked it up and moved it sometimes, and slept with her paw over it, which Erica thought was very cute and had taken a stack of photos of already.

She'd done the dishes, taken Bruce outside for a quick wee, and was watching TV when the dog hopped up next to her on the towel she'd laid down to protect the fabric sofa in case the dog wanted to sit there. She leant over and gave the dog's velvety head a kiss. It was fast becoming her favourite spot on the creature. And then she stifled a laugh as they both let out a long, deep sigh of contentment. Careful not to dislodge the dog, she dragged her phone from the arm of the sofa and quickly snapped a couple of photos and sent some to her friends, who she'd been keeping up to date with the adventures of Bruce, the funeral industry – always being discreet, of course – and her life in Melrose.

Her phone pinged with a series of messages containing expressions of love and awe and a collection of related emojis.

'Sorry,' she said to Bruce when the dog grunted and shifted position slightly. 'Am I disturbing you, miss?' she said, giving the solid tummy a pat and then the belly a scratch when it was presented to her.

Later, as she got into bed herself, Erica firmly told Bruce to get in her bed, which she did, her green dinosaur toy beside her, having carried it in when she'd followed Erica and watched her cleaning her teeth and getting ready for bed.

'Good night, Bruce,' she said, turning out the light. As she lay in the dark, Erica tried hard to not see the similarities to the night she'd had Daphne stay. But the déjà vu was there and the flicking of images, followed by grips of emotion and anxiety.

It's okay; we're fine, she told herself, as she put her headphones in and selected a guided meditation track.

Erica was disappointed to wake again with a start – she hadn't for a couple of mornings, she didn't think. Though this morning was different, as was the cause of her abrupt departure from slumber. As she came to, memories flickered into focus.

Bruce! She opened her eyes. The dog was lying on the bed beside her with her head on Erica's chest, her face between her breasts, her nose disconcertingly close to Erica's chin; she could feel puffs of warm breath. She imagined big brown eyes looking up at her, but it wasn't quite light enough in the room to see.

'Good morning,' she said. 'Who's a good girl, but doesn't understand personal space?' she said, and reached out and stroked the dog's head. 'Yes, you're lovely,' she assured the dog, who tried to shuffle closer. 'But you're very heavy,' she said, the previously comforting weight suddenly becoming stifling.

'Come on, time to get up,' she said, and eased herself upright. As if signalling Mission Accomplished, Bruce jumped off the bed and went over and sat to attention at the bedroom door. 'You'll have to wait a sec – I need to get dressed.' *Please be able to wait.* Erica blinked a couple of times to try and get her addled brain in order. The morning was unfolding too quickly; she wasn't used to this. Yes, being jolted awake, she was, but she was accustomed to getting up and taking a few moments to get organised to go for a walk.

Right, clothes.

'Hang on. Slow down,' she said, more to herself than the dog, and then almost laughed as Bruce lay down with her head on her paws in the doorway.

Her brain was a muddle and insisted on staying focussed on the déjà vu feeling of how similar this was to the night of Kayla's disturbance with Daphne. She tried to force aside the flickering images trying to come through. Actually, she vaguely remembered tossing and turning and cuddling Bruce at one point last night. Didn't she? She might have even called her Daphne. She did seem to have the same sensitivity, if in a completely different outer appearance. Maybe it was a working dog thing – emotional intelligence as well as whatever the other type of intelligence was.

It was then that Erica noticed the amount of natural light in the room and that the grey frame around the curtains said it was a lot later than four-thirty or five o'clock. At the same time of this realisation and reaching to her phone to check it, there was a ping signalling the arrival of a message. She dragged it off the bedside table and put her code in. There were two messages from Jimmy. *Oh, shit, sorry.*

The first was from over half an hour ago asking if she wanted to come over for a hot chocolate. The second, just now, was asking if everything was okay. Oh wow; it was just after six.

Her brain scrambled to formulate a reply to tell him she was on her way. But then Bruce gave a 'Woof' and she suddenly realised this morning was very different. She began typing: *Sorry, I slept in. I know, strange ...* but then told herself to stop explaining. She deleted what she'd written and typed, *Sorry, can't this morning.* Would that work? Fully aware she was overthinking it, she pressed send.

But then she remembered how fragile Jimmy was. Thus, not including an explanation – namely that it was her and not him – wasn't quite suitable, she decided. She brought up the text box again and typed: *I can't because this happened …* and then quickly snapped a pic of Bruce, added it to the message and pressed send.

Sorry, girl, I know it's not the most flattering shot of you. 'Yes, I know you don't care,' she said with a laugh as Bruce had a big yawn.

'And I'm talking to a dog about image quality, for goodness' sake. Clearly, I'm losing my mind,' she muttered, getting up and shaking her head at herself. *And I could have just sent one of the dozens I've already taken, anyway. Gah!*

She began dressing from the clothes laid out on the chair. Her phone pinged with another message from Jimmy: *Gorgeous. I love dogs. Bring her over.*

But, bakery = health regs etc, right? she typed and then sent.

Jimmy: *Come to the van instead.*

Erica sent a thumbs up emoji and quickly finished getting dressed, put the phone into her jacket pocket, and hooked the lead onto Bruce's collar.

'Sorry, I hope you don't mind going to different places. If you do, you'd better adjust quick smart.' Erica loved the idea of having the company and mentally crossed her fingers that Bruce would be like Michelle's Daphne, who was the perfect companion – and saviour. She leant down and gave Bruce a cuddle.

'You're such a gorgeous girl,' she said, a rush of emotion taking over – so much so she had to blink back tears. 'You're loved now, and perfectly safe. We're going to have lots of fun together.' She gave her a kiss on the head and stood up. 'Come on. You can have a wee and anything else, and then meet Jimmy. He's a man, but I think you'll like him.'

Chapter Thirty

Downstairs, as she waited for Bruce to finish her wee, Erica really hoped she was doing the right thing – wasn't taking things too quickly with the dog. But better Bruce was with her where she could see if she was upset than alone in the flat, she decided. *Boots and all, Bruce, boots and all.*

'Come on,' she said. Erica crossed the road with Bruce trotting alongside perfectly, and opened the side gate, taking extra care to be quiet. She went to the caravan, noting there were no lights on in the bakery, and tapped on the door.

Jimmy opened it. 'Oh, aren't you lovely?' he said. 'Both of you,' he added self-consciously.

Bruce strained at the lead to hide behind Erica's legs.

'Aww, poor darling,' Jimmy cooed.

'Sorry, I don't think she's very fond of men. I suspect she might have had a rough time along the way. I can probably leave her out here – the yard seems secure,' Erica said, looking around. Though she really didn't want to, and was already regretting bringing the dog over with her.

'No, she's welcome to come in, if she wants to. I'm fine if she is. And I'm sure Gemma won't mind. It's okay, sweetie, I won't hurt you,' Jimmy said to Bruce. 'I'll come out so I'm not looming over her looking all big and scary.'

'Here we are. Better now?' Jimmy squatted away a little from Erica and Bruce. He held his hand out and Bruce stretched her neck to sniff him. 'That's it. See, I'm okay,' he said, standing up straight again.

'Good girl, Bruce,' Erica said, bending down and rubbing the dog's chin.

Bruce moved towards Jimmy and stood looking up at him, her tail waving back and forth. And then suddenly she was standing on her hind legs with her front paws on his thighs. 'Oh. Hello there! You've decided I'm a friend, then? Excellent,' he said, stroking her head.

'Sorry, I'm new at this dog ownership business, and Bruce is new at being a house dog. Down you hop, there's a good girl.'

At that Bruce took her paws off Jimmy and sat down.

'Good girl,' Erica cooed again.

'There you are, beautiful,' Jimmy said, and gently gave her chin a rub and then her ears. 'Come on, in you come,' he said, and turned and made his way up the steps.

Erica was last in after Bruce had bounded after Jimmy without need for further encouragement. Two full mugs were already on the small table. Jimmy and Erica sat down on opposite sides on the plush booth-style seating with Bruce on the tiny space of floor below between them and the bench containing the row of kitchen appliances.

'Now, did I hear right – she's a she and her name is Bruce?' Jimmy said.

'Yep. Not my doing, I can assure you. But given she's an adult, I don't think I can really change her name. And, honestly, I'm getting used to it. I kind of like that she's a little bit of an enigma.'

'Yeah, more interesting than Blue or Spot. And a good conversation starter. And, anyway, who's to say Bruce shouldn't be a female name, anyway? Be who you want to be, and all that, I reckon,' Jimmy said.

'Sorry about earlier. I woke up as usual, but must have actually fallen back to sleep – I guess because of feeling safe and secure with Miss Bugalugs here,' Erica said, reaching down and giving the dog a pat.

'What's her story, anyway? Is she yours or just visiting?' Jimmy asked.

'She's straight off a farm. No idea how skilled and if she worked sheep or cattle, or both, but they were probably going to shoot her if we didn't take her. Well, Walter, my boss. Have you met him yet? Technically he took her.'

'No. But Gemma speaks highly of him.'

'He's lovely. Not a dog person – neither am I, really, for that matter; I love them; I'm just clueless – but Walter's a softy at heart and an all-round good egg. So we went to organise a man's funeral and left with a dog.'

'That's taking customer service to a whole new level,' Jimmy said, grinning before sipping from his mug.

'It sure is,' Erica said. 'And I don't know what we'll do if more people ask us to take their unwanted pets. Fingers crossed that doesn't happen.'

'God, I can imagine you guys ending up with quite the menagerie over there – birds in cages, a couple of cats, more dogs, guinea pigs ...'

'Yes, it doesn't bear thinking about, really. It's a bit sad, because she seems a little afraid of people – well, men in particular. Which is why I have her and not Walter. But it's my gain, isn't it, girl?'

Bruce looked up at Erica adoringly.

'Aww, that look. She loves you. Such a gorgeous girl,' Jimmy said.

Erica was just about to ask Jimmy how he was doing when Bruce got up and went to the door and sat.

'Oh. Do you think she needs to go out?' Jimmy said.

'It looks that way. Sorry to cut this short, but I'd better not tempt fate and ignore her. Thanks for the hot chocolate,' she said, draining her mug and getting up.

'Thanks for visiting.'

'I'm really going to have to start returning the favour,' Erica said.

'No need: this is fine with me.'

'Oh,' Erica said, hand on the door ready to leave, 'do you want to come for a walk with us? If you'd rather go to sleep, I completely understand …'

'Um … You know, actually, I think I might give it a shot,' he said, getting up and grabbing a coat that was lying on the end of the nearby bed.

'Really? That's great. You can tell me what's going on with you since Bruce and I have hogged the conversation.'

Outside Erica strode ahead, not wanting to put Jimmy under the spotlight. But when she turned back after opening the gate, he was only halfway from the caravan to where she and Bruce stood. Even in the pale light she could see the fear etched in his features, and in the colour of his skin. She wasn't sure what to say to him – whether to be gentle or stern with her encouragement – and was still deliberating when she noticed him take several really deep breaths. His chest and overall height inflated in response, then he hoicked his shoulders up and moved forwards on long strides.

Outside the gate he took audible breaths, puffing out condensation into the cold morning air.

Erica closed the gate behind him. 'Okay?' she asked.

'Yep. All good. Well, not quite, but still … You know, now I'm out, I'd actually really like to walk along the creek. Since we've got Bruce here to protect us.'

'Um. Sure.' Erica shoved aside the ripple of anxiety that ran through her. 'Come on, then. The walking track is this way – that's the sign,' she said, pointing to a sign that was too far away for them to read. 'I have to admit, I've been too chicken to do this walk before now and have just stuck to the streets.'

'I've not actually been on a walk at all,' Jimmy said quietly as they walked side by side along the street to the edge of town.

'Seriously?' She tried not to turn her head to take a good look at his physique, which seemed very toned for someone who didn't exercise, from what little she'd seen. 'I guess kneading bread and all the lifting you do would keep you fit.'

'Maybe. But I skip – as in with a rope – in the yard and do push-ups and squats et cetera. Very exciting stuff. Gemma has been amazing – she even does my groceries for me.'

'But aren't you going a bit mad locked away? Sorry, that was …'

'Yup. I'm sure I am going a bit loopy.'

'Are you okay?' Erica stopped and looked at him. 'I mean, okay with being out now? We can go back if you want – just say.'

'You know what? I'm jittery, but I'm hanging in. I think learning from you that there's no possibility of bumping into Kayla was the push I needed. And being with you and Bruce helps. I really need to do this.'

'Fair enough. I know what you mean. Can't let them have that much power over us, either, right?' Erica said.

'Exactly.'

'Have you heard about the play? I think your Gemma's going to have a part.'

'Yeah. I've heard about it. No way I'd act, but I'd love to help by building the set or something. That's one of the reasons I need to get over this agoraphobia, or whatever it is. Are you going to have a part?'

'Nooo waaay. I'm happy to stay well behind the scenes, thank you very much. And not because of … you know …' she said, waving a hand.

'Fair enough.'

'I'll be doing the makeup. Jennifer, who's organising it, is lovely, so we'll all be in safe hands, I'm sure.'

'She's very good on the lead,' Jimmy said, nodding at Bruce after they'd been silently walking for a few minutes.

'Yes. And I'll bet it's a very new concept for her, too. Though sadly being on a chain is not, I don't imagine. Uh, here we go.' Erica pulled out a bag from the little plastic container attached to the lead as Bruce stopped and squatted. 'Ooh, clever girl, right by the bin. Thank you, miss.'

'Poor dog. I feel the need to turn away and give her her privacy,' Jimmy said, and did just that.

'Yes, the indignity of it all,' Erica said, bending down and carefully picking up the warm pile with the bag, cringing as she did. 'Thank goodness you're such a lovely girl – makes this bit much easier to bear. And I'm so glad I don't have to carry a warm bag of poo around for the next half hour,' she said, putting the bag in the bin. 'Good girl, Bruce.'

'Yes, quite. Good girl, Bruce.'

Erica noticed Jimmy expanding again with the taking of a big, deep breath and letting out another large puff of condensation from his mouth.

'Good to be out?' she asked, smiling warmly at him.

'Yup. Can't believe I've been locked away for so long.'

'I can. I don't know how I'd be if I hadn't taken this job, a big part of which is talking to people.'

'Hmm. It's just mind over matter, isn't it?'

'Yes and no. It's a very real fear and a perfectly valid reaction to what you've been through, in my opinion. But I'm no medical expert. Remember, you had the additional and longer-term stress of the unknown that I didn't have. Sorry, not that I'm making comparisons. It's not a competition. What I'm saying is to be kind to yourself. We all can only cope with what we're dealt the best way we can.'

'Yeah. Thanks.'

'You'll get there,' Erica said, touching his arm. 'I've been listening to some guided meditations. Walter put me onto a great app. It might not be your thing, but it's helping calm me right down. Here,' she said, stopping. 'I'll text you a screenshot so you'll have it. Just in case. No pressure, though. Sorry, can't do two things at once – walk and text, that is.'

'Haha. And here I was thinking all women were the queens of multi-tasking,' he said, waiting beside her.

'There you go. Might be useful,' she said, putting her phone back into her jacket pocket and walking on.

'Thanks,' he said as they both heard his phone click.

'Multi-tasking?' Erica said. 'Load of bullshit. Not that we – I – can't. But I do think you run the risk of doing a whole heap of things badly. I'm more about focussing on the one task and doing it well. Like you and your cakes and baking.'

'Hmm. I hadn't really thought of it like that. Haven't really thought at all about multi-tasking – we men don't have that same pressure put on us. We're just considered incapable meat-heads who can only do one thing at a time, which suits me just fine.

'I think women have got a raw deal all round – this pressure to be everything to everyone at the same time: career, smashing glass ceilings, raising kids, doing most of the housework et cetera. And all while being paid less, when you *are* in paid work, and ultimately ending up with a shitload less super. It's pretty fucked up.'

'I agree. It sure is.' *You'll make someone a great husband one day.* But she kept the words to herself.

They trudged on, having to go single file once they got to the narrow dirt walking track that was the result of many feet of people making their way beside the creek. It was running and, though beautiful, the trickling of the water over the rocks made conversation difficult, especially now they weren't walking side by side. Poor Bruce was often having to slog through the grass alongside the track, too.

'This is so lovely, Erica,' Jimmy said, catching up to Erica when the track became wide enough again for the three of them to fit. 'Thank you for pushing me to come out.'

'Hey, that was all you. Shall we go across the bridge or keep going up that way? It looks like most people go this way, judging by the wear on the track,' she said, pausing.

'Yep.'

'I hope we're not going to get lost. Though, as long as we keep the town in sight, we'll be okay, I think,' she said, as if to herself.

'I've been taking note, so we can always turn around and head back the way we came if we find we can't go full circle,' Jimmy said.

'Oh, good one. I haven't. Walking and taking note being too much for my addled brain.'

A few minutes later they were standing before another bridge – this one suspended by cables, very narrow and lined with timber boards. A sign said there was to be no swinging or running.

'I'm going to wait until you get across,' Jimmy said.

'Hmm. Not sure how Bruce is going to go. Can you go first, miss?' The dog looked at the bridge. 'Please don't tell me I'll have to carry you – you're heavy.'

'I don't mind carrying her, but it'll be hard because of the instability of the bridge. Just take it slow and sort of nudge her along. It's perfectly safe because of the mesh at the sides, so she can't fall off.'

'Go on, off you go, Bruce,' Erica urged. The dog placed a paw on the timber and then another.

She was going fine until Erica had left the bank and the bridge began to move. Bruce stopped and crouched down.

'Uh-oh. Keep going, there's a good girl,' she said, giving the dog a gentle shove with her leg. She didn't want to bend down, which meant letting go of the sides. 'I don't like it either, but it's not far.' As if having become used to the movement in those few moments, Bruce suddenly got up and carefully made her way forwards.

Safely on the other side, Erica watched while Jimmy came over, the bridge swinging scarily from the tiniest movement.

'Phew, thank goodness for that,' he said. 'I think I'll give this a miss next time.'

'Yes, me too.'

'Lucky Bruce having such a low centre of gravity.'

They were at the back of the caravan park and Erica knew exactly where she was now. They walked out to the street and along to the office with the bakery across the road and stopped.

'Thanks so much for your company,' Erica said, and found herself flinging her arms around Jimmy and hugging him.

'Thank *you*. It's been great. Amazing,' he said, squeezing her back. 'Thank you, Bruce,' he said when they had parted. He bent down and let the dog sniff his hand. He was rewarded with a lick. And then Bruce jumped up and put her paws on his thighs again.

'I think you've just been approved of – again,' Erica said. 'I really probably should be telling her off for jumping up, right? But I can't bring myself to.'

'No. I know what you mean. She's lovely.'

'Good girl,' Erica said, giving the dog a pat when she was back on all four feet. 'Just no doing that with muddy paws or with small children and frail old ladies, or anyone else who wouldn't appreciate it,' she said, ruffling the dog's ears.

'Okay, I'll see you tomorrow – or not; up to you,' Jimmy said. 'See ya. Have a good day.'

'You too.' Erica waited until Jimmy had closed the gate behind him and waved as he let himself into the caravan. Erica waved too, and then continued around the back to the entrance to the flat. As she was climbing the steps, her phone pinged. She dragged it out and paused. It was a text from Jimmy: *Thanks for waiting. I really appreciate it.*

No worries, she wrote back, adding a thumbs up emoji.

'What a perfect morning, Bruce. Breakfast time,' she said, unlocking the door to the flat and letting them in. She unclipped the dog lead and smiled as Bruce went to her bed and curled up in it out of the way. 'Good girl.'

As she stood unable to take her eyes off the lovely dog, she marvelled at how relaxed they both were. *This is a perfect moment*, she thought, and made a conscious effort to commit it to memory. She was thrilled with how quickly and easily Bruce had settled in and also felt really good about helping Jimmy take that next step to freedom. Not that she'd done much.

Jimmy also gave a very nice hug, she thought as she got bowls out for her and Bruce.

Chapter Thirty-one

Erica was just packing up for the day when the front office door opened. She looked up to see Jimmy looking about him, eyes big and darting, skin ashen.

Oh. 'Hello there,' she said, unable to keep the surprise from her voice and no doubt from her features. 'You're out and about!' *Der. Way to state the obvious, Mum*, she heard Mackenzie's voice say in her mind.

He swallowed several times before speaking. 'Yes. Hi, Erica. I'm ...'

She moved out from behind the counter. Bruce followed and went over to Jimmy and looked up, her tail waving back and forth.

'Hello there, Bruce. Have you had a good day?' Jimmy said, rubbing the dog's ears.

'Hello,' Walter said, appearing from down the back hall.

'Walter, this is Jimmy – who lives behind the bakery,' Erica said.

'It's great to finally meet you,' Walter said, holding out his hand.

'Likewise,' Jimmy said, accepting Walter's hand. 'Sorry I didn't come to your dinner that night at your place,' he said. 'Thanks for the invitation. I just ...' He blushed slightly and gazed at the floor.

'You're welcome. And it's not a problem at all. There'll be a next time,' Walter said.

Erica watched Jimmy take a deep breath, as if summoning something from within.

'I've had a few issues with crowds of people. Well, being with people, really,' Jimmy said, looking up. His cheeks were flaming and Erica's heart surged towards him at seeing his discomfort. 'But I'm getting better.'

'That's the main thing,' Walter said. 'Good for you.'

'Thanks to Erica and Bruce here,' Jimmy added.

'That's excellent news. I'll get out of your way. I'm heading off – just going to leave some paperwork on the desk for you, Erica,' Walter said, moving past them.

'Sorry if I'm disturbing you,' Jimmy said.

'You're not. Not at all,' Walter said. 'Bye, Bruce,' he said, patting the dog, who had turned towards him, as he passed. 'You're a good, good girl.' He ruffled her ears and was rewarded with a lick when he finished.

'See, Walter,' Erica wanted to say, 'she's fine with you.' But she was still a little stunned at Jimmy being there in front of her. He also looked a bit different, she realised, and couldn't place how or why for a moment beyond the fact he was in the wrong context – she was used to only seeing him at the bakery or his caravan or in the pale light of early morning.

Ah, that's it, he's dressed up more than usual. He was usually in khaki or navy workwear, but here he was in well-fitting jeans, navy jumper and relaxed chocolate brown suede coat.

'I was wondering if you'd like to have an early dinner at the pub with me,' Jimmy said as the silence began to stretch into awkward territory. *As in a date?* Erica wondered. *Oh dear. I hope not.* 'You'd be welcome to join us, Walter.' *Excellent, not a date, then.*

'Oh, thanks, Jimmy, but I'm a bit weary to be honest. I need to get home. Next time?'

'Okay. No worries.'

Erica couldn't say no to the pleading look in Jimmy's eyes. He seemed almost frightened that she might. And she sympathised with how hard just walking across the road at this hour – in broad daylight – to ask this question might have been for him. 'I'd love to join you,' she said. 'Oh. But I have Bruce. Not sure I should leave her unattended yet in the flat.' She looked at the dog, who looked back at her, tail swaying.

'You could leave her here – in the office,' Walter suggested. 'Or I'm sure if you go to the pub down that way,' he said, pointing, 'they'll let you have her in the beer garden. They have those big heaters, but you might still be a bit cold. Anyway, I'll leave you to it. See you tomorrow, Erica and Bruce. Jimmy, it was lovely to meet you. Enjoy your evening.'

'You too, Walter,' Jimmy said. Erica noticed he seemed a lot more comfortable now.

'Wait there, Jimmy. I'll just get my handbag and coat and Bruce's lead,' Erica said, moving back behind the counter again. 'Let's try the beer garden and if it's a problem I'll bring Bruce back here. Okay, let's go. Come on, Bruce, there's a good girl.' She put on her thick coat and hooked the lead onto the dog's collar.

'Thanks so much for this, Erica,' Jimmy said, waiting outside on the step with Bruce while Erica locked the office door behind them.

'Thanks for inviting me. It's hardly an imposition, Jimmy. I'm keen for a meal out and, just between you and me, I'd rather have company. So, you're doing me a favour.'

'Oh. Great.'

Erica noticed his shoulders and also facial features seemed to relax.

'They won't take meal orders until six, so do you want to go for a walk first?' he said.

'Um. No, not dressed like this,' Erica said.

'Oh, yeah, sorry. I didn't think.'

'It's okay – no need to apologise. I'm happy to go now and sit and have a drink. But only if you're up for that,' she said, putting her hand on his arm for emphasis. 'Honestly, you need to do what you need to do. I know just being here now is a big step. Sorry if I'm sounding patronising. I don't mean to.'

'You're not. You're being a good caring friend. And I'm really grateful. You know what? Let's go and be normal people – me, that is, not you; you're very normal already – and sit and linger,' Jimmy said.

'Are you sure?'

'No. But it's what I think I need to do.'

Erica watched as he took a deep breath and stepped off the final step and onto the pavement. 'Come on, Bruce, you'll look after us, won't you?' she said.

Erica was pleased to find the outdoor courtyard area was furnished with artificial turf so Bruce had something soft and insulated on which to lie down. She hadn't quite thought about that and idly wondered if she should get some kind of mat to carry with her. She hated seeing dogs on hard, cold – or hot, for that matter – concrete while their owners socialised. Thankfully they were also in a corner out of any breeze and under the heater, which was so efficient Erica had to shed her coat. She wondered if the hotel staff even noticed Bruce at their feet. There hadn't been anyone to ask when they'd arrived – the only person they saw was the young woman behind the bar who took their orders and also eventually brought their meals out.

They enjoyed a drink – both sticking to lemon, lime and bitters – and then a schnitzel before leaving at around seven p.m. Erica made a mental note to tell Issy and Mackenzie she might have found an even better schnitzel than the ones they'd had at the pub at the other end of the street.

'Thanks so much again, Erica,' Jimmy said, as they left.

'No worries. Happy to help. How are you feeling?'

'Okay. Good, actually. It was almost a bit of an anticlimax – in that I'm now thinking: what was I so worried about?' Jimmy said.

'I know what you mean. The worry and procrastination is often worse than the actual thing you're bothered by. What's that quote? I think it's "We have nothing to fear but fear itself", isn't it? Or something similar. It's so true, but still we humans worry …' she said, shaking her head sardonically.

'Yes. Exactly,' Jimmy said. 'Honestly, I feel like a new man. I used to be quite sociable once, before …'

'That's great. I think it's like riding a bike – you're just out of practice and have to get your confidence back again.'

'Yes. I think you're right. Fingers crossed.'

'Would you like to come up for a cuppa?' Erica said as they stopped at the corner by Walter's office. 'I'll understand if you're exhausted or just don't want to. No pressure at all.'

'I know it's only early, but I am a bit knackered, actually. And I've got the usual early start.'

'Fair enough. Don't underestimate what tonight will take out of you emotionally – and physically, for that matter. Stress is exhausting, as is facing and overcoming fears.'

'Yeah. Thanks so much for understanding,' he said, hugging her.

'I do. You're not alone,' she said, feeling a surge of maternal protection towards him.

'Thanks, Bruce – you're a big help too,' he said, giving the dog a pat. Erica had almost forgotten the dog ambling along beside them. 'See you in the morning?' he said, looking at Erica.

'At this stage, yep.'

Again, she waited for him to cross the street and close the gate behind him. As she did, she thought she might have to be careful she didn't leave Bruce somewhere; she was so quiet and well behaved. She returned Jimmy's goodbye wave.

As she went around the side of her building to the back, she had the strange and fleeting thought that this was what Renee meant about people coming into your life right at the perfect moment and for a reason. She'd had Walter. And now Jimmy had her. It was bizarre that they'd had such similar experiences – and positively freaky that it was due to the same person – but it felt good to make a difference in his life.

'You're such a good girl, Bruce,' she said as the dog bounded up the stairs in front of her.

Chapter Thirty-two

'Okay, ready to go? Where's Bruce?' Walter asked on Thursday afternoon.

'In her bed in reception. I just checked,' Erica replied.

They were in the hallway just about to place Milton Barrow in the hearse for his final journey to the nearby cemetery. Erica had done a few of these trips, but today she felt a cloak of overwhelming sadness around her. Knowing it was probably all about Bruce and Erica projecting human emotions onto the dog didn't seem to help. Every time she'd looked at her curled up in the soft bed, she thought the dog looked forlorn. She'd noticed Bruce was occasionally still a little wary near Walter, which made them both sad and him a bit frustrated. Erica could tell. She regularly shuddered at idly wondering what the poor dog might have been through and had to overcome.

They'd discussed taking her with them, but Walter had said it was too soon. Erica agreed they couldn't risk the dog getting in the way and tripping someone over by getting underfoot. And there was the lingering question over the comment about her being too nippy. She supposed it just wasn't worth the risk until they knew her better. Though she'd spent a lot of time with Bruce and hadn't had any issues – the dog had been beautifully behaved.

She did of course have in the back of her mind Michelle's story about the time she'd taken Daphne into the child care centre she managed – where she'd caused utter mayhem – as a reminder that dogs could be unpredictable at any time. Apparently, Daphne had taken the kids' squealing with fear as squealing with delight, and when they'd hidden under the desks she had sought them out, thinking she was playing hide and seek. And Daphne was impeccably well trained and behaved!

'Never again,' Michelle had declared. 'I see why they say never work with children or animals; what was I thinking mixing both?' Thankfully no one had got into any trouble, though they had brought in a counsellor to talk to the scared kids, just in case. But it had been an 'absolute headfuck', Michelle had said a week later after downing several quick glasses of wine – purely medicinal and absolutely necessary, she'd declared when she'd looked up and noticed her friends' raised eyebrows at both her drinking and spray of foul language, in neither of which she usually indulged. All the while Daphne, causer of said mayhem, had sat beneath the table with a smug grin on her face.

Having noticed the dog, Renee had laughed and said that perhaps the poor dog hadn't relished spending time with children, either, and had deliberately got her wish for it to be a once-off event.

'As if she's that clever,' Michelle had said.

But it had left Erica wondering. Renee always said animals were smarter than humans gave them credit for. And often smarter than humans, full stop. Michelle usually agreed, but had been mentally too scarred by Daphne's recent shenanigans to do so right then.

Bruce had barked several times spontaneously and randomly and had even growled on a few occasions. At absolutely nothing, as far as Walter and Erica could tell.

She didn't tell Walter, but it triggered her trauma and she became jumpy all over again – not that she'd completely stopped being like that.

'Maybe there *are* ghosts in here,' Walter had said idly while going through some paperwork at the desk, not pausing or looking up at one bout of barking.

'Stop it, Bruce,' he'd commanded and the dog had. Erica hoped the dog's behaviour had something to do with its previous master still being in the building and that peace would reign after today's service.

'Right. Good to go?' Walter asked when they were all loaded and seated in the hearse in the garage at the back of the building.

'Yep,' Erica replied and snapped her seatbelt closed as the roller door behind the hearse went up.

At the cemetery, Erica wished whoever was in charge had planted some trees. As it was, it was quite desolate. She thought this every time she came out here. They obviously needed to leave space around the perimeter to keep extending the area, and she supposed there wasn't enough of a gap between the rows of graves for planting. It was neat and tidy, which was more important, she decided. And at least out here it was unlikely anyone would be required to take their relative's headstone because the grave was needed for someone else, as she'd heard was happening in the city, where they'd run out of space. Here paddocks left bare or planted with crops came up to the fence.

They'd just finished getting everything set up and greeted Jennifer, who was officiating, when the first car arrived. Today was just a graveside service – no church or hall portion first.

They'd come out earlier and set up the portable gazebo for shade. It also doubled as protection from rain, but today was fine.

As they'd left to go back to get Milton, Erica had been about to query if it was safe to leave the gazebo unattended – she'd have offered to stay with it – but then reminded herself that this was the country.

They greeted Edith and Aiden and the rest of the family surrounding them and ushered them to their seats. Erica noticed Edith was now using a walker with wheels and seemed to have aged a lot since they'd seen her standing outside her house just a matter of days earlier. It caused another wave of sadness to roll through her, but she pushed it away to focus on the event.

It turned out to be a small gathering – they'd ended up printing far too many of the service sheets.

They had just pressed play for the first piece of music in the service when out of the corner of her eye Erica noticed a dog trotting across the gravel towards them. It was a blue heeler who looked just like ... Bruce ...

Oh, fuck, it is *Bruce!* She tried to catch Walter's eye, but he was looking at the ground at his feet on the other side of the grave from Erica. Erica watched the dog trot over to Edith Barrow and sit not at her feet, but right on top of them, her head between the old lady's knees, her eyes looking up at her. Edith patted the dog and then leant forwards and wrapped her arms around Bruce's face, having to bend down low and close to the dog.

'Bruce!' Erica heard one of the young granddaughters exclaim, only to be silenced by a glare from her father and a tap on the hand by her mother on her other side.

Erica held her breath, not sure what to do. How the hell had the dog got there?

No, it must be a different dog, she thought, relaxing slightly. Bruce didn't really have any distinguishing features; she was just a blue stubby thickset cattle dog. No doubt she was sister to this one. She relaxed a little. Yes, that was it. Bruce was locked up safely back at the office – they'd made sure.

But hadn't the girl said her name? She must have misheard. Erica looked up at the same moment Walter did. His mouth went into an O shape and she was sure accompanying the tilt of his head towards the dog and the frown etched in his face were the mouthed words, *What the hell?* Erica made her eyes wide and shrugged slightly in response. She thought she heard Jennifer clear her throat.

Soon the service was almost over and she was handing out flowers to those present to toss into the casket along with their final thoughts or words. Today it was heads of lavender in their basket – from someone's garden and dropped in earlier that morning by a friend of the family.

After a while the scent started to bother Erica. Her nose really *had* become super-sensitive since leaving her job on the ground floor of David Jones. It didn't help that everyone seemed to be inadvertently crushing the lavender heads – or perhaps on purpose – before releasing them.

When the casket had been fully lowered and the small crowd dispersed, Aiden Barrow came over and, ignoring Jennifer but glaring from Walter to Erica and back again, hissed, 'What the fuck is that stupid dog doing here?'

'Oh, so it *is* Bruce, then?' Walter said.

'Of course it's bloody Bruce! It's your bloody dog. Well, you took it in.'

Suddenly Erica wondered where Bruce had gone – she'd got caught up with finishing the service and had lost track of her.

She and Walter turned and looked over and there was Bruce still sitting at Mrs Barrow's feet.

'With all due respect, Aiden, she doesn't seem to be doing any harm,' Walter said.

'In fact, your mother appears to be enjoying her company,' Jennifer chimed in.

Without another word, Aiden stalked away and gathered his wife and son to him. Then, as if as an afterthought, he went to his mother – left alone with one of the young grandchildren and Bruce. He was clearly the head of the remaining household. The other adult siblings stood by silently, having been herded into a small group. Erica gasped as he gave Bruce a shove with his foot. She glanced at Walter, who said in a growl, 'Aiden. Don't you dare be cruel to the dog.' Erica was a little shocked, but wanted to throw her arms around Walter for defending the creature.

'Yes, Daddy, don't hurt Bruce,' the child said.

'Aiden,' Edith said, in a half-hearted warning tone.

Erica watched them leave and, when they couldn't see her, looked at Walter, who had his lips pursed and was shaking his head slowly from side to side. She'd never seen him look so stern. And it was her fault – she'd assured him Bruce was locked up safe and sound.

Keen to mitigate some of the damage, Erica strode over to where Edith Barrow was being shoved into an empty wheelchair by her son.

'I can walk,' Edith snapped. 'I'm not dead yet.'

'Edith, Mrs Barrow, I'm really sorry about Bruce's intrusion.'

'I'm not; it was a lovely surprise.'

'Oh. Um, well, does that mean you want to take her back?' Erica held her breath as she waited for the reply. She looked from Edith to the child beside her, who she thought looked about eight.

'Dad won't let us have her,' said the child.

'And I can't: I'm being put into the home. Thank you for taking her,' Edith said.

Erica was careful to let her breath out quietly. 'She's a lovely dog. Though, a little bit naughty, judging by today's antics,' she added, smiling.

'Can I come and visit Bruce some time?' asked the girl standing beside her grandmother.

'Yes, of course you can. Any time you like,' Erica said, a little startled at realising how young the child looked up close. 'Perhaps I could bring her to visit you at the home, too, Mrs Barrow.'

'Oh. That might be nice. But only if it's no trouble. Thank you,' Mrs Barrow said, and gave Erica's hand a squeeze.

'Come on,' Aiden Barrow said.

'Thanks for everything,' Mrs Barrow said to Walter and Erica as she was pushed past them.

Erica suddenly remembered Bruce and reached down and grabbed her collar as she was about to move past.

'Sorry, Bruce, you naughty girl, you're with us. God, Walter, I am so, so sorry,' Erica said when the family was out of earshot. 'I can't believe she slipped past me and out the doors at some point without me noticing. But she must have.'

'I didn't see her escaping either, and she would have had to go out under the back roller door. We'd better be more vigilant in future – for one, we don't want her getting hit by a car. As for today, what's done is done; no point worrying about it now,' he said with a wave of his hand.

'I thought it was a great addition to the service,' Jennifer said, with a cheeky twinkle to her eye. 'Well, I must be off. I'll see you good people again soon. And you, Bruce – you were the star of today's show. Made my day, you did – no offence, Walter and Erica,' she added as she patted Bruce.

The three of them hugged briefly and said goodbye. Erica held Bruce's collar while Jennifer drove away, before letting her go while they packed up.

'I shouldn't say it, but some services leave you feeling disappointed in humans,' Walter said as they were packing the gazebo into its carry case. 'And that was one of them.'

'Hmm,' Erica said, nodding. She followed Walter's gaze as it landed on Bruce, who was now sitting in the sun, the picture of innocence.

'Well, at least we know Bruce can behave with other people. You're not nippy at all, are you, lovely girl?' he added, bending down to ruffle the dog's ears.

Erica joined in. 'Aiden was pretty pissed off,' she said.

'Yes. But something tells me that's probably just his usual MO. Did you get the impression Edith didn't want to give up Bruce?'

'I did. And I also thought it looked like she was being made out to be frailer than she really is. Though that could be my imagination,' Erica said.

'No, I think you're spot on. I suspect she's being shipped off into an old folks' home before her time to get her out of the way, but I didn't say that out loud.'

'Elder abuse, you mean?' Erica said.

'Yes, but obviously I have no proof. And financial abuse could be at play, too – out here with generations of farming families it wouldn't surprise me if they both went hand in hand.'

'So, what can we do?'

'Nothing. We have no evidence of anything untoward. Unfortunately, being grumpy and disrespectful isn't a crime. And every family is different. Take your pick of clichés.'

'But that's a bit, um …' Erica was lost.

'Defeatist?'

'Yeah.'

'It's none of our business. As I said, we have no proof of anything untoward – certainly not illegal. You'll go mad if you take on other people's problems and try to fix them, Erica. Our job was to treat everyone with respect and give Milton a satisfactory send-off based on his and his loved ones' wishes. And that's exactly what we've done. And, remember, each person handles loss in their own way. What we've seen is maybe their grief and how they're dealing with things.'

'I guess.'

'Anyway, don't forget, we've technically gone way beyond our duty in taking in our friend Bruce here.'

'She's so lovely. I still think it's awful they didn't want her.'

'Well, it's our gain. I've seen a lot of callousness out here. Don't let the media reports of everyone banding together during emergencies fool you that these places are warm and fuzzy all the time. A lot of terrible things go on behind closed doors and behind silos when no one is looking. You just haven't been here long enough to see it or hear about it. I hope you only ever come across the good, but, sadly, that's unlikely. They don't say life on the land is hard for nothing. I think in a lot of cases it makes you hard, too.'

'That's sad.'

'Yep, and it's a fact, which is why we can't afford to get too caught up in things that don't directly affect us. If we become jaded, we can't do our jobs well.'

'No, I suppose not.'

'Sorry, I'm rambling now. I agree, it's sad. And I hear you. But it is what it is and not our business.'

'I guess at least they can't really come and demand Bruce back now we've changed her registration details, can they? I'd be devastated.'

'True. But we'll have to keep a better eye on missy here, who has proven to be a slippery little sucker, haven't you, you naughty girl?'

'I wonder if she knew it was Milton in the car or just didn't want to be left behind on her own,' Erica mused.

'No idea. But, like you say, she's proved she can be trusted to be included. Or not trusted to be left behind, actually,' Walter said with a laugh. 'Just what have we taken on?' He sighed as they clambered into the front of the hearse, with Bruce climbing onto Erica to get into the centre seat, where she sat up looking out of the window, appearing to be very pleased with herself.

'Are you right there?' Erica said with a laugh to the dog.

'Apparently,' Walter said, giving Bruce a pat. 'Lucky this car has a bench seat. I wish she had her harness on, though,' he said, as he started the vehicle.

Chapter Thirty-three

On Friday afternoon, Erica was sure she'd just heard the office's front door open and close, but when she looked up a few moments later, after finishing her note so as not to forget, there was no one there. She frowned and tried to ignore the shiver creeping up and down her spine. *There are no ghosts in here*, she told herself firmly. *Oh. Bruce.* The dog's demeanour would be a sure indicator. She turned to check if the dog was still snoozing in her bed, and almost leapt out of her chair.

Bruce was in fact in her bed. But sitting cross-legged beside her, just a couple of metres away, was a little girl dressed in the local primary school uniform of maroon windcheater and navy pants. Erica stood up so she had a complete view of the office in front of the reception desk in order to check for the whereabouts of the child's parents. But the space was empty. She sat back down.

'Hello, there,' Erica said, facing the dog and the child.

'Hello,' said the child quietly, looking up at Erica. At that moment Erica knew who she was – the granddaughter of Bruce's former owner. The girl who'd been beside Edith Barrow at the funeral.

'You're one of Milton Barrow's granddaughters, aren't you?' she said.

'Yes, she was my grandpa's dog. I've come to say goodbye to her properly. I didn't really get the chance yesterday at the funeral.'

Oh. God, you poor child.

'I'm Eliza, by the way,' the girl said.

'Hello, Eliza, I'm Erica.'

'I know. I remember you,' Eliza said, having turned back around to face Bruce.

'Um, how did you know where she'd be?'

'Well, this is where *I'd* put her bed if *I* had a dog in an office,' Eliza declared.

Right. Okay, then, Erica thought, trying not to smile too broadly. *You're quite the cutie, aren't you, Eliza?*

'Thanks again for taking her. And having her inside. Bruce, you're going to be very happy with Walter and Erica, okay? You'll be safe. There's nothing to be scared about here. And it's not your fault my dad doesn't like you, okay? You're lovely,' Eliza said, stroking the dog's head rhythmically.

'Is there a reason your dad doesn't like her?' Erica wondered if there was something she and Walter should know, and while she didn't think it was perhaps quite ethical to quiz a small child – was she even eight? – without a parent present, she went ahead nonetheless. She was keen to know as much as possible about the dog.

'Because she was Grandpa's dog – they didn't like each other very much.'

'Oh, why's that?'

'Because he's a mean old bastard – Grandpa, apparently.'

Erica had to force herself not to smile at the precociousness and matter-of-fact delivery.

The child's hand stroking Bruce didn't miss a beat. 'That's what Dad says. But he's mean, too, so he can't talk. Adults are very confusing,' she said, frowning. Erica watched as Eliza's shoulders rose and fell. The child took a deep breath and then sighed it out.

'Yes, they can be,' Erica said, choosing her words carefully. She watched as Bruce stretched out and exposed her belly, clearly happy with all the attention she was receiving.

'Do your parents know you're here? Are you meant to be in school?' Erica said, suddenly thinking to check her watch. *Primary school kids don't have free periods, do they?*

'No. And yes,' Eliza said.

'Um, okay …?'

'Yes, I'm meant to be at school. And, no, my parents don't know where I am,' Eliza said, her slight exasperation evident.

'Because you're meant to be in school?'

'Exactly.' Eliza returned her attention to stroking Bruce's belly.

'You're going to get me in trouble,' Erica said. She longed to gather the child to her and give her a big hug.

'Sorry.' But Eliza made no move to get up and leave.

'Are you missing your grandpa?'

'Hmm. A bit. Can I tell you something?'

'You sure can.'

Eliza stared down at Bruce's tummy. Erica watched her fingers drawing circles on the smooth, soft skin.

'I think he's better off dead,' Eliza finally said.

'Oh.'

'I know you're not allowed to say that. It's not because I think he's in heaven or a better place, or whatever – that's absolute bullshit, if you ask me. It doesn't even make sense.'

'Right. Just between you and me, I quite agree. But don't tell anyone,' Erica said.

'Okay. I'm good at keeping secrets.'

I bet you are, Erica thought, though she couldn't help wondering what she might be holding onto if she was this open about these aspects of her family life. The thought made her uneasy. 'So why is your grandpa better off dead?' she asked.

'Because he was in pain.'

Ahh. 'Because he had a stroke, right?' Erica said.

'No. His heart hurt.'

Erica frowned to herself. She was sure Milton Barrow had died from a stroke.

'It was broken a long time ago.'

'Oh?'

'It's why he and Dad didn't get along.'

'Did something happen?'

'Yes. Dad blames him for my little sister dying. And Grandpa blamed himself.'

Oh shit. Oh my god. Erica swallowed. She was a little lost with how to deal with this. She could also sense impending doom, that somehow this was going to come back and bite her later. She was glad the girl had her back to her. 'I'm so sorry, Eliza.'

'Thanks. It's okay. I still have a brother. But I do miss Milly, though. She drowned in the dam. At Grandpa's place.'

Oh. Oh, Milton. 'That's so sad. I see why you say your grandpa had a broken heart.'

'Yes, he never forgave himself. That's what Mum says. She's still sad. Dad's just angry. It's all a bit of a mess, really.'

Oh, sweetheart.

'Do you know what I think, Erica?' said Eliza, who had turned and was now looking up at her, her big blue eyes filled with tears. Erica tried to swallow down the lump lodged in her own throat.

'What's that, Eliza?' she said.

'If people were kinder, the world would be a much better place,' Eliza said.

'Yes, you're so right there,' Erica said with a croak. She cleared her throat a little noisily. 'Are you able to talk to your parents about how you're feeling? Or maybe your teacher?'

'Kind of. Not really. No one listens. I'm just a kid,' she said sadly, bending down and kissing Bruce's belly. 'I'm not allowed to be sad. I have to put on a happy face. And Mum and Dad don't need me to worry about, on top of everything else. So, basically, everything is pretty shit. But it will get better.'

'It will,' Erica agreed.

'When?'

'I don't know. Sorry. Sorry, I know that's not helpful.'

'That's okay. Adults often aren't.'

'We don't always have the answers because sometimes there is no answer, unfortunately. I've lost people I loved myself and I know that I'm at times very sad and … and some days are less sad than others. But, and I know this is going to sound like one of those horribly annoying things grown-ups say that doesn't really make sense, but I think your grandpa would like you to be positive about the future and enjoy your life. And make the most of it. Does that make sense?'

'Sort of. You mean he wouldn't want me being upset because of him, don't you?'

'Exactly.'

'I wish I could have Bruce. Sorry, I know she's yours now and that would make you and Walter very sad. And, anyway, it's never going to happen …'

'Are you absolutely sure?'

Eliza nodded. The big glistening eyes were now trained on Erica. 'We don't have sheep now, so no use for a sheepdog and no money to feed an extra mouth not pulling its weight. That's what Dad says. You'll be okay, Bruce,' she said, burying her face in the dog's tummy. 'Grandpa loved you. And I love you. I'll never forget you.' She gave the dog a kiss on the face and scrambled to her feet. 'I'd better go. I don't want you getting into trouble, too.' She kept her gaze down, but Erica knew she must be in tears. How could she not be?

Before Erica could say a word, she was being hugged and kissed on the cheek. 'Thank you,' Eliza whispered, and then ran around the counter to the front door. She disappeared outside and the door clunked closed behind her a moment later.

Erica went and poked her head outside to make sure Eliza got back to school safely, returning to her desk only after she'd seen the child run through the gate and disappear. For ages Erica tried to engross herself back in her work, but kept being distracted by thoughts of the encounter with Eliza. Her heart ached for the child and she longed to help. But she knew she couldn't. She swivelled her chair around to look at Bruce. The dog looked fine.

'Greetings! I'm back!' Walter said jovially, coming in from the back. 'Oh. Are you okay? What's happened?' he asked, looking at Erica.

'Nothing really.'

'But something's up, because you look like you've just dropped your last dollar down a drain.'

'I just had a visit from Eliza, Edith Barrow's granddaughter. The one with her at the funeral.'

'Oh?'

Erica took him through the encounter.

'Oh my god. The poor thing,' he said, sitting down heavily on his chair. 'I didn't know anything about that. Mary and I weren't engaged to do the service and I don't even recall hearing whispers.

That's odd, though perhaps not, given they live so far out of town – they're not really Melrose locals. It puts rather a different slant on things. And I suppose goes some way to explaining why Milton was buried in the Melrose cemetery just down the road. I wonder where young Milly is interred – I'm thinking not there, because the family didn't hang around to visit any other graves. How utterly heartbreaking.' He shook his head slowly. 'That darling little girl … Unfortunately, adults have a knack of disregarding children and being overprotective all at once. A bit like what might have gone on with your parents and your brother's death, maybe. Disappointing to think how often history repeats …'

'Hmm.' *God, you're right. Probably nothing has changed and it's four decades on.* But there was no point dwelling on it. 'She seemed both really young and fragile and very grown up,' Erica said.

'Well, sadly, I think that's what life on the land can do. Kids are introduced to harsh realities from a very early age and at times in a very matter-of-fact manner. I think it's both a blessing and a curse – in many ways. Hands-on and practical; they're instantly quite grown up. But also, I suspect, emotionally stunted – that's a bit harsh, but I can't think of a better word; short-changed, maybe – because of not working through that side of things adequately, due to being so capable physically. If that makes sense? I'm not a medical expert, obviously, so it's just my observation.'

'I guess it's a bit like how they say children aren't *born* racist, but life makes them like that, and by life, I mean we, adults.'

'Yes. Exactly. Sadly, hurt people hurt people – themselves and others … Oh, hello. Thank you. Yes, you're a beautiful girl.'

Erica turned her chair back around to find Bruce had got out of her bed and was sitting in front of Walter with her head on his knee, looking up at him. He rubbed her face.

'How could anyone not want you is a mystery to me,' he said. 'And I'm so sorry you've had a rough life and you don't fully trust me.' He bent down and kissed her on the head. And when he lifted his head, Erica saw tears in his eyes. 'Oh god,' he said, rubbing his face with his hands. 'I seem to have got something in my eye.' He pulled a tissue from the nearby box, and blew his nose. 'I'm being a sentimental old fool,' he muttered. 'Look what you're doing to me, Bruce, love. I'm not even a dog person. Well, I don't know about you, but I need a cup of tea after all that,' Walter said, getting up. 'How about you, Erica?'

'Yes please. White English breakfast, thanks.'

'Coming right up.'

Chapter Thirty-four

Erica became anxious when a little later she heard the door open again. She was sure she was going to be told off by one of Eliza's parents, or a teacher. But it was someone she hadn't met. He looked a bit familiar – most likely he'd been at one of the funerals. Lots of people were now familiar to Erica – all of the same people seemed to attend most funerals. He was a man in his late seventies or early eighties, she estimated. He looked around, taking in the space as if he was looking for someone or something, or perhaps not entirely sure where he was. Erica stood up.

'Hello. Can I help you?' she said.

'Sadly, yes.'

Erica grabbed a clipboard with an empty form and space for notes, came out from behind the counter and around to the front.

'I'm Erica,' she said, holding out her hand. He changed the grey fedora-style felt hat he held in his right hand to his left and accepted her hand.

'David Turner,' he said. 'I need to organise my wife's funeral.'

A lump lodged in Erica's throat in response to seeing the tears in his eyes.

He cleared his throat before speaking again. 'She's just gone. In some ways a blessing, but ...' He shrugged. 'If they haven't already, the nursing home in Laura will be calling Walter shortly.'

'I'm so sorry for your loss. Come through here,' Erica said, ushering him into their reception room. 'Can I get you a cup of tea?'

'Oh, that would be lovely, thank you.'

'You have a seat and I'll be back in a moment.' Erica pulled the door closed, but was careful not to latch it so she could push it open in a few minutes with her hands full with two mugs. In the kitchen she poured another mug of tea for the newcomer. 'A David Turner has just come in,' she explained to Walter. 'His wife has just passed. He said the nursing home in Laura will call you.'

'Right. Okay. I know the name, but I don't think I've met him or his wife before. Are you okay to ...?'

'Yes, fine, thanks.'

When Erica went back across to the room, she was surprised to notice the door was ajar. Had David Turner changed his mind and left? She pushed it open fully with her hip and stopped when she entered at seeing Bruce curled up on the chesterfield leather couch beside him, her head in his lap. The man was stroking the dog's sleek blue-grey coat while murmuring quietly to her.

'Here we are,' she said, putting down the mugs. 'I hope she's not bothering you and you're okay with dogs,' she said. She thought to shut the door, but left it open in case Bruce needed to get out.

'Oh yes. I had to give up my wonderful companion a few years ago to move into an aged care facility. I've missed her so much.

I hadn't quite realised just how much until this lovely thing joined me. My Suzie was a blue heeler too. Very intuitive and clever creatures.'

'This is Bruce.'

'Oh.' The man frowned and looked down at her.

'Yes, she's a she named Bruce. That wasn't our doing,' Erica said, offering a crooked grin. She wanted to say: 'She's a rescue; though I'm not sure who's rescuing who.' But she refrained.

'It's nice to be an individual, isn't it, Bruce?' David Turner said.

Erica longed to get out her phone and snap a picture of the scene in front of her, such were the times. Instead, she resolved to commit it to memory.

'Tell me about your wife,' she said, carefully extracting the pen attached to the clipboard, ready to take note of anything that might be useful for a service.

'Agnes.'

'Tell me about Agnes,' Erica urged.

Erica wrote as David told her about his wife – how they met, their life together, which had been spent farming and being heavily involved with horses: competing in the early days and then both as judges and coaches of several disciplines until very recently. All the while he stroked Bruce. At some point his eyes had closed.

Erica didn't notice Walter enter until she heard the click of a photo being taken. That wasn't surprising because David was quite loud – most likely a bit on the deaf side, she concluded. She stayed in her position making notes, but sent silent thanks to Walter for being on the same wavelength. With his eyes still closed and too engrossed in his story and interaction with Bruce, David didn't seem to notice Walter moving around the room taking shots from several angles.

Checking David still had his eyes closed, Erica looked up at Walter and smiled and mouthed the words *Thank you* as he moved back towards the door to leave. Walter nodded and winked and left the room quietly. She hoped they weren't breaching some kind of privacy code or industry ethics, but that was Walter's department. And he was honest through and through, so wouldn't do anything untoward.

She returned her attention to David's voice.

'Thank you – you've been lovely,' David Turner finally said after his second cup of tea and having gone through details of his wife's service with Erica, which was going to be held at the farm, now being run by their two daughters, with Agnes's ashes scattered beneath her favourite gum tree. 'That's a huge weight off my mind.'

'I'm glad,' Erica said.

They left the room together.

'And thank you, lovely Bruce. You've warmed the cockles of this old man's heart. A great idea to have a dog on hand. It really helps,' he said to Erica.

She nodded and smiled.

Walter was behind the desk. He stood up. 'David Turner?' he said.

'Yes.'

'I'm Walter Crossley,' he said, coming around and shaking hands with their latest client. 'Firstly, I'm so sorry for your loss. The nursing home in Laura has just this moment called so I'll be heading off very soon. Please rest assured we'll take very good care of Agnes.'

'Thank you. I know you will. We haven't met properly before, but I know of you and your business by reputation. You're the best there is around here.'

'I appreciate you saying – thank you. Now I really hope you don't mind and please tell me if I'm overstepping, and I'll absolutely abide by your wishes if … Well, I noticed you with Bruce and I couldn't resist snapping a few photos. They're quite something, I'm sure you'll agree.'

'That'll be down to your skill and the lovely Bruce, I suspect, rather than this sad and tired old codger,' David said.

'Come around here, please,' Walter said, leading the way to back behind the desk. 'I'd like you to see. And …' He pointed to the computer screen.

'Oh. Goodness me. Could I perhaps trouble you for a copy? I'd like to print it out. You see, your dog reminds me so much of my old girl. And I agree, it is a lovely shot of both of us – if I'm allowed to be so bold as to say.'

'Actually, I was wondering if you would agree to us using one or more of them on our website and social media – show them online, to the public. You see Bruce here is a very new addition to the business: a valuable one, we think, too. We'd like to promote that fact, being as it's a point of difference for us, too – and a candid photo is much better than a staged one.'

'What a great idea – having a dog as part of things, that is. I was just saying that to Erica. Yes, I'm fine with appearing online. That's perfectly okay with me.'

'Thank you so much. In return I'd be very pleased to have some printed for you and supply them on a USB stick if you wish. Or in addition to.'

'Great. Thanks. I'd like that – both options. I'd better go now. I told my daughters I'd be out to see them at four. Thank you again for taking a huge weight off my mind,' he said, clasping first Erica's and then Walter's hand in both of his.

'It's a difficult time. We understand that. You have our card. Please don't hesitate to call if you think of anything else,' Erica said.

'Yes, goodbye,' Walter said with a wave.

Erica and Bruce walked David Turner to the door.

'Oh, one other thing,' David said, turning back.

'Yes?'

'Would Bruce be able to attend to, you know, offer some additional support? I'll have plenty of family around, but I just …'

'Oh. Yes. Of course. I'm sure she'd like that, wouldn't you, Bruce?'

The dog stepped forwards until she was underneath David's hand. She stood looking up at him with big brown adoring eyes and her thick tail waving slowly back and forth behind her.

'Thank you,' he said, giving her ears a rub. 'Almost makes it bearable,' he muttered. 'Cheerio, then,' he said and raised his hat.

'Bye for now,' Erica said, and closed the door behind him.

'You'll never know how beautiful and important and wonderful you are, Bruce,' she said, bending down and patting the dog.

She went back to her desk and sat down and looked at Walter, who was now sitting in his chair. 'Wow,' she said.

'Yes, that about sums it up,' Walter said.

They both watched as Bruce settled herself in her plush bed with a deep sigh.

'She's something special all right. How lucky are we?' Walter said.

'Yep. Incredibly.' Erica made a mental note to phone Renee and – at the risk of her friend kindly saying 'I told you so' – point out the incredible timing and circumstances. She really was beginning to see what Renee meant when she went on about everything fitting together in the great puzzle that was life.

'Well done on those photos, Walter,' Erica said.

'Thanks. I wasn't sure it was quite the right thing to do, but couldn't resist. All's well that ends well. At least on that score. And now I'd better head off and collect poor Agnes.'

Chapter Thirty-five

Over the weekend, Erica was disappointed not to have had Jimmy's company while walking, and he couldn't make it the first couple of days of the new week, either. It was now Tuesday evening. He'd texted saying he was busy helping Gemma, and sent some images. Erica hoped he was doing okay and that that wasn't an excuse – that he'd retreated again. She was hopefully seeing Gemma that night, so would tactfully enquire after him.

Erica had received a text on Sunday saying the first meeting for the play was at Jennifer's house in Port Pirie on Tuesday at seven p.m. Walter had made some phone calls and she was soon to be collected by Roy, Gemma's father, who was apparently insisting on taking his vehicle – a seven-seater four-wheel drive. Erica liked the idea of being part of a group excursion.

'Hi, Gemma,' Erica said, a little breathlessly, having almost run late. She'd been talking to Bruce and having trouble tearing herself away. The rest of the group was already settled in the vehicle, with the exception of Gemma who'd had to wait outside to let Erica in.

'Hiya,' Gemma said, standing back to allow Erica past.

'Thanks,' Erica said as she clambered through the gap behind the seat bent forward and into the very back of the large vehicle. As she did, she was surprised to see Jimmy seated just ahead of her and next to Peggy.

'Hi, everyone,' Erica said, putting her seatbelt on. 'Thanks so much for this, Roy,' she said.

'All good,' Roy said from the driver's seat, waving his hand in acknowledgment. 'I hope you're okay all the way back there.'

'It's great – I've got a good view from here,' Erica said.

'You were more than welcome to bring Bruce – I was expecting to meet this dog I keep hearing great things about,' Roy said. 'Right, if we're all correct and accounted for, we'll get this show on the road,' he added, putting the vehicle in gear and pulling out from the kerb.

'I thought I'd spare us all the doggy breath and your car from dribble,' Erica said. 'She's adjusted very well to life inside, though.'

'As in, she's sprawled across her bed and didn't show any interest in heading out again?' Walter said, turning to look back from the very front seat beside Roy.

'Exactly,' Erica said with a laugh. 'We've been trying to teach her to fetch in the office, haven't we, Walter?'

'Yes, and at this point it's safe to say we're the ones doing all the fetching – and getting the most exercise in the process, for that matter. I reckon she thinks she's too old for games. Or perhaps too clever. The look of disdain she offers is quite hilarious, isn't it, Erica?'

'Oh yes. I swear, sometimes she's got her eyebrows raised as if to say, "Really?" It's too funny.'

'She sounds like quite the character,' Roy said.

'She's that all right. Certainly keeping us on our toes, right, Erica?'

'Yep. But enough of us going on like proud new parents,' Erica said. 'How are you going, Peggy?'

'Doing okay, thanks, Erica.'

'Good to hear,' Erica said.

'Hi, Jimmy. It seems like ages since I've seen you. How's everything?' She reached forwards and gave his shoulder a squeeze.

'Yes, I've missed you. It's all been a bit hectic. The weather warming up means events and catering – weddings, anniversaries, birthdays …' Jimmy said.

'And thank goodness I've got you, Jimmy,' Gemma said. 'It means I can take on more. And Geraldine Jones's death means Jimmy's had to step up to offer fancy cakes too now. I hate to profit from that, but …'

'Someone has to – it may as well be you,' Peggy said. 'I knew Geraldine well and I'm sure she would approve.'

'Thanks, Peggy,' Gemma said.

'Yes, thanks for saying, Peggy,' Jimmy said.

'That's fantastic. So, you're, um, doing okay, then? I've loved seeing the pictures of your cakes and the functions you've sent through,' Erica said.

'I'm loving it. I've even done a consultation by myself with a bride and groom, and with a couple celebrating their fortieth wedding anniversary, and I've been fine. I didn't even get freaked out being in the crowd at a wedding on Saturday.'

'That's fantastic. Well done. Are you going to still be able to help with the play?' Erica asked.

'Possibly not on the night, but I can work on sets whenever. I've found a whole lot of energy I didn't realise I'd lost.' He shifted

in his seat, turned around and beamed at her. There was barely a
hint of the nervous man she'd last seen. Her heart soared. She was
thrilled for him. In fact, the whole car was alive with buoyant,
effervescent energy.

'I hope Jennifer has found enough people,' Peggy said.

'She must have, otherwise I suppose we wouldn't have been
called to a meeting. Would we?' Roy said.

'You're right. It must mean it's going ahead,' Peggy said.

'Sorry, I didn't mean to sound so blunt,' Roy said.

'It's okay, I didn't take it that way, Roy. I'm fine. I've got a
thicker skin than that,' Peggy said.

'Goodo.'

It had been a little over a week since Walter's dinner and the
first mention of the play. Erica wasn't surprised Jennifer had
gathered them so soon, though she had been starting to wonder if
it would go ahead.

'I wonder what play you're going to be doing,' Erica said.

'Still not going to have a part yourself, then?' Jimmy said.

'Nope. Definitely not,' she said.

'I'm disappointed, but also a bit relieved I don't have the time
for an acting role. Doing that might have given me the confidence
to be in front of cameras and then maybe I could apply for one of
the bake-off TV shows,' Jimmy said.

'Well, maybe you'll be just fine without it. I mean, being
on TV, just as you are,' Walter said, turning partially in his seat
towards them.

'Yes. That's exactly what my friend Renee would say,' Erica
said in an attempt to expel the sudden rush of anxiety that was
gripping her. *Just hormones*, she told herself. *Be gone, please. Breathe
through it.*

She admired Jimmy's desire to push himself to overcome this fear of being the centre of attention and a part of her wished she had the same strength. She held a similar fear within, not that she was confessing it to anyone.

She wasn't sure where it came from – perhaps it had just always been part of her. Though weren't most people terrified of public speaking? *So, I'm just normal, right?*

Why then does thinking about the stage give me the absolute heebie-jeebies – and when I'm not even contemplating doing it?

Erica reluctantly allowed herself to wonder whether the anxiety might not actually be related to her hormones and menopause. Something inside her had clearly been triggered.

Oh my god. Stage fright! I was in that school play. In primary school. Well, I was meant to be … Hang on a second …

She remembered practising lines, over and over, with class-mates. A dress rehearsal. Lights. Bright lights. And then flickering ones. Ah, a spotlight onstage. And then cameras. Some kind of commotion. *What happened?* But just like every other time, it all began slipping from her mind.

'I don't mind making a fool of myself,' Walter said. 'I reckon that comes with advanced age – losing the self-consciousness.'

Oh god. Not me. No way. Not again. Her face began to flame. One thing she thought was certain back then; she'd made a fool of herself. Another jolt of fear bolted through her. Something had gone horribly wrong. Erica really didn't want to remember how or why and this time was content to let any recollection slip away. She returned her attention to the chatting group in the car, thankful that she was in the back where no one could see her discomfort.

'Which is why you will be brilliant,' Peggy said.

'Well, we'll see about that.'

'You might uncover a whole new talent and passion you didn't realise you had, Walter,' Peggy said.

'I think my issue might be remembering my lines. The old memory isn't quite what it once was,' Walter said, tapping the side of his head with a finger.

'My excuse around that is having too much other more important stuff going on up here,' Roy said, taking one hand briefly off the steering wheel and tapping his head too. 'There's only so much you can fit in. Well, that's my story and I'm sticking to it. I kind of hope the play is a comedy so if we stuff it up the audience will still laugh – even if not in the expected way. She didn't say what it was the other night, did she?'

'No, she didn't. I fancy a whodunnit – Agatha Christie style,' Peggy said. 'Or even a modern take on one.'

'Yes, that would be fun,' Gemma said.

Despite being right on time, the group was the last to arrive. Jennifer ushered them inside and into her lounge room where they were introduced to several other people already seated, including Phillipa and Lloyd, who Erica had met at Walter's dinner party. They mumbled greetings and took their seats.

'Righto, folks, bit of shoosh, thanks,' Jennifer said. 'So, we're all go, people. Firstly, we have a play. But we'll discuss the nitty gritty of that in a bit.' Erica noticed a stack of paper on her lap under her notebook. 'A friend of Ingrid's here, Claire Thomas, is an emerging playwright, and she'd love us to put on her new play, and, best of all, not charge us anything for the privilege. So, win-win. It's called *Beware the Price of Progress!* and is described as: *A cautionary tale about telling the truth, being kind, minding your own business and looking out for one another in the age of social media and internet scams,*' she read. 'It has something for everyone. A bit of humour, a gentle crime running through it, and a lesson for all of us,' Jennifer added.

There were oohs and aahs and a general air of excitement and anticipation in the room. Now she knew what it was about, Erica was able to ignore the jagged unease of anxiety passing through her.

'And, if you're all in agreement, I'd like it to be a fundraiser for something in the area of mental health, anxiety support or suicide prevention – I haven't decided which area or particular organisation as yet. Feel free to send me your suggestions, if you have any.

'So, I'm thinking the best bet is to have our performance on the October long weekend – Saturday the first,' Jennifer continued.

There was a collective intake of breath.

'Yes, it's not far away. It gives us a month. But I think it's achievable. And I reckon if we don't have a tight timeframe, we might lose our steam along the way. Hopefully we can get some audience from further afield that way too – because of the long weekend, obviously. So, hands up who agrees with that – well, everything really?'

All hands went up.

'Any issues or questions at this point? Just on what's been mentioned so far.'

Everyone shook their head and murmured no, they had no questions.

'Brilliant. That's settled, then.' She made a note in the notebook on her lap. 'I'd like to have our performance in the Melrose Hall, if that's okay with you all. My reasoning is, other than the town's gorgeous aesthetics, it makes sense because lots of people tend to head up that way for long weekends and school holidays. I've enquired and it's available, so have made a tentative booking. Any objections?' No hands were raised and there was much nodding and agreement around the group of what a good idea that was.

Next Jennifer went through the list and descriptions of cast members, allocating each person to a role in the play and outside of it – front of house, set design and the rest – and then asked if anyone had any issues.

Erica was amazed at how smoothly this was going. She'd been on several committees connected with the girls' schooling and it had been nothing like this.

'John from John's Hardware here in town has very generously agreed to donate anything we need for set design, including delivery or loan of a ute for transporting, if necessary. So, Jimmy, if it's okay with you, I'll put you in touch with him direct to sort all that out in due course …'

Jimmy nodded.

'… and also writer Claire Thomas to discuss her vision for that side of things. We want to do it justice. Oh, and also someone for lighting once I know who. John thinks his niece, Sahara, might be interested – she's young, creative and a whiz with tech, apparently, and also happens to be an electrician, which I'm sure will be a bonus. So, fingers crossed!'

'Yep. All good with me,' Jimmy said.

'Excellent. How exciting. You're all being brilliant!'

That's because we have a brilliant leader, Erica thought with awe.

'Thank you so much, everyone. This is a long-held dream of mine, so it means such a lot that you're all here and willing to help me realise it. And our chosen organisation will be very grateful for whatever funds we raise, too, I'm sure. Right, so any questions?'

'How come you're not having an acting role?' Robert, Ingrid's husband, asked. They had just been assigned the lead roles.

'Oh god. I don't want to be onstage. I think you'll all agree I'm best off being the producer-director.'

'Not necessarily. I think you'd be great in any of the roles,' Walter said.

There was a round of murmurs of agreement.

'You're too kind, Walter – and you all – but I'm happy in my role, thanks. And I think it's best I leave myself available to organise the ancillary events. I'm hoping, if I can swing it, to make quite the weekend of it – afterparty on the Sunday with spit roasts. Another fundraiser. But we'll see. First things first.'

'I think that's a great idea. We should be able to help with catering, shouldn't we, Jimmy?' Gemma said.

'Absolutely,' Jimmy said.

'Thank you. But as I say, that's a discussion for another time. I haven't quite got my head around how that looks at this point.

'How about Tuesday evenings and all weekends going forward for rehearsal – starting with this next one, obviously? And the other question is, do you want to alternate the venue for meetings? The options are Walter's office – okay, Walter?'

'Yes. Absolutely. I'm thinking the garage might be even better – it's clean enough and there's stacks of space when the vehicles are out.'

'And Robert and Ingrid have kindly offered to have us to their home in Laura, too. We'll most likely have to pay to hire the hall, so it's not really feasible to do all our rehearsing there. Thoughts?'

A discussion ensued, which ultimately went around and around several times until Jennifer stepped in. 'How about Ingrid and Robert's place in Laura this Saturday at nine-thirty a.m. and then take it from there? See how we feel after that. Okay?'

There were murmurs of agreement. Erica marvelled at how quickly Jennifer could wrest control back.

'I'm happy to do lunch for us all this weekend – off the top of my head, sandwiches, quiche and salad. Perhaps even lasagne. I need to have a think,' Ingrid said. 'So, let me know – and perhaps Jennifer, too – if you have any dietary requirements.'

'You beat me to it. I was going to suggest we all bring our own, but that's great if you want to do it. Now, I think that's most things on my list covered. Here are your scripts,' she said, handing out the booklets.

'Do you want a contribution for printing costs – for these and what's going to come up later?' Jimmy asked.

'Oh. I wouldn't mind. That would be a big help,' Jennifer said.

'And I'd be happy to offer my office facilities if necessary, too,' Walter said.

'Great. Thanks, Walter. I'll keep it in mind,' Jennifer said.

'How would twenty dollars each work – to start with?' Jimmy said. 'I'd be happy with that, though I don't have any cash on me at the moment.'

'Fine with me,' Walter said, getting out his wallet.

'I'm happy to contribute that amount, too, but don't carry cash on me these days, either,' Ingrid said. 'I can get some out when I do the groceries and give it to you Saturday – okay?'

'Same – the amount is fine with me – though I'm in the same boat with not having cash on me as well, sorry,' Robert said.

'And it'll have to be an IOU from me, too, I'm afraid,' Phillipa said.

'Hang on a sec, folks. Firstly, that's very kind, and I accept with much appreciation – thank you – but how about I provide you all with direct deposit details and we do it that way? I've opened a new online account specifically for the play,' Jennifer said.

There was another round of nods and murmurs of agreement.

'Okay then, that's on the to do list,' she said, writing a note. 'Thanks again, everyone. Now, Erica, your Issy and Mackenzie seemed keen, that night at Walter's, to help with publicity their end. Do you think they still would be?'

'I'll ask them and let you know. I'm sure they'll be fine, but I don't like to presume – I've learnt that lesson along the way.'

'Yes, I can imagine,' Jennifer said with a laugh. 'Thanks.'

'I know that lesson well, too,' Ingrid said quietly, leaning towards Erica and grinning.

'Actually, I'll just text them now,' Erica said, getting out her phone. 'Though I probably won't hear from them until tomorrow. Issy was actually hoping we might be doing a musical she could have joined a chorus for – given she's so far away.'

'Oh well, maybe next time. Or perhaps if this gets a decent response, we could do a talent search type event another year. God, listen to me. Focus, Jennifer. First things first. One thing I almost missed on my list is how we're all going to communicate. We need to sort that out. I'm wondering if email is okay – that's my preference. I'll set us up as a group. But I might be persuaded to go the Facebook group route, if anyone has strong views. Bearing in mind, this is just our communication – between ourselves. I'll set up a Facebook page for the event. Sorry, they're the only two mediums I'm the slightest bit up with. I'm happy to discuss other social media options anyone is au fait with for promoting the event, but can we leave that until the weekend? So, hands up those in favour of using email. Oh. Okay, email it is then. Please fill in this form with all your contact details,' she said, handing around a single-page spreadsheet.

'Oh, this is going to be fabulous,' Jennifer said while she waited for the form to come back around. 'I can feel it. Thanks, everyone.

I think we're close to being done for tonight. Unless anyone has anything pressing to add?'

There were mumbles of no, all good and plenty of shaking of heads.

'No? Okay, then, I'll type up my notes and email as an attachment. Of course, I hope things don't change, but nothing is for certain. So, please, if you need to pull out or anything happens, please, please, *please* let me know at your earliest convenience so I can shuffle things if need be. And, that's me. Thanks again, people. Oh, and to make life easier, can we please do our best to keep email threads to separate topics and make the subject clear up the top?'

There was another round of nods and rumblings of agreement.

'No doubt I've forgotten something,' Jennifer said, reading down her notes.

'As if, Jennifer,' Ingrid said.

'Yes, that's highly unlikely, I would think,' Walter said.

'Too kind, too kind,' Jennifer said. 'Feel free to email me if you think of anything at all. I might be bossy, but I'm not above being corrected. So, with no further ado, I declare our first meeting officially closed. See you Saturday – the address will be in the first email. Please do your best to memorise your parts. Now, I'm really sorry, folks, but I'm going to have to kick you all out now on account of it being a "school night",' she said, adding quote marks above her head with her fingers. Erica smiled at how much the gesture reminded her of her girls. She missed their company and mannerisms – even their sarcasm and eye-rolling and telling her to get with the program or the times.

'I'm excited,' Walter said when they were all back in the car and heading home.

'I like that she runs such a tight ship,' Peggy said.

'I don't think I've ever been to a meeting that has only gone for an hour. That's pretty impressive,' Walter said.

'Yes, it gives one great certainty, which is a comfort, I find,' Roy said.

'I'm not sure anything to do with the theatre can be certain, Dad,' Gemma said.

'No, you're probably right there.'

'Or comfortable, for that matter,' Peggy said.

'No, true,' Roy said.

'I really hope it all comes together okay. It will be good to help fulfil Jennifer's dream and raise money,' Erica said.

'Yes,' Walter said.

'The long weekend is a good idea, but it's a pity that rules you out, Gemma and Jimmy,' Roy said.

'Yes. Well, don't write us off just yet, Dad – we'll see how bookings go and what they are. We might end up being available on the night, yet. And I'm sure we can fit in some extra catering for everyone,' Gemma said.

'Yes, that's an important part of it. Anything can go wrong and we'll all still be happy if we've got full bellies,' Peggy said.

'I agree with you on that score, Peggy,' Walter said.

'I'm glad we won't have to be sewing costumes,' Peggy said. 'My eyes aren't what they were for that sort of thing.'

'Yes. Helpful that it's a contemporary piece and ordinary characters,' Roy said.

They lapsed in and out of silence and were all yawning heavily and regularly when they finally drove into Melrose and then pulled up in front of Walter's house, despite it only being nine o'clock.

'See you outside the bakery again on Saturday at nine a.m., if not before,' Roy said.

Walter paused with his door open. 'Are you okay to take your car and drive again?'

'Oh yes, no problem at all.'

'I'm happy to contribute petrol money,' Walter said, getting out.

'So am I,' Jimmy said.

'And me,' Erica said.

'Thank you, but it's not necessary,' Roy said.

'Well, if you change your mind, let me know,' Walter said, and climbed out. 'Thanks for the ride.'

'I can walk from here too, Roy, to save you the trouble,' Erica said. She didn't want to, but it felt right to at least offer.

'Yes, me too,' Jimmy said, with even less exuberance than Erica.

'Honestly, it's really no trouble. There's more palaver involved with getting you out from back there. Anyway, there's no proper pavement up here or decent lighting; I'm not having twisted ankles on my watch! So, just sit tight for a few more moments.'

'Thanks, Roy, I appreciate it.'

'Are you up for a walk in the morning?' Erica asked Jimmy as they stood on the pavement.

'Probably not. I'll have to let you know.'

'Okay. No pressure.'

As Erica let herself into the flat, she marvelled at how quickly she'd got used to Jimmy's company on her walks and craved it, even after just a few days. She'd enjoyed their couple of conversations about the US and a few other places they'd both been, and she liked being distracted from her own thoughts for a while. But at least she had Bruce, poor conversationalist that she was.

'Bruce, I'm home,' she called. The dog, with a just-woken-up tiredness to her eyes and gait, strolled across the flat towards her, pausing to have a big stretch on the way. Erica felt bad for waking her.

Part Three

Chapter Thirty-six

The weather gods turned on a beautiful early spring day for Agnes Turner's funeral at the family farm, which was aided by the two p.m. timeslot – being a perfect time after the sun had burnt off the overnight chill and before the cool of evening rolled in. Also warming Erica, but this time from the inside out, was her bursting love for and pride in Bruce, who was seated beside David on the wooden bench beneath Agnes's favourite tree, where her ashes would be scattered later. The dog had leapt up and straight away laid down beside David, with her head on his lap, just as back in the office a few days prior, and then sat up and to attention during the eulogy read by his two daughters and four teenage grandchildren, who were dressed in matching riding attire ready to perform the team riding demonstration, choreographed to music, which they'd been working on with Agnes. Erica had been excited, as had David sounded, when he'd called the day before to tell her the kids were okay to go ahead. Their matching grey ponies stood nearby, tacked up ready, held by a couple of friends.

Erica had been introduced to everyone earlier but she'd promptly forgotten the friends' names in her determination to not get any of the identities of David's nearest and dearest wrong – his daughters, Carol and Tina; and teenage grandchildren, Joel, Alice, Toby and Evie. Well, she hoped she had the grandkids right – they were all so alike dressed in matching cream jodhpurs, short brown boots, Bermuda blue jackets and sunglasses.

As the ponies moved past, she tensed in readiness to leap the few metres and attempt to stop Bruce if she decided to disgrace herself and chase after them – not that she thought she'd ever be quick enough to catch the dog if really put to the test. Thankfully Bruce remained perfectly still, clearly as enthralled as everyone else there, possibly encouraged by David's arm around her, and Erica relaxed. Out of the corner of her eye she thought she saw Walter and Jennifer ease in their stance too, stood behind the rows of chairs set out for the seventy or so mourners.

The music took Erica by surprise – all she'd been told was that the kids needed a total of twenty minutes in the schedule for a display of some sort. ABBA's 'Chiquitita' caused her to choke up – it was one of her favourite songs of all time.

As she watched the kids pair up, split off, become a row of all four together, and cross tracks in single file, all the time going around in time and with paces that matched the music's tempo, she thought she'd never seen anything so beautiful, nor any better tribute by grandchildren to a grandmother.

With the song only five and a quarter minutes long, she was disappointed when their display was finished and all four lined up facing David, who stood, his cheeks streaked and glistening in the sun, and returned their salute with a firm nod. He then began to clap, joined in loudly by everyone.

A ripple of laughter rang out when Bruce stood up and let out an equally hearty, 'Woof, woof,' which set off a bout of cheering. The kids grinned and responded by bowing down low over their horses' necks before straightening up again and riding off to leave the arena and untack their steeds ready for the final part of the service – the scattering of Agnes's ashes – just before afternoon tea was served.

The shadows were long when Walter, Erica and Bruce headed back to the office. (Jennifer had left a bit earlier for an appointment with a bride and groom for their upcoming wedding.) Carol and Tina walked with them the rest of the way out to the car after saying goodbye to David, who had been waylaid by the grandchildren showing him something on one of their devices. Out of their father's hearing Carol and Tina excitedly told Walter and Erica they'd found a beautiful adult male blue heeler called Ted and were driving to Whyalla the following day to collect him from the RSPCA shelter. They'd gone on to say that David couldn't have Ted at the nursing home, but he would live at the farm with them and be there whenever he visited and, if he turned out to be as amenable as Bruce, they'd take him regularly to Laura to visit him and the other seniors. Erica was thrilled for David and she and Walter spoke over the top of one another when they asked them to send some pictures of Ted and for David to keep them updated and to also please bring the dog in to meet them at the office before too long.

'Did you hear that, Bruce?' Walter had said, looking into the rear-vision mirror as they drove off, more buoyed than ever before after leaving a funeral service. 'It's thanks to your wonderfulness that David Turner will have a canine companion in his life again. And a rescue one at that. How fabulous.'

'Thank goodness she didn't decide to chase or round up the horses. Wasn't the kids' riding display incredible? I could have watched that for hours. And that song: beautiful, but it was a bit of a sad reminder. I'm a huge ABBA fan, thanks to my parents – though I don't recall much, if any, music being played in the house after Mark died.'

'Hmm. I can imagine. I've been a bit the same since losing Mary. I used to turn up the volume inside so we could hear it when we were out in the garden, but I haven't recently. I'm actually quite the closet ABBA fan myself,' Walter said, shooting Erica a cheeky grin.

'Oh, Walter, why keep it in the closet? We'll have to do something about that! Speaking of parents – and I hope you don't mind me completely changing the subject –'

'No. Not at all. What is it?'

'The play. This is sort of tongue in cheek, but goodness, it's all a bit close to home for me – what with the step-siblings trying to sort through their parents' messy financials and them being in a nursing home and everything.'

'Yes. I can imagine it's triggering all sorts of things for you. I really appreciate you running lines with me – that's what Jennifer said it was officially called, didn't she? I'm really not up with the lingo – but do say if it gets too much for you. I will completely understand.'

'I will. Thanks. I'm sure I'll be fine, and I'm really enjoying doing it.' With all the happenstance she'd discovered, or accepted, recently, Erica couldn't help wondering if there might be a reason for the play and her involvement in it – albeit on the periphery.

'Two heads are always better than one, I reckon. But go on, you were talking about the content of the play being all too familiar.'

'Oh, it doesn't matter. It just makes me wonder how different – harder or easier – everything would have been if Mark were still alive. And of course it's a reminder that I'm on my own and have to deal with all this stuff alone now Stuart's gone. Just when you start to think you're getting on top of the grief or through it, or whatever, it comes back and slaps you in the face. Sorry, I'm ruining the mood,' Erica said.

'Don't be. And you're not. I get it. It's good to talk about these things. As I say far too often, and you're probably sick of hearing: grief is a complicated business. I'm not convinced that ever changes – just gets a little more comfortable to live with over time.

'But back to the play: I find it a little triggering myself, mainly due to my advancing age. I get far too many of those scam phone calls. I'm so mindful of saying "speaking" in response to the "Is that Walter Crossley?" question in case it's recording the "yes" ready to then drain my bank account or something. I probably come across a bit pompous or blunt to some clients but so be it. And then there's the emails – so easy to inadvertently click on one of the malicious links. It's a damned minefield. *Beware the Price of Progress* indeed – perfect title for the play!'

'Yes. I shudder to think of people like your character Edwin and Peggy's Olive getting roped into giving the scammer remote access to their computer and having their funds drained. Not to mention their adult children having to pick up the pieces – like Ingrid and Robert as Heidi and Martin,' Erica said.

'It happens quite a bit by all accounts. It doesn't help that we're all trying to remain independent for as long as we can so don't want to ask for help – in so many areas. Especially technology, I think, because the young ones can be so impatient. Not so much recently, but my Peter has been known to get quite exasperated.

And I like to think I don't do too badly with the tech side of things.'

'Honestly, I think technology is just the current theme for discord; doesn't every generation say the young ones are perpetually annoyed with their elders and vice versa?'

'True. Since the dawn of time, I'd bet,' Walter said. 'I do like that Claire has written something that focuses on a pertinent and current issue, and has handled it in such a clever and entertaining way. But goodness, yes, it's a bit close to home in parts. I have to say, I love her twist at the end where it turns out it's the granddaughter of one of the other residents who is the scammer. That's clever.'

'Yes. And it means we get a rare instance of closure with the perpetrator being caught and the victim getting their money back. So, yay for that,' Erica said.

'How someone would even go about hacking a computer or setting up a scam boggles my mind.'

'Hmm. Mine too. Speaking of technology, has Peggy told you Jimmy's taught her how to use video calling and is helping her with her lines?' *I really hope he's feeling okay about the storyline, being as the perpetrator turns out to be a young woman.*

'Yes, isn't it marvellous? They've become firm friends. I'm so pleased for them both – and it does go to show young ones and older ones can knock about together quite well. Well, obviously, look at us, for that matter!' Walter said.

'Exactly!' Erica smiled to herself. She took a slightly deeper breath and luxuriated in the warm sun coming through the window.

'And I think he's quite enamoured with young Sahara – wasn't she a boon find for our lighting and backstage?' Walter continued. 'Everyone is fantastic, but her arrival on Sunday was a surprise breath of fresh air. I don't want to jinx things, but so far it's all working brilliantly. And her idea for doing a soundtrack for extra voices, since we don't have enough extras, well, that's pure genius. Not that I know anything at all about theatre goings-on.'

'Yes. I thought that was absolutely brilliant as well. As was Jimmy's idea to do the cut-outs of extra people standing and sitting so that when they're turned around they become trees and shrubbery for the garden scene. That positively blew my mind!'

'Mine too. We're surrounded by so many clever people. And I'm having an absolute ball being entertained and distracted and feeling part of something much bigger than just my little life. I've never really found a local organisation that does what this is doing for me – though I might not be saying that in a few weeks when I'm having trouble remembering my lines and I'm scared of letting Jennifer and everyone else down.'

'You're going to be great, Walter. I know it. Your enthusiasm will get you over the line. And, remember there's some leeway for you to ad lib – I like that about the script, too.'

'Thanks for the vote of confidence. Yes, good point about the script. At least we can work on it in the office – I really appreciate you helping me, in case I haven't already thanked you.'

'You have. And it's my pleasure.' Erica felt a little left out, not having a part, but also kept reminding herself that her main job was on the night doing the makeup. That was important too. And she'd also told Jennifer she was happy to do any fetching and carrying, and had committed to Jimmy to lend a hand painting the sets when they were ready. Not that it was significant, but she'd also committed to providing biscuits or cake for the weekend sessions to help keep everyone going after the choc chip ones she'd made on a whim the Saturday just gone had been such a hit. Also heartily embraced had been Bruce, who she'd taken along after checking it was okay with the group.

'Jennifer's timing couldn't have been more perfect. I feel like spring has sprung in the most magical way – and right across my life. I honestly can't remember when I last felt this bright about things. Maybe I'll be completely done in and fed up by the time the performance is finished with – and thank goodness my part mainly involves remaining seated – but right now I can't help being disappointed that it'll be over all too soon. I have a feeling the time is going to simply fly by.'

'Hmm. Me too.'

Chapter Thirty-seven

Walter was right about the rest of the month leading up to the play passing by very quickly and Erica knew for certain she would remember the time as one of the most enjoyable of her life. She'd found utter joy in mixing with her new group of eclectic friends and preparing for the play and festivities afterwards.

What had started as Jennifer's idea to put on a play for fun and entertainment and raise a bit of money in the process, had quickly – with the speed and intensity of a hurricane, they all joked – turned into an entire weekend carnival-style fundraising event, with, in addition to the main catered lunch, live entertainment, sideshow attractions, market stalls and several auctions – silent and otherwise.

Adding to Erica's good vibe, too, she knew, was spring having settled in with warmer weather, brighter light all round and an eruption of fresh green foliage. The whole group had been bubbling with excitement this last week at the gorgeous weather they'd scored for their event, which also meant an influx of visiting fair-weather cyclists and grey nomads. There was a vibrancy and congestion in the street that Erica hadn't known before, and she thought it was wonderful.

Though nothing could quite compare to the liveliness and noise going on around her earlier backstage and onstage behind the closed burgundy curtains while the set was being finalised for their final full dress rehearsal. People had been shouting and racing about and bumping into each other and scurrying in circles and back and forth like mice, or ants in the case of the backstage staff dressed all in black. The nervous energy, general chatter and last-minute panicky exclamations and enquiries of where is this or that or who had even caused Erica's hands to begin to shake and her nerves to jangle in response while doing the hair and makeup. But thanks to the meditation she'd incorporated into her daily routine, she'd taken several deep breaths, steadied herself and managed to get everyone done in plenty of time to be available in case there was anything Jennifer or anyone else needed.

And then, if she hadn't witnessed it for herself, Erica would have scarcely believed just how quiet so many people could suddenly become, particularly a group that had earlier been so boisterous. But when Jennifer held up her hand beside Erica, at the left of stage, the actors behind her fell silent. Then, after receiving confirmation via the radio headsets from each back of house team member, including Erica, she'd counted down in the hush, her voice quiet but clear in Erica's ear.

But as the main spotlight lit up the setting of Peggy and Roy (playing the bewildered and upset grandparents who'd just discovered they'd lost a fair proportion of their life savings to a scammer) and Robert (playing Peggy's stressed-out, I'm-really-far-too-busy-for-this son) seated in the lounge area of an upmarket boutique-style nursing home, a flash of déjà vu and brief roar of anxiety shot through Erica, causing her to almost gasp audibly.

Needing to regain her composure and aware of the necessity for silence and the tight space around the stage in the old hall, she stepped back out of the way of Ingrid (playing Walter's character's daughter and Robert's character's step-sister) who was ready to stride into the scene. Her focussed breathing matched the whoosh of the curtains separating and the groan of the mechanism overhead and she welcomed the cold breeze that swept past her as the gathering fabric came to a halt. Settled again, she repositioned herself ready to feed lines if needed. She doubted anyone would forget anything, though; their rehearsal the previous night, specifically held at the same time as tonight's performance in order to do a final test of all the lighting, had been perfect.

All went splendidly and, after what seemed like it could have been mere minutes or several hours, the curtains closed again. They were ready for tonight's performance.

Still in the wings, Erica could practically feel in her chest the thundering applause and cheers from the small but effusive audience comprised of the crew's nearest and dearest and playwright Claire. Smiling and feeling like a proud mother all over again, and so thrilled to be a part of what was promising to be a hugely fantastic event, she became introspective as she watched the cast onstage holding hands and bowing to the continuing small but mighty roar below them.

She was a little sad that this one would be their last such gathering – it was all ending too soon. Walter had been right. She tried not to think about how after the weekend this would be completely over, because whenever she did she became quite sad and disappointed – like now. For the past week she'd tried to keep the thoughts at bay, but they'd kept poking their way into her consciousness.

While at times it had all been quite exhausting, joy had been the overriding emotion. She'd really miss the busyness, fun and distraction and sense of satisfaction of being part of something for the greater good. Particularly enjoyable had been their painting sessions, which had always started out as readings of the play and ended with raucous karaoke – them all loudly singing into their paintbrushes, rollers and whatever else they could find with a handle to vaguely replicate a microphone. There were also bursts of dancing at tempos ranging from downright lively by the younger ones to little more than a gentle sway on the spot from those of more advanced age. While ABBA and tunes from the eighties were firm favourites, the more youthful in the group, including playwright Claire Thomas, who had tried to get to most weekend meetings, and Chloe, Phillipa and Lloyd's teenage daughter, who had been cast in the role of scammer-slash-computer hacker, had introduced them to some of the latest hits. Walter and Roy trying hard but completely butchering rap lyrics had caused Erica to laugh so hard she'd come awfully close to peeing herself.

Though Erica had also found another hobby to fill some time. She'd been asked to do the makeup for two wedding parties on separate weekends, but had declined – not easily, because the requests had come via the office from long-term clients of Walter's and she hadn't wanted to cause any issues for him. Thankfully he too had been aghast – more affronted than even Erica – at the nerve of both groups of people expecting her to provide her services, equipment and transport for free.

Stuart had tried to push her down that path as a business years earlier and she'd declined. Back then her lack of interest had been as much about not giving up her weekends and being available for her daughters; protecting family time was too important. Now she knew she deserved better than to be taken for granted, no matter how flattering the compliments became. She was allowed to put herself and her needs first, and did.

But, in addition to the focus and setting of the play already front of mind, the requests had given her an idea: offering her services to nearby nursing homes doing nails, hair and makeup for residents wanting such on a big or special birthday, or similar important occasion. She'd been several times and loved every minute of it, especially feeling so valued by her clients, despite her voluntary status. Walter was happy for her to do it during their quiet days, too.

A few of the homes were even keen for her to take Bruce in and on one of her visits she'd chanced upon Edith Barrow, who'd smiled broadly and clapped her hands at seeing the dog approaching, as did precocious granddaughter Eliza, who also happened to be visiting at the time. Erica had beamed back and enjoyed a thoroughly lovely time with them. When she'd left, she'd encountered David Turner and his daughter Carol entering with their blue heeler, Ted, who Walter, Erica and Bruce had already met at their office a few weeks back. The humans had hugged before David had said, 'Great minds think alike, eh?' while grinning and nodding at the two similar-looking dogs, who were happily wagging their tails and sniffing each other as they got reacquainted.

Driving home in Vera with Bruce in the back, thinking about Edith and Eliza's and David and Carol's contented dispositions, despite their recent bereavements, Erica thought she finally saw what Renee meant when she said wealth was about a whole lot more than numbers on a bank balance.

When Jennifer announced that the worthy recipient of their efforts would be a new South Australian charity being started up to train and provide assistance and therapy animals, Erica had been thrilled to the point of needing to swallow down a tightly lodged wedge of emotion.

Like Erica, Jennifer had been stunned and impressed by Bruce's intuition and calming presence, not only at David Turner's wife Agnes's funeral, but at the heart-wrenching service the following week for a seven-year-old boy who'd died after falling from a silo on a farm.

Jennifer and Erica had stood back watching Bruce roam the crowd, as if looking for the person most in need of her succour, and stopping for a cuddle, before moving on again. They'd quietly sighed and mused over how incredible it would be if each school could have a dog like Bruce on hand to help kids deal with these moments and ease the passage of life, or another type of suitable animal.

Erica had told her daughters all about it. Then, just last week on the phone, Issy had declared she now knew what she wanted to do career wise: she was going to study sociology and psychology and ultimately have her own counselling practice, with a focus on animal therapy.

Mackenzie had chimed in that she was going to follow in their father's footsteps and study business so she'd be able to keep her little sister and her business on track when the time came. She'd quipped that someone had to save Issy from herself – she couldn't help a jibe. But both girls were serious, even having already been in contact with their chosen university and got the ball rolling.

They'd both also applied to do some volunteer work with the RSPCA over the upcoming summer – before their uni courses started – in the area of dog handling, and were discussing doing a short course on animal care and training too. Erica couldn't have been prouder of them. She still beamed whenever she recalled the conversation, though at the time she'd almost suggested they should be focussing on finding a flatmate to help with the finances instead. The latest prospect, a guy from Mackenzie's work, had been fired after being caught stealing from the till, which had given them all pause for thought. So far as a team they were keeping on top of expenses. Also, if it wasn't really necessary, Erica knew she'd rather not have someone else in the house when she was finally able to return for a visit. Following this thought she hadn't mentioned the subject again.

Nailing down the charity had served to put a new rocket under the already very driven Jennifer, too. It had been incredible to witness and Erica had been thrilled and honoured to assist her brilliant leadership – even while worrying that her new friend had taken on too much, so much so she'd expressed her concern to the woman herself. But Jennifer had reassured her she was fine, that she was a different person with better coping strategies than when she'd lived in Sydney – namely, a quieter life all round and much lower cost of living.

She'd shared a big chunk of her life story in explanation. Erica had been shocked to learn of how she'd burnt out and that the big business she worked for had shown scant care about her state of mind. They'd sucked her dry and then spat her out, she'd said. And she wasn't alone; apparently treating human resources as inanimate, expendable cogs in the larger corporate machine was a common theme playing out in plenty of businesses all over Australia and probably right around the world. Erica both marvelled and scoffed at the idiocy and short-sightedness of Jennifer's former bosses and the entire company.

Erica had also marvelled at the transformation in Jimmy. He'd blossomed, unfurling like the lotus flower in the logo of her meditation app.

She found it hard to reconcile the new Jimmy with the one who so recently had been housebound, practically paralysed with agoraphobia. He'd turned into a fun, chatty and animated companion with a great sense of humour. They'd continued to walk with Bruce, when they could – venturing onto some of the longer trails just above the town. Erica joked she might have to walk the whole Heysen Trail to combat the amount of food she was consuming as chief taste tester of his various creations.

Gradually the applause dimmed and the cast made their way down the steps and past Erica, offering her high-fives and thanking her for the compliments she uttered as they went, their voices accompanied by the hollow clatter of feet on the polished timber. The noise and excited chatter, starting up as suddenly as if the pause button on a recording had been released, successfully dragged her from her brooding and, recomposed, she joined the end of the group as they moved out into the hall to be debriefed by Jennifer and anyone else who had anything to contribute. Erica made her way across to the empty seat saved for her by Mackenzie and Issy, who had arrived that morning, bringing a welcome breath of fresh air to everything – words spoken by Jennifer, though Erica had been thinking the same thing. Jennifer had got to know them quite well via text and email as they'd willingly assisted from Adelaide with selling tickets, as promised, and even taking over social media. She was going to introduce them to the organisers of the charitable organisation they were fundraising for, too.

Erica was looking forward to seeing Steph, Michelle and Renee, who were arriving that afternoon, just in time for the play, having booked a cottage beside one of the pubs. Erica couldn't wait to see them.

'Oh my god, Mum, you guys were fantastic,' Mackenzie said, as Erica slid in beside her.

'Yes, that was incredible,' Issy said, leaning behind her sister and patting Erica on the shoulder.

Now she wasn't paralysed with fear whenever she thought about being onstage, a tiny part of Erica was really regretting not having an acting part. Yes, she had other important jobs to do, but they were adjacent. Thankfully Jennifer did her best to make everyone feel just as important. But still … Erica's eye was drawn to their lead, Robert, as he held his phone to his ear, and moved away with a finger in his other ear. She then noticed his wife Ingrid move after him towards the hall's front door.

'Okay, listen up, people,' Jennifer said, clapping her hands and then waiting for the roar of excitement and nervousness to completely die down.

Erica turned back to face their leader.

'That was excellent, everyone. Well done. You've all surpassed my wildest expectations. Sorry, I seem to have a little something in my eye,' Jennifer said, blinking and then dabbing at the corners of her eyes with a tissue.

A few people chuckled.

'Okay. So, that's the play under control. We have a few hours to rest up for those who need it. I have a good feeling about tonight. So, really, that's all I have.'

'Yes. You were all great. Thank you. You've made my dreams come true already,' playwright Claire said, turned towards them from her seat at the end of the front row against the left side of the hall. She was smiling but seemed a little uncomfortable with so many pairs of eyes on her.

'Darling, you ain't seen nothing yet,' Roy said.

'I don't want to freak you out, but it looks like a full house, right, Roy?' Jennifer said.

'Yup. It's sure shaping up that way,' he said, checking the notebook he held.

'Right, so I'll leave you to it. Back here at four p.m. sharp, unless you hear otherwise from me. Keep an eye on your phones but please leave them on silent so we don't have any embarrassing mishaps tonight. Okay?'

Murmurs of agreement rambled through those present.

'Righto, you lot, off you go. I need a quiet moment to clear my head and consult my list.'

Chapter Thirty-eight

The room gradually became quiet. Jennifer checked her running sheet. Erica, Issy and Mackenzie hung back along with Peggy, Walter, Jimmy, Gemma, Roy, Phillipa, Lloyd and Chloe. There was still plenty to do behind the scenes and for everything going on tomorrow.

Jimmy looked a little frazzled, but was smiling; he was clearly in his element, Erica thought. She was the same – actually quite enjoying this type of stress and excitement.

She gazed around, taking another moment to admire Jimmy's set – well, sets, plural. There was the interior of the nursing home, which when the panels were turned around became the garden outside of it, and then there was the bedroom of the young hacker that also quickly became the bedroom of her grandfather – one of the residents of the old folks' home. He'd cleverly put concealed wheels on everything so each piece could be turned around or moved quickly by just one person and with minimal effort. The way he'd thought it all through had blown Erica's mind and shown him to be a man of many skill sets and a very clever mind.

Her gaze idly followed Jennifer as she walked across the room, thinking how incredible she was. Not only was she full of energy and passion, but there had been no shouting and everything had been run smoothly: like a well-oiled machine, as her dear old dad would have said.

Erica frowned. *What's happened?* There, over by the wall, were Jennifer and Robert, Ingrid and Claire. Even from this distance Erica could see the paleness of all their faces and the strain in their features, the slump of their shoulders. She stood up and made her way through the chairs towards them, but then stopped. Jennifer was making ushering movements and saying, 'Go, go. Of course, you must go.' Claire was speaking too, but her voice was inaudible, though her waving hands seemed to be reiterating Jennifer's words.

Suddenly the room was quiet, the only sounds being Ingrid's and Robert's hurried footsteps clattering on the wooden floor – clack, clack, clack – and then the clunk of the heavy timber doors closing behind them. Then Jennifer was calling for a bit of shoosh from those still assembled. That was the rest of the cast and crew, actually, Erica realised. As one, they turned and watched while Jennifer, followed by a teary-looking Claire, clomped her way purposefully across the front of the first row of chairs and then sat down heavily on the stage, her legs dangling. She began rubbing her hands across her face.

'What's happened?' Walter said.

They all got up and crowded around.

'Sorry, folks, but the show's off.'

Claire nodded and with her head lowered concentrated on drying her eyes and blowing her nose quietly.

Exclamations of 'What?' 'But why?' 'What's happened?' rumbled through the group.

Jennifer held up her hand. To Erica it seemed she was making an extraordinary effort to stay calm. Her face was ashen now, and her features seemed to have aged a decade during that walk across the hall. Tears were in her eyes. Erica's heart lurched towards the woman – their indefatigable leader appeared broken.

'Sorry, everyone. It can't be helped. Robert and Ingrid needed to leave. Robert's parents have had a car accident. It's serious. They're being airlifted.'

There was a collective gasp and Erica experienced a déjà vu flash in her mind of the same occurrence with Stuart's parents, his almost identical words to her on the set of the film she was working on all those years back in the US. She shuddered at how her career had all but ceased to exist from that moment. Of course they'd discussed that she would pick up where she'd left off later – return to the US in due course or perhaps work on local film and TV. But it had never happened. All that flashing in her mind made her dizzy and nauseous. She felt behind her for a chair and sat down.

'No,' and 'Fuck,' were the murmured words filling the space.

And then Mackenzie's clear, earnest voice cut through the rabble: 'No. You can't give up.'

'But we don't have a leading pair of actors and we never had enough interested parties to have understudies,' Jennifer said. 'We have to cut our losses.'

'But it's not just any old play. It's *Claire's* play,' Phillipa said. 'It's your rare and really important chance to have your play properly performed, isn't it?'

Claire nodded again. 'Yes, but it *is* only a play. I'm sure there'll be other opportunities.' Though to Erica's ear she didn't sound convinced.

'And the fundraising,' Issy said. 'It's such an important cause.'

'Yes, there's got to be a way,' Mackenzie said.

Jennifer shrugged helplessly. 'Ingrid and Robert urged us to replace them, didn't they, Claire? But they're in shock: there *is* no one else,' she said, rubbing her face.

'I know! Mum. You and Jimmy can play the leads – I saw you guys in the wings, ready to give the lines. You know them, don't you? You said you've been helping Walter rehearse all this time.'

'And, Jimmy, you've been helping me,' Peggy said.

'Yes, but I don't think I know all of them – well, not well enough,' Jimmy said.

'No, me neither. I'm always reading from the script,' Erica said.

'You've got hours before the opening. You could learn them,' Issy said. 'I bet you know more than you realise,' she added.

'Exactly. You'll have soaked them up during rehearsals, too. You've both been at all of them, haven't you?' Mackenzie said.

'Well, yes,' Erica said.

'True, but ...' Jimmy said.

'Yes, at least give it a shot. That's better than giving up,' Gemma said.

'I agree,' Roy said. 'If it's a flop – and I absolutely know it won't be, sorry to even suggest that, but – well, then we can apologise and give everyone's money back. Or they'd totally understand, what with the last-minute substitutions.'

'And if the worst happened – and I agree, it won't – it's such a worthy cause that I really think people wouldn't even want to be reimbursed. It is, after all, only the cost of a main meal in the pub,' Peggy pointed out.

'True,' Lloyd said.

'I agree,' Phillipa said.

'Hang on a second,' Walter said, raising his voice and holding up a hand. 'I love your enthusiasm, everyone, and belief in your mother and Jimmy, Issy and Mackenzie, but I rather think it's up to them to agree to do it – be comfortable doing it – and not for us to badger them into anything.'

'Yeah, sorry,' Issy said.

'You're absolutely right, Walter. We're getting carried away. Mum, Jimmy, it's completely up to you,' Mackenzie said. Both girls looked downcast.

'Yes, please don't feel you have to do this for me,' Claire said.

'I'm to blame too. My apologies,' Roy said.

'Yes. Sorry,' Phillipa said.

'Entirely up to you. Knowing the lines is one thing, but getting the nerve to get up onstage is a whole other ballgame,' Lloyd said.

'It's okay, everyone, I'm the one who should be apologising. I'm as much to blame,' Jennifer said. 'I'm in a bit of a state of shock, to be honest. But, yes, thank you, Walter, you're absolutely right. When it comes down to it, as Claire said, it *is* only a play – this is not life and death. My apologies, Jimmy and Erica. Please don't feel pressured. At all. It is a big ask, I know, and you have every right to decline, for any reason. And without explanation.'

'Thanks, Walter and Jennifer, but I think I'd really like to try and step up, actually. Remember, I was originally keen to have a part but Gemma and I thought we'd be too busy this weekend – and the wedding that was meant to be tomorrow has been cancelled. Gemma?'

'I'm good if you're good.'

'Everyone has put in so much work. It'd be a real shame to just let it go to waste. Count me in,' Jimmy said.

'Yes. I really appreciate you saying, too – letting me off the hook,' Erica said. 'But I'm with Jimmy. I'm keen to give it a go. If you're okay to take a risk on me, that is?'

'Yes, it's your play, Jennifer, and yours, Claire – do *you* want to take the risk with me?' Jimmy asked, looking from Jennifer to Claire.

'If you want to do it, I'd absolutely love to have you on board. But only if you're sure,' Jennifer said.

'Oh my god, it would mean the world to me,' Claire said. Her eyes glistened with tears. 'But, as Jennifer says, only if you're absolutely certain.'

Jimmy looked at Erica with his eyebrows raised in question. 'So, we're doing this?'

Erica nodded. 'Yep. If you're in, I'm in.' While she wasn't entirely convinced she *wanted* to do it, she did feel she *needed* to – for herself and for Jimmy, first and foremost.

'Oh, I'm so pleased,' Jennifer said, regaining some colour and movement. 'Thank you.'

'Thank you,' Claire croaked, dabbing at her eyes.

'Good on you, Mum and Jimmy – you're going to be awesome!' Issy said.

'I agree. You totally are,' Mackenzie said.

'No pressure, then,' Erica said, smiling wryly at them. 'Just kidding,' she added, putting a hand on each of their arms when they again looked a little chastised.

'Okay, folks,' Jennifer announced, 'the show is going ahead, thanks to Jimmy and Erica.'

A spontaneous round of applause erupted.

'Jennifer, I've had an idea for something that might help Mum and Jimmy with remembering some lines,' Issy said, once it was quiet again and some people had moved away to chat amongst themselves.

'What's that, Issy?' Jennifer asked.

'Well, maybe we can enlarge and print out some pages and stick them to the coffee table you sit near and the floor, for just in case,' Issy said.

'Oh. That *is* a good idea,' Jennifer said.

'And, you know, even if it all goes wrong and the worst happens, you could simply pull the chairs back and have a dance floor – turn up the music,' Issy said.

Oh dear, Erica thought. She loved her girls' enthusiasm and efforts to help, but turn it into a disco? Or nightclub, or whatever they were thinking?

'I could tell some jokes,' Roy offered. 'If it came to it. Some are even clean,' he added with a slight chuckle.

'No, it won't come to that. I'm sure,' Walter said. 'Sorry, Roy, I didn't mean that about you and your jokes. I was thinking aloud and stuck back a bit in the conversation.'

'No worries. All good, Walter, old mate.'

'You're all brilliant,' Jennifer said, looking around the group. 'We're going to give it a damned good shot. And like you've said, I'd put money on people not wanting a refund anyway.'

'Right. Jimmy, you and Erica go and swot up. If you're still sure, that is?' she added, looking at them.

Erica nodded and stood up. She felt decidedly queasy now. But she couldn't let Jennifer and everyone else down. And she wouldn't let herself down like she had last time she'd tried acting many years ago.

'We can do this,' Jimmy said, threading his arm through hers.

She nodded and whispered, 'I'm terrified.'

'So am I. But I can't let Jennifer down. Remember there is nothing to fear but fear itself. If I can make the progress I have and you can pack up your life like you did to move up here, then this'll be a piece of cake. It's one night. Just one night.'

'But I had stage fright last time,' she whispered. 'Like, *really* badly.' While somewhat curious to discover what had happened, Erica was also very glad not to know the cause of the shame that burnt inside her, though, thankfully, less intensely now.

'That was then and this is now. You're not that person any more.'

'You should be on the inspirational speaking circuit,' Erica said. She wanted to laugh, but couldn't manage to push aside her anxiety enough to.

'Well, I've been listening to you,' he said.

'You've got this, Mum. And Jimmy,' Issy said, coming up to them.

'Yep. You're going to be fantastic; we know you are. We wouldn't have suggested this if we didn't believe in you.'

'Yeah, thanks for dumping me in it,' Erica said wryly. 'Again, just kidding.'

'It will do you good,' Mackenzie said, phraseology and tone Erica recognised as her own and her mother's before her.

'Well, I'm going to give it my best,' she said.

'Me too. Come on, let's go and find a quiet spot,' Jimmy said.

'That's the spirit,' Mackenzie said. 'And our birds fly the nest. Here, we see the adults being coddled by the children. Life has come full circle,' she said in her best David Attenborough drawl.

'Yes: fly, butterflies, fly,' Issy said, making ushering movements with her hands.

'Oh haha, you two,' Erica said. She pulled away from Jimmy, turned and wrapped her arms around both of them, gave them each a kiss and then released them.

'Your girls are awesome. Cute and funny too,' Jimmy whispered.

'Yeah. I got lucky,' she whispered back.

'Nothing to do with luck from where I'm standing.'

'Right, Jennifer, give me a pen. I'm going to change the actors' names on the programs,' Mackenzie said.

'But there are hundreds of them,' Jennifer said. 'It's not simply a matter of typing in a few lines – like I'm about to do for the online stuff.'

'So we'd better get cracking, then,' Issy said. 'Unless there's something you'd rather we do?'

'I'll help,' Chloe said.

'No. No, that would be great. If you're happy to do it,' Jennifer said. 'Here you go,' she said, handing her a pen. Walter pulled two from his pocket and handed one to Mackenzie and another to Chloe. 'Thanks, girls,' Jennifer said. 'The programs are at the front on the table.'

'My pleasure,' Mackenzie said.

'Mine too,' Issy said. 'Mum and Jimmy are going to pull this off and I want everyone to know who they are,' she added.

'Good for you. But we could reprint them. Or print stickers to go over that bit,' Walter said.

'Nope. We're not wasting paper and ink – it's twenty-twenty-two, Walter! Sorry, no offence. Really.'

'Oh, Walter,' Chloe said with exaggerated exasperation complete with a deep sigh. Erica had to turn away to stop from cracking up laughing.

'Okay. Good point. And no offence taken,' he said cheerfully.

Chapter Thirty-nine

Erica had managed to remain calm and steady when doing the makeup for everyone. Issy and Mackenzie had offered to step in, but Erica thought the distraction would be useful. And it had been. She'd kept her earbuds in with calming binaural tones coming from them and she'd remained relatively at ease. She'd worked hard to talk her anxiety into becoming excitement. She'd once heard someone say that anxiety and excitement felt the same inside. They were the same jingly, jangly vibration.

She and Jimmy had done their best. They'd run through everything three times and then agreed that if they didn't know it then it was too late. They'd also agreed that they didn't want to be so prepped that they became robotic. The play had a certain amount of room for ad libbing and they'd agreed to do their best to exploit that and appear more natural.

In the wings, Erica now trotted up and down on the spot to get rid of some of her nervous energy and prepare for the moment she stepped onto the stage, which was actually at a fast walk. Jimmy was seated in the dark with Peggy and Roy on set in the nursing home's lounge, waiting for the lights to come on and the curtain to open.

'Ready?' Jennifer said, beside Erica.

'Yep. As much as I'll ever be. Let's do this.'

'Good girl.'

'You're going to be awesome, Mum,' Issy whispered from behind her.

'Yes, go break a leg,' Mackenzie whispered.

Erica put her hand behind her back and gave them a wave before moving into position out of sight behind the set. They'd had lots of hugs before, but now she was trying hard to keep her first line on her lips and herself in character.

'John, Sahara, good to go?' Jennifer said quietly into the walkie talkie handpiece.

'Roger that. All systems go,' John replied.

'Yes, I'm ready. Lights good to go,' Sahara said.

Jennifer counted down: 'And, four, three, two, one. Go.'

Erica felt a rush of anxiety when the lights came on and the curtain opened and she heard the hushed arguing voices of Walter, Peggy and Jimmy already onstage. *Oh god. What was I thinking? I can't do this!* Her heart hammered against her ribs and her mind began grappling to recall the words of her first line that had just slipped from her lips. *Oh fuck! Oh fuck. What is it? Please, don't do this to me ...* She heard a gasp from behind her and a whispered, 'Go on, you're fine,' from John. It served as an effective circuit-breaker for her. *Oh. I've got it.* With shaking fingers slick with sweat she walked onstage and pushed the set's back door open, glad, as she did, there was no knob that needed turning.

She stood facing the dark audience for a moment, looking around at the seated cast members of Walter, Peggy and Jimmy, as directed in the script, the spotlight in her face. *Just don't use their real names: it's Edwin, Olive and Martin you're looking at. And I'm Heidi.* Behind her eyes came a flashing montage of images of the last time she had been onstage in this same position – standing under a spotlight facing the audience, ready to speak. It came back to her in gruesome clarity and the image froze, just like she had then in the bout of serious, crippling and unrelenting stage fright that she saw in an instant had changed everything for her. She'd opened her mouth and instead of words … nothing. And then several more seconds of nothing. Then members of the audience gasping and shifting in their seats. Someone had hissed the words from beyond the stage. Instead of uttering them, she'd burst into tears, and sobbed, before being bundled offstage by someone – her dad? She couldn't remember, but knew it had been an older man.

This time will be different, she told herself, as Jimmy's character Martin turned towards her from his position seated in a floral upholstered armchair and said, 'Finally! What took you so long?'

'Well excuse me for not being able to drop everything the minute you call! It's all right for you not needing to get kids to school on your own. Hi, Mum, hi, Edwin,' she said in a gentler tone, looking sympathetically from Walter to Peggy. Both appeared suitably distraught and she had to work hard to not break character and smile at them. Seeing Peggy sitting in front of her dressed in a floral dress and with a pink bow in her hair was really quite disconcerting, too, even though she'd seen her like this in rehearsals. 'Right, what's happened?' she said.

Walter as Edwin opened his mouth to speak, closed it again, and offered a demure shrug.

'Edwin?' Erica as Heidi said.

'She's your mother. Olive, tell her,' Jimmy said, folding his arms tight across his chest.

Peggy said, 'Okay. Well, I only clicked on the link once. It was an important email from the bank. And it said it was urgent. So, I followed the instructions on the screen. Just like you've taught me with the internet banking.' The perfectly innocent tone and demure expression from the normally quite brash Peggy caused a titter to run through the audience and Erica the need to bite down on the inside of her lip to keep her own composure.

'It sounds like you weren't actually in the online banking, Mum.'

'Well how was I to know? It looked real enough to me.'

'How many bloody times have I told you, "Don't click on the bloody links in emails"?' Jimmy said.

'But it said it was *urgent*. And the time on the message said it had been there since midnight. The account was going to be closed if I didn't. Time was of the essence. I'm really sorry.'

'I know. It's okay, Mum,' Erica said, sitting down on the chair beside Peggy and patting her hand.

'Well, the account's now closed and all the money's gone, so well done! And, Heidi, it's not bloody okay – what about this don't you get?'

'Don't yell at me. Or Mum. Shouting won't help anything.'

'And neither will you being in denial. Oh for god's sake, you people! Last week it was the scammer on the phone, this time the bloody email. This is why I didn't want them having smartphones or tablets. Well, for the record, they're not living with me when they get chucked out of this place because they can't afford it.'

'Duly noted. Why are you even here if you're not going to be useful?' Erica said.

'Yes, that young lass was very smart,' Walter said. 'She was from the Australian Tax Office – it doesn't pay to muck them around. Oh no,' Walter's character said knowingly.

'Dad, she *wasn't* from the ATO, she was *pretending* to be. And, yes, thank goodness she was smarter than you and you couldn't figure out how to give her any money. That's at least something,' he added.

'No, Martin, she was adamant. I wasn't running the risk of having Olive frightened out of her wits when the police turned up to arrest her for not filing her tax return.'

'Oh my god. I can't handle this.' Jimmy stood up and started pacing while rubbing his face.

'Really, I would never have guessed,' Erica said with her eyebrows raised and her head tilted towards him. 'And I take it, as usual, I'm going to have to deal with everything. How you manage to run your own business beats me. Right, firstly, have you called the police?'

'Of course I've called the police – well, not me, Bernard, the manager of this place has. He's probably still off talking to them now.'

At that moment Lloyd, playing the nursing home manager, came through the door. 'The police are on their way,' he said.

Time raced and it seemed to Erica as if just moments after that first scene the curtain was coming down on the first half and the audience was clapping and cheering.

Erica left the stage. She had a costume change.

'Oh my god, Mum, you were, *are*, amazing. You all were, *are*, oh whatever!' Issy said.

'Yes, fantastic,' Mackenzie said.

Erica's daughters patted Erica on the back as she moved past them and down the steps to go to the back dressing room area, followed by the rest of the cast.

'How are you? Okay?' Jennifer said, as they all filed in and surrounded her. 'Excuse my language, but that was bloody brilliant.'

'Oh my god. I'm loving it,' Erica said. *I feel so alive.*

The rest of the production went without incident and far too quickly in Erica's opinion. She wanted to stay up there making those below laugh, gasp and sigh forever. There was something really satisfying in moving people like that.

And now as she got changed and wiped her stage makeup off, she really wished she'd never given up her dream. Because she now knew that this had been her true career dream. Not makeup. That had been the next best thing. She shook her head with wonder and disbelief. *Bloody hell.* She'd heard of people uncovering repressed memories, but had always struggled to believe it was really possible.

A part of her wished they had planned to do more shows. Perhaps they could take it on the road to the other towns. Or even further. She glanced across at Jennifer, who looked wrecked. Poor thing. She'd wait before making any such suggestion. And, anyway, she was on a high. Perhaps she'd feel differently in a few hours or days, or whenever this wore off. Erica hoped it wouldn't, but this kind of internal energy couldn't be sustained for too long – it would be exhausting, as debilitating as being stressed all the time maybe. No doubt she'd come back down to earth with a thud on Tuesday or when they did the next funeral, which was booked for Thursday.

The cast and crew ambled up the road in small groups and gathered in the pub with their nearest and dearest. After a couple of drinks, they dispersed, warned by Jennifer that they had another big day tomorrow with all the fundraising, which began with a fried bacon and egg breakfast. They were all expected to help out. A few groans were greeted by apologies from Jennifer, who admitted she might have bitten off more than she could chew. They all mumbled encouraging words in reply and then dragged themselves up off their chairs and home to bed. It was, after all, only one weekend. They could keep up the momentum for another day. The hardest and most stressful bit was over – the play. Hospitality was a doddle; it was what small country towns excelled at and were famous for. But doing it hung over wouldn't help, they'd all agreed.

Erica felt a bit bad that she'd hardly seen Michelle, Steph and Renee, particularly when they'd come up from Adelaide especially, though they'd seemed cheerful enough. Hopefully she'd see more of them in the morning. It was as if her old and new lives had been combined but also kept a little separate – a bit like the small bowls of olive oil and balsamic vinegar that had been sitting on the pub's tables.

Erica had to put it out of her mind for now. They were her dear friends, and they would understand. If they didn't, she couldn't make them.

'Thanks so much for being here,' she said, hugging the three of them to her.

'Are you kidding?!' Steph said. 'Wouldn't have missed it for the world. It was brilliant. You were phenomenal.'

'No. Exactly. You were fantastic,' Michelle said.

'I feel like we've just witnessed the start of something big,' Renee said quietly.

Erica almost told her about her idea to take the production on the road, but said instead, 'Sorry I'm distracted and not seeing much of you. I'm afraid tomorrow might be more of the same.'

'We can always come back and visit you another time – the cottage is fabulous,' Michelle said. 'And next time I'm bringing Daphne to play with Bruce – I just know they'll love each other. I'm going to enjoy seeing more of your gorgeous dog tomorrow, too.'

'Michelle's right – we'll be back. Anyway, we're big girls – we don't need looking after,' Steph said.

'Or entertaining,' Michelle said. 'Though you've just done that in spades,' she added.

'Totally,' Renee said.

'Just go and get a good night's sleep,' Michelle said.

'And let us know tomorrow if there's anything we can do to help,' Steph said.

'Thanks, you guys – you're the best.'

Erica fell into bed and was surprised she didn't lie awake tossing and turning due to her high, but instead drifted off to sleep, her arm around Bruce.

Chapter Forty

Sunday beneath Mt Remarkable dawned bright and sunny, but not too warm. Erica was enjoying a few sips of water and soaking in the atmosphere seated alone in the grassy area beside the caravan park, which was surrounded by food trucks and market stalls. Issy, Mackenzie, Steph, Renee and Michelle had taken Bruce for a wander. They'd headed off just after the TV reporter and camera operator had left – after interviewing Erica – and when the local newspaper journalist had appeared and asked her for a chat. Erica was loving feeling like a celebrity, having had lots of people come up and tell her how well she'd done the previous night, but was also starting to feel a little weary. She'd been awake early to help set up the sea of stacking plastic chairs and the round tables where she now sat, trying to stave off the early signs of a mild headache.

'Hello. You're Erica, aren't you? The lead from the play?'

'Hello. Yes.' Erica looked up, holding her hand to her eyes to block out the sun. A tall, lean woman around her age with short grey hair and dressed in faded denim jeans and black T-shirt stood above her.

'Mind if I sit?' the woman asked.

'Not at all.' Erica indicated the chair next to her with a wave of her hand.

'Michaela Rodgers,' said the woman, sitting down and holding out her hand. 'You were fantastic last night,' she added.

'That's kind of you to say. Thanks very much,' Erica said.

'What a great event,' Michaela said, looking around. 'And such a fantastic cause to support.'

'Yes, it came together really well. But it was all Jennifer,' Erica said, following Michaela's gaze.

'One should never underestimate the therapy animals can give us humans without even trying,' Michaela mused, as if not hearing Erica.

'I agree. Are you a journalist doing a story? Because Jennifer over there …' she said, quickly looking around and then pointing '… is the best person to talk with about the fundraising efforts.'

'Oh. No. I'm a prod—'

'There you are! I thought I'd lost you!' Erica looked around at hearing another unfamiliar female voice and saw a smiling woman who looked to be a similar age to Michaela and was a head shorter. She had grey hair pulled back into a ponytail and was dressed in jeans and a wraparound bright multi-coloured top with short sleeves.

'Chelsea Richards,' the woman said, offering her hand. As she shook it, Erica experienced an instant warmth.

Chelsea pulled out another chair from the table and sat down. 'Brilliant performance last night. And I hear you had to step in at the last moment.'

'Thanks. Yes, it was a bit of a clamber.'

'Have you spoken to her?' Chelsea asked Michaela.

'Not yet, darling. You interrupted us.'

'Oops. That's me. A bit overzealous,' Chelsea said, wincing at Erica.

Erica started feeling uncomfortable under the scrutiny. *Who are these people and what do they want?*

'Um, are *you* a journalist?' she asked.

'Haha, god no. Sorry, not that there's anything wrong with journalists ...' She offered Erica another cringe before beaming again and taking a sip of the drink she held.

Erica smiled back.

'Erica, Chelsea and I are here looking at locations,' Michaela said.

Do you mean property? Real estate? 'Well, it's a lovely area.' Erica swivelled around, looking for Lloyd. 'See that man over there, and the woman to his left – they're local real estate agents,' she said. 'They'll be your best bet.'

'Oh, no. Sorry, did I not say? I'm a TV and film producer,' Michaela said.

'And I'm a talent agent. I was holding back, but my darling wife here seems to be having trouble getting to the point.'

'That's because you keep interrupting me, sweetheart.' Erica couldn't tell if her gentleness was natural or forced. Nonetheless she thought, *What a lovely couple.* Cute, she could imagine Mackenzie saying.

'We'd like to talk to you, actually,' Michaela said.

'Oh?' Erica said. 'I haven't been in town long. Walter, over there, funeral director,' she said, pointing, 'he'd be the man to ask.'

'No, I don't want to talk to you about locations,' Michaela said.

Erica frowned. Her brain wasn't working. She frowned harder when they each handed her a business card.

'Thanks,' she said. She stared at them. One was quite corporate looking – navy and white – and the other had marbleised swirls of bright colour on one side. Erica turned them over to look at the white side with lines of text – navy on one and pink on the other, but all the text was moving like liquid and she couldn't seem to regain her focus.

'Sorry, I'm a little confused,' she finally admitted.

'We've clearly had too much wine or too much sun,' Chelsea said, and giggled.

'Yes, clearly,' Michaela said. 'Oh dear. *Erica*, our primary purpose for being here was hunting for the right locations, yes. I didn't think for a second that I'd *finally* manage a crucial bit of casting all the way out here. But I have. You're perfect for a supporting role in the film I'm putting together right now. Incredible timing your play being on!'

Sorry, what? Erica blinked.

'And I'd like to represent you,' Chelsea chimed in.

'Sorry?' Erica said, finally managing to speak.

'Be your agent,' Chelsea said.

Isn't that a conflict of interest? Erica thought, looking at them. *Oh, what would I know? And of all the things to go through my mind right now. Utterly ridiculous.*

'But I'm not an actor, or actress,' Erica said.

The two women sitting close to her on either side looked at each other with quizzical expressions.

'Hang on, you're Erica – from the play last night, right?' Chelsea said.

Michaela dragged out a crumpled, folded copy of the printed program and held it out. She pointed to where Issy or Mackenzie had handwritten her name in. She couldn't quite tell which from this distance. 'Erica Cunningham? I watched you onstage. So …'

'Yes, that's me. I'm Erica Cunningham. But the play last night was a one-off. I'm a funeral director's assistant. Hair and makeup artist by trade, actually,' she added.

'But you're a natural,' Chelsea said.

'Yes. Please say you'll come and be in our film,' Michaela said.

'You want me to go somewhere and audition?' Erica said. Random thoughts and emotions were pinging all over the place inside her brain and stomach.

'No. I'm offering you a part.'

'Michaela …' Chelsea said in a warning tone.

'Ah, I'll clear it with the big bosses – you know how persuasive I can be,' Michaela said with a dismissive wave of her hand. 'It's a feature. Already funded and not far off of starting filming,' Michaela said. 'The location hunt is for another production. It's all happening in South Australia's screen industry right now.'

'Not just in terms of the number of productions, but also the great roles and fantastic opportunities on offer for women. It's finally our time,' Chelsea said.

'That's great news,' Erica said, amazed she'd managed to utter something intelligible at all.

'It sure is. It's been a long time coming, especially for women of our age. And you're exactly what I've been looking for. The role is for the mother of the lead, which is already cast, so the right look is significant. And you're *it* to a tee. Plus, I've seen you act, so we know you have the talent. I think this could be the start of big things for you. I can't say too much yet, but you could also be perfect for a new TV drama series we have in the works,' Michaela said.

'Yes, and doing the film role would really set you up. Sorry, it's a lot to take in. But I'm serious. *We're* serious.'

'Well, you're very kind, but I'm not an actress. Not really. In fact, I was terrified last night,' Erica admitted.

'Well, it certainly didn't show. And given you stepped in at the last moment, I think you did an incredible job,' Michaela said.

'Thanks.'

'Yes. And a film set isn't nearly as nerve-racking as live theatre,' Chelsea said.

Erica stared at them with her mouth slightly open. *No way.* Any moment she expected someone to jump out and cry, Gotcha! She'd heard of models being discovered – plucked out of obscurity – but did that also happen with actors? She didn't see why it couldn't, especially if they were looking for someone or something with particular attributes. Renee went on about synchronicity and fate and cited examples all the time.

Gradually her mind and eyes began to clear. She blinked and looked at the cards again. She hadn't heard of Michaela Rodgers or the name of her production company. But that wasn't surprising – she was well out of the loop and hadn't even been inside a movie theatre for months, thanks to her belt-tightening. She'd used to stay right until the final credits – had always loved film.

The ember that had begun to shine inside her flamed. She'd pushed this desire deep down into her so long ago and piled so much life and other stuff onto it. So much so that before last night she'd all but forgotten it had even existed. Yes, she'd trained to do hair and makeup for film and embarked on that career, but only because of her humiliation at her last acting attempt – her debut.

Now Erica glowed inside with excitement and yearning and a feeling she couldn't quite describe: acceptance? Maybe. She'd felt it before: it was a watered-down version of what she'd experienced on her first day on the film set in the USA several decades back: the feeling of having found her place, her tribe.

'Sorry, we're being far too pushy,' Chelsea said, cutting into the silence and dragging Erica's attention back to the present.

'Yes. I forget sometimes not everyone is as passionate as me,' Michaela said, clearly deflated.

'What's the film about?' Erica asked.

'Are you a reader – of novels, particularly relatively recent ones?'

'Not really, no.'

'Well, the title might not mean anything to you then. It's called *Out of the Gully*. It's an adaptation of a lovely heart-warming story by Australian author Imogen Manfredi about a woman in her early twenties finding her feet after trauma, heartbreak and upheaval – it's a lovely, gentle journey of self-discovery.'

If she wasn't so out of kilter, Erica might have laughed and told them how much it sounded like her own life.

'It'll be atmospheric, with a big focus on setting; gorgeous cine-matography. Sorry, I'm getting carried away. Anyway, nothing gory or scary or sexual.'

'Well, there's a bit of swearing … Sometimes there is no better word than *fuck*, is there?' Chelsea said with a grin.

'Oh, yes, I quite agree,' Erica said, with a laugh. A vague memory crystallised. *Oh*. 'I've actually heard of it. Your film. I do read the paper sometimes – well, online mostly.' She remembered the many write-ups – it was a huge deal for not just Australia but in this state, and she thought she remembered the publicity around it being a majority female production. 'You've got the South Australian Government right behind you, haven't you?'

'Yes. So, eek, no pressure.' Michaela arranged her features into a wince.

'That's brilliant. Well done,' Erica said.

'Well, it's a little soon to be popping the next bottles of bubbly. We haven't started filming yet. We've been delayed,' Michaela said.

'Yes. Someone's not feeling quite right about the options found to date for the lead's mother,' Chelsea said, her eyebrows raised knowingly.

'What can I say? I'm a perfectionist. Nothing wrong with that. If it's worth doing, and all that …' Michaela said.

Erica began to come out of her slight stupor and became a little excited. *I would be perfect. The story could be about my own kids; we're living a version of it right now.*

That thought caused reality to seep back in and the excitement inside her to fade. She was a woman on the cusp of turning fifty with a brand-new, secure, full-time job she was damned lucky to have. Michaela and Chelsea might be right about women her age now having their time in the limelight of the screen industry, but she didn't have the desire or energy for more upheaval or stress in her life. It was all well and good for Michaela and Chelsea to be passionate and flattering and demanding, which was fine given what they were trying to achieve. But they didn't know her circumstances. And, anyway, anything could happen – film projects probably fell over all the time, for any number of reasons. No; it was too big a gamble.

'I'm very flattered …' she began, but stopped. She didn't want to say the next words; she wanted to hold onto the remaining tiny glimmer of excitement for longer. Forever, if she was being totally truthful.

'Don't just be flattered,' Michaela said, in almost a whine. 'Say you'll do it. Please.'

Out of the corner of her eye she noticed Walter laughing with Jennifer and several others. *Exactly*, she thought. *My place is here.* 'I'm really sorry ... But I can't.'

'Could you at least think about it?' Michaela said.

'I'm sorry,' Erica said, pursing her lips and shaking her head.

'Come on, Michaela, we'd really better get going, else we'll be late,' Chelsea said, standing up and touching her wife on the shoulder. 'Well, it was wonderful to meet you, anyway. And, seriously, you were brilliant last night.'

'Yes,' Michaela said, also getting up. 'You really were fabulous. The offer's there and you have my card, if you change your mind.'

'And mine if you want representation,' Chelsea said quietly. 'See ya.'

'Goodbye,' Michaela said.

'Thanks. It was great to meet you. All the best with everything,' Erica said. She stared after them.

Wow. Wait until you hear this mind-blowing coincidence, Renee!

She'd think Michaela and Chelsea might be scammers if she hadn't heard of the book adaptation being a big coup for South Australia, the State Government having poured a heap of money into it et cetera.

But, actually, they could still be scammers – cat fishers, like in the play last night. Learning that would relieve the lingering residual disappointment.

She got out her phone and fired up Google. Just because they knew the name of the book – she did too, she thought as she typed it in. When the results came up, she clicked on images. And there was a photo of Michaela Rodgers – the spitting image of the woman who had just been sitting and chatting with her.

Well, okay, then. Totally legit. She sat back in her chair feeling chuffed at not only having met some famous people, but that strangers with real credibility had heaped such high praise on her.

Chapter Forty-one

Erica was still sitting sifting through her thoughts and emotions when Issy and Mackenzie reappeared, startling her slightly when they sat down next to her.

'Mum,' Issy said.

'Yes, darling?' she said. Out of the corner of her eye, Erica saw Bruce flop onto the grass and laughed to herself at the dog's melodramatic action.

Mackenzie sat down on Michaela Rodgers's recently vacated chair.

'Can we talk to you about something?' Issy continued.

'Of course. What's up?' Erica said, looking from one to the other.

'Firstly, I know we should be talking about this in private – back at the flat – but I don't think we're going to get a chance ... And, well ...' Issy said.

'Yes, it's a bit time sensitive,' Mackenzie said.

'What is? What's happened?' Erica asked. 'Have you found someone suitable to move in with you?'

'No. That's still a work in progress. This is something completely different,' Mackenzie said.

'Okay?'

'We're not even sure if you want to know at all,' Issy said.

The girls shared what seemed to Erica to be a questioning look.

'Well, I won't know if you don't tell me what you're on about. And I get it's a very hectic weekend, I'm sorry about that –'

'Don't be. It's not your fault,' Issy said.

'And we're loving it,' Mackenzie said.

'But …? Come on, what is it?' Erica prompted.

Issy took a deep breath. 'Okay. You know how you said about your box of things from school days, back at home? Well, you haven't mentioned your brother Mark again, or that box, so we're not sure …'

'But we looked,' Mackenzie said.

'Oh. Right,' Erica said.

'Do you want us to tell you what we found out?' Mackenzie said.

'Yes.'

'Are you sure?' Issy said.

'I'm sure. It can't hurt now. Tell me. Where was I at school in 1984?'

'It still blows my mind that you can forget something like that,' Issy said.

'We've established that. And it's not the issue at hand, Issy: stay focussed,' Mackenzie said.

'Yes, sorry.'

'Orroroo, Mum. You were in year seven in 1984 and at Orroroo,' Issy said. 'And we've found out something else as well – two things, actually.'

'Oh. Okay?' *How strange that I went to Orroroo the other week …* Time seemed to stop for a moment as she ruminated on that. She shuddered inwardly at remembering how she'd felt being back there.

'Not in the box; it was something else Grandpa said.'

'Sorry, what was that?' Erica said, pulling her attention back to the here and now.

'Issy, stay on track. Mum, Mark's name wasn't Mark – well, it kind of was – Mark was his *middle* name. His first name was Stephen. He was Stephen Mark Tolmer. That's why you couldn't find him on the Find A Grave website.'

'Oh. I had no idea. How bizarre,' Erica said, her brain starting to whirr again with random, disjointed thoughts. *How could I have not known that either?*

'Which brings us to the other thing,' Mackenzie said.

'Yes. We know where he's buried,' Issy said, becoming a little excited.

'Really?'

'Yes. Orroroo. And he's buried, not cremated and scattered or in a wall with a plaque. Here, we've got a photo,' Issy said, pulling out her phone.

'Do you want to see?' Mackenzie said.

Erica's whole being was slowing. She nodded and held out her hand.

'He doesn't have a headstone, but there was a community group – Lions Club or one of those – who put these little white crosses up on any unmarked graves,' Issy explained as Erica squinted at the image on the phone screen, her hand cupped around it to make it clearer in the sun.

She stared, not really feeling anything at seeing a small, white wooden cross – she assumed it was wooden – with her brother's name and birth and death dates on it in black. A moment later she experienced a surge of disappointment in her parents for their abandonment of him, both in not giving him a proper headstone and also in leaving him, because she knew they'd left soon after. Fragments of memories were trying to push their way into her consciousness, but, as usual, they didn't fully form before drifting away again. Her whole childhood had been experiences of packing and unpacking. She couldn't grasp any particular memories of the time when they'd packed up without Mark. Had it been the year she'd gone and stayed with Steph and her parents – her favourite auntie, Irene? Ah, really, what did it matter – her remembering, or how her parents had behaved? She knew all too well that parenting included plenty of occasions where it was a matter of damned if you do, damned if you don't. And while she'd lost a husband, she hadn't lost a child.

She looked from Issy to Mackenzie. Losing Stuart was bearable – just; helped by her anger towards him. Losing one of her daughters wouldn't be. She knew that. So she had no right to question her parents' actions.

And then a shard of memory did poke through. The school play – the one she'd spectacularly fucked up. The beginning and end of her dreamt-of acting career. She'd tried to go ahead when she'd just found out about Mark – she wasn't going to let his selfish actions in dying ruin her chance. She'd been angry. She'd wanted to go that night to the water hole. He'd told her he didn't want his little sister tagging along; that she was a pain and an embarrassment. So she'd stood there onstage, under the bright, glaring lights, determined to prove herself to him, despite his recent death, and not let anyone down. And she'd continued to stand, not uttering any of the several lines she had, until someone – one of her parents? – had walked onstage and tried to usher her off, her trying to refuse but eventually being picked up, held around the middle and carried off with her arms and legs flailing. How embarrassing. And life changing. It had literally changed the course of her life. Though, really, there was no guarantee she would have succeeded as an actor. But she also had no proof she wouldn't have. And now she knew she did have the talent. She'd just been told. So …

She dragged her attention back at hearing Issy's earnest and then Mackenzie's concerned voices from beside her.

'Mum, say something,' Issy whispered.

'Yes, are you mad at us?' Mackenzie said.

'No. Of course not. I'm glad. It's just a bit of a shock, that's all,' Erica said.

'We weren't sure if you wanted to know or not – you haven't mentioned it again since,' she said, seeming a little helpless.

'I'd like to go and see his grave while we're here,' Issy said.

'Yes, me too, which is why we had to tell you now. Sorry, again, for telling you like this.'

'Hello, what's up?' Steph said, appearing beside them. 'God, who died? Shit, sorry, that's completely insensitive,' she said, plonking herself on a nearby chair.

'We've found where Mark's grave is – Mum's brother,' Issy said.

'Oh. Orroroo, you mean?' Steph said, frowning slightly.

'You knew? You *know*?' Erica stared at her cousin. *How come I didn't think to ask you?*

'Of course, silly. What's going on?'

'Mum couldn't remember,' Issy said.

'I'm not surprised. It was bloody traumatic. Mum, Dad and I came up to get you. Do you remember that?' Steph said.

Erica shook her head. 'We had a guy drown here recently and it triggered something, but I seriously can't remember much at all about Mark or any of what went on then. It's been bugging me.'

'Why didn't you ask me?' Steph said.

That's a very good question. Erica shrugged and shook her head. 'Why didn't you tell me?' she said.

'I didn't know you wanted to know and that you didn't remember it. I'm amazed you managed to get up there last night, considering … I thought the school play was why you decided against acting. Until then, you'd been adamant, though you were pretty young. I mean, who *ever* ends up in the career they say they want at that age? At the same time, I was insisting I was going to be a ballerina, remember? That lasted until I discovered it meant years and years of starvation and exhaustion. No thanks.'

'What? You were there that night? At the play?' Erica asked.

'Yup. It was Dad who dragged you offstage.'

'What are you talking about?' Mackenzie said.

'I had a case of stage fright. Like, major. Seriously embarrassing,' Erica said.

'Yeah, but to be fair, you shouldn't have even been up there. You were in no state,' Steph said.

'I can't believe you remember it.'

'I can't believe you don't. What's that you're clutching?' Steph said, tugging at the business cards Erica still held, until she released them.

'A film producer and talent agent? Huh?' Steph said, reading the cards.

'Wowsers, Mum,' Issy said, peering over.

'Yeah, cool,' Mackenzie said.

'Yes. They offered me a job,' Erica said.

'What, in makeup?' Steph said.

Erica shook her head. 'Supporting actor – the main character's mother – in *Out of the Gully*. It's the adaptation of –'

'I've heard of it. Seriously?' Steph was staring at her, wide-eyed.

'No way,' Issy said in awe.

'Fuck, Mum, that's fucking incredible. It's been all over the news. They're meant to be starting filming soon. I think there's been a delay. Oh my god,' Mackenzie said, with her enormous eyes on Erica.

Thankfully there was enough noise from the PA system broadcasting music from the local community radio station in Port Pirie, and everyone else around them, that no one was turning around staring at them.

'So, are you moving back?' Mackenzie said.

'Yay. Brilliant,' Issy said.

'I told them no. I can't,' Erica said.

'Oh. Okay. But ...' Issy started and stopped.

'I'd love to be back in Adelaide with you and near your grandpa, but I'm really enjoying feeling settled and that life is a bit more predictable again. It's different at your age when you have your whole lives ahead of you. But, to be honest, I'm enjoying being here in Melrose with Walter where I feel like I'm able to catch my breath.'

'I get it. You have been through an awful lot recently,' Steph said.

'Hmm,' Issy said.

'Also, it wouldn't be right to let Walter down,' Erica said. 'He gave me a chance when I desperately needed it and he needs me. He's given me so much more than just a job.'

'Well, you always have been one of the most loyal people I know. It's an admirable quality. Maybe if there were more people like you the world would be a much better place. You need to do what's right for you.'

'We love you for being you. And I reckon if anyone deserves your loyalty, Mum, it's Walter. I think he's awesome. I don't blame you, Mum,' Mackenzie said. 'And, yeah, it would be the shortest new career in the history of new careers if you did leave,' she said with a laugh and gave her mother a gentle nudge with her shoulder.

Erica sighed with gratitude, contentment and the tiniest bit of sadness and regret. 'And, anyway, I can't cry when I've got makeup on, remember. So, I'd be useless if I had to do that,' she added.

'I'm sure you could learn,' Steph said. 'It's probably psychological – counselling and or hypnosis would no doubt sort it. Maybe it's something to do with the trauma from the play all those years ago, or something, which might mean you've inadvertently overcome that last night too.'

'They have tricks for that sort of thing – stick some drops in your eyes that make them sting or water or something, I think,' Issy said.

'Yeah,' Mackenzie said.

'Anyway, my mind is mush these days. I wouldn't be able to remember my lines.' *Actually, no, that's not true, it's better since I've been doing the meditation, but still …*

'Seriously?' Steph said, staring at Erica. 'Are you forgetting what you just did last night? A whole play – not just a scene. And without proper rehearsal? I get that you have to say no, but don't put yourself down.'

A moment later the nearby PA speakers crackled and then the sound of a throat being cleared was heard. They all lifted their heads to listen. Erica took the business cards Steph put back onto the table and tucked them into the back pocket of her jeans. 'Come on, folks, gather around for our auction. Over this way. Roll up, roll up,' Jennifer's voice boomed out all around them.

'I love how chilled-out this place is,' Mackenzie said, getting up.

'Yeah, I can totally see how you wouldn't want to leave, Mum,' Issy said, putting her arm on Erica's shoulder. 'Come on.'

'You go. I'll just wait here with Bruce,' Erica said.

'Okay, then. Be back soon,' Issy said.

Chapter Forty-two

'What a weekend, hey, Bruce?' Erica said, bending down and giving her darling dog's ears a ruffle. She was rewarded with a glance up, a lick and a few solid thumps from the stubby tail.

When she sat back in her chair, she noticed Michelle and Renee walking towards her. They sank into a plastic chair each on either side of Erica.

'Hello, lovely Bruce,' Michelle said, leaning over and giving the dog a quick pat. 'Crikey, I'm a bit light-headed. And exhausted,' she added with a sigh as she brushed some loose strands of hair out of her face. 'Why does the first warm weekend always take me by surprise? At least it's not raining.'

'Exactly,' Renee said with an exaggerated sigh.

'So, not partaking in the auction frenzy, then?' Erica said. Thankfully the auctioneer's voice coming from the nearest PA speakers was at a lower volume than Jennifer's call to attention and they could hear themselves speak without raising their voices or straining.

385

'I bought a shitload of raffle tickets and put a few bids on some silent auction items,' Michelle said. 'I could do with a new little SUV.'

'Me too. I'm getting a bit peopled out, to be honest,' Renee said. 'All this socialising and being in the masses is exhausting.'

'Yes. I know what you mean,' Erica said.

'You must be nearly ready to drop yourself, or are you still riding the adrenaline wave?' Michelle said.

'Teetering between both, I think,' Erica said with a weary laugh.

'I should have asked first – are you wanting to be alone or okay for us to sit?' Renee asked.

'Of course. Sorry – yes, sit. I was just using Bruce as an excuse to stay out of the way, really. Though, don't get me wrong, I am generally having an absolute ball.'

'So, are you going to tell us?' Michelle said, her raised eyebrows trained on Erica.

'Tell you what?'

'I don't know.'

'Steph said you'd had some sort of news, but that we had to ask you about it,' Renee explained.

'Oh. Um. Which bit?'

'No idea, you're telling the story,' Michelle said, and laughed.

'It's been a big weekend, to say the least,' Erica said.

'Oh, come on, spill. What's going on?' Renee said.

Erica searched her mind for a moment over where to start and if she should mention both Mark and Michaela and Chelsea, or just the encounter with the latter pair. Weariness was descending. And she was rostered to help clean up later. But, really, the loss of Mark was too big a part of the other to leave out.

'Okay, so, settle in, this is going to take a while and quite possibly blow your minds ...'

'Wow, that's a lot for you to process,' Renee said, when Erica had given them a quick rundown of the Mark situation and the connection to her performance.

'Yes. Christ, Erica,' Michelle said. 'I'm so glad you were able to overcome your stage fright. So, I guess there's proof right there that the truth comes out eventually, huh?' she added.

'Yup,' Renee said knowingly. 'And of how everything is connected. I keep trying to tell you, not to mention pointing out all the moments of synchronicity. There's no arguing with fate – well, no point trying to, anyway.'

'Which I guess brings me to the next bit. The weirdest part of all,' Erica said.

'There's more?' Michelle said.

'Oh, there's always more,' Renee said. 'Tell me,' she said, clapping her hands together excitedly.

Erica pulled the two business cards out of her pocket and placed them face up on the table in front of them. 'I've been offered an acting role in a film,' she said as her friends leant in close to read the cards.

'You what?' Michelle's eyes were huge. 'Oh my god. That's awesome.'

'Of course you have,' Renee said. 'You totally deserve it.'

Erica glanced at her youngest friend and struggled to read her expression.

'Did you know? Do you know Michaela and Chelsea?' she asked.

'No. And no,' Renee said.

Erica frowned quizzically at her. *Huh?*

'Well, you enjoyed last night, right – you loved it?' Renee said slowly.

'Yes.'

'And recently you've been feeling good about where you are in life – your new job, being here in Melrose, your bunch of great new friends, your independence and feeling like you're back in control of a few things again? And generally being positive about the future, right?'

'Yes, to all of that. I don't remember when I was last so content. So ...?'

'Well, that's what has made room for the job offer.'

'Great. So just when I get settled and happy the universe shakes things up again? Is that what you're saying?' Erica said, rolling her eyes.

'I can't know for sure. It's your journey. Maybe you've been sent out here as a pause to prepare you for the next wonderful thing to happen, and this is it,' Renee said, tapping the cards.

'Life is so bloody complicated. I'm tired just thinking about it,' Michelle said, frowning.

'Well, thinking about it is what you shouldn't do. You need to just let it happen. That's the problem with us humans; we try to control everything. You know this, Mich, we've talked a lot about it. A lot,' Renee said.

'I know. I'm just tired.'

The blood roaming around Erica stilled and she became a little cold and clammy. 'So, I shouldn't have turned it down, then?' she asked quietly.

'No way,' Michelle said, the words coming out more like a long sigh.

'Oh. Did you? That's entirely up to you. And you know my feelings on the word *should* – that it *should* be erased from our vocabulary. Full stop.'

'I agree. Though I still use it. Far too often. You turned them down? Why?' Michelle asked.

'I like it here. I feel like I've found my place. I'm at peace. And I'm tired. I don't have the energy for a mid-life crisis, which this would kind of be – a bit like running off to join the circus, right? Also, I do feel a certain loyalty to Walter.'

'I hear you. And one of the things I love about you is your selflessness. But I keep hearing that fifty is the new thirty. Maybe Renee is right that your time here was for recuperation. Or maybe just to find out about Mark? God, I don't know. I'm confused,' Michelle said, rubbing her hands across her face.

'Tell me about it. Renee? Help.' Erica said.

'It doesn't matter what I think. It's your life. The offer could be the universe testing your resolve – seeing how much you want to be here. Or it could be offering you a way to get your life back to where it was before all the trauma of your brother's death, now that you've learnt whatever life lessons you needed to.

'Remember, all the worrying in the world won't change the outcome – it might just delay it. You'll always find your destiny eventually – the universe, cosmos, whatever you want to call it, will make sure of it.'

'Well, here and now it feels right for me to say no. That I do know,' Erica said.

'And that's all that matters. You might feel differently in an hour, tomorrow, next week – some time. Or not. But if you do, you'll find a way to make it happen. So, don't worry about it.'

'Easier said than done,' Michelle said.

'Remember, Michelle, how you told me you realised it was only when you stopped worrying about what your mother thought that you finally got your dream job?' Renee said, staring Michelle down.

'Yup. It's true; the easiest way to succeed is to let go. But it's also really hard to do – doing nothing totally goes against society's expectations of us to always be working and striving; doing *something*. Not to mention the legacy of being raised by a complete control freak.'

'Well, you've freed yourself from her. That's something to be very proud of,' Renee said.

'Exactly,' Erica said.

'Thanks. Only twenty-odd years too late, but hey … I know, better late than never,' she added, holding her hand up. 'Renee's right, though, Erica: sometimes the best thing you can do is nothing at all. It's bloody hard to do at times, though. Knowing and doing – two completely different issues. I need a reminder tattooed on my arm. God, I need a drink. Is it too early for a G and T?'

'Did I hear the squawk of a parched throat?' Erica, Michelle and Renee turned at hearing Steph's voice. She was approaching with Issy and Mackenzie beside her. 'Here we are, ladies,' she said, raising the stack of plastic cups she held in one hand and the jug of clear, bubbling liquid with floating wedges of lemon in the other. 'Gin and tonics all round?'

'Oh my god, Steph, you're a bloody lifesaver!' Michelle cried.

'See, the universe always provides,' Renee said, smiling at Michelle with her head tilted and eyebrows raised.

'Yep, it sure does. And always with impeccable timing,' Michelle said, grinning back.

'God, I love you guys. Thanks so much for being here,' Erica said, looking around the seated group while Steph poured them each a cup and Issy handed them around.

'Always,' Michelle said.

'Yup, what Mich said,' Steph said while concentrating on her task.

'Just don't forget us when you're famous,' Renee said.

'Oh haha, Renee,' Erica said.

'Have you changed your mind, Mum?' Issy asked.

'No. Renee's just being funny.'

'Okay, folks, a toast,' Steph said, holding up her cup.

They each held up their own towards the centre of the table.

'To life,' Steph said solemnly.

'To life,' they each repeated and tapped their cups together.

Chapter Forty-three

Monday morning had seen Erica, Issy, Mackenzie, Steph, Renee and Michelle meet for brunch before they left to return home to Adelaide. Erica had almost invited Jimmy until she remembered how little time she'd spent with her three Adelaide friends after them driving all that way for her. Then she hugged everyone and waved them off, both cars going in different directions with Issy and Mackenzie taking a detour to Orroroo to see Mark's grave in person.

Erica was content with her decision to not go and see the grave herself, and for her forthrightness in not capitulating. She just didn't see the point or what it would achieve after all this time; it wouldn't give her any answers to her many questions about him or her parents. She'd let too many people sway her in the past and gone against her intuition too many times.

After her big weekend she was glad for the peace and tranquillity of the flat and Bruce's company. But what she now wasn't content about was her decision to turn down Michaela and Chelsea. It wasn't plaguing her like the overthinking she used to do prior to discovering meditation, but the two women had begun to drift in and out of her thoughts a lot. She'd determined not to worry about it and instead let the universe sort it out – as Renee had counselled yesterday and many times before that. The guided meditations and music tracks were proving a big help too.

She hadn't been able to stop picking up their cards from the kitchen bench where she'd left them. And every time she did, a stream of what ifs and images of herself performing – not onstage like the other night, but under booms and in front of cameras with cast standing about not far away – ran through her. Her excelling; the director shouting, 'Cut. That's a wrap. Job well done, everyone. Erica, that was fantastic.'

She had this exact dream on Tuesday morning after waking far too early and slipping back into sleep. She so rarely dreamt or remembered having done so that it had left her rattled. Renee had once asked the group if they dreamt in colour or black and white and Erica didn't have a clue.

In the shower, getting ready for work, the fact she remembered the dream in such vivid, colourful detail gave her the answer.

Back at work, she was wasting the day on trying to settle back in while summoning the courage, the words, and the opportunity to tell Walter she was leaving. She dreaded it, felt nauseated about it, but knew he'd be kind and supportive – would only say the right things. She just hated the idea of letting down someone she thought so much of. She also hated that she couldn't discuss it with him matter-of-factly, due to his involvement. He'd become such a treasured confidant.

She'd turned down Jimmy for a walk that morning, too, and now regretted it. She wanted to be told she was making the right decision. But, no she didn't. She was – she *had* made the right choice. She just didn't want to hurt anyone and sadly that was exactly what she was about to do.

'Walter?' she'd ventured several times when she'd heard him in the kitchen area, in with the filing cabinets, or coming around the corner. But for the whole day they hadn't got further than agreeing that the weekend had been fantastic but exhausting. After that it had all been him holding up his finger in a hold-that-thought gesture and answering his phone as he walked away from her.

She'd heard only snippets of his side of the conversations. He'd always been one not to take or make calls in company, so that wasn't odd. But what was weird was the amount of time he'd spent on the device that day. He looked serious and spoke professionally, so it was discussions with or about business of some sort – well, she assumed. But not once had he come over and sat behind the desk to discuss a death or upcoming funeral or said he was heading out to collect a body or see someone about their recently departed relative.

Erica became concerned it was health-related – he had that sort of serious vibe about him – but forced herself to instead speculate that Jennifer might have embroiled him in something else related to the weekend.

It was mid-afternoon when Walter finally sat down heavily in his chair beside Erica. She didn't like the look of his colour and her mind went back to his health. But she didn't want to pry. His face was tight and etched with concern and she found her features mimicking his.

'What a day!' he said. 'Sorry, you've been trying to pin me down for most of it. Now. You have my undivided attention. And then there's something I need to discuss with you. So, how about we turn our phones off for a bit, eh? At least put them on silent.'

Erica did so and placed hers face down on the desk and then watched as Walter reached over and took the landline phone off the hook. She was a little surprised; she had never seen him do that before.

'Right. I'm all ears,' he said, sitting back in his chair with his loosely linked hands lying in his lap.

'Wasn't it a fantastic weekend?' Erica began and then stopped.

'Yes. We've established that. Several times, in fact. You were brilliant, Jennifer was pleased, lots of money was raised and heaps of people had an excellent time – we've gone over all of that. The fact you're starting with small talk suggests a difficult conversation is about to happen. Aren't we past that now? The small talk, not the other, that is,' he said, smiling kindly. 'Please don't beat around the bush; just tell me.'

Erica swallowed and took a deep breath. 'I've been offered a job. Back in Adelaide. And I'd like to take it.' She'd taken a risk, not having called Michaela yet, but it had felt right to speak to Walter first. She had her fingers crossed the job was still available, but was also prepared to accept that if it wasn't then it wasn't meant to be.

Please say something.

Erica had trouble reading him. He looked almost nonchalant as he gazed at her. Hang on, was that relief spreading across his face? A smile, even, at the corners of his mouth?

'Don't worry, it's not in funerals,' she said, feeling the need to say something as the silence continued. 'Not that it matters, I guess,' she found herself blundering on, a little disconcerted by his reaction, or rather non-reaction. Time seemed to have stopped or gone into slow motion. 'A film producer and talent rep approached me over the weekend. They –'

'I heard there were some film people lurking about. Not at all surprising – lots of movies have been filmed in and around the Flinders Ranges; the region's a very popular location.'

'It's all strangely coincidental. Ridiculously so, some might say. Though my friend Renee doesn't believe there is any such thing – she says that everything is connected and pre-ordained. My friend Michelle, too. And I'm really starting to see what they mean.'

'I tend to agree. I wonder, too, though, if coincidence, serendipity or fate – call it what you will – might actually be hope in disguise.'

'What do you mean – that coincidences happen so we don't lose hope?'

'Yes. Imagine what a sad and depressing life it would be without all the many magical and inexplicable things we take delight in or look forward to.'

'That's true.'

'Oh, and I just remembered. Imagine where young Jimmy might still be if not for wonderful happenstance. I'm so pleased he's managed to put that behind him.'

'Yes. Thank goodness. So, you're really okay – not at all upset about my decision?'

He took a deep breath and let out a long, loud sigh. 'Yes and no. I'll miss you. Of course I will – you've become very special to me.'

'But …?' she prompted when he didn't continue.

'But … what?'

'So, you're not going to tell me how unstable a career in acting will be and try to talk me out of it?'

'Nope. You're a big girl. You don't need my or anyone else's approval. For anything. And you're going to do just fine – not fine: you're going to be brilliant. No, I'd be telling you you were a fool if you didn't at least give it a shot – though I would hope I would find a better choice of words. If I'm honest, I'm thrilled to have played a small part in setting you back on your feet – and on your way.'

'But what will you do? You said you spent ages looking for someone before I turned up. I feel terrible about leaving you in the lurch.' *Not that I'm arrogant enough to think I'm indispensable.*

Walter's warm smile became a cheeky grin. 'So, you know all the phone calls and palaver I've been up to today?' he said, looking at her with his eyebrows raised.

'Yes? I thought something weird was going on.'

'Well, speaking of coincidences – they're everywhere today! I've been made an offer, too – on the business. Months ago, actually. But now I'd really like to take it. Retire a little early, if you will.'

Erica stared at him, her mouth dropping open slightly as she took in his words.

'Before there wasn't any point. But I don't want to make the same mistake I made with Mary now I have Jennifer. We seem to have inadvertently fallen in love somewhere along the way. I know it appears to have happened very quickly, but I'm sure Mary would approve and agree that at our age you need to jump at any chance of good companionship you can get. This weekend taught us that we weather the stressful times okay and work together well, and still like each other tremendously.'

'Oh, Walter. I'm so happy for you – for you both. That's fantastic news.' She leapt up and across the space and wrapped her arms around him, causing him and Bruce, in her bed nearby, to let out startled, stifled *oomphs*. They hugged tight before Erica drew back and returned to her chair.

Erica knew Walter and Jennifer's relationship had progressed beyond friendship. She might have not experienced the rush of excitement and dizziness and delirium of sprouting love for many years, but she could still recognise it when she saw it. Even people in later middle age weren't immune and couldn't hide the effects. So, that part of Walter's news wasn't entirely unexpected. Being in love was a magical and beautiful thing, and Erica felt privileged to have been there to watch it unfold – more the speed of a Christmas gift being torn open by a child on the big day than a change of seasons. But, whatevs, as Mackenzie would say. She could hardly scoff, given her own sudden desire to change careers – and to acting of all things.

She wondered if Walter and Jennifer had realised the strength of their rapport at that first funeral just a few days after Erica's arrival. She sure had. She'd thought they were just used to working together, but apparently, it had been Jennifer's first time working with Walter, and her first funeral service full stop. Erica had only found that out quite recently.

'I've been in a bit of a pickle over how to tell you. I've actually been making a couple of calls on your behalf, trying to secure you alternative employment not too far away,' Walter continued, dragging Erica's attention back.

'Oh, Walter, bless you. I've been so worried about letting you down and how to tell you,' Erica said.

'Me too. I've been freaking out a bit, as your darling daughters would probably say. God, we're a fine pair of galahs,' he said with a laugh, clearly releasing some of his relief and tension.

'So, what are you and Jennifer going to do? Or will you be putting your feet up and admiring the roses? I have to say, Walter, I can't quite imagine you as the pipe and slippers kind of guy.'

'No. That's the quickest way to end up in one of those caskets in there,' he said, indicating his head towards the front room. 'We're going to buy a caravan and join the masses of grey nomads wandering around this wonderful country of ours. I'm not sure that's me either, but we'll see soon enough. Nothing ventured, and all that.'

'I'm thrilled for you, I really am,' Erica said.

'And I, you,' Walter said. 'What's the movie?'

Erica told him in a rush of words until she was breathless. She was excited but also relieved to have it out in the open.

'Well, you're going to be fantastic. I look forward to seeing you on the screen and a red carpet down the track.'

'Thanks. I'm excited, Walter. But I'm really going to miss you and this place.'

'We'll be in your heart and you'll take that wherever you go,' he said, reaching over and patting her hand. 'It's been quite the couple of months, hasn't it?' He sat back in his chair and looked up at the wall planner. 'Have you told them you're taking the job?'

'Not yet. I didn't want to until I'd spoken to you. How about you, with the offer on the business?'

'No. For the same reason,' he said, smiling kindly.

'Well, you'd better hop to it before they change their mind,' Erica said, putting on a slightly scolding tone.

'Ditto,' Walter said. 'You don't want that producer having to make do with a second-rate actor.'

'I think they're going to want me quite soon, though – the film's already been held up with looking for the right person, though that might have been just what they told me …'

'You go as soon as they need you.'

'But we've got a service on Thursday and one booked for next week.'

'Don't you worry about that. People are always going to be dying – and at inconvenient times. I'm sure Jennifer will help out if necessary – she's officiating at both services anyway. So, don't you concern yourself about me – I think it's time for you to be a little selfish, my dear. I'll take this out the back,' he added, getting up with his phone in hand.

Erica dragged hers off the desk. Her heart was hammering with excitement as she brought up the number and pressed the green button. She'd already put Michaela's and Chelsea's numbers into her list of contacts.

The call was answered immediately. 'Hello, Michaela speaking.'

'Hi, Michaela, this is Erica Cunningham. We met on the weekend at –'

'Erica! I couldn't forget you! Please tell me you're calling to accept the job.'

'Yes. I am. I'd love to. If it's still available.'

'Very funny – *if it's still available*,' Michaela gently mocked. 'When can you start?'

'When would you like me to?'

'Oh, that's what we like to hear,' Michaela said with clear relief in her voice.

When she didn't actually answer the question, Erica added, 'I could be back in Adelaide in time to start Thursday afternoon. If that would work for you.'

'Oh, yes please! You are a lifesaver – you've no idea. I'll get some things sorted and let you know. We might have to wait until Monday or the following week to start filming, but you'll need some prep anyway. To get the ball rolling, I'll shoot the script straight through and some other employment guff. Hang on, Chelsea's here; I'll put you on speaker.'

'Fantastic news, Erica!' she heard Chelsea chime in.

'Thanks. I'm really excited.'

'Good to hear. Do you want me to represent you? No drama if you don't – I could give you some other names. Or you could go it alone while you thought about it.'

'No, I'd love you to represent me, thanks.'

'Well, my first instruction as your agent is … breathe. Right?'

'Got it,' Erica said with a laugh.

'Oh, and can you text through your email address, thanks? We might have to wait for a while to celebrate, because shit's going to get very real very quick when you get back. So, buckle up for a fun but hectic ride.'

'Sorry to cut this short, ladies, but I've got to go now and herd some cats. Ciao!' Michaela said.

'Okay, bye. Thanks so much, again,' Erica said, disappointed with her lack of inspired vocabulary.

'Take care. I'll be in touch and will see you Thursday,' Chelsea said.

Erica hung up thinking it was lucky she'd instantly liked both Michaela and Chelsea so much because otherwise it might get tricky.

'How did you go?' she asked Walter as he came around the corner.

'Thunderbirds are go. Jennifer said congratulations.'

'Thanks.'

'Now, more to the point, how did you go?' Walter asked, perching himself on the desk.

'Good. But, um, I said I'd be there Thursday afternoon. Are you sure about Mr Jones's funeral?'

'Absolutely. Jennifer has just confirmed too. I hope you don't mind me having told her. I asked her to keep it to herself, which I know she will.'

'No, that's fine. God, my head's spinning. This is all happening very quickly,' Erica said.

'As you know, the best things often do. Like you coming here in the first place – remember that? Just go with it, I say.'

Erica nodded. 'I'm going to miss working with you, Walter.'

'And I'm going to miss working with you. But sometimes the universe has other plans, and ignore them and your intuition at your peril. So, farewell dinner at my place on Wednesday evening, then? Okay with you? Oh. Lordy, that's only tomorrow night.'

'I don't need a –'

'You absolutely do so need a farewell, and a bit of fuss made, my girl! I'll have no arguments on that score. I'll gather the usual suspects – just an informal, quiet evening to send you off. Not too late, so you can rest up for your drive back.'

'That sounds perfect. Thank you.'

'Oh, hello there – is someone feeling left out?' Walter said as Bruce got up out of her bed and moved to sit between them, dinosaur in her mouth. She dropped her favourite green item on the floor between Walter and Erica and looked back and forth as if trying to demand a treat, seeing who would crack first under the pressure of her gaze. Walter rubbed her ears. The dog seemed to have now well and truly got over whatever issue she'd had with him.

'Um, Walter, what about Bruce?'

'What do you mean?'

'Can I keep her – take her back to Adelaide with me?'

'Oh, Erica. I can't believe you even think you need to ask. She's yours – of course she is. I could never be knowingly responsible for tearing apart a bond such as yours. I think she's gorgeous, but you two are special together. And I've seen how much she's helped you. I hope you don't mind me saying this, Erica, but I'm not sure any of this next wonderful bit in your life would be happening if not for this cheeky beast. I've seen how she's transformed you.'

'I think you're right.'

At that moment Bruce let out two barks, 'Woof, woof,' before picking up her dinosaur again, taking it back and dropping it into her bed before flopping down onto it heavily.

Walter and Erica both laughed.

'See, she agrees,' Walter said.

Chapter Forty-four

'Okay, Bruce, I think that's us ready to go.' Erica had already finished packing the car. She'd just come back upstairs to do a final check – mainly underneath the beds – as her dad had taught her as a small child. A quick check under the beds was always the last thing they did before closing the door behind them on any move or after any overnight stay on holidays. The habit had stayed with her.

Looking around the flat, which had been her cosy home for just a couple of months, made her both sad and excited. She might not have been there long, but a lot had happened. She'd changed so much. And made wonderful bonds.

Her thoughts went to the image of her new friends – Walter, Jennifer, Jimmy, Gemma and Roy – standing on Walter's driveway the night before, waving her off after the dinner party Walter had put on for her, ably assisted by Jennifer.

She would really miss these people, though she reminded herself of her certainty that these were connections she'd made for life. She'd keep in touch and hopefully would see them again before too long. And the most important new friend she'd made in Melrose was standing right beside her: Bruce.

Looking down at the patient blue-grey thickset dog, with her big brown eyes staring up adoringly at her, caused Erica to tear up. She squatted down and hugged the dog and indulged in a little cry into her fur before standing back up again. It felt suddenly wrong to have said goodbye to everyone last night and insisted they not come around this morning – that she was leaving early; most likely taking Bruce for her last Melrose walk in the dark. Now she regretted that decision.

'Come on, girl, let's get on the road,' she said. 'Time to go.' She turned off the lights and pulled the door to the flat closed behind her. 'Goodbye, flat – you've been a wonderful home,' she whispered, and made her way slowly down the stairs behind Bruce. At the bottom, she placed the bunch of keys on the small hall table.

'Goodbye, Walter and Crossley Funerals,' she whispered. 'Thank you for everything.'

She closed the outside back door to the business behind her and took a deep breath to steady herself, biting her lip against the newly forming pressing flood of tears.

I'm meant to be happy, for goodness' sake – I'm going on to a fantastic new life. Stop it.

She leant in and clipped Bruce into the centre of the back seat, and gave her a kiss. God, she wished she could have her right beside her in the front for the journey, but safety first: Bruce was as precious a cargo as one of Erica's human children. If something happened and the airbags went off, the dog would be crushed in the front seat.

Erica closed the car door and leant back against it, looking up at the looming mountain behind – Mt Remarkable. *Remarkable – you sure are that*, she thought, breathing in the cool, clear air and giving her mind time to catch up in case there was something she'd forgotten. She was calm but a little sad.

A part of her wanted to unpack the car and return upstairs to the cute and cosy flat with its plush furnishings. She'd arrived there damaged and lost, needing cosseting while she got back on her feet. This place, particularly its people, had transformed her in just under two months. It was hard to leave that sort of support.

She stood concentrating on a few more deep breaths. Thank goodness she'd discovered the meditation tracks. They were yet another wonderful gift Walter had bestowed on her. She closed her eyes and took several more breaths. And when she opened them again, the sight greeting her caused her to grin and her heart to expand painfully under her ribs. Tears filled her eyes again.

There was Walter, hand in hand with Jennifer, coming around the corner of the building. And behind them were Jimmy, Gemma and Roy. The crunch of gravel was loud in the quiet morning under their feet as they made their way across the car park towards her.

While she was thrilled to see them there, she couldn't say she was completely shocked; she doubted anything could surprise her in the way of timing, after all that had gone on.

'Oh, you guys,' Erica said, putting her hands to her face, and the balloon holding the tears and emotion back broke and she began to weep.

Big fat tears raced down her face in two streams, burning her eyes and skin. She looked at Walter's wet eyes and glistening cheeks before sinking into his embrace. They held on tight, both sobbing.

Slowly the tears stopped.

'You've become like a daughter to me, Erica, so if there's ever anything you need, I'm only ever a phone call away, okay?' Walter said, into her hair.

'Oh, Walter,' she said. 'I love you. Thanks for everything. Especially this,' she added, shrugging helplessly.

Jennifer joined them when they parted slightly. 'We couldn't let you leave without a proper send-off committee,' she said, and wrapped her arms around Erica.

'But that was last night. And I said ...' Erica started, but more rising tears stopped her from speaking further.

'Yes, dear,' Jennifer said, now holding Erica by the shoulders and looking into her eyes. 'We know what you said. But sometimes you don't know what's best for you. You're too close. So here we are.' She cupped Erica's face with both her hands. Her eyes were red and full of tears too, which caused Erica's to spill over again. 'You're going to be brilliant. We are so, so proud of you.' And with a kiss on the cheek, Jennifer released Erica, who took a deep breath.

Jennifer and Walter stepped aside and Jimmy moved towards Erica. 'Sorry, but I have no words,' he said, his lip quivering. And then he burst into tears. Erica opened her arms and gathered him to her. 'You've become my best friend,' he sobbed into her hair. 'Thank you for saving me.' They both cried as they clung together. It took a few moments for Erica to bring herself back and for both of their chests to still. She drew away and put both her hands on his chest. 'You are always welcome to visit – and there will always be a bed, for as long as you want it.' *Thank goodness the girls didn't fill the other room in the end!* 'Don't be a stranger. Go knock the culinary world dead.'

She hugged Gemma and then her dad and then they all stood apart wiping their tears away.

'I just need a final cuddle with Bruce, and then you're good to go,' Walter said, opening the car door and leaning in.

'And me,' Jimmy said.

A moment later they'd finished saying goodbye to Bruce, retreated, and closed the car door.

'Now, please go, before I lose it again,' Walter said, standing back and smiling weakly at Erica.

Erica got in the car and turned on the key. *Come on, then, Vera.* She drove past the short line of people, waving as she went. With the exception of the raised hands, it could have been a guard of honour at one of their funerals. *How blessed am I?* She struggled to swallow the hard lump in her throat.

As she drove out of Melrose, she looked back at the magnificent and magical blue mountain looming large in the rear-vision mirror and silently thanked it.

I'll be back to visit; this isn't forever. Maybe I'll be in a film here, she thought, remembering Michaela and Chelsea being up there hunting for the right location. That was just three days before. It could have been a lifetime ago.

'Well, Bruce,' she said, glancing now at the dog in the mirror, sitting up and staring out through the windscreen in serious concentration, 'as your new human siblings would say, that was the shortest new career in the history of new careers! I hope you're ready for an exciting new life filled with more people to love you.'

'Woof, woof.'

'Excellent,' she said and returned her gaze to the road in front, taking a deep breath as she did.

A bit more than three hours later, after a stop for a quick break and a wee for both her and Bruce along the way, Erica pulled into her suburban street and then drove up her driveway, noting as she did that it seemed both familiar and a bit foreign.

'Here we are, Bruce – welcome to your new home. I hope you'll love it here as a city dog.'

'Woof, woof.'

Erica turned around and smiled at the dog, who looked excited. 'You do already – that's what you said, isn't it, my good girl?'

'Here you are!' Mackenzie cried, and made her way down the front steps.

'Yay!' Issy said, skipping behind her sister.

Mackenzie went to the boot and took the first of Erica's luggage to the house while Issy leant into the back of the car to cuddle and then unclip Bruce, and then led her out. Erica remained seated behind the steering wheel, looking up at the house, savouring the moment, trying to take stock of the range of thoughts and emotions rumbling through her.

After a few moments she got out.

'Welcome home, Mum,' Mackenzie said.

'It's so good to have you back,' Issy said.

Erica gathered Issy and Mackenzie to her and they held on tight.

When they parted, they all bent down and made a fuss of Bruce.

'Welcome to the city, Bruce,' Issy said. 'You've got a lovely big backyard and there are bound to be lots of other dogs at the park to make friends with.'

'And Daphne,' Erica said. 'Michelle's bringing her over later.'

Erica, Issy and Mackenzie made their way through the house and out into the garden so Bruce could have a wee and stretch her legs. The trio stood with their arms linked at the edge of the vast entertainment area, while Bruce did a few laps of the lawn, sniffing everywhere, before checking out the garden beds.

'Look, Mum,' Issy said, giving her a gentle nudge and indicating her head to their left. Nestled in the garden bed was a smooth, round stone the size of two cupped palms side by side, painted in the same colour brown as her late brother Mark's jumper.

'Oh, you guys, that's lovely,' Erica said, tears welling. She'd told them about Walter's tribute to Mary in his garden.

'You can change the colour if you like,' Issy said.

'No, it's perfect,' Erica said.

'We've got some more for Gran and Dad – even though his ashes are inside …' Issy shrugged instead of finishing the sentence.

'Yeah. We thought they should be here together,' Mackenzie said.

'I reckon orange for Dad and pink for Granny,' Issy said, 'But we wanted to check with you first.'

'Thanks, but that sounds perfect,' Erica said. She'd suggest sky blue for her dad when the time came, which probably wasn't too far away. She was sad to think about that, but relieved she was now back and close by if it did happen soon.

Epilogue

One month later.

Erica sat down on the flat sandstone slab bench in front of the clear glass fence around the enormous terrace perched high above Adelaide. She'd already marvelled at the twinkling lights of the city below and the shining stars in the clear sky above. It was breathtaking. Now she was seated with her back to all that beauty, watching the crowd mingling. She smiled at Bruce snuffling around with Michaela and Chelsea's two dark caramel spaniels, having made herself at home.

Michaela had commented on how beautifully behaved Bruce was, even going so far as to say perhaps they should do a film about her life – along the lines of a heart-warming family movie similar to *Red Dog*. Erica thought she was joking, but couldn't be sure. Michaela was passionate and threw ideas around all the time; some of them clearly stuck, others drifted by the wayside to be used later, or maybe never.

She watched her old friends mingling with her new friends – her two worlds perfectly combined. Issy and Mackenzie were working the room beautifully. She wouldn't be surprised if they ended up in the film industry at some point too. She smiled, remembering how when they'd arrived earlier Issy had said under her breath, 'Holy shit,' and Mackenzie had told her to close her mouth; she was being embarrassing, despite her own eyes being as big as entrée plates.

She was thrilled that Walter, Jennifer, Jimmy, Gemma and Roy had come along and that they didn't seem at all out of their comfort zones. She'd seen Jimmy in deep conversation with Michaela earlier and had wondered if he was being offered a job or industry lead. He was so talented and in all sorts of areas. The 'jack of all trades' title fitted him, but the other part of the idiom sure didn't. He was a brilliant carpenter, cake maker and decorator and exceptional caterer.

At this stage he'd decided to stay in Melrose helping Gemma. Erica hoped that had nothing to do with the fact Kayla was somewhere in this city – yes, locked up, but still possibly too close by for his comfort.

Walter and Jennifer seemed to have dropped at least a decade from their ages. Grey-nomading certainly suited them. No doubt it helped that Walter's son Peter was in the throes of relocating back to Adelaide from London, new fiancée in tow, child on the way. The revelations of late had avalanched. Walter would make a brilliant grandfather. Erica couldn't wait to meet them all too. She was so blessed to have found him. He was such a dear and special friend.

Erica looked up to see Renee and Michelle walking over. They sat down on either side of her.

'How can you not be looking out at that gorgeous view?' Michelle said.

'Because, Michelle, you were absolutely right; it's all about the people,' Erica said, sighing contentedly. 'I'm so lucky.'

'You made your own luck,' Renee said sagely. 'You made this all happen.'

'Yes. Renee's right. And you so deserve it,' Michelle said.

'Thanks. Who said turning fifty was horrible – that we women suddenly became invisible with no new prospects?'

'Men. Men say shit like that,' Michelle said. 'Sadly, it's up to us to show them they're full of crap.'

'Do you ever just feel so incredibly blessed and grateful that you're too full to breathe?' Erica said.

'Yep,' Renee said. 'That's being at peace with who you are and your place in the universe.'

'You're right. It feels like I'm exactly where I'm meant to be in life. And the future isn't even scary because I've had so much proof that things somehow do turn out okay. It's unsettling and comforting and exciting all at once,' Erica said with a long contented sigh. 'Who would have thought?'

'Well, me, Erica. I told you,' Renee said, grinning, before tilting her head and nonchalantly taking a sip from her Champagne flute.

'It's been fantastic to see you start to thrive again,' Michelle said. 'And this is just the beginning. But it still blows my mind how, on the one hand, everything can change so quickly – literally overnight – but we've actually been preparing or building up to this for most, if not all, of our lives. I believe in it, but still find it all a bit mind-boggling when I stop and think about it.'

'Tell me about it,' Erica said.

'That's why you need to focus on the present – accept that the past can't be changed and the future can't be controlled.'

'I can totally see what you mean, Renee, about how you can't outrun or avoid or ignore your true self or passion indefinitely. I spent a ridiculously long time trying not to listen to my heart. I might not be on the cusp of fame or have smashed through a glass ceiling or anything, but I'm pretty content with my simple little life. I feel free,' Michelle said.

'That's when you know you've made it, Michelle. It's disappointing to see so many people following the wrong narrative and trying to buy contentment with *stuff*. Whoops, soapbox alert! I'd better stop,' Renee said, shaking her head as if trying to remove the thought.

'But you're always spot on, Renee,' Erica said. 'You know, I think I'm glad this has happened for me now – I mean, at this age, rather than earlier,' she mused. 'I'm so much better prepared emotionally and mentally. I could do without all the online and social media bullshit that's around now, of course.'

'At least it's unlikely nude photos or anything unsavoury from your past will be unearthed. I, for one, am so glad my years of silliness occurred well before the internet and particularly the era of selfies and putting everything *out there* online,' Michelle said.

'I reckon if it's not already happening, there'll soon be people you can pay to scrub clean your online presence,' Renee said.

'I think you're right. And, sadly, a whole new angle for scammers. I'm glad I've never really embraced social media to the point of commenting on political or contentious stuff either. I've only ever shared funny memes, cute cat videos and missing pet or person posts,' Erica said.

'Oh yes, me too. Not that I'm ever going to be famous or anything,' Michelle said with a wave of her hand. 'But, yes, please continue to be super careful about what you post and expose yourself to online. I'm happy to keep Googling on your behalf and letting you know what's safe for you to see.'

'And me,' Renee said.

'I really appreciate it. I'm so lucky to have you guys. And thank goodness for Chelsea and Michaela, too – they've been fantastic.' The three friends sipped silently from their glasses.

'Yes. I really like both of them,' Renee said a moment later. 'And guess what?'

'What?' Erica said.

'Yes, what?' Michelle said.

'Guess who's been offered a place on the design team?' Renee said.

'You have?' Erica said.

'Yup,' Renee said.

'Oh my god. Well done,' Erica said.

'That's fantastic. I'm so happy for you,' Michelle said.

'Thanks. I'm a wee bit excited,' Renee said.

'How good is life right now? Come on, I need to look out and wish upon those stars and that view,' Michelle said.

They stood up and turned around. Erica held back while the others went closer to the balustrade – she wasn't at all keen on heights.

She became mesmerised by the twinkling again and her thoughts began to drift back to their conversation. All the pieces that had come together over her lifetime to put her there were too mind-boggling to contemplate. But one thing she was sure of, in her soul, was that now was absolutely the right time for this, with who she was and what she'd learnt. She couldn't have pulled a role like this off all those years ago if she'd had the opportunity. Not even a year ago. She could see that now. And the most incredible part of this was that it was all so perfect it couldn't fail, or, rather, wouldn't. She knew that. And if something did appear, on the surface, to go wrong in the future, then she knew she could deal with it. *Nothing is ever quite as it seems. Closing doors aren't actually necessarily a negative thing.* God, those in charge of the messaging in greater society had a lot to learn. Like Renee said: too many people took too much notice of what others thought they needed, including random strangers, rather than listening to themselves and chasing their own dreams.

She looked up. *Stu, I made it. I know you know. You had a hand in all this. I love you. I miss you. I wish you were here. But I'm okay. I'm fantastic.*

Cursing the lump forming in her throat, she turned back around to face the people – her new workmates, new tribe – and smiled. There was nothing snobby or arrogant about these film people, though perhaps that was the nature of Adelaide. God, she loved this place, with Melrose a very close second.

'Where's the birthday girl and our future leading lady?' she heard Michaela's voice call via a microphone. 'Oh, there you are. Over here, please, Erica. We need to mark this milestone properly.'

Erica held out her elbows so Michelle and Renee could link arms with her.

'No, you go. This is your time to shine,' Renee said, shaking her head and leaving her arm by her side.

'Yes. Exactly. We're right behind you,' Michelle said, smiling warmly.

Erica blew a kiss off the tips of her fingers to each of them, took a deep breath, swallowed down the rising emotion and turned and made her way forwards.

'Got a blowtorch for all those candles,' Erica heard Walter mumble as she walked past. She turned back. He winked at her. She grabbed him and gave him a quick hug and kiss on the cheek.

'Haha. There's always one cheeky bugger,' Erica said.

'Or maybe a fire extinguisher?' Steph said, hugging Erica before she could move past. Holding her at arm's length she said, 'But seriously, Erica, I'm so, so proud of you. You've made it. On your own merits. This is all you,' she whispered.

A chant accompanied by clapping started as she made her way through the parting crowd, 'Speech. Speech. Speech …'

'Righto, righto,' Erica said. 'Give me that microphone. You might regret this, people.'

Acknowledgements

Many thanks to:

Sue Brockhoff, Nicola Robinson, Annabel Blay, Jo Munroe, Johanna Baker, and everyone at Harlequin and HarperCollins Australia for turning my manuscripts into beautiful books and for continuing to make my dreams come true.

Kate O'Donnell for her editorial expertise and guidance to bring out the best in my writing and this story.

The media outlets, bloggers, reviewers, librarians, booksellers and readers for all the amazing support. It really does mean so much to me to hear of people enjoying my stories and connecting with my characters.

Special thanks to Sergeant Sean Patton of South Australia Police for his assistance with police procedure, Meredith Pammenter of Northern Areas Funerals for her assistance with the funeral industry, and Ashleigh Knott and Lisa Scott for their assistance with the film industry. Any errors or inaccuracies are my own or due to taking creative liberties.

And, finally, to my dear friends who provide so much love, support and encouragement – especially Mel Sabeeney, Bernadette Foley, NEL, WTC and LMR. I am truly blessed to have you in my life.

Turn over for a sneak peek.

Sunrise Over Mercy Court

by

FIONA McCALLUM

Available April 2023

Chapter One

Elsie was in the pantry tidying up the jars and tins and checking that all was neat and in order and everything was correctly labelled. A lack of labelling wasn't a problem for them – well, so far – with both of them knowing, for instance, that the icing sugar and not the cornflour occupied the bulbous shaped old coffee jar and the cornflour the taller, squarer and more slender glass jar, despite their contents appearing identical through the clear glass. But they didn't want to cause more of a kerfuffle for daughters Janine and Corinne after their demise – on their own terms, if all went to plan – than was inevitable. Thus, they were in an organising and sorting frenzy, performing whatever was the opposite of nesting. Purging, Elsie thought it might be termed. That probably wasn't quite right either, was it? Hmm. She frowned before letting it go. Anyway, this was one of the items on her and Howard's to-do list, that they were gradually making their way through. They both loved being orderly and getting things done and out of the way. And there wasn't a whole lot else to do at their age of seventy-eight, in between the medical appointments – just general maintenance;

they had no health issues – and attending the funerals of their peers, which was happening far too regularly.

Elsie was enjoying being deep in the pantry: it meant less of the disconcerting occurrences where she thought the movements out of the corner of her eye grabbing her attention were their dear old dog Maisie, who had succumbed to age a month ago. Maisie had never been into the pantry – the space was a bit too tight for a human and a large German shepherd and the dog had remained cautious to the end.

Elsie still felt guilty for not being there with her and Howard at the final moment and also at the thought that she was glad she hadn't been. The best thing about Maisie's passing – though, god, she missed her more than she could probably put into words – was that they hadn't had to make the decision to have her put to sleep after all. They'd spent ages fretting over it, questioning each other over and over about how they'd know when the time was right. The dear old dog had kept them on their toes and on tenter-hooks for the last few months of her life. One day she'd seem to be reasonably energetic and bright, the next she'd be spread out on the floor looking like her demise was imminent. They'd had a great vet, a kind, gentle, patient and reassuring woman. But she wasn't living with the dog and didn't do house calls. Lucky that, Elsie had often thought, otherwise they probably would have spent a sizeable chunk of their remaining superannuation having her popping in to check on the dog. As it was, several times they had rushed poor Maisie in to see her – thankfully the dear old dog didn't mind the vet surgery and loved being in the car – only to have the dog brighten up completely and be sent home again after a quick check-over. That roller-coaster had been hard and a strain on their nerves. But the last time, Howard had been at home alone with her, Elsie having, finally, after all the Covid palaver, felt safe enough from the dreadful disease to meet a friend, Judith, for coffee and to go to a movie.

She'd had her phone switched off, and had forgotten to turn it back on once she was on the bus heading for home. She was so out of practice with catching the bus – it was her first time in around three years – that she'd been caught up in remembering to tap her card and put it away again, and checking her phone had completely slipped her mind. She'd never been as keen on the thing as Howard – useful, yes, but also a bit hard on the eyes, she found.

She'd entered the house, humming to herself, and wandered down the hall only to come out into the open-plan kitchen, dining and living area to find Howard at the kitchen table, head in hands, sobbing. Slowly he'd revealed that soon after Elsie had left, Maisie had collapsed on the floor – actually flopped from standing, this time – and he'd not been able to find a pulse. He'd rushed her to the vet – only a few minutes away by car – and urged them to revive her so Elsie could have the chance to say goodbye.

As Elsie stood there with her arms around Howard, head on his shoulder, sobbing herself now, the pain, relief, guilt had started. The relief at not being there and having to help make any decisions and the guilt of not being there to support Howard and also not holding Maisie's paw – never leaving her; being there for her right to the end, like she'd promised her so many times. How he'd even had the strength to lift the large dog into the car and then into the vet from the car park – and hadn't done his back in – was beyond both of their comprehension.

Her grief had begun in a split second, as grief always did. She'd walked into the house, keen to discuss the movie, cheerful, buoyant, feeling finally fear-free about being out in public properly after the Covid years and look what she'd come home to. In an instant there was a big hole in their lives and souls, and the maelstrom of emotions attached to it all.

In the first minutes, all she could do was apologise over and over for her inattention regarding the phone. Howard, of course, her darling Howard – best friend of seventy-four years, husband of fifty-nine – was his usual beautiful self; sad of course, but not at all upset with Elsie. He was more concerned about her not having the chance to say goodbye. That was the reason for the eight missed calls on her phone, he'd explained later. They'd revived dear old Maisie and he'd wanted her to say goodbye. When she'd died soon after, they'd gently said this was it. She'd gone. Gradually he'd pulled himself together enough to ask for her to be cremated and to let him know when to collect her ashes, paid and driven home.

Elsie ranged from being bereft and sick with guilt to glad and relieved that her last goodbye had been that morning as Maisie had followed her to the front door. She'd said, 'I'll see you later, darling girl. Remember, you are loved,' as she had every time she'd left the house. They had both told the dog they loved her many times throughout the day, because the precious thing had arrived from the RSPCA after an apparently horrendous former life, which had left her timid and malnourished, and they'd taken it upon themselves to reassure her as often as they could.

Elsie sighed, let her reminiscing slide into the background, and returned to her task in the pantry.

She blinked and stared at the two tins of chickpeas she'd just found buried right at the back of the cupboard. When had they bought these? Though 'why' was the more pertinent question. She racked her brain for a recipe they might have needed them for once – a salad, perhaps? – but came up empty. They hadn't entertained in ages – their first time having people other than their daughters around since the pandemic was next Thursday.

She left the tiny room, carrying the tins, frowning, and crossed the space to where Howard was in the study working through the many photos. His current task, also on their to-do list, was to sort the digital photos and scan all those in the many albums and save them so Corinne and Janine would have a copy each of everything in digital form. They could fight over the physical albums at a later date.

'Howard?' she called from the doorway, holding up the cans of chickpeas.

'Hmm,' he said, eyes still on the screen in front of him. *Damn stock market, when are you going to start going up again?* he thought with a sigh and shook his head. He'd checked it while taking a break from sorting the photos and wished he hadn't.

'Any idea why we have two tins of chickpeas in the pantry?'

Howard backed his chair back and turned fully around to face Elsie. 'Um, let me just think for a moment.' He took his glasses off and rubbed his face. 'Oh, I know. I remember now,' he said a few moments later. 'We got those that last big shop we did just as the supermarket went completely mad with the people hoarding toilet paper and everything. They were the last thing on the shelves, so I grabbed them.' He shuddered in response to the flood of memories. How traumatic those last days in the supermarket just before lockdowns had been. All that jostling and fear and panic. He'd got caught up in it and was a little embarrassed to admit he'd been influenced. Hence the damned chickpeas, which he knew nothing about – other than the fact they apparently came in tins.

'What? Because they were lonely?' Elsie said.

He grinned at his darling wife and rolled his eyes. *Trust you, cheeky minx.* How wonderful – and incredible, really – to still have a wife you adored, loved and regularly found hilarious after nearly six decades. 'Very funny. No, because I thought they'd be useful – you know, if the worst happened. Nutritionally, I think was where my mind was going. Remember back then, the chaos? We didn't know what would happen with the supply chain, or if we'd be able to buy food in lockdown, et cetera. Remember?'

'Oh god, yes, that's right.' Elsie shuddered as the memories flooded back. It was quite incredible how quickly she seemed to forget the details of major parts in her life. She shuddered again. 'Okay, so what are we going to do with them?' she said.

'Eat them, I suppose,' Howard said. 'We're not throwing them out, if that's what you're suggesting.' He frowned. *Do we even like chickpeas? I sure hope so.*

'No. Now come on, Howard, when would I ever advocate for wasting food?'

'Sorry, no, of course. I'm being a bit tetchy. I'm trying to sort through a stack of images that are almost identical, within hundreds. Damn this digital photography that's made it so easy to end up with thousands of photos with the mere press of a button. Oh well.' He sighed and gave his face another rub.

Elsie stood there with the cans, and waggled them. She really wanted to deal with them, despite being aware she was being slightly obsessive about them. Though they both were, about all sorts of things. It seemed to have come with retirement fifteen years ago. And more recently had stepped up a notch in their determined effort to get their affairs in order and move on to the last item on their list.

'Let me see,' Howard said, wheeling himself back to the desk. Now facing the computer screen, he tapped on the keyboard. 'Ah, we could make hummus. We like that, don't we?'

'Yes. Oh, yum.'

'Okay, here's a recipe with plenty of five-star reviews. We'll also need tahini. What's that when it's at home?'

'Sesame seed paste, isn't it?' Elsie said.

'Ah, yes, you're quite right. Well, why don't they just say that, then? They're fine with peanut paste – don't need to give that a fancy name.' *Why does everything have to be so damned complicated?*

'Who's they, dear?' Elsie said, just for fun. She loved when he muttered about the strangeness of the world. They enjoyed great long conversations about how screwed-up everything was – another major reason for this final plan of theirs. But Howard ignored her, simply waved his hand and kept on peering at the screen and tapping on the keyboard.

'And how the hell did I get to this age without knowing that?' he muttered, shaking his head. 'Right,' he continued a moment later, making a note on the back of an old envelope on the top of the stack beside him, 'tahini. Garlic, salt, olive oil and lemon juice we have plenty of. Might get some fresh ones. Hmm. Cumin. Do we have any cumin, dear? It's a spice, by the looks.'

'Yes, that's in the cupboard. I saw it yesterday when I inventoried the spices. You know – it's the one we use in stews and curries.'

'Great, well, I'll just print this recipe out and we're good to go.' He carefully tore off the portion of the envelope containing his list and, after a final tap on the keyboard, turned to the printer as it roared to life.

He tucked the scrap of paper into his pocket, collected the page from the printer and got up. 'I'll see you in a bit,' he said as he handed Elsie the recipe on his way past. 'You can bone up on this, if you like, while I'm gone.'

'Are you going now?'

'I thought I might. Good to have a mission. I need to clear my head for a bit – this is doing me in,' he added.

Elsie sympathised. He'd been doing this for months, on and off right through last year. Before that it was research on the family tree. He'd loved that. But this task was dragging on and he often complained that it was driving him spare. Why did old people use that term? What did it even mean? she wondered, before letting it go. She blinked it away just before Howard kissed her on the forehead.

'Anything else?' he said, moving past her.

'No, I don't think so.' It didn't matter, anyway, Elsie thought, Howard trekked to the supermarket at least once a day, sometimes twice. She knew it was partly because of how much he missed Maisie – their gentle walks together and also her presence. She'd noticed his patience with the photos had shortened considerably since he'd lost his companion, whom he used to mutter to almost constantly as she snoozed in her bed or sprawled out on the floor. She too understood the impact of this large missing piece from their lives and the accompanying constant haze of grief, so she didn't rib him about how often he traipsed back and forth to the shops. It was very convenient for her, too. As part of their planning, it also made sense to keep less fresh fruit, veg and meat on hand than previously. Also, because Howard preferred to walk to the shop and there was only so much he could carry. At their age they had to pace themselves – in all areas. It was a vicious cycle, really – not much food in the house because he didn't want to carry much food from the supermarket. Or rather, a friendly cycle, she decided, because it kept her darling husband occupied.

'Okay, back soon. Call if you remember anything,' he said, holding up his phone. Elsie nodded as she made her way to the table to read the recipe in preparation for Howard's return.

*

'Here we are,' Howard said, reappearing in near-record time. He put a jar of tahini paste and three lemons on the bench. He'd rushed and was slightly out of breath. It hadn't been an altogether fun trip to the supermarket.

'Great. Do you realise we only need half a cup of tahini for each tin of chickpeas?' she said, looking at the large jar, turning it over to see how much it contained.

'Oh. Well, it was the only one they had. Damn. Regardless, I should have checked. It was in the spreads section.'

'So perhaps we could use the rest of it on our toast in the morning, or something, just as it is.'

'It must be what people do, on account of it being where it was. The lad I asked knew straight away, was on the verge of sighing at me in that exasperated way so common with the young ones. We love sesame seeds and sesame oil, so it might be nice for a change,' he said with a shrug as he opened the third drawer full of assorted kitchen utensils and took out the strap wrench.

Elsie watched as he undid the lid, marvelling, as she did every time either of them used the device, how effortless opening jars was again. For years they'd had to resort to belting them with the back of a heavy knife to break the air seal, but that was fraught with issues.

Once they'd never needed to give such an activity a second thought. They'd laughed off struggling with the odd tricky lid, which they'd always somehow manage to conquer after passing the offending item back and forth between them a couple of times. But about a decade ago, they'd both ceased to be able to get any jar open at all.

More than being simply frustrating, it had served as a stark indication of the ebbing away of their independence. But worse than that was the additional reminder of their increasing isolation and lack of belonging to a community. They were the last of the long-term residents in the cul-de-sac and everyone moving in these days seemed keen to keep to themselves. So, while the natty contraption Howard was currently using with ease couldn't cure their invisibility, at least they could easily open their own jars again!

Elsie was so grateful for whomever in one of their Facebook groups had raved about this device. They'd been so desperate to try it that they'd even stumped up for the full delivery fee, ridiculous for a single item, to have the thing delivered the other year during Covid from the hardware store's plumbing tools section. Now she told everyone she could of its existence. It was a godsend, for want of a better term. Howard and Elsie were not religious, by any stretch. Quite the opposite – thought it was all a con and the Bible a work of fiction. Every time they used this wrench, they extolled its virtue and then thanked it before popping it back in the drawer. Elsie thought it deserved to be mounted on the wall, or something more befitting of its value, rather than tossed into the third drawer along with various other utensils – all useful now; they'd finished sorting the kitchen drawers.

'Oh, that's hideous. Bitter,' Howard said, screwing his face up, having just dipped a teaspoon into the freshly opened jar of tahini. He was cringing with distaste, making a good imitation of one of Rowan Atkinson's Mr Bean expressions. He opened the top drawer again, retrieved another teaspoon, and handed it to Elsie. 'It's definitely not off, I made sure – I always do.' He stood looking at her with his eyebrows raised, waiting to see if she felt the same way. They had similar views about most things.

'God, you're right. That's awful. I don't like it one bit,' she said. 'People spread this, just as it is, you reckon?' she said, staring at him, sticking her tongue out.

'Apparently. Well, I certainly hope it tastes better once turned into hummus along with the chickpeas and other ingredients. And I sure hope we like hummus still, after all this.'

'Um, you do realise that we'll have to buy more chickpeas to use up the tahini now? We don't want to waste it,' Elsie said.

'No. Oh, god, this is a right can of worms we've just opened, isn't it?'

Elsie giggled. 'It's turning into a saga! No, no, I can see it becoming a hilarious skit,' she said, beginning to laugh loudly.

'I see what you mean,' Howard said, also beginning to chuckle. 'We could have an endless cycle of buying chickpeas and tahini until both run out at the same time on our hands. That could go on until we die.'

'Exactly,' Elsie spluttered and began to laugh hysterically.

Howard joined in and soon they were doubled-over, laughing uproariously. They fed off each other for several minutes, a new bout of laughter starting up every time they stood up, holding their stomachs, and looked at each other. Eventually they gave a final splutter, and then wiped their eyes.

'Oh, I needed that,' Howard said after clearing his throat.

'Yes, me too. Bless the chickpeas,' Elsie said, causing them both to giggle again.

'Let's make sure we like homemade hummus before I go back for the next lot of chickpeas, shall we?' Howard said.

'Good idea, dear,' Elsie said, grinning at him.

They worked together side by side, as they often did, and after around half an hour – twenty minutes or so of it spent standing waiting for the legumes to cook, key, according to the recipe's author – stood back from the bench with a half cracker each slathered in their fresh hummus.

'Ready?' Howard said.

'Yep. My fingers are crossed,' Elsie said.

Looking into each other's eyes, they popped their samples into their mouths.

Elsie closed her eyes to get the full experience and knew Howard was doing the same, when he spoke. She could always tell, by the way his voice sounded.

'Hmm. Well, that's an improvement on the tahini paste, I must say,' he said.

'Yes, it's actually rather good.'

'I agree,' Howard said. 'Right, so that's one problem solved. Next is, there's rather a lot of it. The hummus, that is. Shall we freeze some? Can we, do you think?'

'I don't see why not. And then of course the next big question is, just how many lots do we have to make to get to a point of having zero tahini and zero chickpeas? Because we're really not going to do anything with either ingredient again. Are we?'

'No, definitely not.'

'I'll tackle that question a little later.'

talk about it

Let's talk about books.

Join the conversation:

 facebook.com/harlequinaustralia

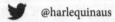 @harlequinaus

 @harlequinaus

harpercollins.com.au/hq

If you love reading and want to know about our
authors and titles, then let's talk about it.